The Art of Adapting

Cassandra Dunn

Cassandra Dunn

TOUCHSTONE

New York London Toronto Sydney New Delhi

Touchstone
An Imprint of Simon & Schuster, Inc.
1230 Avenue of the Americas
New York, NY 10020

First Touchstone trade paperback edition July 2015

TOUCHSTONE and colophon are registered trademarks of Simon & Schuster, Inc.

For information about special discounts for bulk purchases,
please contact Simon & Schuster Special Sales at 1-866-506-1949
or business@simonandschuster.com.

The Simon & Schuster Speakers Bureau can bring authors to your live event. For
more information or to book an event, contact the Simon & Schuster Speakers
Bureau at 1-866-248-3049 or visit our website at www.simonspeakers.com.

Interior design by Aline C. Pace

Manufactured in the United States of America

1   3   5   7   9   10   8   6   4   2

Library of Congress Cataloging-in-Publication Data
Dunn, Cassandra, 1971–
The art of adapting : a novel / by Cassandra Dunn.—First
Touchstone hardcover edition.
pages   cm
"A Touchstone Book."
1. Brothers and sisters—Fiction. 2. Family life—Fiction.
3. Domestic fiction. I. Title.
PS3604.U5576A89 2014
813'.6—dc23
2013039950

ISBN 978-1-4767-6160-2
ISBN 978-1-4767-6162-6 (pbk)
ISBN 978-1-4767-6161-9 (ebook)

For Zoe and Maia:
I love you up to the sky

The Art
of
Adapting

1

Lana

The drugstore was filled with Valentine's Day decorations and chocolates—the last thing a woman wanted to see just after being left by her husband. Heart-shaped Mylar balloons and chalky conversation hearts mocked Lana as she chose cards for her kids. She knew they were too old for it—saccharine photos of puppies holding stuffed velvet hearts in their mouths, cards from their mother on Valentine's Day—but it was tradition. And with her present in turmoil, and her future uncertain, tradition was comforting.

Lana pored through the trite and sappy options looking for something metaphor-free and Asperger's-appropriate for her brother, Matt. Her old neighbor Dixie, mid-sixties and tanned from her new residence on a golf course, rounded the corner, headed her way. Lana turned away without thinking about where to go, why she was hiding from her friend. It made no difference—Dixie spotted Lana as she pivoted away.

"Lana, dear!" Dixie trilled, beaming as she came up to Lana.

"Hello, stranger," Lana said, beaming back to the best of her ability. She gave a friendly wave with the cards in her hand. Dixie was trim and well preserved, tucked neatly into a dark green polo shirt and white tennis skirt.

"Card for Graham?" Dixie asked. "I just love Valentine's Day, don't you?" Her hair was shorter, smoother, shinier than the pre-retirement version of herself, now more silver-blond than the flat gray she used to sport. She looked amazing, like a blissed-out retiree. Lana looked like she'd decided to give up personal hygiene for Lent. Not that she was Catholic. Or knew anything about Lent. She looked exactly like a woman spending Valentine's Day alone after nineteen years of having someone to celebrate it with. Like she'd been awake half the night feeling sorry for herself, then had slunk to a drugstore nowhere near her house to reduce the chance of running into neighbors or friends or coworkers in her disheveled state. A lot of good that had done.

"Actually, they're for the kids. Graham . . ." Lana held up the tacky cards and felt-covered rose-shaped pens that she was also giving her children—the kind of pens they'd likely never use. She wanted to finish the sentence, allow the truth to roll out of her like the brown sludge dripping from the chocolate fountain for sale behind Dixie, but she couldn't do it. As if it weren't bad enough having her marriage end, there was the painful act of telling everyone. How many times did she have to say those words, suffer the stunned look on someone else's face, fight the urge to comfort them as if it were their tragedy to swallow?

"How is Graham? Still working on that book?"

Graham was not working on a book, and never had been, but it was a conversation starter he lobbed around at parties, his idea for a science fiction novel about a space colony that survives the destruction of the earth. Lana gave a vague smile and a shrug.

"He's keeping busy." *Dating,* she was tempted to finish. *He's keeping busy dating a redhead.* But Dixie meant well, and snarkiness wasn't going to fix the situation, so Lana let it go.

"How's the new place?" Lana asked. "You look phenomenal."

"Oh, you're too sweet," Dixie said. She touched her hair, a whiff of self-consciousness rising from the gesture. "Is it too much?"

"Dixie, you look twenty years younger than you are. I can't even compete." Lana held up her arms to show off her oldest jeans, her faded powder-blue sweatshirt from the kids' elementary school. They were now in high school.

"I can give you my hairdresser's card," Dixie said. She snapped open her miniature beige calfskin purse and extracted a dark purple card. The front of the card read *Janelle Monroe* in tiny script, followed by a phone number. Nothing else. No address, not even a salon name. Was minimalism the newest marketing fad?

"Wonderful. Thanks," Lana said. She dropped the card into her big mommy purse, the bottomless one she kept meaning to downsize from. "Please say hello to John for me."

"Oh, I'll do better than that!" Dixie said. "We'll have you and Graham over for dinner!"

Lana sighed. Really, there was no way around her humiliation. She just had to barrel straight on through it, over and over.

"I'm sorry, Dixie. I'm afraid that won't happen. The truth is . . . Graham moved out."

Dixie narrowed her pale blue eyes and touched her hair again. "Why on earth would he do that?" she asked.

It wasn't at all the reaction Lana was expecting, and it struck her as equally tragic and hilarious. Indeed. Why would he? Dixie knew nothing of Graham's late nights working, Lana's loneliness, the arguments, the silences, the threats to leave one another. She knew Lana and Graham from dinner parties, where they were always on their best behavior.

The Mylar balloons swayed overhead in the man-made breezes of central air-conditioning while piped-in Rick Springfield crooned about wanting Jessie's girl, and Lana couldn't help laughing at the horror of it all.

"I have no idea," she said.

"Oh, my sweet dear," Dixie said. She pulled Lana into her, one of those half hugs women do, where they chicken-wing their arms and grip the other person's shoulders, a modified chest-bump of affection.

Dixie and John had been married since college, a good forty-plus years for them. They were living Lana's dream: one spouse, for life. They and their three perfect children and five cherubic grandchildren were beating the odds, while Lana was on the verge of becoming a statistic. Lana returned the half hug, surprised at how frail Dixie felt beneath her glossy sheen of newness. Would Lana be alone when the forward march of time caught up to her? Dixie stepped back and looked Lana over. "Please give Janelle a call. She can do miracles. It'll make you feel so much better."

Dixie touched her hair one last time before giving a little wave, a ripple of four fingers, then she turned on her white tennis shoe and walked away.

Lana paid for the cards, the pens, a couple of boxes of candy for each kid, Matt's beloved yogurt-covered pretzels—the yogurt coating a horrid Pepto-Bismol-pink for the occasion—and headed home. Janelle's purple business card rode shotgun within Lana's purse, a chatty copilot listing all of the ways she could make Lana over: cover her gray, give her long loose layers, make her look less like a mom and more like a woman a man might actually desire. And while Lana wanted all of that, she also resented the feeling that she had to repackage herself for the market. Graham was graying, thinning in a spot on the crown of his head, and had put on a little roll around his middle, but he seemed to be having no trouble getting dates.

Lana compromised by swinging by her favorite nail salon, where the fumes gave her a headache but the attentions of beautiful delicate Mai always made her feel better. Mai complimented Lana's nails, her shapely fingers, her skin, and while it was likely just a means of earning her repeated business, it did make Lana feel better. The manicure also fell within Lana's tighter, post-separation budget, while she was fairly certain a Janelle Monroe makeover did not.

"Sit, please," Mai said. She could have been eighteen or thirty-five. It was impossible to tell. Lana sat. Mai set out four color choices and Lana pointed to the red—appropriate for Valentine's Day. Mai held the bottle up to Lana's cheek and squinted, giving the faintest shake to her head. She held up a bottle of rose-pink polish and gave a shy smile. Lana nodded. She wanted someone else to make the decisions.

Being single meant Lana got to be in charge all the time, do things the way she'd always wanted them done. She no longer had to wait until Graham was done watching TV before starting the noisy dishwasher. She didn't have to budget for the fancy-label wine he preferred. She could wait an extra thousand miles before getting her oil changed. But it also meant she had to be in charge even when she didn't want to be. That she'd had to be the one to fire the gardener she could no longer afford. That she'd given up her beloved winter fires because Graham told her she needed to get the chimney cleaned first and she had no idea who to call for such a thing. Or how much it would cost.

Mai finished massaging Lana's hands with lotion. Before starting to paint her nails, she gestured to Lana's left hand.

"You want to put your ring back on before I paint?"

Lana had no ring to put on, of course, but Mai didn't know that. It had been months since she'd worn her wedding ring. Maybe months since she'd had a manicure.

"No," Lana whispered. Stupid Valentine's Day. She smiled but felt her eyes moisten. Mai ducked her glossy head of beautiful black hair and got to work. With Lana's hands busy lying flat on the table between them, she had no way to wipe her eyes. She caught a lone, errant tear on the shoulder of her sweatshirt.

With lovely pink nails, an armload of valentines, and renewed resolve boosting her spirit, Lana headed home to wait for her kids to return from their overnight visit at Graham's. She expected to find Matt in the kitchen, eating a generously buttered English muffin, drinking milk from his favorite blue cup, but the kitchen was empty and the house was quiet.

Lana set out three piles of Valentine's Day gifts on the kitchen table and signed the cards. She still had a couple of hours before Graham brought the kids home. She weighed her options. Heading back to bed was too depressing. Exercising held no appeal. Eating was a dangerous way to pass the time. She texted her kids.

Happy Valentine's Day! I love, love, love you! Mom

Abby wrote back immediately:

Can we come home now?

The proper answer was no, because it was Graham's time with them, but it wasn't like they had an official visitation schedule set up. Graham saw them when he wanted to see them, brought them home when he was done. Matt emerged as Lana was trying to formulate a response.

"What's that?" he asked, gesturing in the general direction of the piles of stuff on the kitchen table.

"It's Valentine's Day," Lana said.

"Oh," Matt said. He set about making his breakfast. He showed no interest in the pile of gifts before his seat at the table or the envelope bearing his name.

If it's okay with your dad, Lana wrote. That seemed fair enough. Defer to him, but give the kids permission to influence him.

He says fine, Abby wrote back.

Lana sent a text that she was on her way and fetched her keys. "I'm going to go pick up the kids at Graham's. Want to come along?"

Matt looked at his uneaten breakfast.

"You can bring it," Lana said. Matt picked up his food and headed for the garage.

Lana's mood was instantly lifted the moment she pulled onto the sunny street and turned toward the ocean, headed for Graham's place in Del Mar. Once her children were home it'd be a happy holiday. Valentine's Day wasn't meant to be spent alone. Of course, fetching the kids early meant Graham would be spending it alone. The thought made Lana smile. But the smile made her feel guilty. She flipped on the radio to a soft-rock station she normally hated, but knew would be playing the sappy brand of love song appropriate for the day, maybe something to remind her of happier times. What she found was even better. Adele's "Someone Like You." The perfect anti-love song.

Lana was singing along when she noticed the colored lights flashing behind her. A police car, on her quiet little suburban street. It was so unlikely that she kept driving for a moment, sure it wasn't meant for her.

"Oh, no," Matt said, peering in the side-view mirror. "What happened? What did you do?"

"It's fine," Lana said, pulling over. "I'm sure it's nothing. Maybe I have a brake light out?"

Matt ducked down in his seat, curled himself into a ball, fetus-style. His plate of breakfast fell to the floor mat.

"Please stay calm, okay? It's fine," she said. But as the buff cop climbed out of his car, adjusted his belt, and strutted toward her window, she got that horrible clenched-stomach feeling of being in trouble.

She unrolled her window just as the police officer came up next to her. She put one hand out protectively over Matt, hovering just above his skin, trying to transmit some calming force onto him.

"Do you live in this area?" the cop asked. He had on sunglasses and a hat, the brim pulled low over his eyes, his pad already out, flipping to a blank page.

"Um, yes. Back on Meadowlark?"

"So then you must know there's a stop sign back there? On Coventry?"

"I missed a stop sign?" Lana said. It seemed impossible. She was an annoyingly cautious driver.

"No," Matt said. He raised his hands to squeeze his head and started to rock his body back and forth against the back of his seat. "No, it's not on Coventry. It's on Capital. It's on Capital, and she stopped. A California stop, they call it. It wasn't a long stop. Not the five full seconds. I always stop for five seconds. It was barely one second. But I counted one second. She had her brake fully pressed for one second. And it counts. If you look in the driver's handbook even one second counts." He rocked and rocked, knees to his chest, fists poised at his temples.

"It's okay, Matt," Lana said. She watched helplessly as Matt punched his ears once, twice, and rocked steadily. The car shook with him. The anxiety in the car was rising. The officer was suddenly more interested in Matt than in Lana.

"Is he okay?" the officer asked.

"Yes, fine. He, um, he just . . . Police officers intimidate him." That was true. She nodded in agreement with herself. She pulled out her license and handed it to the officer. She'd take the ticket. Anything to get out of there before Matt lost it.

"He doesn't look okay," the officer said. "Sir? Do you need help?" He was nearly shouting at Matt, which just made Matt withdraw deeper into his tight ball, made him cover his ears more fiercely, punch them a third time, a fourth.

"Oh, please don't raise your voice. He's sensitive to loud noises. He gets overwhelmed. He's got Asperger's?" She didn't mean to make it a question, but it hung there between them, a plea for understanding. The officer slowly took Lana's license from her, still eyeing Matt. He peered down at Lana's license, studied it thoroughly. And smiled. He leaned to his left to look around Lana for a better view of Matt, who continued to rock against the seat, eyes shut, ears covered, a turtle hiding from a predator.

"Matt?" he said. "Matt Croft?" Both Matt and Lana startled at the sound of his name. How would the officer know him? Lana wondered if he was the same one who'd pulled Matt over for his DUI and scared the hell out of him with his blowhard threats. That would be bad. That would push Matt over the edge for sure.

"Officer, if you can just write the ticket. My kids are waiting for me, and Matt here is . . . He'll calm down as soon as we go."

"It's okay, Lana," the officer said. He held Lana's license out to her. "Matt here's right. The sign's on Capital, not Coventry. And even a one-second stop counts. My mistake."

Lana, confused, accepted her license. He was letting her go? Matt opened his eyes and took in the officer in his own safe way, casting sidelong glances at him, mostly checking him out with his peripheral vision. Matt pointed a finger at him. Leaned forward, across Lana, to point vigorously at the officer's chest. Lana fought a surge of panic. Was that an aggressive move? Would the officer grab Matt and pull him from the car, slap handcuffs on him and take him away, for pointing?

"You're Nick Parker," Matt said. He withdrew his pointing finger and returned to rocking absentmindedly, but his hands were in his lap and not punching himself in the head anymore. He seemed to be calming back down. "You were in the Marines. You were at

Camp Pendleton and you wore too much cologne and you had shorter hair and it wasn't gray yet, and you said you'd teach me to hit a baseball, but you never did."

Lana slowly took in the police officer, who was now smiling very clearly at her. "Nick?" she asked. Sure enough, the gold pin on his uniform read PARKER. It had been nearly twenty years since Lana had seen him. Since Graham had stolen her from him.

"So you married him," Nick said. He removed his Wayfarers, and without the glasses, Nick emerged. The same high cheekbones, deep-set dark eyes, striking physique. He had aged beautifully. "I saw on your license. Lana Foster now?"

"Oh. No." Lana laughed, suddenly self-conscious. She touched her messy hair. "I mean, yes. I married him. But I . . . um. We . . ."

"They're separated," Matt said. "They don't live together anymore. The kids are at Graham's. Lana gets sad when they're with Graham. And today is Valentine's Day. Which is a silly holiday. A Hallmark holiday. But Lana was sad about it and then when it was time to get the kids she was happy. Until you pulled her over. Then she was scared."

"Shh," Lana said, laughing nervously. Nick laughed with her.

"Nice to see you again, Matt," he said. "You're right. I promised to teach you to hit a baseball before I shipped out."

"Then you and Lana broke up and you never did. She met Graham and she liked him better, and you stopped seeing her, and me, and forgot to teach me to hit a baseball."

"I'm sorry I let you down," Nick said. He opened his notebook and started writing. Lana's gut writhed. So was she getting the ticket after all? Because Matt had spoken the blunt truth, as he always did, and made Nick angry? Lana's body was a taut wire of tension. She really couldn't afford a ticket. Nor the humiliation of being given one by an ex-boyfriend from decades ago. Nick ripped off the sheet of paper and handed it to Lana. It was his name, email, phone number. "Maybe we can get coffee sometime? Catch up?"

"Oh, I'd love that!" Lana said, too loudly. She laughed, embarrassed for herself. "So how long were you in the Marines for? And are you married? Kids?"

"If I tell you everything now, we'll have nothing to catch up on," Nick said, giving her that sly grin of his, the one that had lured her in so long ago. "Happy Valentine's Day." He gave her shoulder a squeeze, gave Matt a salute, and slid his sunglasses back on. As he did so, Lana noticed that he had no ring on his left hand. Lana watched him walk back to his car in her rearview mirror. It was a very nice view.

"The kids are waiting," Matt reminded her.

"Right," she said. She started the car, but waited for Nick to drive off first. He slowed next to her and waved, and she waved back, her fearless, long-forgotten twenty-four-year-old self re-emerging temporarily. The bright-eyed girl of hope and promise, the one who didn't take life so seriously, who loved sex and kissing and hand-holding but didn't need a man in her life full-time. It was time to dust off that version of herself.

"There are three more stop signs on this road," Matt said. "You should do a five-second stop. That way there's no mistaking that you stopped. I always stop for five seconds. I can count if you don't know how long that is. Most people don't know how long a second is. Not really. Not exactly."

Lana drove toward her children, Nick Parker's information in her hand, and Valentine's Day laid out before her, ripe for the picking. "You do that," she said. "You count for me."

She was on such a high that even the sight of Graham, freshly showered and well dressed, smiling, relaxed, and happy to be free of her, did nothing to rattle her. She embraced her children as if they'd been gone more than just sixteen hours. She wondered briefly if she should be concerned that her mood that day had swung so quickly from insomnia and tears to ecstatic, effusive joy.

"Happy Valentine's Day, my loves!" she sang, kissing both kids, knowing how her gushing affection embarrassed them. Abby rolled her eyes and Byron shrugged her off.

"Oh, right. Happy Valentine's Day," Graham said. Lana gave him a smirk and turned away. As if there were any chance she'd been talking to him. She floated down the steps toward her car, still holding Nick's note.

2

Matt

Matt waited in the car when Lana went up Graham's steps to get the kids. His heart was beating too fast and his ears were still buzzing. He didn't feel like rocking anymore, but he didn't feel like walking up two flights of stairs, either. He'd thought it would be a nice change, getting out of the house, going for a ride, but it had been a mistake. The police officer, even though he turned out to be Nick Parker, just Lana's ex-boyfriend and not the bullish police officer who'd yelled at Matt for drinking, had still managed to upset Matt. And Matt's breakfast was ruined, dropped on the floor of the car. And he was hungry.

The kids came toward the car, backpacks on and carrying armloads of clothes and books as if they weren't wearing backpacks that the clothes and books could go into. They were talking too much, too fast. Lana held up her hands as she smiled at Matt, made a show of covering her ears. He nodded, covered his ears, and waited. He closed his eyes while he was at it. He felt the car doors open by the suction then barrier-breaking feeling, pressure building then snapping, followed by a gust of fresh air. Then he felt the kids' voices more than heard them. Abby chirping like an excited bird, the high-pitched energy raising the hair on Matt's arms. Byron's voice was a deep grumble, the vibration carrying through

Matt's seat and into his spine. Matt kept his ears covered until they got home. Waited until Lana and the kids were inside the house before he uncovered his ears and rubbed them. They were itchy and sweaty. He sat for a moment in the silence of the car, shut safely in the garage. It was a perfect bubble of calm and quiet. But only for a moment, before Lana remembered Matt's spilled breakfast and came back to clean it up. She was always cleaning something up. But she was smiling, happy now, and didn't even scold Matt for the butter on the floor mat. At least his milk cup had been in the cup holder so he hadn't spilled that.

Matt headed for the comfort of his room, the only place in the whole house that was just his. He was learning to like his new room. His bed was firm and the cornflower-blue sheets were soft stretchy cotton. T-shirt sheets, they were called. But they were even softer than Matt's T-shirts. The room was fine. It was the window that posed a problem. The window faced east, letting in early morning light, which woke Matt up before he wanted to be awake. The sun refused to be stopped. Like Buddha had said, "Three things cannot be long hidden: the sun, the moon, and the truth." Matt's sister Becca liked to quote Buddha, and he liked that one the best.

Matt's old room at Spike's had faced north, so no sunrises or sunsets had glared their way into his space there. Every change brought new problems, which was one reason Matt tried to avoid change. But moving to Lana's house was a change Matt just had to live with. Like the window, and the sun. Matt had tried closing the blinds, but the light still found a way in. He added a sheet over them for reinforcement, but the effect was all wrong: rumpled sheet, slats of light visible through it, dust motes escaping out the bottom. Eventually Lana had brought home blackout curtains for him. They were much better at muffling the morning light, but they were a deep maroon color. Matt preferred blue curtains. He preferred blue everything. But it was Lana's house, even if it was Matt's room. So he tried to like the maroon curtains. Lana seemed to prefer shades of red to any other color. Lana was sad sometimes, and Matt didn't want to make her more sad by telling her he didn't like the curtains.

Matt was not good at sleeping. Even without the sunlight in-
terfering. His mind kept him awake at night. He liked to take
walks or work on his computer at night when he couldn't sleep.
He also used to drink and use Spike's pills to sleep. The pills
and the drinking weren't allowed anymore, doctor's orders, and
mostly Matt was good about that. He missed the drinking all
day long, but it was the worst whenever he wasn't busy thinking about something else. He'd found some bottles of alcohol in
Lana's garage, in an empty red toolbox. Drinking them a little at
a time helped at first, but they were empty now. The pills he only
missed at night, and he missed them most nights. One night it got
so bad he used Google to map the route from Lana's house in the
suburbs to Spike's apartment near campus. He figured out how to
walk there, and how long it'd take, but hadn't gone. But he saved
the route. Just in case.

Aside from the pills to help him sleep, Matt didn't miss Spike.
For one thing, Spike didn't seem to like Matt much, except when
Matt was giving him money. The good thing about Lana was that
she liked Matt no matter what. When she bought the weighted
blanket for him, he felt how much she cared about him. That blanket was Matt's favorite new possession. It was thick and soft and
so blue and so heavy that it sometimes could make Matt's body
stay asleep even when his mind wanted to be awake.

Lana had also bought Matt a noise machine. He was trying to
choose the right sound for each night. He wasn't sure how much
it helped, but it gave him interesting things to listen to as he lay
awake in the night. He liked the birds on Monday, a bustling forest
waking at dawn. He liked the rushing stream sound on Tuesday,
little trickles and drips across small pebbles beneath the roar of
white water. Wednesday he used the raucous traffic noises. He'd
never lived in a big city, and he wasn't sure he'd like it, all those
people, but he liked the car noises, trying to figure out what kind
of car each one was from the sound it made. Thursdays he always listened to Bach. He was still figuring out the right sounds
for sleeping on the weekends, because the routine in the house was
different then—the kids were up later and Byron was usually in the

kitchen eating around two a.m., just as Matt was trying to figure out what to do with himself.

Those were the times when Matt most missed his nighttime walks. He and Spike had lived in a neighborhood where college kids were out late, and there were always a few of them on the street while Matt walked. Lana was worried that if Matt walked around her quiet neighborhood, even just doing a few laps around the block at three a.m., the neighbors might think Matt was suspicious and call the police. Matt never wanted to talk to the police again. Except maybe Nick Parker. To learn to hit a baseball.

Matt was also still adjusting to Byron and Abby, Matt's only nephew and only niece, fifteen and five-sixths and fourteen years old, sophomore and freshman in high school, Taurus and Libra. They were loud. That was the main problem. They yelled across the house to each other even when they had nothing to say. They sang and whistled and banged cupboards and slammed drawers and argued a lot. And they were messy. Not that Matt was never messy, but he never left dirty dishes all over the place with half-eaten food on them. Matt tried not to waste, and he definitely tried not to leave food out that might attract ants or, even worse, roaches. Not anymore, not after what happened at Spike's. Plus there were the germs. Food left out for even a short period of time was a perfect breeding ground for microorganisms. Matt wanted to explain this to Byron and Abby, but even when his words came easily, they didn't seem to understand him.

Lana's house was big and full of echoes, while Matt and Spike's apartment had been rather small and full of quiet. He missed the quiet. But Lana's house also had a front room, a formal sitting room that no one ever used, with a huge picture window that looked out across the green lawn, the tiny hedges, and into the world beyond. Matt's apartment had windows, but Spike never wanted the curtains open. Sitting and looking out Lana's front window was one of Matt's favorite things to do now, once the kids were off at school and Lana was either at work or out doing whatever she did when she wasn't working.

Matt couldn't drive anymore, so the window was all he had.

Or he could drive just fine, but they wouldn't let him. One night he'd had the same number of beers he always had, but while he was driving to the library a cyclist had distracted him and made him swerve. A police car had pulled him over and he'd gotten into trouble for it, for driving after the beers. The police officer was a huge hostile man with a bushy mustache who wanted to scare Matt, and did, but Matt didn't understand why. He'd only swerved a little, not even across the yellow line, and hadn't hit anything. He'd never had a car accident or even a ticket before, because he knew every traffic rule there was. But the big angry mustached police officer didn't care, and Matt's license was revoked.

After that Matt stayed home more, with Spike and the beers and the whiskey and the pot, and Matt slept a little better, but then there were Spike's good pills, which really helped Matt sleep, until one time Matt slept too much, too hard, and too long, and Spike couldn't wake him.

Matt had woken up in a white hospital room under starched itchy white sheets. He was strapped to the bed and in terrible pain. His body was full of tubes and wires and nose-burning antiseptic smells. His throat ached so much that he couldn't talk, and when the nurse came in and asked how he was feeling, Matt could only tip his head back to show her his raw throat. It felt like it had been scraped with metal on the inside.

"We had to pump your stomach. Your throat will be sore for a little while," she said.

The nurse undid Matt's restraints, rubbing Matt's arm where they had been, and it felt like being slammed by a hammer, the sudden and unexpected graze of her cold fingers just above the inside of his left wrist. The jolt of pain spread throughout Matt's body in one hard fast shock wave and he'd jumped away from her. Matt didn't like to be touched. He could feel the touch of people's breath, the prickly sensation of their eyes on him. Actual physical contact could hurt his skin in a way that nobody else seemed to understand. He could tell by the nurse's wide eyes that she didn't understand. And with his throat on fire he couldn't speak to explain. He hated hospitals and doctors and nurses in general. They were always saying they wanted to help you before they caused you some sort of pain.

The nurse left and a doctor came in. Matt knew he was a doctor because his name badge said so. Aside from that, he could have been anyone. He was middle-aged, graying and fat, with ill-fitting glasses that carved deep impressions on either side of his nose. And he smelled like cigarette smoke. Matt didn't like him. The doctor breathed through his nose and it made a whistling sound so distracting that Matt could barely hear him over it. How could Matt trust the advice of an obese doctor who smoked?

The doctor told Matt that his liver was compromised, like that made sense, like there was a negotiation going on inside his body, but there wasn't any negotiating—Matt's liver was broken somehow and he was to blame even though he'd known nothing about it. He felt like he should apologize, like he'd violated some rule, when he was always so careful to follow every law and rule. He didn't like troubling people. He could feel the doctor's disappointment. It filled Matt up from his chest to his head, made the buzzing start inside his ears, and he didn't know what to do with the feeling or the sound. Sometimes he hit his ears to stop the sound, but he knew the doctor wouldn't like to see that. Most people didn't like to see it, although Matt didn't understand why they cared what he did to his own body.

The doctor told Matt that he had to stop the alcohol and drugs and take Wellbutrin to stay calm instead. He told Matt that he had Asperger's syndrome and that's why he wasn't like other people, but Matt didn't know what other people were like so it didn't mean anything to him, except that he couldn't drive or drink or smoke pot anymore, and could only take the pills the doctor told him to, and never sleeping pills in case he took too many again. The doctor's nose whistled and whistled and Matt agreed so that the doctor would go away and take his noises and disappointment with him.

But being alone in the hospital room wasn't better. The room was too bright and the antiseptic smells made Matt feel sick. Then he'd had to go to the bathroom, but the rolling IV stand wouldn't fit in the small bathroom with him. He really had to go, though, so he pulled out the tube in his arm so he could shut the door and before he'd even finished peeing the nurse was back and yelling at him and there was saline and blood all over the dirty white linoleum floor and then the doctor came in whistling, whistling, shaking his head, even more disappointed.

"Asperger's," the doctor said to the nurse, and they both nodded like it was code for something Matt couldn't see or feel. He tried to be good after that, holding very still while they put the IV back in his arm, but it hurt too much to bear, and he flinched and they yelled at him like he was a bad child. Matt kicked the IV stand away and it hit the nurse in the chest and then they left him alone. Moments later two huge orderlies came in and restrained Matt again, and they gave him a shot of something that made the room go all fuzzy.

When Matt woke up he was still restrained, and the IV was back in his arm, and the scratchy sheets still hurt and his throat burned even more because he'd screamed when the orderlies had pinned him down. But Lana was there, the warm rose-petal smell of her competing with the antiseptic to soothe Matt's nerves. She stood next to Matt's bed, her back to Matt, her arms crossed and legs locked and strong like when they'd been little and she'd told other kids to leave Matt alone. And then he felt safer. Not completely safe, because he was still in the hospital, but better, calmer. Or maybe it was the doctor's new pills that made him feel calmer. But only until a social worker came to visit and said she was worried about Matt going back to live with Spike. She had short blond hair, messy and wet-looking even though it was dry. It was full of some product that smelled like men's cologne. She had lots of earrings on one side and only half as many on the other, and red-framed glasses. She didn't seem like she wanted to help Matt, even though she said she did. She spent more time looking at her phone and clipboard than she did at Matt or Lana.

The social worker tried talking to Matt but he couldn't stop counting her earrings: nine on the left and four on the right. Why nine and four? He needed to count again and again, trying to find the significance, and she became very irritated with him because he couldn't stop counting to answer her questions. Then she talked to Lana instead of Matt, which was fine with him. She cleaned her red-framed glasses on the hem of her shirt and told Lana that Matt needed more care, maybe some help from the state, maybe a facility that would better fit his needs, as if Matt had any needs, aside from the need to get out of the hospital and away from all the sick people there with germs they couldn't contain, not really, even with all of the antiseptic. Matt could feel the germs in the air, getting into his lungs with each breath, and even with the calming pills he couldn't sit still and had to rock against his restraints to stop thinking about the germs on every surface around him.

Then suddenly Lana was angry. She used her loud voice to tell the social worker to leave and never come back. And then it was decided, before Matt even knew they were deciding. He was going to live with Lana.

And so he'd moved into a house of red accents: burgundy curtains and cranberry-colored throw pillows and a huge Persian rug with golds and greens dancing on a sea of maroon, and he'd fit in his soothing blues wherever he could.

3

Abby

Abby passed her time at the dinner table flexing and relaxing her abs, glutes, and thighs over and over, counting reps until she could escape back up to her room. She was on twenty, headed for a hundred. She hated meals. Especially listening to other people eat: the click of a fork against someone's teeth, the chomp of their teeth coming together as they mashed food, even the gulp of swallowing—they all revolted her. If she'd been allowed to listen to her iPod at the table to drown it out that might've helped, but it was against her mom's rules. Abby thought maybe when her dad moved out there would be fewer rules, since Graham was the one who always needed everything just so to relax after work each day, but the rules stayed even without Graham there to care.

Uncle Matt was just as restless, rearranging his fork, knife, and napkin over and over, carefully lining them up, waiting for his food. Lana kept watching him as if this stressed her out. Abby thought Matt seemed calm enough, almost robotic a lot of the time, but Lana treated him like he was always about to blow a fuse or something.

Matt was Lana's new project, now that Abby's dad had moved out. Lana hadn't even asked what Abby or Byron thought. She just came back from visiting Matt in the hospital and told Abby and

Byron that he was moving in. She assumed they would be fine with having their weird uncle thrown into the mix just months after their family was ripped in half. Not that Abby wasn't fine, mostly. But she wanted Lana to care about the times when she wasn't. Her mom didn't even seem to notice.

Abby had been a straight-A student for years. Forever, actually. Until now. But did Lana make as much of a fuss about Abby's falling grades as she did about Matt's dinner? Well, it was only one grade, but that was bad enough, a total humiliation to Abby, who had always been the "smart" kid. (Byron was the "athlete," never mind that Abby was a pretty good soccer player.) Abby had pulled a C on her chemistry midterm and tanked her whole grade and perfect GPA. She'd pretended it was just a onetime brain-freeze to blame, and her mom had bought it, because she wanted not to have to care, Abby could tell. But then her teacher, Mr. Franks, had emailed her mom and said Abby was behind on lab reports, too. The jerk. Lana sighed and hugged Abby like it was Lana's fault somehow, like the separation had caused Abby to temporarily forget how to take a simple test or do her lame labs. Abby was relieved to dodge a lecture on the bad chem progress report, especially when Lana agreed not to tell Graham about it, but Abby also felt annoyed that she was turning into a screwup and her mom didn't even ask why. Not that Abby would've told her.

Lana finally served Matt and Abby, sat down, and started putting a steady stream of bites in her mouth like she was in an eating contest. It wasn't the way Lana ate before, with Graham still in the house, but it was how she always ate now, shoveling and swallowing without much time spent on chewing. It reminded Abby of back when they used to go to the beach and she and Byron would play sea turtles. They'd dig a hole in the sand, throw a couple of rocks or shells in to be the eggs, and use their hands like flippers to chuck sand behind them, trying to fill the hole in before a big wave came up and did the job for them. Abby wasn't sure what hole Lana was trying to fill these days, but she didn't want to have to watch.

Abby's stomach was a mess. She was hungry and queasy at

the same time, all the time. She pushed the food around her plate and watched Uncle Matt. He had to arrange everything a certain way before he could eat. Matt used the same plates and bowls for his food every meal, and he got all freaked out if things were out of sync. No food could touch other food. If his corn and slab of meatloaf collided, Abby was pretty sure he'd have a quiet, choking meltdown, like someone having a seizure.

Abby thought she was the only one with food issues until she met Matt. She had nothing on him. She ate a bite of corn, but regretted it the moment it was in her mouth. The little kernels gushed their sweet contents as she bit down on them. She could taste the sugar, the calories, and something about the way the mushy corn-guts oozed onto her tongue, like fish eggs popping, made her ill. Then there were the pulpy remains of the corn, that weird shiny skin that hardly seemed like food. It gave her the willies. Abby tucked the corn into her cheek and started another round of her exercises, tightening and releasing while her mother ate, two feet away, oblivious to how annoying her ravenous eating habits were.

Abby was always thinking about food, which was a funny pastime for someone who hated eating. For breakfast every day she had a bowl of Cheerios (the plain kind, not the sugary ones) and a glass of chocolate milk. She'd decided to give up the chocolate milk, but she hadn't quite gotten around to it yet. It was little-kid food, and she was fourteen now. Plus, it was empty calories. She was always starving in the morning, and usually a little light-headed, and the protein-sugar combination seemed to do the trick to get her going each day. So maybe she wouldn't give up the chocolate milk. She'd just lose the calories from somewhere else.

"Are you eating or playing?" Lana asked. Abby looked up to see if her mom was talking to her or Matt. Of course it was her. She pointed at Uncle Matt, to show he was also doing weird and unnecessary food rearranging. Lana narrowed her eyes at Abby. Matt had Asperger's, which was fancy medical-speak for not having normal manners. Abby took another bite of the corn, chewing slowly with her eyes shut for her mom's benefit. It was all she could do to make herself swallow it. Her throat tightened and threatened not to let it go down, but she chased it with a big gulp of water and down it went. She sighed, relieved. Throwing up on the table would probably send Matt into a conniption. Lana shook her head and clucked her tongue. Abby used to be her mom's favorite child, but lately it seemed like nothing she did really made her mom happy. But Byron, who was skipping yet another dinner at home to mooch off his friend Trent's family, could do no wrong. Absence made the heart grow fonder.

"The corn is cold," Matt said.

"Yeah, it is," Abby agreed.

"Well, it was warm when we started. If you both ate when you were served . . ."

"I can't eat corn before meatloaf. Brown, orange, yellow," Matt said. He pointed from his meatloaf to his carrots to his corn. Abby had to stifle a laugh. He had a crazy color code to everything he did. It was kind of cool, to see an adult acting like a kid, but it was also kind of annoying, because he got away with it.

"Why does brown have to come first?" Abby asked. Her mother shot her a look, but Lana was the one who kept telling her and Byron to treat Uncle Matt like a normal part of the family, and that's the kind of question you'd ask in a normal family.

"Because it's a blend of three colors. Orange is a blend of two. Yellow is a primary color," Matt said. He wasn't snippy about it. He seemed to like the question. Abby nodded and looked at Lana, who was also nodding. It was still nuts, but it seemed less crazy when you knew the system.

"Where does the milk come in?" Abby asked.

"Last, of course," Matt said. "White is the absence of color."

"In paint, sure, but in light, white is all of the colors together," Abby said, proud that she knew this. Her mom gave her another look, no doubt for mucking with Uncle Matt's system. Matt was looking around his plate, taking this in. He shook his head.

"Food isn't light. These vegetables are from plants. Many paint colors come from plant matter."

"But milk doesn't. It comes from cows. So does the meatloaf."

Matt stared at his plate some more. She'd gotten him there. The system had holes.

"It's turkey meatloaf," Lana said.

"Yuck," Abby said. As if she'd like cow meatloaf any better.

"Eat your dinner," Lana said to her. She rose and took Matt's bowl of untouched corn and warmed it up in the microwave.

Matt waited, zombielike, until the warmed corn had returned, and then he went back to eating. Abby guessed the conversation was over.

"Can I be excused?" she asked.

"You hardly ate."

"I have chemistry homework."

Lana looked at Abby's plate. "I can make you something else to eat," she said. "You can take it up with you."

Then Abby felt bad. She didn't mean to reject her mom's cooking. She just didn't feel like eating. Matt was done with the browns and oranges and on to the yellow food, eating his corn in careful bites, seven kernels at a time on his favorite spoon, like always. Abby just couldn't watch it anymore.

Lana made Abby a sandwich, even though Abby said she wasn't hungry, and Abby took it up to her room along with her ice water. She pulled out her chemistry book and set her journal inside it, just in case her mom checked on her. Abby kept two journals, which was pretty time-consuming, but everyone knew that it was best to leave a decoy journal full of mindless blather out for your mother to find, while you hid the real one full of your secret feelings somewhere safe. Abby was pretty sure that Lana didn't read even her fake journal—she seemed too busy scrambling around cooking and cleaning stuff for that, but it was still better to keep up both journals, just in case. Abby finished an entry about how happy she was to get a goal in the last soccer game, set that journal on her desk, then pulled her real journal from under her mattress. These days she mostly wrote about Gabe in that one.

Abby was pretty sure she'd be doing fine in chem if Gabe Connor weren't in her class. He made it hard to concentrate. Gabe was the captain of the boys' soccer team at school, and he was broad and tanned and flawless in every way. He was also oblivious to Abby's existence, despite the fact that he usually helped out with the girls' soccer team. Once he'd helped Abby get up when slutty Caitlin tripped her with her cowlike inability to get out of the damn way. Gabe's hands were the perfect balance of soft skin and callused palms. Abby was a goner the moment he'd touched her.

Gabe helped with his dad's construction company sometimes, and all that hammering meant his chest and arms were just as muscular as his soccer-toned legs. He even smelled amazing. Gabe's mom used these lavender-filled dryer pouches from Trader Joe's in the laundry. Abby had seen them peeking out of the top of his mom's grocery bag once when she came to pick Gabe up, back before he got his license. The lavender was subtle, earthy, not as girlie-smelling as you might think, and you had to be real close to pick up on it. Abby used them in her own laundry now. Lana thought they were a waste of money. Abby didn't bother to explain, because her mom wouldn't understand anything to do with having an interest in boys.

While her dad was dating, first a blonde, now a redhead, as Abby had detected from the stray strands of hair on his couch and the second pillow on his bed, her mom hadn't had a single date in the seven months since they'd split up. Not one. And it wasn't like she wasn't pretty. Lana had a good nose, full lips, wavy dark hair, and these amazing light brown eyes that were flecked with so much gold they were almost orange, like tiger's-eye stones. Abby had light green-yellow eyes, pale and sickly, and her father's flat dirty-blond hair. She was invisible on top of ordinary. Also, Lana had breasts, which Abby did not. Fourteen was the age of breasts, she'd noticed at school. But somehow the gene pool had dried up just when Abby came along, because there was nothing there.

Abby was tall for her age, but she wasn't what they called a "big girl," which she was grateful for, because the queen bees at school were merciless to fat girls. Abby liked her long arms and long legs, but she worried about her stomach and she had bigger thighs than she wanted. If she squeezed the flesh on her thighs hard enough, she could see the pucker of cellulite under her pale skin.

She wore clothes that hid her thighs, and she did her daily workout to keep them under control. She wished she had something else going for her, something really likable. Being smart didn't count, or it didn't back when she was still smart. The popular girls mocked the straight-A girls, and boys were oblivious to them. At least the boys Abby liked. Like Gabe, who had been dating one of the ditziest girls at school all year. Caitlin, who was as busty as she was dumb. The exact opposite of Abby in every way. So it was stupid that Abby was in love with Gabe, since she clearly wasn't his type. But she really couldn't help it. The harder she tried not to think about Gabe, the more she thought about him.

Abby took out her aggressions on the peanut butter and honey sandwich her mother had made her. She mashed it flat and then rolled it into a tight ball. It held the sphere form pretty well. She opened her bedroom window and chucked it over the fence and into the neighbors' yard, where she knew their dog would appreciate it. She hated to waste food, and at least that way someone was going to eat it. Of course, as soon as she tossed it away her stomach started to growl. She drank the whole glass of ice water in about ten seconds, and that shut her stomach up.

Abby pulled out her exercise chart and got to work. She did two hundred crunches a day, four kinds of leg lifts (fifty reps each), and forty push-ups. She hated the push-ups the most, so she did those first. The leg lifts were the easiest. She'd seen these mountain-climber exercises in a TV ad, and she wanted to add them to her routine. They were half ab workouts and half leg workouts. She'd start with forty and see how it went. Working out was the best way to make any dark thoughts disappear, Abby had found. Afterward she felt exhilarated, invincible. Exercising made her light-headed and dizzy, but it was a good kind of dizzy, the kind where the warm fuzziness of her brain comforted her. The other kind of dizzy happened at school, or really anytime she sat up or stood up too fast. Pinpricks of light would scatter and dance before her eyes, her own private fireworks show, and her face would get hot, and sometimes she had to sit back down in a hurry to keep from going somewhere she didn't want to go.

Abby finished her journal entry by writing her name a few times, adding Gabe's name to it. *Abby Foster Connor. Abigail Leigh Foster Connor. Abigail Connor + Gabriel Connor.* She admired the similarities of their first names. *Abigail* and *Gabriel* looked good together, and had almost the exact same letters. She was pretty sure neither one of them liked their full first name, since they were both quick to correct substitute teachers during roll call in chem. But written next to *Gabriel*, *Abigail* looked nice. Like they were meant to go together.

4

Byron

Byron resolved to quit smoking. Again. He straightened from his stooped coughing position and beat against his chest with the side of his fist, trying to kill the ticklish spot in his lungs that could only be quieted by another cigarette. He'd had a good run with it so far. He'd made his impression with the in crowd, had bridged the gap between the jocks and the rebels, and had worked his way into both groups, but now it was starting to affect his performance in the pool and on the track. Sometimes at top speed it felt like his lungs were stuffed with fiberglass insulation. All itchy and cottony. And according to his little sister, they put fiberglass in cigarettes, so he guessed the analogy was right. She was another reason to quit. Not because he wanted to set a better example for Abby, because there was no way his goody-two-shoes sister would ever smoke, but because if she'd figured it out, their mother couldn't be far behind. And he really didn't want his mom to know. Lana had enough going on without worrying about him developing lung cancer forty years down the line.

Byron leaned against the porch railing waiting as Trent skate-boarded down the sidewalk toward him. Byron heard him coming long before he saw him: the click, click, click across the sidewalk dividers. Trent stopped in the middle of the sidewalk, pulled out his phone, and started typing a text message. Byron heaved his backpack onto his shoulder, sauntered across the lawn, past the hedges, to jump the low picket fence that ran along the side of the yard. He was trying out some free-running techniques he'd seen on the Internet. He kicked his heels to one side and easily swung the lower half of his body over the fence without breaking stride. He nodded at his success and nudged Trent with his elbow.

"Dude, that's not to my mom, right? I texted you from her phone." Byron used his mom's phone sometimes, because his tight-wad dad had him on the cheapest phone plan. If Byron or Abby went over their texting limit, they had to pay Graham for the extra charges out of their allowance. Luckily Lana liked it when they used her phone. She thought it showed how much they all trusted each other.

"I know you did, jackass. I can tell what phone it came from. Hers says Lana. Yours says moron." Trent kept typing.

"So you're not texting my mom?"

Trent hit send, cocked his ear as he listened to the swoosh of a message going out into cyberspace, and gave Byron his new half-smile: arrogance layered on mystery. It was a new expression he'd been trying out. Byron had caught him practicing it in the mirror. Trent dropped into a crouch and karate-chopped Byron in the upper arm. Hard.

"Asshole," Byron said, shoving Trent aside.

"You're the asshole," Trent said, pocketing his phone.

Trent liked to flirt with Byron's mom for reasons that Byron couldn't begin to comprehend. Trent claimed she was hot, for one, which wasn't true. It was his *mom*, for crap's sake, wasn't that against some code or something? But luckily Trent's flirting was so inept that Lana hadn't seemed to notice. Once in a while Trent sent her little smiley-face texts, which creeped Byron out, but made Lana happy, so he left it alone. Mostly.

"No texting my mom, asshole."

"You can text mine," Trent said, smirking again.

Byron liked hanging out at Trent's house best. His mom, Tilly, was definitely not a hot mom, she was three hundred pounds of nonstop chatter, but she was nice enough, and she was a great cook who always had leftovers to feed them. Tilly was divorced, alone, and needy, the loneliness seeping out of her pores as she watched them eat, wiping her sweaty forehead and neck with a wadded-up paper towel that lived in her left hand. Sometimes she tucked the paper towel into her cleavage when she thought Byron wasn't looking. Tilly was a nervous talker, prone to asking a simple question, then talking for the next twenty minutes solid without giving the other person a chance to answer the damn question. It annoyed Byron at first, but he'd gotten used to it. She just wanted someone to listen, and he could do that while he ate.

"What'd you have for dinner last night?" Byron asked, hopping onto Trent's skateboard.

"Some manicotti thing. Pretty good. You'll like it."

"Awesome."

Dinner at Byron's house wasn't the same after his dad moved out, so he avoided it as much as he could. Nobody talked anymore, there was never any laughter. It was strange that it was any different, because Graham was a late-working type who had rarely made it home for dinner anyway. But something about the fact that he wasn't coming home just as they finished up each night had changed everything. Lana fretted over every little thing, and weird Uncle Matt had all these systems and rules for eating, and Abby just sat there sulking until she was excused each night. Eating with Trent, making faces at each other while Tilly gossiped through dinner, was a lot better than that.

They picked up speed, Byron skating and Trent running around him, trying to make him crash with sudden swerves and stops. Byron had pretty good balance, and with his new free-running training it was getting harder for Trent to throw him. When the taunting didn't work Trent resorted to kicking the board out from underneath him. Byron jumped in the air at the exact moment Trent's foot connected with the skateboard, and the board skittered away sideways, while Byron landed catlike on the ground. Solid.

"Dude!" Byron yelled.

"Fucking awesome!" Trent cheered. "That was so Bruce Lee. Let's do it again."

Trent fetched the skateboard from the bushes for another go.

One of the other reasons Byron liked Trent's house was Betsy. She was Trent's sister, a college girl, and too mature to notice Byron, which just made her hotter. She was big, like her mom, but not the sad kind of fat. Betsy was all curvy and confident. She liked to lie out by the pool in low-cut tops and shorts, reading magazines and chatting on her phone. Whenever she bent over, Byron was mesmerized by her enormous breasts threatening to escape from her spaghetti-strap top.

She went to San Diego State, lived on campus there, and came home without warning whenever she felt like it. She'd bring home big Hefty trash bags of laundry, dump them out in the middle of the kitchen floor, and go sunbathe while her mom washed it all, folded it with love, and talked, talked, talked.

They entered the cool, quiet house and dumped their backpacks. Trent headed straight for the fridge. "Motherfucker," he said into the appliance.

"What?"

"Someone ate it."

"What? Who?" Byron feigned irritation to match Trent's, but inside his belly did a little flip. Betsy must be home. He checked out by the pool. Nothing. Checked the laundry room just off the kitchen. No trash bag of clothes. He sighed, frustrated with the whole thing. Nothing ever worked out the way he wanted anymore.

"Bet my mom took it to work. She's got this new boss, kind of a jerk, but he likes her cooking. I bet they end up screwing." Trent made a face, grabbed a bag of chips, and threw it at Byron. Byron couldn't believe the way Trent talked about his mom sometimes. Trent grabbed a box of cookies and two Cokes. They watched TV, played a new video game where you got to shoot Nazis who shouted German curse words at you before they died, snacked on Doritos and salsa and ginger snaps, and at some point Byron realized he actually missed Tilly and her endless jabbering. It seemed like nobody had a regular family anymore.

Byron wasn't really in the mood for gaming, but there was always the possibility that Betsy would appear, so he figured he might as well camp out and wait. More and more Byron felt like he was always waiting these days, for something, anything, to happen. And then the only stuff that ever happened wasn't the kind of stuff he wanted to have happen, like his parents splitting up.

Last year had been pretty good. Being on track and swim team meant that, for a freshman, Byron knew a lot of upperclassmen, so he never got hazed. He'd worked his way into the jock crowd before he realized that the rebels hated the athletes. So he spent his summer hanging around a couple of members of the lightly rebellious set. And now he was straddling both groups, which gave him decent social status at school. Not that it had done him much good. He was pretty much a third wheel in both groups and Trent was still his only real friend.

School itself was a grind. Byron wasn't a nerd like his sister, so he had to actually earn his grades, wading through boring novels and his fat U.S. history book and biology BS. It wasn't that he couldn't do the work—he wasn't stupid—it was just that he didn't see the point of most of it. Seriously, when in life would he ever need to be able to recite a whole passage from *Macbeth*? Or identify the body parts of a dissected rubbery stinky frog? Or recap the Declaration of Independence?

And then there was his dad. Graham had taken Byron and Abby out to dinner the night before, which meant a tedious hour and a half of sitting in a corner booth in a diner while Abby drank water and ate nothing and Graham lectured Byron on all the ways he needed to "step up." He told Byron he was the man of the house now, and had to take on more responsibilities, not "skate by" anymore. Byron didn't know what Graham wanted from him. Not only was Lana fine taking care of Byron, even happier when she was doing it, but there was Matt now. Wasn't he the man of the house? Didn't Byron get to keep being a kid for a couple more years? Graham had nothing but advice for Byron, always implying that whatever Byron was doing, it wasn't good enough.

"Sports is the key," Graham had said. It was a speech Byron

knew well, brought on by the scribbles Byron always drew on napkins at the table. "I mean, art is a great hobby, but there's no money in it. No career."

"Right," Byron said. He wasn't really considering a career in art. But he also didn't think track or swimming were keys to anything, any more than Shakespeare or frog dissection.

"Now, I don't mean a career in sports, mind you," Graham went on, while Byron sketched the man with a tiny dog who was standing outside the restaurant. It was just getting dark and the streetlight above the man was on, casting a milky shadow. Byron couldn't get it right on the napkin, though. He'd shaded to the point of tearing through the first layer of the napkin. "But a college scholarship in track or swimming, that's a launching pad to whatever you want to do. Business. Law. Hell, maybe even medicine."

Abby snorted and squinted at Byron, cocked her head to one side as if trying to see how Graham could possibly see a doctor in him. Not that Byron disagreed with her, but still. He wadded up his straw wrapper, tucked it into his straw, and blew it at Abby. She dipped her fingers in Byron's water and flicked them at Byron. Byron jabbed at her with his pen, drew a line down her arm. She picked up an ice cube and threatened to go for the collar of his shirt with it, but just as Byron was deciding between calling a truce or smacking her, she popped it into her mouth and smiled, fluttered her eyelashes all innocent-like. All of this childish behavior, super-inappropriate in a restaurant, going on two feet from Graham, and he either didn't notice or didn't care. They never would've acted like this around Lana.

Graham wasn't a bad father, not that Byron had anyone to compare him to, but he was never really all there. He was like a cardboard cutout dad, like one of those life-sized movie star things you saw in movie theater lobbies. He'd ask them what they did at school, but then Byron could tell he wasn't really listening to whatever they said. Whenever they'd stop talking, Graham would look up from his phone or come back from staring off into space or checking out some girl across the restaurant and say, "Oh, that's good. What else?" to get them going again. It was obvious that Graham didn't know what to do with them. Back when their parents were together, Lana took care of everything kid-related, and now, whenever they were alone with Graham, Byron could see how uncomfortable Graham was. They'd lived together Byron's whole life, but they hardly knew each other.

Trent elbowed Byron as a Nazi came around the corner, headed straight for him. Trent took him out just in time. Byron wasn't concentrating on the game and kept getting shot. Trent wasn't competitive, so it didn't hurt to lose to him. Trent never really cared much about anything, which made him pretty easy to be around.

"You ever hear from your dad?" Byron asked.

"Who?" Trent said.

"I mean, birthdays or holidays or whatever. Or is he just, like, gone?"

"I don't know. He has a new kid now, you know? He's all about that little bastard. Doing the second-chance thing."

"You call your brother a bastard?"

"He's my half-brother. And he is a bastard. My dad won't marry her."

Trent was the only guy who knew about Byron's parents splitting up. They didn't talk about it much, but Byron liked that Trent understood without Byron having to explain. He got why Byron didn't want to be at home much these days. He usually made Byron feel better. Only now he had Byron wondering if his dad was going to disappear like Trent's. Take some job across the country and just never come back. Start a new family and forget about his old one.

"But what about you and Betsy? Doesn't he want a second chance with you guys?"

"What about us? We don't need that asshole," Trent said. "Bets and I are fine."

Byron shoved a handful of chips into his mouth, washed them down with Coke, and it made him feel ill for a moment. He needed to get going, back home to Lana and her new nervousness and Matt and his weird food rituals and Abby and her boring perfectness. He had a ton of homework to do, too.

"No worries," Trent said. "It gets easier. Much like you've gotten used to me kicking your ass here." He gestured toward the TV, which Byron wasn't paying any attention to.

Byron nodded and sat up. "Rematch, asshole. I was just getting your confidence up. Now your ass is mine."

"My ass is Fiona's," Trent said. "When we were screwing she dug in so hard she left scratch marks on my left cheek. That shit hurt for a week." Trent smacked his own butt for emphasis, and Byron shook his head. Life was so unfair.

Despite being part of the jock crowd, Byron rarely got invited to the cool parties, and worst of all, he still didn't have a girlfriend. He'd come close with Trina, before she shut him down over some crap about her best friend feeling jealous every time Trina was with Byron. So that was it for them. One kiss, followed by a tizzy from some basket-case girl who called herself a friend, and Trina was no longer speaking to him. No other girls really paid him any attention, except as a guy who could introduce them to someone else—someone more popular, or more edgy, or just less dull. Somehow Trent had managed to hook up with a friend of his cousin's over the past summer, despite looking like a cross between an overgrown hobbit and Spicoli from *Fast Times at Ridgemont High*. Where was the justice?

"We can make sandwiches," Trent said, checking the fridge again as if the leftovers might have magically reappeared. He came back and took the controller for his turn.

"Nah, I'm not really that hungry. Maybe I'm going to go," Byron said, shaking the crumbs from the bottom of the chip bag into his mouth. "I have that history report."

"You even read the section yet?" Trent asked, back to firing rounds at a stubborn Nazi who refused to go down.

"I don't need to. I have Uncle Matt." Byron jumped over the back of the couch and clipped his heel, barely making it. He needed to work on that move some more.

"Lucky dog," Trent said. "I have that calculus test. Is he good at math?"

"He's a fucking genius. He's good at everything."

Byron dusted the crumbs from his hands and pants onto the floor so Sparky, the rumpled little gray mutt, could lick them up.

"Good at everything except being a normal human being?" Trent asked, just as he got taken out by the Nazi.

"Yeah, except that."

5

Lana

Graham had left full closets behind when he moved out. Lana figured he'd come for it all eventually, but as the months passed it was starting to seem unlikely. She touched the familiar fabrics, felt the cool weight of them, marveled that something so simple, so inanimate, could elicit so many emotions. The clothes reminded her that while she'd been willing to stick it out no matter what, still would if he would be willing to work on their issues, he had walked away clean and hadn't looked back. How did people do that? Simply let loved ones go and carry on like they never mattered in the first place?

Lana had the opposite problem. She kept everyone. Even the sitters who'd never cleaned up after the kids though she specifically asked them to, the undependable friends who always canceled last-minute, the father who'd never really had time for her. Lana toted them around with her everywhere she went, weighed down by their unreliability, holding out hope for the day they'd finally rise to her expectations. She missed them when she didn't hear from them. The kids hadn't had a sitter in years, but Lana still kept in touch with the ones she'd used. She still made regular lunch plans with friends who almost never kept the date. She still called her father, trying to time it for when her mother was at her weekly bridge game, to see if he was in there, the dad she'd lost so long ago.

"Well, now, kitten," Jack would say. "What's new out there in Cali-for-ni-ay?"

And Lana would start to tell him about how well her kids were doing in school, how they excelled at sports, how amazing they were. And Jack would launch into a diatribe about something a lot less pertinent than his only grandchildren.

"They're trying to close one of the parking lots here at the villa. Turn it into a putting green. Now, you know I appreciate a man's need to fine-tune his game, but do you have any idea how many golf courses there are in Florida? Or how lousy some of these old folks are at parking? I had my door dinged twice last week by some old fart parking his Caddy too close to me and opening his door into mine. Can't we keep it a parking lot, designate it for people who aren't fit to park among us civilized folk?"

Lana would try a few times to get Jack back into the realm of the relevant, but there was no stopping him once he started talking. Eventually she'd hang up, unfulfilled, frustrated, vowing to stop setting herself up for disappointment. Then a week later she'd miss his booming voice and rants about old ladies feeding pigeons off their balconies, and the bird droppings all over the walkways below, and give him another chance.

As for Graham, it was time to stop waiting for him to come around. He had a totally new wardrobe. He had reinvented himself. He wasn't coming back for these things. Lana had bought five large plastic bins with snap-on lids months ago, then forgot about them. She hauled them up from the garage and started stowing Graham's clothes in them. With each armload carefully folded into a bin, the weight of the room lifted. She finished in record time. Months of procrastination resolved in a half hour of effort. She stood back and admired her handiwork. The closet was wide open, spacious as a promise.

She emptied his dresser drawers next: socks, underwear, an array of ties and cuff links he'd never worn. And that's when she found it: Graham's wedding ring. A simple gold band resting in a carved wooden bowl they'd picked up on a trip to the Grand Canyon, mixed in with paper clips, a memory stick, a brown button, some change. Had he forgotten it? Left it on purpose? She set it on her dresser and tried to decide what to do with it. Ignoring it seemed like the best option for the time being. She still had the bins to contend with.

She hadn't thought about how to get the bins downstairs. They were heavier than she'd expected, crammed so full that some of the lids wouldn't latch. She dragged them to the top of the stairs and considered her options. She was tempted to shove them down the stairs, sledlike, and see what happened. But if they caused any damage to the walls on the way down she'd have no one but herself to fix it. It wasn't like she could ask Graham to help her carry them when he came to drop the kids off. Or she could, but she wanted this to be hers, this cleansing act. He could fetch his things from a dusty corner of the garage like a proper ex.

Matt sat by the front window, staring out at the world passing by, a fish safe inside his aquarium. His blond curls and green eyes were set aglow by the sun, his pale fluttery hands busy in his lap, tinkering with some object she couldn't make out. Lana cleared her throat, wanting to get Matt's attention without startling him, and got no response. Throat-clearing was one of those signals that had to be learned, and Asperger's made it harder for Matt to absorb social cues.

"Matt?" Lana said. He jumped, as always. She hated startling him, but hadn't figured out how to draw him back from his reveries without doing so.

"What's in the bins?" he asked. Lana smiled. How he knew exactly what she was up to without knowing that she was about to say his name was one of the many Matt mysteries.

"Some of Graham's things. I need to put them in the garage, but I'm afraid if I try to lift them by myself I'll fall down the stairs."

"Do you remember when Grandma fell down the stairs?" he asked. Matt had been only four when that had happened. Their grandma had broken her hip, and had never fully come back from it. Lana wondered if Matt remembered visiting her in the hospital afterward, or if he just remembered the stories.

"Yes, maybe that's why I'm afraid to try."

"You're much younger than she was, so I bet it wouldn't hurt you even if you fell," Matt said. Lana nodded, waiting. He turned back to the window, rotating out of the conversation. Lana was being too polite, trying to get him to offer to help. She knew perfectly well that she needed to be direct and blunt with Matt. Subtlety was wasted on him. She'd been so good at dealing with Matt when they were younger, but years of marital diplomacy had taken their toll. She'd become too mousy.

"I was wondering if you could help me carry them," she said.

Matt turned as if surprised to see her still standing next to him. He leaned around her and looked up the stairs at the bins perched on the landing. He nodded. "I can carry them," he said, making no move to leave his window. He tracked a bird fluttering from one branch to another in the big tree out front. Just as Lana was about to prompt him again, he rose and headed toward the stairs. Lana followed him. Halfway up the stairs he turned and glared at her shoulder. "You can wait in the other room," he said. His way of telling her to back off. Motherhood had made her into a hovering nurturer. Being married to Graham had bred a need for attention that she loathed in herself. Matt liked personal space, and lots of it.

"Sorry," Lana said. "Of course you can do this yourself."

Lana had just made it into the kitchen when she heard a crash. She found Matt sprawled on the floor at the bottom of the stairs, a bin on top of him.

"I'm fine," he said before she could say anything. He waved her away. Matt was a strange mix of clumsy with lightning-quick reflexes. He was always knocking things off tables and desks, but catching them before they hit the floor. His gross motor skills were a trouble area. His fine motor skills highly developed.

"Maybe I should be helping you," Lana told him.

"I'm younger than you," he said. "I can fall down the stairs and not break anything. You go wait in the other room."

Lana sighed. What did she care if he dropped them all? They were Graham's things, left behind for her to contend with. Her sister Becca had been telling her to clear out Graham's belong-ings for months. Then she was supposed to light sage and spread the smoke throughout the house to cleanse it of the leftover bad energy of their troubled marriage. If only it could be that easy to clear away two decades of built-up memories, plans, arguments, wishes that never came true.

When Graham arrived to drop the kids off, he stopped on the doormat like there was a force field before him. He rarely offered more than a brief wave through the open door as the kids passed from his world back to Lana's. They usually exchanged a few words of small talk before he turned to head down the porch steps. He seemed to no longer feel welcome in his own house, and Lana wasn't sure if that was a good thing or not. Tonight Lana needed to hit him up for money, so this time she waved him inside. He came in, just barely, his heels resting on the metal threshold strip.

"A couple of things. For one, I wanted to warn you not to speed down the street here in your new car," Lana said. It was such a loaded statement that it made her cringe, but then she patted her front jeans pocket, where Graham's discarded wedding ring rested, and it seemed less petty. "I guess they've set up a speed trap."

"Here? Who are they hoping to catch?" Graham asked.

"Well, sadly, me," Lana said with a shrug.

"A ticket? How much was it?" Graham asked.

"Luckily, I got out of it. Turns out the officer was Nick Parker, if you can believe that." She waited while Graham processed the name.

The first time Lana saw Graham she was nestled in Nick's arms at a party. Graham had done a double-take as he walked by and Lana had smiled at him. She and Nick were days from breaking up, in the tender tail end of their summer romance. Nick had just enlisted in the family business. He was shipping out soon and wanted no strings. It was a bittersweet ending. They were parting as friends. But Graham didn't know that as he flirted with Lana at the drinks table while Nick was in the bathroom. Graham was competitive, confident, determined to steal Lana from chiseled, brawny Nick and his six-pack abs. He pursued her relentlessly. Lana had been loved before, but never like that. Never with such hunger. Graham had been so proud to call Lana his girlfriend, so jealous when other guys talked to her. When had that vanished?

"Nick Parker," Graham said. He shook his head. "Out of the Marines and into the force."

"Yeah, it was strange running into him. Funny thing is, I think he recognized Matt before he realized who I was."

"Well, good that you got out of the ticket," Graham said. He backed up a step, nearly stumbling out the open front door.

"So, the other thing. Byron's swim team fees are due, and Abby's soccer team is taking pictures, and for some reason the water bill is higher than usual this month. I was wondering—"

"I'll take care of it," Graham said. He looked behind him, toward the darkening street. Was he looking for escape, or Nick Parker?

"Oh, thanks. The car also needs an oil change. It's actually overdue." It wasn't, but if Graham was feeling generous, Lana figured she should ask for something extra.

"Yeah, okay. I don't have my checkbook. I can bring it next time. Is three hundred dollars enough?" Lana hesitated, shrugged. He'd always insisted on managing the finances. How was she to know what everything would cost? "Let's make it four hundred."

"Great. Thanks. That extra hundred is probably cheaper than a ticket would've been," Lana said with a laugh. Graham smiled, a humorless pinch of his features, and headed out.

Lana still felt the occasional swell of loss when she watched Graham leave the house. She was fine during the day, as the house had always been her domain during daylight hours. But watching him walk away during the same time frame he used to be arriving home reminded her how much her life had changed, without her permission.

She found Byron settled at the kitchen table, his pen in his left hand, curled into a clublike fist that seemed incapable of creating the fine sketches and beautiful drawings that he left in the margins of every page, on the backs of junk mail envelopes, in the corners of her shopping lists. Matt was the only other left-hander in the family. And the only other one with any artistic skill.

"This one," Lana said, touching a thin line of a forehead, nose, chin. It was barely an outline of someone's profile, but it was a beautiful suggestion of a young woman. "This is great. Who is that?"

Byron slid his elbow forward until the picture was covered. "Nobody."

"Matt has some very nice artwork," Lana said, tackling the dinner dishes, silently reprimanding herself for talking, for distracting Byron from his homework. English, which he hated, but which had been her favorite subject. She wished he'd ask for help, or share his assignment, or just connect a little more, like Abby did. Sometimes. The truth was, Abby had been growing a little more distant with each passing year since about age eleven. At fourteen she could go a full day without uttering a single word. And then other days she'd talk so much Lana couldn't keep up with her.

Matt drifted into the room, handed Lana his empty ice-cream bowl, vanilla with chocolate sauce, same as always. He hesitated, watching Byron.

"Hemingway," Byron said, without looking up. "He was kind of an ass, I guess."

Lana turned to scold him for his language, but stopped herself. He wasn't talking to her. She didn't want to interrupt one of his rare efforts to chat with Matt. Matt mumbled and slid his hands into his pockets, then back out. He smoothed his hair, tugged an ear, adjusted his collar, and tucked his restless hands back into his pockets.

"Hemingway was unhappy. And sick. He had liver problems. Diabetes. High blood pressure," Matt said. "He was an alcoholic. And depressed. He committed suicide in 1961."

"Really?" Byron looked interested for the first time.

"His father, grandfather, brother, and sister all committed suicide. They had hemochromatosis. All of them. It's hereditary. Too much iron in the blood. Toxic levels. The iron accumulates in joints and organs. Supposed to be very painful. Hemochromatosis leads to diabetes, cirrhosis of the liver, heart disease, and depression. The iron affects your brain and moods. A lot of suicide among people with hemochromatosis. It's more common in people of Irish descent. He won the Pulitzer and the Nobel prizes. He had four wives."

"Hm." Byron leaned back, taking in his half-written essay, and rubbed his lower lip.

"Nice. Good shading," Matt said. "The perspective is off a little. With the background. It's morning? I see what you did with the shadow there. It's too light. But definitely looks like morning light."

Byron looked at him questioningly and Matt nodded a few times, his head bobbing as he considered his own thoughts. Matt held his hand out, a curved index finger gesturing toward Byron's paper as his eyes took in the spinning ceiling fan overhead.

"Yeah," Byron said. "It was this morning. The shadow of the tree's pretty good, but something's not right with the hill behind it, the building over here. The perspective is off." He spun the paper around for Matt to get a better look. "You think it's too light?"

"Hm," Matt said. "The hill. Yes. The hill. It's too . . ." His hand fluttered toward the page and Byron held out his pen. Shyly, Matt took the pen, made a few strokes that Lana couldn't see, and they both nodded in unison.

"Amazing," Byron said.

"Better," Matt said. He laughed a hoarse huff and shook his head. "Not amazing, but better."

Byron spun the page back and lowered his head. Lana wondered if Matt had hurt his feelings, if she should explain again the bluntness that comes with Asperger's.

"Steinbeck's next," Byron said.

"Ah, Steinbeck." Matt nodded enthusiastically. "He also won the Pulitzer and the Nobel. But he only had three wives."

"Is his writing better?" Byron asked. "I just can't get into all the bullfighting."

Matt nodded. "Not just better. Amazing."

Byron laughed, a loud bark, and Matt startled at the sound. Matt shook his head, clearing the effects of the unexpected noise, and chuckled himself, a rattle of mini-huffs, like the rumbling start of an ancient car. As he wandered back toward his room Lana raised her eyebrows at Byron. He shrugged, grinning.

"He's funny. Who knew?"

Lana left him to his homework, headed upstairs to check on Abby, who was busy writing in a journal in her room. Abby ignored Lana in her doorway, so Lana left her alone. Lana pulled Graham's wedding ring out of her pocket and set it in the jewelry box where her ring now lived. Maybe someday she'd sell them. Or give them to the kids. Just as she was sinking into a pool of self-pity, her cell phone rang somewhere in the house. She never had it on her, and never got to it before it went to voice mail.

"Mom!" Byron yelled. "Phone!" It drove her kids crazy that Lana didn't keep better track of her phone. They lived on theirs, but nobody really called Lana, aside from her sister Becca. The only people who ever sent texts from Lana's phone were her kids, to keep under the texting limit Graham had set for them. She met Byron on the stairs, holding her phone out to her.

"You missed the call."

"Of course I did. I always do." She smiled.

"Who's Nick Parker?" Byron asked.

Lana opened her mouth and closed it again, wondering if he'd overheard her talking to Graham. It took her a moment to realize the missed call had been from Nick Parker. The perfect, chiseled dreamboat of her past popping up in her present to pull her out of her own wallowing. Twice.

"An old friend," she said. An old friend who didn't have her number. She smiled and hit the call-back button as Byron headed for the kitchen, back to Hemingway.

"Are you a stalker?" she asked when Nick answered. "How'd you get my number?"

"I'm a cop," he said, laughing. "You never called for that coffee, so I thought I'd remind you. No pressure. If you aren't interested . . ."

"How's Friday?"

6

Matt

Matt preferred forty-five-degree angles for most things. Ninety was too sharp. Thirty was too shallow. But forty-five felt just right. Each item just far enough apart to make it easy to grasp without knocking anything else over. Matt hated his clumsy nature, but it was what it was, so he just tried not to crowd things together, and never put anything at the edge of a table. Spacing was important. Spacing was soothing. Spacing was forgiving when Matt's body didn't cooperate with his brain.

Matt arranged his food the same way, separate bowls and plates and utensils a few inches apart, spokes extending out from the wheel of his dinner plate at forty-five-degree angles. He admired the arrangement of objects the way he took in the beautiful alignment of a constellation. Not that constellations were aligned, not carefully placed or symmetric like he liked his food. In fact, it was the asymmetric nature that drew him to stars. So much chaos and chance, scattered all around. But then held in place for eternity. It was infinitely distracting and inexplicably soothing.

But the food, that had to be at forty-five degrees. He started with the dinner plate, and set the blue cup and green bowl of carrots at the proper angles. He liked his blue cup best because it was the hardest to tip over, and he preferred a particular spoon and fork that felt most secure in his hand. He liked the carrots in a small green bowl just for carrots, and the corn on a very small salad plate with slightly raised edges. Lana was just finishing making dinner, and he didn't have his napkin or silverware yet, and the special corn plate was missing, replaced by an extra salad bowl. He didn't want to make a fuss, but he wanted the plate instead of another bowl. He tried to like having the bowl for a change. As he arranged them one by one, the overall effect of the dinner plate, carrot bowl, and corn bowl was very Mickey Mouse. Head and ears. He smiled and looked up, at no one in particular.

"Mickey Mouse," he said. Abby sat across from him and Byron was to Matt's left. They were inches from the Mickey Mouse design, but instead of looking at his arrangement, they turned toward each other. They were always doing that, pulling in toward one another like magnets, instead of seeing what was all around them. He pointed toward the plate and two bowls, but just then his extra salad bowl was lifted away.

"Sorry, Matt," Lana said, replacing the bowl with the corn plate. "I forgot."

Mickey Mouse vanished, and the angles were thrown out of sync. He fixed it just as the napkin and silverware arrived, but they were the wrong fork and spoon. They were the narrow-handled smooth ones that he had a harder time holding on to. He needed the ones with the wide, flat handles, and the pretty flower design around the edges, for extra grip.

"Oh," Matt said, holding up the fork. "I can't. Not these. I need the other ones. The ones with the scalloping around the edges."

"Right, sorry," Lana said. She sighed, frustrated, and the feeling filled Matt's chest as she took the fork and spoon and came back with the right ones. He wanted to keep things simple, to just have everything the same every day, but somehow that ended up making them harder. He didn't understand why.

Lana waited while the kids served themselves. Byron filled his plate in a messy heap, everything touching everything else, exactly the opposite of how Matt liked his food. Abby took a small scoop of corn, some salad, and a few slivers of halibut. Lana asked Abby if she wouldn't like more food, and Abby said no, as always. Matt wondered why Abby came to dinner at all, since she rarely ate anything. Then Lana started eating, too fast to taste her food. Lana was sad again, or maybe mad, Matt wasn't sure which, but her happiness was gone and her unhappy feelings filled Matt's whole body until he could barely move. Then Abby asked for more water, and Byron told her to get it herself, and the tension in the room and in Matt's body just got worse.

Dinners, which had always been a quiet time for Matt, were quiet no more. The kids talked at the same time, tonight about swimming and driving and movies and money, and they got louder and louder, talking over one another until the noise hurt Matt's ears and muscles and bones. He covered his ears to make it stop. It was better with his hands dampening the noise except that he couldn't eat with his hands over his ears and he was hungry.

He decided to try again, but when he removed his hands the talking was even louder, now about driver's training and an expensive soccer camp and getting jobs and swim team fees, and there was a scraping sound, the horrible screech of metal against ceramic as Byron separated bites of fish with the side of his fork. Matt raised his hands to his ears again.

An unexpected prod to Matt's shoulder, not rough but a harsh jolt of unanticipated contact, nearly knocked him to the floor. It was Lana, smiling, holding an empty TV tray, nudging him with it. She gestured for him to put his food on it, but he still had no free hands, just the ones on his ears, which were busy keeping the noise out. She set the tray down, mouthed something he couldn't hear, and loaded up the tray for him. She pointed from the tray down the hall toward his room, as if he had suddenly sprouted an extra set of arms and could now carry the tray of food away from the noise while covering his ears to block out the noise. Matt stared at it, wondering how it had all gotten so complicated so fast. He just wanted dinner. The weird ground-turkey meatloaf he didn't care for, not on Mondays, but he refused to eat the halibut the rest of the family was eating, because Matt didn't eat fish. So he got leftovers of other food he also didn't care for. But he also got corn, which he loved. And it was getting cold.

The tray rose before him and Lana led the way. Matt followed her out of the kitchen, into his room, where she set the tray down beside the bed. He would have to rearrange the food. Everything was in the wrong place again. Lana closed the door, shutting herself in the room as well. Matt removed his hands, grateful for the quiet. Well, it was considerably quieter, but he could still hear them: the higher pitch of Abby's voice carrying above the lower tone of Byron's. Byron's voice was changing, getting deeper, getting easier to mute with doors and hands, it was more of a vibration than a sound these days. But Abby's shrill pitch just couldn't be stopped.

"Sorry. They're a little excited tonight," Lana said.

Matt nodded. Excited. Not the correct word. *Agitated* was closer. *Argumentative*.

"They're mad at you," he said. Lana flinched, as if he had said something hurtful, and he wondered if he had. Wasn't it true? Wasn't it obvious? "Because you and Graham aren't together anymore. And they think they could have all of these things if he was still here. You have less money without him. He makes a lot more money than you do. You aren't a CPA like him. So they're mad at you."

"I heard you," Lana said, hands on her hips. Her hips were bigger. Not much, but enough that her jeans had little horizontal wrinkles running between her hips. The jeans were straining to contain her. Her hands were holding her tight now, too. Even tighter than the jeans. Little wrinkles formed in the backs of Lana's hands as she gripped her wider hips. The gripping meant stress, strain, unhappiness, this much Matt knew. He could feel Lana's unhappiness seeping into his body, settling into his sternum, expanding within his chest. It made it hard to breathe.

"And now you're mad?" he asked. "You're mad at me about wanting a different fork?"

"No," she said. "I'm not mad." She rubbed her forehead. Massaged the pressure points just above her eyebrows. Matt wondered if acupuncture would help her. He wouldn't do it, let someone put needles in his body, needles that might have anyone's germs on them, but Lana was a schoolteacher and was around germs all day long, so she probably wouldn't mind.

"You could get acupuncture," he said, pointing toward his forehead, and suddenly Lana was laughing.

"I'm not upset because you like a certain fork, okay? I want you to feel comfortable here. It's just . . . everything piling on all at once. Sometimes it's too much for me. I don't have all of the solutions that everyone expects me to have."

"Solutions? I think you mean money." Matt finished arranging his food and watched Lana's earrings sway as she spoke.

"True. Teenagers have expensive tastes and hobbies and sports and I don't have the means right now. Maybe after I get a better job."

"You have a job. You said you like your job."

"I love my job. But it doesn't pay enough."

Matt eyed the corn. It was definitely cold now. He touched it with his fingertip. It was cold and not buttered. He pulled out his wallet and looked inside. There were several bills, various denominations. He removed them all and held them out.

"Here. And can I have warm corn? With butter?"

"Matt, I'm not taking all of your money, and yes, you can have warm corn with butter."

She leaned over for the corn, her jeans pulling even tighter, and Matt set the money on the tray.

"I don't really need that money. My friend Bill pays me to do programming for him. He just sends me money every week. I don't even mind the work. It's fun for me. I do it at night when I can't sleep and it helps my mind calm down. And the money keeps coming, but I don't really need it for anything. Maybe you can use some of this money for acupuncture." Matt pointed to his forehead, but he didn't mean for him, so then he pointed to Lana's forehead. "And to get more jeans. You've gained weight and those are too small for you now."

Lana looked up, hands back on her hips, wrinkles back in her hands. Matt tugged at one of the belt loops of his jeans, which were nice and worn from many washes, and showed her how they should fit.

"I wear Levi's. They fit perfectly."

"Yes, they do," Lana said, leaving with both the corn and the money.

Matt sat on his bed, watching the back side of his closed door, waiting for her to return. He needed something on the door. A poster or calendar or something to look at while he waited. He rearranged the meatloaf plate, carrot bowl, and blue milk cup, but it didn't feel right. He needed the small salad plate with the corn before any of it would work.

The noise from the kitchen grew louder, then there were footsteps, too many of them and too loud, getting louder. He covered his ears again just as his door opened and Abby and Byron, very excited now, proper use of the word, jumped up and down in his doorway yelling something he couldn't understand with his hands over his ears. Wouldn't even have understood without his hands over his ears, he was pretty sure.

They were wild and hopping, like rabid kangaroos. Only not Australian kangaroos, since there was no rabies in Australia. Kangaroos were marsupials. Opossums were also marsupials, and opossums were rabies-resistant. So perhaps kangaroos were rabies-resistant as well, even the ones not in Australia. Matt eyed his computer. If the kids weren't jumping up and down in front of it he'd go look that up right now. Could kangaroos get rabies? It seemed very important to know.

Then Lana came back with the corn, and he could see it steaming, a pat of butter precariously balanced on it and ready to slip off. She shushed the kids and Matt risked removing his hands to accept the corn.

"What they mean is thank you," she said, barely above a whisper.

"Thank you!" the kids both whispered, so loudly that it was like the rasp of a rake against concrete. They held up the money, his money, and smiled at him, as if waiting for something else.

"The corn is better now," he said. The kids looked at each other, smiled in their magnet-pulling-together way, and left laughing.

"You're a good uncle," Lana said softly, "and a good and generous brother. But lay off my weight." She shut the door and Matt leaned over the corn, inhaled the steamy aroma. It was perfect. It made up for the meatloaf.

He finished his dinner and looked up the rabies statistics while he waited for his ice cream. Lana was good about always remembering the ice cream. He loved ice cream, but he never got it at Spike's, because their freezer was broken, and Spike didn't want a repairman to come inside to fix it. Spike never wanted anyone inside their apartment.

Matt pulled out his Google map of directions to Spike's apartment. It said it would take him three hours and forty-five minutes to walk the 11.3 miles. That seemed like an awfully long time. Matt didn't know if he was a fast walker or a slow one. He only ever thought about walking to Spike's in the middle of the night when he couldn't sleep. He knew he wasn't supposed to take sleeping pills anymore, but he missed them. The ice cream was better at Lana's, but the sleeping was better at Spike's.

The doctor had Matt on Wellbutrin now, which was supposed to keep him calmer, and he supposed it did. His impulse control was better. He didn't act out anymore; when he got upset he was able to keep it inside until it went away. The Wellbutrin was like a warm fog weighing down on him that kept him from going to that place that he couldn't come back from. He hadn't kicked or thrown anything in a while, and he could see how it wouldn't help the situation to punish inanimate objects. The drug was supposed to help him censor his spoken thoughts better, too. He still said things that he didn't know would upset people, like telling Lana she had gained weight. It couldn't have been a surprise to her. She had to know she was fatter. People got upset when you told them the truth. That's what Matt had learned. The Wellbutrin helped him not tell the truths in his head quite so often.

The job he'd had before programming for Bill had been programming for Annette. She was a nice lady, but she didn't like how

Matt wouldn't look her in the eye or answer her right away. She got in his face and spoke too loud and it was hard to get away from her sometimes. But Matt liked the work. And he was good at it. The best coder on the team. And Annette knew it, too. So she put up with the no eye contact and nonresponses. Until she had a baby and brought it in to show it off, and Matt was amazed at how much it looked like the pig-baby in *Alice's Adventures in Wonderland*. It looked exactly like it. So he told her so. And then he got fired. Because his boss had an ugly baby. The Wellbutrin might've helped back then. Maybe he would have thought about the pig-baby but wouldn't have said it aloud.

Lana came in with Matt's ice cream and picked up his dinner tray.

"Kangaroos?" she asked, and he jumped. "Sorry," she said. She was always doing that to him. She would say a word to him and it'd startle him out of his thoughts. She pointed to his computer screen, to the rabies information before him.

"Some marsupials are rabies-resistant," Matt said.

"Oh, great," she said.

"It is," he said. "It takes many tests to diagnose a human with rabies. Saliva, spinal fluid, hair follicles. Not easy to diagnose before symptoms. You need to be sure, because rabies is a fatal disease."

"Is it fatal?" she asked. "I thought there was treatment. Those stomach shots."

"Treatment only works before there are symptoms. Once you have symptoms, have rabies yourself, it's fatal. Rabies is four thousand years old. Raccoons, skunks, and foxes are the most common rabid animals in the U.S. But mostly bats give it to humans here. Except in Hawaii. No rabid bats there. I don't know why. Also fish, reptiles, and birds. No rabies for them. And not in Australia. No rabies there, just lyssavirus. So no rabid kangaroos. I'm not sure about all marsupials, but opossums are rabies-resistant. Maybe because of their lower body temperatures. Not immune, but resistant. Rare, for an opossum to have rabies."

"Even our opossums?"

"Even ours," he said. He started to eat his ice cream and kept reading. When he looked up, Lana was still there. He didn't know how much time had passed.

"I didn't mean to upset you by saying that you're fatter," he told her. "You're eating more because you're unhappy. Mom ate a lot more when she was sad, too. Do you remember, after Stephen died? She ate all the time. But she didn't want to get fat, so she threw up after she ate. It's not healthy, eating all the time. But throwing up is also bad for you." He pointed to his teeth, which he carefully cleaned twice every day, and which could be stained, or worse, by stomach acid. "You aren't throwing up, so you're getting fatter, but it's better for your teeth, not throwing up."

"I didn't know you knew about Mom," Lana said.

"I notice everything," Matt said. "Well, most things. I notice things that people don't think they show me. And I write it all down." He gestured toward his notebooks. "I like to have data." He thought about showing her a notebook, but then she might touch it, and he didn't like people to touch his things any more than he liked people to touch him. "Once you're happy again you won't eat so much and your jeans will fit again."

Lana laughed and shook her head. "You're like my living, breathing conscience, Matt," she said. "With you around I don't even need my conscience."

Matt took another bite of ice cream and shook his head. "Oh, no. Without a conscience people would do terrible things."

She handed him his melatonin and he swallowed it with the last of his milk. Maybe it would help him sleep for a few hours. He'd just given all of his money to Lana, so he couldn't very well go to Spike's tonight. Spike wouldn't give him pills if he couldn't pay for them. That much he knew.

"Is Nick Parker going to teach me to hit a baseball?" he asked.

"Do you want him to?"

"No. I don't think I care about that anymore." Matt was almost done with the ice cream. It had just the right amount of chocolate sauce left, now melting into a swirling pool of chocolate-streaked creamy vanilla soup. "Maybe he could teach me to shoot a gun, though."

Lana shook her head. She started to say something, then stopped herself. Then she said, "The noise alone would probably do you in." Matt nodded. He had to agree with that. She was probably right.

"Okay, then. Maybe the baseball after all," he said.

"I'll let him know," she said. And she smiled as she held out her hand for his ice-cream bowl. The worried, eating Lana disappeared for a moment, and a happier one appeared instead. Matt liked that one better.

7

Abby

It just wasn't fair. Abby knew life wasn't supposed to be fair, as her father liked to remind her, but this was beyond unfair. She watched Caitlin, slut-in-training and terrible defensive midfielder, fawn all over Gabe. He laughed and leaned toward Caitlin, his face inches from the cleavage barely contained by her V-neck soccer jersey. Abby wore a tank top under her jersey, because if she leaned forward you could see straight down her shirt, and see that she had nothing in there. Plus, sweating in the polyester gave her heat rash, which looked like a minefield of mini-zits. Abby was playing pretty well, despite being low on energy from skipping lunch, and she silently praised herself for this, because nobody else was going to. Coach Zimmerman hardly ever noticed Abby. He even marked her absent a couple of times when she was standing right in front of him.

Abby turned away, unable to watch them anymore, and caught Emily's eye. Em gave her a sympathetic half frown, half shrug, which was nice, but didn't help. Emily had one of those annoyingly perfect bodies: tall and skinny with noticeable breasts, and every boy in school had noticed. If Em wasn't so shy, Abby was sure she'd be dating one guy after another. Or any guy at all, which would still be more than Abby.

Abby ran into position for the next drill and waited with the rest of the team for Caitlin to finish her hair-flipping and bending-over display for Gabe.

"Caitlin!" Coach Zimmerman shouted, followed by three short whistle bursts. "If I have to call you back into position one more time, you're running five laps!"

Abby and Em smiled at each other. Caitlin giggled one last time and sauntered into position. Caitlin never ran anywhere unless she absolutely had to, claiming her large breasts hurt when she did. All the more reason to avoid running laps, right? Apparently not. Abby was pretty sure Caitlin liked any chance to reference her own boobs. Even getting in trouble so she could use them to try to get out of her punishment. Coach Zimmerman turned beet-red whenever Caitlin pointed at her chest and said she couldn't do laps because the bouncing made her breasts ache. But then he'd recover.

"Change sports, or run. Your choice." He said it to her about three times per practice, but still nothing changed.

Caitlin was trouble, anyone could see. And she could hold Gabe's attention like no one else.

After practice, drenched in sweat and splattered in mud, her ponytail failing as wisps of hair swirled out from her head like Medusa's snakes, that's when Gabe decided to finally notice Abby. She was pulling her water bottle out of her bag when he came over to fetch his blue hooded sweatshirt lying on the ground next to her. If she'd known it was his, she'd have sneaked a sniff of it before he came for it.

"Hey," he said, giving her a quick little head jerk as he pulled the sweatshirt on.

"Hey," Abby said back. She was already light-headed from the workout, and Gabe's attention kick-started her heart. She had a floaty feeling as he stood in front of her, like it was a dream. She saw a few colored spots dance on the periphery of her vision. She guzzled water so she wouldn't have to say more. She was less likely to embarrass herself if she stayed quiet.

"You look good out there," Gabe said. "You're getting faster. Those longer legs of yours, I guess."

Abby stopped drinking. He'd noticed her legs? They turned to jelly and she wished she had a place to sit down.

"You ever think about track?" he asked. He cocked his head to the side, looking at her from a near-profile. From this angle she could see every one of his long, thick eyelashes, the gentle slope of his perfectly balanced nose, the fullness of his lower lip.

She shrugged. "I don't know. My brother runs track."

He turned, looked right at her. He had a thin cluster of freckles on each cheek. "Byron, right? He's good. You could be better."

Her stomach did a little flip. She smiled at the ground. His eyes were so deep dark green, it hurt to look directly into them. "Why?"

"Why do I think you'd be better? You're more focused. More disciplined."

She nodded. "Definitely. Byron's a lazy slob."

"He's pretty quick for a lazy slob." Gabe laughed and pushed up the sleeves of his sweatshirt. His forearms were tan and toned, decorated by a thin dusting of blond hair. "How'd you do on the chem midterm?"

Abby drank more water and shrugged. She couldn't tell him she'd tanked the midterm. She was one of only two freshmen in the class. Her and Nori, who was a certifiable genius. They'd both earned top honors in their math class in middle school, so they'd been placed in AP chem as freshmen, which was a big deal. It'd been a proud moment at home when they got the news. Lana had made red velvet cupcakes and everything. And now Abby was floundering, even though she knew she could handle the work. She couldn't very well tell Gabe that it was his fault.

"Not as good as I hoped," she admitted. The chem teacher, Mr. Franks, wanted to meet with her. Maybe he wanted to kick her out of class, have her wait until her junior year like everyone else. She'd never gotten a C before in her life. What did they do to you when you got a C?

"Seriously?" Gabe looked surprised. "I was sure you'd ace it."

She shook her head. She didn't have Caitlin's body, or Nori's brains, but she knew how to get a little sympathy. "My parents just split up, and it's hard to study when I keep getting shipped back and forth between them. I think that's the problem."

"Oh. I didn't know. Sorry." Gabe reached out and touched her shoulder with his long, lean fingers. It was the closest she'd ever been to him. A faint earthy whiff of lavender came with him, lingered after he withdrew his hand. She inhaled and held it, afraid to let it go.

Caitlin came up behind Gabe, neither sweaty nor dirty, makeup reapplied, fluffing her wavy bleach-blond hair.

"I'm fine," Abby said. "Forget I brought it up." The last thing she wanted was Caitlin overhearing them talking about her broken home.

"You know, me, too," Gabe said, pointing at his muscled chest. "My parents. Two years ago. It gets better."

She smiled, bravely looking right into his eyes as she did so, for just a moment, before she had to look down at her muddy cleats so that she could breathe again. He was kind and beautiful, smart and athletic. Could there be a more perfect guy?

"Gabe?" Caitlin called. She sounded testy, like they had plans and he was late. Caitlin waited about ten feet back, her hands on her curvy hips. She was the kind of girl who made guys come to her.

Gabe looked over his shoulder at Caitlin. She waved him over, three quick flicks of her hot-pink-painted nails. He turned back to Abby. Was it wishful thinking, or did he look just the littlest bit annoyed at the interruption?

"I gotta run," he said, stepping forward and lowering his voice, out of Caitlin's hearing range. "But look, if you ever want to talk about stuff or maybe study together, we can, you know, hang out."

Abby's heart sped up. She felt so dizzy her hands went numb and her face got all tingly. "Really?"

"Gabe!" Caitlin barked.

Gabe sighed and turned. "Jeez, Cait. I'll be right there."

"I'm hungry. You know how cranky I get when I'm hungry." Caitlin pouted and whined, gave her boobs a little bounce.

"Sorry," Gabe said to Abby. "Duty calls. See you in chem." He gave her a quick salute before turning and catching up to Caitlin, who was now walking away from them.

"Trotting after her like a little dog," Emily said. Abby turned to see her a few feet away, shaking her head. "But he talked to you for a while. What did he say?"

Abby watched Gabe and Caitlin cross the field. Caitlin did one of those flirty sidesteps to bump into Gabe a few times, but Gabe didn't do anything back. He kept his hands in his pockets and walked with purpose. This gave her hope.

"He said we could hang out sometime," Abby whispered. Had she heard him right? Had he really said that?

"Seriously? When?"

And that's when reality came back. "We didn't exactly make plans. We were interrupted."

"No accident. He looked way too happy chatting with you. That's the fastest I've ever seen her move, when she was booking it over here to get him."

Abby smiled, but she didn't feel happy anymore. She was back to feeling invisible. "Maybe he was just being nice."

Em nudged her. "Maybe he likes you."

"How, when he has her flopping all over him?"

Gabe climbed into the driver's seat of his old blue Honda Civic, and Caitlin stood next to the passenger door like she was above opening it herself. Gabe leaned over and pushed the door open from inside, nearly hitting Caitlin with it. Abby smiled as she watched Caitlin sulk. Gabe didn't move, and eventually Caitlin got into the car. Abby was pretty sure she could see the animated hand gestures of an argument inside the car as they pulled out of the lot.

"She's built, but she's dumb and annoying. You're the full package," Em said.

"Ha. The full package wouldn't have a C in chem."

Em, straight-A student, patted Abby's arm sympathetically. "When's your meeting with Mr. Franks?"

"Wednesday morning, before school," Abby said. She was a bundle of nerves, half worried about Mr. Franks and half angry at the whole world. She felt like this more and more lately, and wasn't sure why. While Em meant well, having her around suddenly irritated Abby. Emily was sweet, but simple. Book-smart, but not people-smart. She thought the world was a rosy place and everything always worked out for the best. She didn't even understand dirty jokes unless Abby spelled them out for her. Abby looked for something to do, some excuse to get away from her, but of course there wasn't anything. School was over, soccer was over, everyone was heading home.

Emily's mom's car pulled into the lot and Emily grabbed her duffel bag of soccer stuff and her backpack of school things. Emily's mom was the director of a preschool, and even more annoyingly peppy than Emily.

"Ready?"

"Maybe I'll just do some studying here," Abby said. "Take the bus home later."

Emily laughed. "Don't be ridiculous. My mom's expecting to give you a ride."

It was ridiculous. Ridiculous to hate her best friend for being happy and perfect, especially since Emily had no idea how pretty she was. Abby forced a laugh.

"Yeah, right. Never mind."

"I know! We can get frozen yogurt on the way to your house," Em said, giggling. She was the same exact girl inside that she'd been when they became best friends in third grade. Only now she had the figure of a budding Victoria's Secret model. Life just wasn't fair.

The thought of sitting down across from gruff Mr. Franks and hearing how she'd disappointed him with her chemistry ineptitude made Abby's stomach hurt. She knew she couldn't eat, but she smiled and nodded. "Sure, frozen yogurt sounds great."

Abby picked up her duffel bag and the spots behind her eyes danced and spun. Her face surged with heat and she got a clammy feeling all over her body. She felt a wave of nausea. A dark fuzzy feeling in her head. Her hands and feet disappeared. She was numb, dizzy, cold, but sweating. She tried to call out to Em, but she had no voice. And then the lights went out.

Abby opened her eyes to the bright sunlight above, and a crowd of faces around her. She was lying on the field, the cool grass beneath her, still in her soccer uniform. She recognized Em, Emily's mom, Coach, and a couple girls from the team. She tried to sit up and the world spun and started to go dark again. She felt like she was going to throw up.

"Easy, there!" Coach said. He was inches from her face, but he seemed farther away. He cupped her shoulder and pushed her back down. "Don't get up too fast. You fainted."

"What?" she asked. "What happened?" Abby's bag was under her left leg, her right arm twisted beneath her, still holding the strap. She wanted to let go but couldn't. Her body was too heavy to move.

"You feeling ill?" Coach asked.

"I'm fine," she said, even though she knew she wasn't. "A little thirsty, maybe." Her mouth felt like sandpaper.

"Probably dehydrated," Coach said. He disappeared from Abby's view for a moment, then came back holding up a bottle of orange Gatorade. "You need to drink up before and after. Try something with electrolytes instead of just water. Drink it slowly, and finish it all."

Abby accepted his advice with a nod, closing her eyes so she didn't have to see the worried, prying faces above her. But the fireworks display was still going on in her dark and fuzzy brain, and the world felt lopsided in there, so she opened her eyes again, squinting in the brutal sunlight. "I'm so embarrassed. I've never fainted or anything before." Everyone was still watching the humiliating Abby show.

"Oh, god, you scared me!" Emily said. She started crying, nearly hysterical. "You were right behind me and we were talking, then down you went into a big heap. Like you were dead or something." She wept into her hands until her mother reached for her, and then she cried into her mom's neck. Abby was grateful for being upstaged.

The feeling had come back into Abby's arms and she slowly propped herself up on her elbows. The world tipped dangerously to one side, and Abby tipped her head with it to line her vision up with the tilting horizon, which didn't help one bit. It just made the world tip more.

"Take some deep breaths," Coach said. He checked her pulse against his watch and nodded, satisfied with whatever he found there. Abby focused on breathing and it helped a little. The feeling in her face was coming back, but her lips were still numb. Coach handed the Gatorade to Abby and she drank a few sips. Her stomach roiled in response. She was definitely going to throw up. As if fainting weren't mortifying enough, she was going to throw up in front of all these people, too. She was beyond humiliated, but so grateful that Gabe was already gone. No doubt he'd hear about it, though. Fainting was the kind of thing people talked about. The kind of story that morphed into an epic tale about falling and striking an object, a cracked-open head and stitches and a near-death concussion, any embellishment necessary to keep the story interesting as it propelled itself down the school halls. Abby realized she was thinking clearer now, and her stomach had stopped threatening to lurch. She sipped a little more.

"Please don't tell my mom," she said, surprised at how small her voice sounded.

"Oh," Coach said, shaking his head. "Now, this is the sort of thing us parents need to know about."

"But I'm fine," Abby said. "I mean, doesn't this sort of thing happen sometimes in sports?"

"Sure, sure, I've seen it happen. Athletes, especially good ones." He nodded at Abby and she felt a warmth toward him. He had noticed her after all. "Well, they push themselves harder, sometimes to the point of fainting, throwing up, collapsing in exhaustion . . ."

"And I won't do it again. It's just that my mom, she's under so much stress already," Abby said. Yes, she was thinking very clearly now. "I don't want to upset her more. Please." She looked to Emily's mother for backup, because she knew the whole separation story, and got a reassuring smile. "I'm not sure she could handle this in her current state."

Emily's mom rubbed Abby's arm. She leaned in toward Abby

and whispered something about "that time of month?" Abby had no idea when her last period had been. She'd only started maybe eight months before and it was pretty irregular, maybe only three cycles since then. But it seemed like as good an excuse as any. She nodded, lied and said she'd been having cramps earlier. Emily's mom patted her like a pet.

"We need to tell your mom something," she said. "That you got dehydrated to the point of being dizzy, really dizzy. That you need to bring something with electrolytes instead of just water from now on. That you need a little more rest, certain times of the month?"

Abby wanted to hug her but she couldn't move that much yet. Her arms were still too heavy. "Yes. I think she could handle that."

Coach shook his head in disagreement, but Emily's mother touched his arm, whispered something to him. His face flushed red, and he sighed.

"Okay, okay. But I'm keeping a serious eye on you from now on," he said. "Electrolytes."

"Electrolytes," Abby said. "Got it."

8

Byron

Byron caught a ride home from school with Paul. Paul was one of the guys Byron had hung out with a little during summer, someone he'd known since kindergarten, but they weren't close. He was a means to an end. Byron needed to be liked by Paul's rebel group of stoners so he wouldn't be labeled a jock jerk, and Paul needed a straightlaced friend to show his parents, proof he wasn't running with the wrong crowd anymore. Which he still was, but whatever. They rounded the corner onto Byron's street, and there was a police car in Byron's driveway, freshly polished and gleaming in the afternoon sun.

"What the hell?" Paul said. He ducked down in his seat, slowed to twenty-five miles per hour on the dot, and cruised right past. "You in trouble?" he asked Byron.

Byron laughed. "No. I'm never in trouble." But as Paul dropped Byron off around the corner, Byron wondered.

"I'm not taking any chances," Paul said. "Don't tell them I gave you a lift, okay? Good luck."

Byron got to walk the block back toward his house imagining all kinds of terrifying scenarios that'd land a cop in his house on a Friday afternoon. A break-in? Something with Matt? Byron hadn't broken any laws. He'd hidden some weed for Paul over the summer once, but it was long gone. He checked the cop car to make sure it wasn't a K-9 unit. As long as there wasn't a drug-sniffing dog, he should be fine, right?

He stepped into the house and the cop and his mom were laughing on the sofa together, sitting with their knees just a few inches apart.

"Hey," Byron said, aiming for casual and striking a note just shy of panicked.

"Oh, hi, sweetie," Lana said. She never called him sweetie anymore, which either meant he was in serious trouble or none at all. "How was school?"

"Um, fine. Good." Byron stared at the cop and the cop stared at Byron.

"He looks just like you," the cop said.

"Does he?" Lana asked. She tilted her head and gazed at Byron lovingly. So then not in trouble, it seemed.

"Everything, um, okay?" Byron asked, regretting it the moment he'd said it. Why call attention to something if he didn't need to?

Lana and the cop laughed, turned toward each other, and laughed some more.

"Occupational hazard," Lana said, and they kept right on laughing. "Byron, this is an old friend of mine. Nick Parker. You remember he called the other night?"

"Right," Byron said, although he didn't remember the name at all. "Okay. Nice to meet you." He gave a half wave at the cop, but Nick Parker wasn't having any of it. He marched over to Byron, his hefty leather belt full of guns and clubs and something in a snapped leather pouch creaking as he made his way across the room. He reached for Byron's sweaty hand and grinned at him as he shook it.

"Nice to meet you," Nick Parker said. He had the high, tight haircut of an asshole. The buff build and movie-star looks of someone used to intimidating people without saying a word. Byron didn't like him. Or how cozy he seemed with Lana. The cop's radio crackled to life and he listened to the call, indecipherable mumbling to Byron, then shook his head and sat back down on the couch, this time about a foot from Lana.

"Hey, I was going to run down to Trent's, if that's okay," Byron said. He usually didn't bother to ask permission, but the cop made him feel like he needed to be on his best behavior.

"Of course," Lana said. "Have fun. Tell him hi for me."

Byron couldn't wait to tell Trent that he had competition. From a guy who looked just like the liquid metal guy in *Terminator 2*. Interestingly enough, that guy had also worn a cop uniform. Byron bailed and booked it over to Trent's, where he completely forgot to tell Trent about the cop because as soon as he walked into the house he saw Betsy's bags of laundry in the kitchen. That changed everything.

Byron was still agitated from seeing the cop, but as soon as he spotted Betsy lounging out by the pool, the feeling started to go away. He settled into a chair and half watched Trent scour Craigslist for a car. Never mind that Trent didn't have a license. Not even a driver's permit. Or the cash to buy a car. Byron sat sideways across the plush purple chair, one leg over its arm, so that he could look both over Trent's shoulder and out toward the pool. Betsy had on a new swimsuit: red with a chain of little gold rings for straps and a little skirt around the bottom. It was very low-cut. She was reading a magazine and talking on her phone at the same time, tapping her foot with its hot pink toenails and tiny gold toe ring. Byron was sketching doodles in the margin of some take-out menu he'd found on the table: an eye, a gentle curve of wavy hair, the corner of her lips. He'd just started the outline of Betsy's shoulder when he got struck in his left ear.

"Dude," Trent said, waving the rolled-up newspaper he'd used to smack Byron upside the head.

"Knock if off, jerkwad," Byron said, striking back with a thick *National Geographic* from the table.

"This is important stuff. Pay attention."

"What?" Byron leaned over to see the laptop screen.

"El Camino or Ranchero?"

"Seriously? You think that's a serious question? El Camino, no doubt." He shook his head. "Ranchero. You're a moron sometimes."

"Your mom doesn't think so."

A flash of anger blew through Byron's gut. "Don't talk about my mom."

"Don't ogle my sister."

"Ogle?" Byron started laughing. "Where'd you hear that?"

"I like it. It's a good word. Say it over and over and it becomes nonsense."

"Ogle, ogle, ogle, ogle," they both repeated until they were doubled over laughing.

"Are you jackasses stoned or something?"

Byron stopped laughing and looked up at Betsy standing before them in her red swimsuit, hands on her curved hips, long pink nails tapping in irritation. Man, she was hot.

"No, but you are," Trent said.

"Don't act like a three-year-old," she snapped. "Where's Mom?"

"Hiding from your shitload of laundry," Trent said.

"Or buried under it," Byron suggested. They both laughed until Betsy swung at Byron with a catlike swipe, smacking him in the back of the head. Hard.

"I expect him to be an idiot," she said, pointing at Trent. "But I had higher hopes for you." She directed a pink nail at Byron.

"Sorry," Byron said sheepishly.

"What a wuss," Trent said, rolling his eyes. He turned back to the laptop, back to listings for cars he'd never own.

"Is that . . . ?" Betsy was looking at Byron's doodles on the menu. At the sketches of her. Byron flipped the paper over, but she had crazy-fast reflexes and snatched it. "Wow," she said. "You actually have talent." She looked from the menu to Byron and back again, and he felt himself blush like a damn girl. "Can I have it?" she asked, barely a whisper.

"Of course you can have it," Trent said. "It's our fucking menu."

Betsy hit Trent with the same newspaper he'd used on Byron. Trent glared at Byron, as if he were to blame. Betsy sashayed over to the fridge, menu of Byron's sketches in hand, and peered inside. She leaned way over, her back arched, her round left butt cheek peeking out under the short skirt of her swimsuit. It took all of

Byron's will not to stare. He focused on the back of Trent's shaggy head.

"Where's the lemonade that was in here?" Betsy asked.

"Your boy toy drank it," Trent said, chucking a thumb at Byron without looking up from his computer.

"Sorry," Byron said, hating how pathetic he sounded. "I can make more."

"Could you?" Betsy asked, hand on her hip. "And bring me a glass?" She pointed toward the pool.

Byron shrugged and launched himself out of the chair, over the arm, and into a standing position with surprising ease. He was getting better at this. He headed toward the kitchen, kicking his legs up and swinging his lower body over one barstool, then another, without even breaking stride. He was on a roll. He looked up and Betsy was watching him with her eyes narrowed and head cocked to one side.

"Parkour?" She nodded toward the stool.

"Excuse me?" Byron asked, looking behind him to see if he'd dropped something.

"That move. Parkour." She sighed and rolled her eyes. "Hopping over stuff without stopping."

"Um, I think it's called free running?" Byron said. "I'm just trying it out."

"It's called parkour in France, where it was invented. But free running is the same thing." She put the empty glass pitcher and tub of Country Time on the counter and slid both toward Byron. "There's a parkour club on campus. You should come watch them sometime. They're badasses."

Betsy strolled toward the sliding glass doors, gyrating all of her curves the whole way there, holding the menu to her chest.

"Hey, Bets?" Byron called. She turned and gave him a bored look. Trent always called her Bets, and suddenly Byron couldn't remember if she liked it or hated it. "You, uh, want ice in your lemonade?"

"I sure do." She smiled, gave him a little hair flip, and stepped outside.

Byron opened the Country Time tub and inhaled the sweet lemony dust that rose out of the container. Trent snorted behind him.

"What?" Byron asked, as if he didn't know what was coming.

"I'm so totally texting your mom later. Just so you know."

Byron was spared from having to kick Trent's ass by the sound of Trent's mom, Tilly, opening the front door. She came in struggling with about six grocery bags, so Byron stepped over to help her out.

"Oh, will you look at that, Trent? Byron helps me carry the groceries in. And I see he's even making lemonade for everyone. Isn't that amazing? Seeing someone pitch in and help like that? Doesn't it inspire you?"

Trent snorted again. "Hey, pool boy, when you're done I'll take a glass with ice, too. And make it sweet. Use an extra scoop of the good stuff."

"Trent Alexander MacAaron, you'll get off that couch and come make it yourself," Tilly said. "Are you staying for dinner?" she asked Byron.

"Of course he is," Trent said, still looking at the laptop.

"Um, actually, I haven't asked my mom, so . . ." He didn't want to sound too eager, what with Betsy within earshot and all. But he really didn't want to go home in case the cop was still there.

Tilly stopped unpacking a grocery bag and wiped her hands on a towel. "Oh, I'll call right now and ask her. I've been meaning to thank her for that stuffed pepper recipe."

Tilly picked up the phone and headed off, leaving the bulk of the groceries still on the counter. Byron's mom would never do that. There was even frozen stuff that shouldn't be left out. Byron started putting the groceries away. It occurred to him as he emptied the first bag that this was exactly what his dad was always harping on him about, how he needed to pitch in more, be the man of the house, take responsibility. It wasn't that Byron never did stuff like this for Lana—just yesterday he'd put the dishes from the sink into the dishwasher without even being asked—but clearly Graham just assumed that he was a lazy slob.

"You know, I'm dying of thirst out there," Betsy said, coming inside. Byron barely gave her a glance as he emptied the second grocery bag and started in on the third. "Are you kidding me?" she asked, watching him. "You're putting away *our* groceries? How is it possible you're friends with my loser brother?"

Byron smirked. "Your mom pays me to be. I'm supposed to teach him some manners." Betsy giggled and smacked him on the back.

"You're awesome," she said. She dug through one of the grocery bags and pulled out a box of Nilla wafers. She stood there eating them, crumbs falling all over the shelf of her chest, watching Byron finish the job. Man, Tilly was raising some lazy kids. Byron folded and put away the empty grocery bags, then finished making the lemonade, since clearly no one else was going to.

After she got off the phone, Tilly came in, saw that Byron had put away the groceries, clapped her hands together like a two-year-old, then kissed Byron. *Kissed* him. Instead of thanking him like a normal person, she grabbed his head in her hot chubby hands, squished his face, and kissed his cheek. It was like seeing his great-aunt Ida at Thanksgiving, down to the gaudy rings that left dents behind and everything. He could see the sweat on her upper lip and the smudge of lipstick on her front tooth as she came at him, but there was nothing he could do except stand there and take it. After it was over he had the overwhelming urge to wipe his face with something, but he knew how rude that would look. Plus, she still had ahold of his head. And Betsy was standing there, munching away, watching him.

"You're an angel," Tilly said. Her palms were sweaty. "I should call your mom back. Tell her she raised you right." She gave Byron's face a little shake that made the fat on her upper arms sway and her breasts jiggle. He tried not to look down, but Tilly was holding him near her eye level, and as his eyes fought to find somewhere else to look, there it was, the paper towel tucked into her cleavage, all wrinkled and full of human body oils and sweat. Suddenly Byron didn't want to stay for dinner. He could grab a burger on his way home, kill time until he was sure the cop was gone.

"You know, now that I think about it, I have this history assignment . . ." he said lamely, pulling his face away from her hands. He tried to remember what they were learning about in history, but his mind was blank.

"Yeah, but you also have Uncle Weirdo to tell you everything you never wanted to know about World War II," Trent offered.

Damn, that was it. Pearl Harbor and Hiroshima. Byron would be able to think clearer if Betsy weren't watching, a dusting of crumbs forming a white *m* across the tops of her breasts. It would also help if he weren't so damn hungry. His stomach chose that exact moment to betray him, letting out a long noisy growl.

Tilly's jaw fell open. "No!" she gasped. "Your mom already cleared it and you're starving." Tilly took Betsy's box of cookies and handed them to Byron. "Here, this will tide you over while I cook."

Byron stood there like an idiot while Tilly started snapping green beans, slicing potatoes, dusting chicken in flour and spices for frying. Byron loved her fried chicken. Betsy sighed and poured herself some lemonade before heading back for the pool. Byron knew he shouldn't watch her go with her mom right there, but it was impossible not to. Her hips swayed with every step. When she got to her lounge chair Betsy turned and smiled at Byron, held up the lemonade like a toast. He just about fell over. Forget the cop. Today was turning into the best day. This was the most attention Betsy had ever paid to him. Trent snorted before the screen displaying his dream cars. Byron looked his way and Trent held up his cell phone, no doubt another reference to texting Lana. Byron couldn't say anything with Tilly there, though. Tilly smiled and pointed to a chair, and Byron sat.

"So, you'll never guess who I saw at the store the other day," Tilly said. "Melinda Bass. You remember her daughter Serena? She went to middle school with you boys, but then they moved away? Well, now they're back. Anyway, Melinda says they just rented the cutest little bungalow in Mira Mesa, which I think means she's divorced and can't afford to buy, even in this market. I mean, her husband was, like, an investment banker or something. Cold, but well off. Did you know their oldest, Jack? He was two years ahead of you. Right after high school he joined the Army . . ."

Byron was trapped. Once Tilly started talking, there was no stopping her. He couldn't see Betsy now that she'd settled into the lounge chair with her back to him. He looked over at Trent, and he was pretty sure Trent was smiling into his laptop, enjoying Byron's suffering, punishment for ogling Betsy. Trent was right, though. It was a pretty good word.

9

Lana

Lana rose on Saturday morning to the quiet of a house without children. She was getting used to her Saturday mornings alone, but that didn't mean she liked them. She headed for the kitchen to make coffee and wait for Matt to emerge from his cavelike room. She knew he could hear her. Matt had the best hearing of anyone Lana knew. Even though she would just be having cereal and he'd have the same English muffin prepared the same way every day, she waited to eat with him. She hated eating alone.

Coffee with Nick the day before had been interesting, but not terribly enlightening. He'd expected to have the afternoon off, but ended up working, so instead of casual Nick she got Police Officer Nick. They met at her house, and then never did make it out to coffee, because a half hour into their catch-up session he'd gotten a call and had to run. Lana had wasted their brief time with idle chitchat and never got his full story, just the basics: Marines, police force, a marriage in there somewhere to a woman with kids from a previous marriage, divorce, and no kids of his own. Lana had ended up with more questions than answers, a desire to pry deeper, but no clear sense of whether or not Nick wanted to go deeper himself. In that way he was the same old Nick: dignified and polite and hard to read.

Nick had met Byron, briefly, and had marveled at how much he'd looked like Lana. She wondered what he'd think of Abby, Graham's look-alike, if he'd met her. Nick was a strange mix of familiar and new, and Lana felt the same, like he brought out a decades-old version of herself that didn't fully sync with the current Lana. She honestly wasn't sure which version of herself she liked better at the moment: the young dreamer overwhelmed by the many options to consider or the responsible, methodical juggler who prided herself on being unflappable in a crisis.

She got her second cup of coffee and started getting impatient. She was hungry, and there was still no sign of Matt. It was time for him to take his anti-anxiety meds. She knocked gently on his door, pills in hand, to offer to make his food for him, and got no answer. She peeked inside his room. He wasn't there. His thick weighted blue blanket was folded neatly in half and resting on the foot of the bed. His shoes were missing. His jacket was gone. His keys were not on the little shelf where he always kept them.

"Matt?" she called. It was impossible that she'd missed him, but still she walked into the main part of the house, expecting him to magically appear by the front window where he camped out when the kids were gone. His window seat was empty. "Matt!" She got no answer. She dialed his cell phone and heard the familiar trill of birds chirping that was Matt's beloved ringtone. She found his phone on his bedroom floor under a pile of dirty clothes.

Lana dialed her sister Becca as she ran through the house looking for him. Thankfully her car was right where she left it, and the kids' bicycles were still in the garage right next to it. So he had no transportation, but Matt was definitely gone. Becca's voice mail picked up. Lana hung up without leaving a message and called Graham. "I need you to keep the kids a little longer."

"Lana, I have plans. You need to give me more warning . . ."

"Matt's missing," she said breathlessly.

"He's a grown man, I'm sure he's fine."

Lana rifled through the papers on Matt's desk, looking for clues. He had star charts and strings of programming codes and recipes and mathematical equations and lists of old movies and flyers for local bands in every color imaginable. Nothing of use. He also had two empty bottles, one of vodka and one of bourbon, tucked neatly behind a stack of books under his desk. She recognized both as belonging to Graham. She'd emptied the liquor cabinet prior to Matt moving in. She wondered where Graham had hidden those bottles so that she'd missed them. And why he'd felt the need to hide them in the first place. She'd always thought she knew Graham so well, that part of their demise was due to stagnant familiarity. But ever since he'd left he'd become increasingly mysterious to her.

"Please," she said.

Graham let out a terse sigh. "Honestly, the way you baby him . . ."

"I'm going out to look for him. He's on foot. He can't have made it far." She willed this to be true as she said it. "I'll call when I'm back."

"Lana . . ." Graham said wearily, as if this sort of thing happened often, as if Lana burdened him with her troubles regularly, when in fact she hadn't asked him for a single thing since the moment he said he wanted to move out.

Lana hung up and dialed Nick Parker. As his phone rang she realized it was the first time she'd ever hung up on Graham. She was proud of herself, but didn't have time to gloat. Nick's voice mail answered. He was the only police officer she halfway trusted, but what had she called to say? Did a half hour of getting reacquainted entitle her to call in personal favors from him? He was the same Nick: still handsome and solid, polite and poised and impenetrable as ever. A gorgeous machine of a man. She still knew virtually nothing about him. Was he even the type to honor personal favors? Lana had no idea.

"Nick, it's Lana. I, um. First off, it was great to see you yesterday. We should do it again soon. I wonder if you could call me back? I seem to have . . . Well, there's a Matt issue I could use a hand with."

She sounded like a stammering crazy person. Her request had

been too vague, but it seemed crazier to call back and leave a second, more detailed message. She rounded the rooms of the house a second time, a third. But of course Matt was gone and frenzied searching wasn't going to reveal him. She took a deep breath, fetched her car keys, and set out. She called Becca again.

"Two calls in ten minutes? You must miss me desperately," Becca said with a laugh. Lana started the car and backed out of the garage. She headed north. She'd cover a grid, street by street.

"Matt's missing."

"Oh, crap," Becca said. "How long?"

"I don't know. Last time I saw him was when I went up to bed last night, around ten."

"Well, he could be anywhere by now."

"That's not helpful, Becca." Lana felt a surge of bile, pure acidic panic, rise up her esophagus. She'd had two cups of coffee and no food. Of course her stomach was upset. Matt was fine. He had to be. She'd just gotten him back. He was safe now.

"Okay, okay, I'm sure he's not in Mexico or anything. Did he bring his wallet with him?"

"Yes. And a jacket. But not his phone."

"Well, can he cross the border with just his ID?"

"I don't even want to think about that," Lana said. She didn't know the answer. She was sweating now, little trickles of failure dampening her armpits and dripping between her breasts. In the past few months Matt had gotten a DUI and ended up hospitalized for an overdose. He needed supervision. Lana had arrogantly assumed she was up to the job. What had she been thinking?

"Okay, probably not Mexico. Matt doesn't like dirt or germs or people. He's a creature of habit, right? So what are his habits?"

Lana hit a cul-de-sac and stopped the car. "Outside of the house? I don't know. He's never gone anywhere."

"Maybe you should call the police?" Becca said.

"I just called Nick and left a message."

"I meant a cop you haven't slept with," Becca teased.

"I'll find him." Lana doubled back to cover the streets south of her house. "And if I can't, I'll call Nick again." The grid idea wasn't working. The streets were long loops of similar houses interrupted by cul-de-sacs. There was no grid, which she knew, as she'd lived in the curving-road development for fifteen years. She couldn't think clearly. Where would Matt go? She knew he missed his nightly walks, but he'd only taken them around the neighborhood, just a stroll around a block or two, until Lana had taken them from him, worried about what her neighbors might think. How far would he wander without her there to stop him?

"San Diego's a pretty big city," Becca said. "And Matt's brain is . . . well, it's Matt's brain. I mean, who knows what he's thinking? Maybe the police already picked him up."

If the police had Matt, that wouldn't be good. Especially if Nick wasn't available to intercede. That pissy social worker who'd wanted to put him in a state facility would no doubt hear about it, and would probably interfere with Lana getting him back. Maybe rightfully so. "Let's just pray that they don't," Lana said.

"Never knew you were much for praying," Becca chided. Her levity irritated Lana.

"I guess this is as good a time to start as any," Lana snipped. Lana had said mini-prayers before, like after watching Abby go down hard on the soccer field once, unable to move for a few endless seconds because she'd had the wind knocked out of her. As Lana had sprinted toward Abby's unmoving body she'd offered up a quick, *Please, please, please let her be okay*, to whatever force controlled such things. That was prayer, right? And it had worked. Abby was fine.

"I don't pray, per se," Becca said. "But I've been doing these meditations. You visualize what you want, put it in this glowing, spinning ball, and you send it up to the universe and ask for 'this or better.' It's very relaxing. And empowering."

"Well, can you ask the goddamn universe for this one for me?" Lana said. She was starting to cry, which wasn't helping her look for Matt. She couldn't see a thing. She pulled over and wiped her eyes on the sleeve of her sweatshirt.

"Lana, he's fine," Becca said. "He's Matt. He's . . . protected by angels or something. You know what I mean?"

"He's fresh out of the hospital where he almost died," Lana reminded her.

Becca sighed. "Okay, I get it. Keep looking and I'll keep you company." Becca lived in Virginia, so she couldn't help look for Matt, but her voice carrying across thousands of miles calmed Lana's nerves. Mostly.

Lana found a wadded but probably clean tissue in a side pocket of her purse and wiped her eyes. "Just when I think I've gained the upper hand over my train-wrecked life, something has to happen to remind me it's all still in flux." The harder she tried to stop crying, the more she cried. She hadn't slept well, never slept well anymore, and that always made her more emotional. She'd hated it whenever Graham pointed that out to her, but he'd been right. "I'm coming undone, Becca. Unspooling like one of Graham's golf balls. Byron sawed one open the other day and it had these endless loops of rubber inside. He unraveled the guts of the ball, turning it from something to nothing in moments. That's me."

"Healing is like that," Becca said. "You're right where you need to be: unformed and full of promise. It's a process of undoing the very things that have been binding you together your whole existence."

"And then what?" Lana finished blotting her eyes and kept driving.

"You ask for better. You make manifestation lists. You give yourself permission to have everything you need. And just hope to hell that in the end all of that work will be worth it."

"Is this from your meditation crap?" Lana asked.

"It is."

Lana turned around in another cul-de-sac and sighed. "Can I have a copy?"

"I'll send it as soon as we find Matt," Becca said. "So, let's try to think like Matt." She was silent for a moment. "Never mind. Doesn't he have any friends you can check with?"

Lana hooked a left and sped out of the familiar development, squealing her tires and causing an old man to stop trimming his roses long enough to glare at her. Matt didn't really have anyone that Lana would call a friend. But she suddenly had an idea of where he might be.

"I'll call you back," she told Becca.

Lana pulled up outside Spike's apartment complex. There was no sign of Matt, but why would there be? He knew better than to return here. The doctor, the social worker, and Lana herself had all made certain Matt understood that the only way he'd get better, the only way his liver counts would return to normal, was to avoid Spike and all of his drugs.

She knocked on Spike's door but got no answer. She didn't have a number for Spike. She didn't even know his real name. It was probably Charles or Henry or Lawrence, something befitting his banished-rich-kid status. She knocked again, louder.

"Spike?" she yelled at the door. The apartment complex was vast and boring, beige blocky structures loaded with college kids—Spike's clients, living all around him. Along the walkways were bicycles and skateboards and empty five-gallon jugs of drinking water waiting for pickup. One of them was half full of murky water and had a goldfish swimming in the muck. Lana shook her head. These were UCSD kids. Supposedly smart ones.

She pounded the door a final time and it opened a crack, revealing one of Spike's green eyes, red-rimmed and clearly under the influence of something. A stale and rank aroma wafted out of the apartment. Spike was small, thin, pale, and jumpy. Your stereotypical strung-out-looking drug addict. He was in his twenties but he looked about forty. A man-child in a child-sized body. Everything about him emanated lost soul. Spike wasn't angry, never seemed violent, he was just Spike. At another point in her life, he might've become one of Lana's pet projects. He needed someone to care about him, that was clear.

"Yeah?" Spike said. He'd met Lana before, but she didn't expect him to remember her. He was either high or sleeping each time she'd stopped by to pick up Matt for one of their occasional lunches.

"I'm Matt's sister, Lana. Do you know where he is?"

"I know who you are, sister," Spike said. He smiled, revealing a gap where he was missing a molar. Spike shuffled and a metal base-ball bat clattered to the floor next to him. He swept it aside with his foot. The top of his white sock was stained with something red. Lana hoped it was ketchup. It seemed likely. Fast-food bags littered the room. According to Matt, Spike had flunked out of college and was cut off by his well-to-do parents after a stint in rehab didn't take. She wasn't sure how he and Matt had met up. She'd been busy trying to resurrect her slipping marriage at the time. Clearly she should've been paying more attention to Matt back then. She was trying to make it up to him now. She just needed a little more time. *Please*, she prayed to whoever might care, *let him be okay. Give me more time.*

Lana looked around for witnesses, but it was before noon on a Saturday in a college town, and everyone was still sleeping off the night before. She saw a form on the couch behind Spike. In the darkness she could just make out a dark blue sock hanging pre-cariously off one foot. She pointed toward the form.

"Is that him?" she asked.

Spike smiled, braced the door with his bony shoulder. "What's it worth to you?"

"Oh, I don't know," Lana said sweetly. "A call to the police, maybe?" Maybe it was time to stop being so nice to people. It never got her anywhere. She brought up Nick's number on her phone, poised to call.

Spike frowned and opened the door. "You don't play fair," he said.

Matt was passed out on the couch. On the coffee table in front of him was a bong, a small glass pipe, a tinfoil package of Lana-didn't-even-want-to-know-what, an open orange pill bottle, a half-empty bottle of tequila, and a box of Pop-Tarts. There were food containers and discarded clothes everywhere. She stepped inside and was hit with the smell of urine.

"He pissed himself," Spike said. He dropped into the nearest chair and propped his feet up on the table. "You going to clean it up?"

Lana made her way to Matt and felt his cheek, his chest, his neck. He was warm, breathing, his pulse thumping steadily in his throat beneath her two fingers. He looked so young, with his rosy cheeks and blond curls. So helpless. She sighed and fought back tears. This wasn't how it was supposed to be. She was still holding her phone. She looked at the screen, debating. How much could she trust Nick? He was as by-the-book as they came. Spike was watching her closely.

"Careful, sister," he said. "This doesn't look good for him."

A seething rage filled her up. Who the hell was this little shit, to do this to her brother? And now threatening her? She palmed her phone and hesitated. He was right. It was clear that Spike was breaking an assortment of laws, but Matt was still finishing off his DUI suspension. And he'd only been out of the hospital for two months since his overdose. That social worker had wanted to put him in a state facility. What kind of ammunition would this give her? Lana battled a sense of powerlessness. Matt deserved better. She switched her phone to video and lowered her hand, pretending to be done with it.

"What exactly did you do to him?" she asked. He had Pop-Tart crumbs all over his chest and Lana dusted him off.

"Gave him my special Matt-sleeping cocktail. Don't worry. He didn't OD this time." Spike laughed as if it were all a great joke, the destruction of Matt's psyche and liver and everything that was good and pure about him. Lana turned her phone to get a good shot of Spike, a wide pan of the drug-paraphernalia-strewn table and surrounding space. She tried to avoid getting any part of Matt's body. She lifted her phone and quickly emailed the video to herself.

"Hey, now," Spike said. He scrambled toward her but stumbled over his own heaps of crap and couldn't get to her in time. The phone whooshed that the message had been sent.

She held up her phone. "My insurance policy. You want me to be the only one who has that video, you never see him or interact with him again. You hear me?" She had no idea if the police would care, but she was banking on the hope that Spike didn't want to find out.

Spike shook his head, fell back into his chair, and rubbed his bristly head. "You can't save him, you know. He's a goner. Just like me."

Lana dropped the phone into her purse. "Help me get him into my car," she said. "And give me a blanket or a towel to put under him. I need to get him to the hospital."

"He doesn't need any hospital, sister. He took one tiny sleeping pill, that's it. He didn't have enough cash for more and charity's not my thing."

Spike didn't move. Lana had sixty dollars on her. She hoped it was enough to buy five minutes of Spike's time and one dingy towel. She held it up. He eyed the cash, then shrugged. "I'll get a bedsheet."

With Spike's help she got Matt into the car. She turned and glared at Spike, wanting to say something hurtful and frightening, but out in the bright sunlight of the day Spike had lost his smugness and swagger. He was nervous and exposed, glancing around him. He was small and worn, a shell of anxiety and fear. He reminded Lana of her mother in those hard months after losing Stephen. Gloria had developed that same wounded look, that same forlorn weight about her. She'd become a black hole of emotion, sucking joy from the air around her, swallowing it, and leaving only emptiness behind. Lana wondered what the source of Spike's pain was, what he was trying to numb.

"You aren't a goner," she said. "Neither of you are. Please get some help before it's too late."

Spike laughed in her face, but it was forced, betrayed by his wounded eyes. She could see that in choosing to be kind instead of cruel, she'd managed to hit him in an even deeper, softer place.

Once at home, she had the issue of how to get Matt out of the car and into bed. Or into a much-needed bath and then bed. She checked his breathing and pulse again. Both were within normal range. She was grateful she'd had enough CPR training to know this. She called his name and shook him, and he was able to open his eyes and glare at her before turning away, but she couldn't get him conscious enough to get him on his feet. He'd have to sleep it off in the car. She was staring at him when her phone rang. For once, she had it on her. It was Nick.

10

Matt

Matt had worn the wrong shoes for an 11.3-mile walk to Spike's apartment. He realized that now. The problem was that he hated tennis shoes. The laces never stayed tied. It seemed so easy for others, but laces always gave him trouble. He wore his favorite slip-on loafers, but they weren't comfortable enough for miles and miles of walking. He had a blister on the back of his left heel. He should've worn his boots.

He also brought along a jacket because it was cold in the night when he left Lana's house, but then it got warmer, and he didn't feel like carrying it. He considered leaving it, maybe hiding it in a bush somewhere so he could fetch it on his return, but the best hiding places were all damp with dew or shot through with spiderwebs and he liked his fleece cobalt-blue jacket and didn't want it ruined. But he was confused now. He didn't seem to have his jacket anymore. Where had it gone? Lana was calling his name from somewhere very far away, and he tried to open his eyes, not to answer her, but to look for the jacket, his favorite one ever, only his eyes refused to open. They were glued shut. Had Spike glued them shut?

Matt wondered if he'd made a bad decision, walking to Spike's apartment. He realized now that he could have just called Spike from Lana's house. He could have asked Spike to drive over in Matt's car, the car that Spike had demanded as payment for the ant and roach cleanup from all the beer cans Matt forgot to re-cycle, to drop off something to help Matt sleep. That was all Matt wanted. Sleep. If he'd stayed at Lana's he would've had his favorite breakfast, not Spike's Pop-Tarts. The Pop-Tarts didn't feel right in his stomach. But he probably would not have slept. He'd been having one of those nights. One of the ones when the melatonin had only worked for two hours, and the blackout curtains and the noise machine and the warm milk and the weighted blanket did nothing to help.

He'd forgotten to bring his cell phone with him on his walk, or he could've called Spike before he got the blisters. Matt wasn't good at remembering about phones. He hated talking on the phone.

Google Maps said it would take Matt three hours and forty-five minutes to walk to Spike's. It took more than four hours because his feet started to hurt. He could've taken a bus, if he knew the routes. He could've asked someone about the bus, because there were people outside their houses doing yard work and fetching newspapers, but making conversation with people was exhausting for Matt. He decided he'd rather walk, blisters and all.

There were some things he missed about living with Spike, but some things he didn't miss. Spike didn't try to have conversations with Matt, which was good, but sometimes he yelled at Matt, which made Matt feel anxious and restless, like he might do something bad if the feeling kept building inside him. But then Spike had the pills and pot to make the anxious feelings less overwhelming.

Matt had woken up at one a.m., but waited almost three hours before he set out to walk to Spike's for the pills to help him go back to sleep. He was nervous at first, because Lana had told him that he needed to stop his neighborhood walks in the middle of the night because her neighbors were the type of people who might call the police if they saw a man wandering around at that hour. But nobody was awake and no police came. And then by five a.m. there were a couple of joggers in the neighborhood. That made him feel better. Not that Matt looked like a jogger. But he figured it was less suspicious to be out among the joggers. Matt didn't want to talk to the police ever again. Except maybe Nick Parker. If he was going to teach Matt to hit a baseball. Matt didn't even like baseball, but Nick Parker had liked Lana and wanted Matt to like him and they both seemed to think that Nick teaching Matt to hit a baseball would make Lana happy. Then Lana met Graham and broke up with Nick and Matt forgot about baseball until he saw Nick again.

After walking for several hours Matt had to sit down and take off his shoes. He found two blisters, a big one and a little one, side by side on the back of his left heel. There was an old newspaper in the gutter and Matt tore a piece off, folded it carefully, and slid it over the blisters, under his sock. He tried walking in a circle to test it out. It didn't help. It still hurt to walk. He sat down again on the curb. A cat wandered up to him, tail raised, eyes wide, ears forward, asking for attention. Matt wasn't a cat person. Especially not outdoor cats. He liked birds. Songbirds. The seemingly cute pet cats were killing off the local songbird population. People didn't seem to care what their cat was doing when it was running free outside their house. But Matt cared.

The cat was small and looked jet-black, but when the sunlight hit its fur in just the right way Matt could see that it was actually a striped cat, it just had black stripes against black fur. Matt figured the cat would be soft and feel good against his hand. But he also figured it had eaten more than its fair share of songbirds. He wadded up the paper from his shoe and threw it at the cat, but missed. The cat pounced on the wad of paper and batted it playfully, pretending to be cute and harmless instead of the bird-killer it really was.

"Murderer," Matt said. The cat swatted the paper wad and skittered sideways, dancing up high on its toes for a sneak attack on the little ball. Matt couldn't help but smile, but he still refused to like the cat. He took his shoes off. He couldn't decide whether it was better to walk the rest of the way barefoot or in socks. The socks would offer a little protection from germs or any sharp objects on the ground, but then he'd ruin his socks.

"Can I help you?" a man's voice asked. Matt turned and saw a balding man in a T-shirt, boxers, and a bathrobe, his big belly straining to be free from both the shirt and the robe, on the door-step of the house behind him. He was holding a newspaper and eyeing Matt suspiciously.

"Is this your cat?" Matt asked.

"Yes, that there's Bucky. He's a sweetheart, isn't he?"

"He's a murderer," Matt said. "He's killing birds and you need to stop him."

The man swatted the newspaper across his palm. "Why don't you move it along there, buddy? Find somewhere else to sit."

So Matt walked on in his socks, carrying his shoes, and hating Bucky the bird-murderer and his owner who didn't care. Matt had ruined his favorite dark blue socks and his only feet by the time he finally made it to his old apartment. He was hungry and thirsty and hurting and exhausted enough to sleep, probably without Spike's pills, but he was ready to lie down and sleep for a long time, so he still wanted the pills. He knocked on his old door, what was now Spike's door, and it felt funny not to just walk into his own home. Except that it wasn't his home anymore. He waited. It was prob-ably only eight in the morning. Spike would still be sleeping. Matt pulled out his wallet and removed a twenty-dollar bill. It was all he had. He pounded on the door until it flew open. Spike's bloodshot eyes and a metal baseball bat greeted him. Matt held up the money.

"I can't sleep," he said. "And I'm hungry and thirsty."

"Holy fuck, Matt," Spike said. He set the bat down and rubbed his red face. Spike had terrible acne. He saw the money and grabbed it. "Come on in and let's fix you up."

The last thing Matt remembered was Spike handing him the Pop-Tarts and sleeping pill. And then this. Matt was lying in his bed, tucked under his blue weighted blanket in his room at Lana's house. His head felt cottony and he was desperately thirsty. He could hear voices. Lana and the kids, he decided. But something wasn't right about the kid voices. The pitch was all wrong. There was only a male voice, and it wasn't Byron's. It had a gravelly quality to it that meant it wasn't Graham's, either. Graham had a nasally voice. Matt pulled himself out of bed. He had no clothes on. Matt never slept without clothes on. He got dressed and tried to remember how he got to his bed, but couldn't. He didn't know what time it was, but it felt late. He opened his door and there was Nick Parker, drinking coffee in the kitchen. It was Nick Parker but not the same Nick Parker, because this Nick Parker wasn't in uniform.

"You're up," Nick said.

Lana jumped up from the kitchen table and came at Matt to hug him. She barely got her arms around him, her forearms grazing his shoulders, sending a ripple of pain down his arms and back, before Matt's body flinched and buckled in response. Matt pushed her away as he backed up, warding off her painful touch, nearly falling backward as he tripped over his own feet. Lana almost fell, too. He was worried she'd land on him. Nick came at him, whether to help him or hurt him he wasn't sure.

"No!" Lana said. She held out her hand and Nick stopped moving. "Sorry, Matt. Reflex. I didn't even think about it. I shouldn't have touched you. I'm just so relieved. Are you okay?"

"I'm thirsty," Matt said. He was leaning against the cabinet and he was afraid to move. His legs weren't under him and he wasn't sure what to do about that. They watched him as he struggled to stand. His legs were sore and heavy and his blisters hurt. He made it into a chair and smiled, not because he was happy, but because they were looking at him and it made him anxious and sometimes when an uncomfortable feeling was too much inside him he smiled.

"Glad you think this is all so funny," Nick Parker said.

"He's not laughing. It's a grimace," Lana said.

"He's lucky he's not dead," Nick said. Matt didn't think luck had anything to do with it, but he didn't say so. He'd forgotten his Wellbutrin that morning but he was still able to censor himself. That seemed like a good thing. Nick wasn't someone you wanted to say the wrong thing to. Nick leaned forward quickly and Matt jumped away from him. "I had to carry you from the car. Strip your dirty clothes off of you. Bathe you. Your sister here was panicked this morning. You care about any of that?"

"Please," Lana said. "Let me handle this."

"I'm sorry, Lana," Matt said. "I couldn't sleep. Spike has these pills that help me sleep."

"I know," Lana said. "But those are the same pills that put you in the hospital before. You can't take them, even if you can't sleep. Your liver is damaged. It needs time to heal. And you can't drink while on the Wellbutrin, remember? It can cause seizures."

Matt shook his head. "I didn't drink. I just took the sleeping pill. I didn't take anything but the pill. I drank it down with tap water. Straight from the tap, because Spike's glasses were dirty. And the Pop-Tarts. They were cherry. I don't like Pop-Tarts, or cherry-flavored things. But I was hungry and that's all Spike had."

He was smiling again, and even though he knew it was making Nick mad he couldn't stop. He didn't understand why Nick was there, or why he was so angry. Matt just wanted to sleep. Why did anyone else have to care so much about him wanting to sleep? He remembered his long walk, his run-in with Bucky the bird-killing cat.

"I hope you don't have an outdoor cat," he said to Nick. "They're killing off the songbird population."

"I'm allergic to cats," Nick said. He was watching Matt closely, and not in a nice way. "Lana said there was a pipe of some sort? What was in it?"

Matt shook his head, smiled harder, tried to stop but couldn't. "I'm so thirsty," he said. His mouth was so dry it hurt to talk. He was hot and cold at the same time. He remembered his missing jacket. "Where's my jacket?" Matt asked. "My blue fleece one?"

"You didn't have a jacket when I found you," Lana said.

"No," Matt said. "I had it. I brought it. It's my blue jacket. The one I like. The only one I like. Did you lose my blue jacket?" The feeling in his chest was building: sharp little points of anxiety growing, spreading, trying to break out.

"I'm going to pay a little visit to Spike," Nick said. "Shut down his little pharmacy. I can look for it when I'm there."

Lana said something, but Matt couldn't hear her because the feeling was getting too strong in his chest, the ringing in his ears too loud, the tension in the room too overwhelming. He covered his ears and closed his eyes. He pressed harder and waited until it was quiet and then looked up. There was a tall glass of water in front of him, his Wellbutrin pill beside it, and he was alone in the kitchen. He could hear Lana and Nick in the front room, talking quietly. Matt placed the pill on his tongue and drank the water. It was the best water he'd ever tasted. He drank it all and filled the glass again, using Lana's pitcher of filtered water. It was much better than Spike's tap water. He made an English muffin, which was the only breakfast he ever wanted. He was about to sit back down to eat when he heard the front door open, and Byron and Abby's voices. Matt picked up his food, ready to hurry to his room, but his head was still cottony and his legs were still heavy and he couldn't move fast. He heard the kids stomp up the stairs to their rooms and he relaxed. He couldn't carry his food and cover his ears, so if they'd come to the kitchen in their noisy way he would've had to leave his breakfast behind.

He could hear Nick's gravelly voice and Graham's nasally one going back and forth, could hear Lana in the middle of them, but he couldn't tell exactly what they were saying. They were laughing but it wasn't a real laugh, not a happy one. It was like Matt's anxious smile. The kind of laughter people did when there was nothing funny at all.

11

Abby

Abby showed up for her morning meeting with Mr. Franks ten minutes early. Her mom said that would make a good impression, would show that she was serious about his class. She'd been too nervous to eat that morning. Was still so nervous that she couldn't stop fidgeting. She hoped that wouldn't ruin the good impression. She was wearing a new sky-blue blouse and the locket her grandma Gloria had given her when she was twelve: one side held Abby's eighth-grade school picture and the other side held a picture of her grandma as a teenager looking so much like Abby they could've been twins. Abby adjusted the necklace, her sweater, and checked her earrings. Her hair was tightly braided and holding fine. She looked just like the straight-A student she was. Or had been, until Mr. Franks came along.

Mr. Franks poked his graying head out the door and nodded at Abby. She came in and fidgeted some more as he dug through the papers on his desk. She waited for him to sit behind the huge wooden desk that filled one corner of the room. He only ever sat on the front corner of the desk during lectures, but she figured he must use the actual chair on serious occasions, like scolding students for tanking midterms.

Instead, Mr. Franks carried his papers over and sat next to

Abby on one of the teetering metal stools at the big lab table. He rested his loafers on the rung of the chair and put his elbows on the black countertop like any high school kid. It made Abby even more nervous, having him at her side. She'd rather be lectured from across the room, with the big desk between them. He was so close that Abby could see every pore on his nose. He had some blackheads there. Abby looked away, stared at the sleeping Bunsen burner and white filmy beakers in front of her. No matter how many times they washed the beakers, they never got clean.

"So, Abby." Mr. Franks picked up the papers and smacked the edge of them on the tabletop, as if to line them up, even though they were already neatly stacked. "How are things at home?"

She looked at him in surprise. Even though he was leaning back, she could feel him invading her space. His light brown eyes were intense, almost glowing, magnified by his glasses. She shrugged. "Things are okay, I guess. I mean, my parents sort of split up."

"Sort of?" he asked, rotating the stack and tapping it on the table again.

"I mean, they did. My dad moved out and everything. But we're okay. I'm okay."

Mr. Franks nodded and put the papers down. He folded his hands on top of the pile and twiddled his thumbs. He almost seemed nervous himself. On top of the stack was a slim, glossy brochure. All Abby could make out was a black shadow of a young girl's silhouette on it. Mr. Frank's hands were covering the words below the girl. Abby could tell the girl wasn't wearing obvious clothes. *Oh, god*, she thought, *what if he's a pervert?* And here she was, alone with him behind a thick door, in the lone lab building at the back of school, and hardly any students at school this early. If she screamed, who would hear her?

"I've noticed that you don't eat in the cafeteria anymore. I used to see you in there every day. Now you're usually on the track running at lunch. Is that right?" he asked.

He wanted to know where she was all the time. Like a stalker. Abby sighed and tucked her cold, nervous hands under her legs. Maybe he was just trying to recruit her for track? Because Gabe was right, she had gotten faster. She was timing herself now. And Mr. Franks was chummy with the track coach. Abby had seen them together at lunch, carrying their sandwiches and coffees and laughing. Maybe Gabe had said something to them about her new speed?

"I play soccer. Running helps with that. But I don't have any real interest in track. I mean, my brother runs track, and I guess he likes it, but . . ."

"You've lost quite a bit of weight this year, haven't you?" Mr. Franks said. It didn't sound like a question. He had been watching her. Way too closely.

Abby pulled her sweater shut and crossed her arms. "Not really, I don't think. I mean, I don't weigh myself obsessively, so I don't know exactly what I weigh. But I eat breakfast every single day. It's the most important meal of the day." She needed to stop talking. It was always the talking that got people into trouble. "You know, I've grown some. Maybe I look thinner because I'm taller?"

"Maybe," Mr. Franks said. He stared at her until she had to look away. This was even worse than him being a pervert. "I don't mean to make you uncomfortable, but I can see you're under some stress lately, and I don't think the classwork is the issue. I feel like your troubles are something else."

"I'm not in any trouble," she said defensively. But of course she was in trouble, or she wouldn't have been there, suffering under his judgmental look.

"I heard that you fainted last week."

"Dehydration. Coach Zimmerman said it sometimes happens with serious athletes who push themselves too hard. Gatorade is my new best friend." She smiled, hard, while her heart hammered in her chest.

"I hope that's all it was," Mr. Franks said. "But is it possible there's another explanation?" Mr. Franks slid the brochure across the table, gave it a little spin so the words beneath the shadow-girl were facing her. *Anorexia Nervosa*, it read, in thick black bold italics. Abby's stomach clenched. If she'd had any food in it she would've heaved for sure. "You see, it's my responsibility as a teacher to let Mrs. Geller know if one of my students is struggling with an issue like . . ." He tapped his index finger on the brochure.

Mrs. Geller was the guidance counselor. She was ancient and had a shaky voice and big white dentures and a habit of calling everyone "dear" in this fake whisper voice that Abby didn't trust. And she smelled like baby powder. There was no way Abby could handle having this kind of conversation with her.

"Oh, please don't do that. There's no need. Really." Abby pulled the brochure closer. "I'll look this over. I really don't think this is my problem. I mean, I eat three meals a day. And snacks. I'm a very healthy weight. There's an obesity epidemic in this country, you know? There are other kids who should worry you more."

"I know," he said, staring at her. "It's just that . . . I have a daughter. She's in college now, and doing much better, but there was a time, when she was about your age, that this"—he touched the hip of the girl on the brochure, very nearly touching Abby's hand—"was a problem for her. She was just your size. About your height. That same gauntness . . ." He stroked his cheek with his knuckles as he stared at Abby's face. She squirmed. It was stuffy in the lab, and she was feeling claustrophobic.

"I promise to read this, okay? There's no need for me to see Mrs. Geller." Abby opened the brochure for good measure and pretended to look inside. There was a list of warning signs. The word *control* in huge script in the background. She closed it again. "Can I do something about the midterm? I thought that was what you wanted to talk to me about."

Mr. Franks waved his hand. "No worries there. You already racked up the most extra credit points in the entire class. Do well on the final, get your labs in, do the rest on time, and you'll be fine. But . . ."

Abby had already gotten up and now she had to sit back down.

"You know, it can affect your concentration, and your recall. Undereating."

Abby was pretty sure *undereating* wasn't a word, but she didn't say anything. She had been having trouble concentrating, hadn't she? She couldn't focus in class, or on her labs. And she couldn't remember simple things, like how to take a midterm without cracking under the pressure. But that didn't make him right.

"I promise it's not that," she said. Her voice was shaking. He looked her over one last time, and reluctantly dismissed her.

Abby took the brochure and fled. Her hand was trembling as she tucked it into her bag, and her legs felt wobbly and weak. She needed to run. Just three and a half hours until lunch, and then she'd have a chance to run off the shaky feeling. But if she ran today, would Mr. Franks be watching? This was a disaster. Worse than getting yelled at or kicked right out of class. What if he called her mom about this?

Emily met Abby at her locker. "So, how was it?" she asked.

"Not terrible. I need to get my labs done right away and ace the final. With my extra credit, maybe I can still pull a B." She had no idea what grade she was headed for, and it felt strange to lie to Emily, but it wasn't like she could tell her what they'd really talked about. Abby shook her head, shoved her books into her locker, taking extra care to hide the brochure between her chemistry and history books.

"So that's not so bad," Emily said.

"A B? Not bad? It'll blow my whole average."

"I know. I'm sorry." Emily gave her the sympathy she was fishing for, laying one of her long arms across Abby's shoulders. "What can I do to help?"

Abby, now suddenly self-conscious about Emily touching her body, shrugged off Emily's half hug.

"Nothing, I guess." Abby quickly undid her braid and combed out her hair with her fingers. She'd braided it wet and now it was pressed into crimped waves. It was probably going to frizz. Not that she cared. The day was already a disaster. She heard a pair of girls giggle a few lockers down and knew without looking that it was about her. Snickering kids had been following her around since she'd fainted. She was getting tired of laughing it off, chalking it up to dehydration and hating the taste of Gatorade. When she'd been invisible she'd wanted to be seen. And now that everyone noticed her she wanted to be invisible again.

Abby's scalp prickled and she turned to look behind her. Gabe was standing with his cluster of jocks, staring right at her. He smiled and gave her a little wave, and she smiled back before she had to turn away.

"Oh, my god," she whispered.

Emily giggled. "Never mind. I think help just arrived."

"He smiled at me," she said. "And waved. In front of his friends."

"And . . ." Em nodded toward something behind Abby. Abby held her breath as she turned. There he was, walking up to her, the glowing tan of his skin setting off the whiteness of his teeth, the tiny crooked bottom tooth that she loved shining right at her.

"Hey," Gabe said.

"Hi."

Emily made a cross between a cough and a giggle and excused herself, leaving Abby to humiliate herself without backup. *Thanks a lot*, she thought as she watched Emily's thick black ponytail retreat, swinging like the tail of some exotic animal.

"I saw you coming out of Mr. Franks's room this morning. You looked kind of upset."

She sighed. Here it was. Let the humiliation begin. She knew Gabe knew about the fainting, because Caitlin was one of the biggest gossips in school, and she'd personally mentioned it to Abby no less than four times. Acting like she was concerned about Abby, then giggling when Abby explained, again, what had happened.

"Yeah, I met with him about my blown grade. I'm not upset, just bummed. Mad at myself. He said I'll be okay if I get my labs done and ace the final."

She tugged on her charm bracelet, spinning the little Monopoly silver shoe around and around the chain.

"You can do that, no problem," he said.

"I hope so. I have two labs to make up. Plus the one due Friday."

Gabe eyed her bracelet, nodding slowly. He reached over and touched the charm with one finger, stopping Abby from her nervous spinning.

"I haven't finished mine yet, either. We can work on it together if you want."

She would've responded if she could breathe, but she couldn't.

"Who gave you this?" he asked, fingering the charms one by one.

"My dad. Right after he moved out. He got this little Monopoly shoe, because he thought that's what I always was when we played. I'm always the dog, though. Byron's the shoe."

Gabe smiled and pushed up his sleeve, revealing a big silver watch with a blue face and lots of shiny dials.

"From mine. Dive watch. I don't dive."

They laughed together and Gabe looked around. Abby figured he was making sure Caitlin wasn't coming. He narrowed his eyes at the girls behind Abby, who were still giggling away.

"What?" he asked them.

"Make sure she doesn't faint from the sheer shock of you speaking to her," one of them cackled. Abby recognized her voice as one of Caitlin's cronies. She refused to turn around and look at her, though.

"Make sure you get your ass out of here before I tell Caitlin you two went dress-shopping without her. She finds out you bought that dress she had her eye on, it'll be like *Carrie* at the prom."

Abby heard a locker slam and two pairs of feet stomp away. She could not have loved Gabe more than she did in that moment.

"I actually have a bunch of stuff this week, but how about next Tuesday after school?" he said. "For our first joint study session."

"Sure. I think I'm free." Did he say *first*? Like there could be more than one?

Gabe rubbed his face. He was one of the boys who was already shaving. "And what are you doing for the science fair project?"

Abby had been excited that every student in her chemistry class was required to submit a project to the school science fair, up until today. Now she shook her head and a queasy feeling took over. She suddenly hated everything about chemistry.

"I've had a bunch of ideas, but I haven't had time to pick one, let alone get started. I'll probably do something lame like one of those elementary school volcanoes."

Gabe laughed. "I loved those!"

She smiled as she tucked her frizzing hair behind her ears. It jumped back out from her head, refusing to be tamed. Gabe smiled at her lame efforts to smooth it back.

"I like your hair like that," he said, and she stopped touching it. "So, you know we can do our project with a partner, right?" Abby knew, all right. "So, do you have a partner?"

"No," she whispered. She cleared her throat. "I was planning to fly solo. I don't really know anyone in the class except Nori, and she's the lone wolf type."

Gabe shrugged, raised his eyebrows, and gestured to himself with his thumb. If he was saying what Abby thought he was saying, she might faint again. She smiled and nodded, because her voice was long gone.

"Awesome," he said. "It'll be more fun to work with a partner. Especially one of the smartest ones in the class." Abby smiled and laughed. He had a point. He was one of the smartest ones in the class, and that could only help her. Then she realized that he meant she was one of the smartest in the class, and she blushed a deep, horrible red. Gabe smiled. She raised her hands to her cheeks to hide the depth of her blush. "I'm partial to the hat myself," he said, gently tugging the shoe charm on her bracelet, pulling her hand away from her face. "But I haven't played in years." He released the charm and his hand grazed Abby's before he tucked it into his back pocket.

"Me, either," Abby lied. She loved Monopoly, and had roped Byron and her dad into playing with her last time they visited him. There wasn't much else to do at her dad's apartment. He didn't even have cable.

12

Byron

"Why are we here again?" Trent asked. He took another lap around the gurgling fountain on his skateboard.

Byron retied his sneakers, as if he'd be joining in the fray. "I just want to see them, see what they've got."

"You know Betsy isn't going to be here, right?" Trent asked. Byron leaned back over the edge of the fountain and snagged a penny from the scummy bottom of the pool. He waited for Trent to circle the fountain again and snapped the penny between his fingers, sending it flying at Trent's chest as he passed by. His aim was lousy and the penny glanced off Trent's shaggy head, very close to his left eye. Byron flinched at the too-close near-miss, but was glad he'd made his point. Enough with the Betsy teasing. They were here for more serious business.

The parkour club was supposed to put on a demo, or whatever they called it, at four p.m. But here it was 4:10 and there was no sign of them. Maybe Byron had the day wrong. Or the time. The website looked a little undermaintained, just a stark list of times, dates, and locations. Maybe he had the wrong part of campus. It wasn't like the fountain had a sign with its name on it.

San Diego State's campus was crawling with hot girls in beachwear, so Byron couldn't figure out why Trent was acting like he had somewhere better to be. Just sitting there was pretty entertaining. A little brunette, tan and bouncy with a high ponytail and super-short red shorts bopped by and Byron waved to her.

"You know if this is the East Commons?" he asked.

"I know exactly what this is," she teased, fists on her narrow hips. She looked like a cheerleader, all trim and toned and perky and used to attention. "I know lots of things."

Normally he would've been blown away to have a college girl saying something that flirty to him, but he wasn't there for that. He sighed.

"Thanks for your help."

The girl relaxed the hands on her hips and shook her head, the ponytail swinging with the sway of her body. "Did you get stood up?"

"No," he said flatly.

"Well, this is the East Commons. So you aren't lost. But that's also the commons, on the other side of the library. What does she look like?"

"I'm not waiting on a girl," Byron snipped. He grabbed his backpack and started to head toward the library. Damn. He'd probably missed the whole thing.

"Whoa," he heard Trent say behind him. Byron turned and saw a slender guy scale a good six feet up the side of a building and scamper sideways, walking on air, before gripping the ledge of a second-story window. He hung there for a nanosecond before twisting and leaping down onto the grass below. He hit the ground in a forward roll and ended up in an all-four sideways run, crablike. The guy kicked one leg over his body, spinning like in some kind of break-dancing move. He landed standing and then kicked his legs up again, throwing his body into a handstand. He walked on his hands over to the edge of the fountain, where he did some sort of backflip thing back down onto all fours. A wave of guys behind him performed similar moves, covering every solid object in sight with crazy leaps and rolls, like an invasion of bizarre four-legged aliens taking over the quad. Byron headed back toward the fountain. Trent was watching, mouth hanging open, eyes wide, still standing on his skateboard, which was inching forward in slow motion.

"Awesome," Byron said. He elbowed Trent and knocked him off the board. "Now do you get it?"

"Holy crap," Trent said. "You better quit smoking."

"I did. Mostly." Byron watched the ripple effect of a dozen athletes unleashed, building speed, defying gravity, hurling themselves around the perimeter of the grassy area, ricocheting between trees and bounding up, over, and around fences. "You think they're all gymnasts?"

"Martial arts, maybe," Trent said.

"I took tae kwon do when I was seven. We never did anything like that."

The group split into two and fanned out in opposite directions. They took two different routes but ended up together as a single entity again on the other side of the grass. They started coming back toward Byron and Trent, still moving like some hyperactive army of acrobatic ants.

"Well, you're going to have to do more than track to master all those moves," Trent said. He stepped back onto his skateboard and carved a slow circle around the fountain, still watching the guys travel in their crazy, high-energy, never-stopping fashion.

"Well, I swim, too. I mean, I'm in pretty good shape. I have the same build as a couple of those guys, right?" A few of them were broader and taller than Byron, but most were rope-muscled little guys with zero body fat. Byron was on the slim side, but he didn't have that muscle tone.

The parkour group finished their performance and collapsed in a circle on the grass, high-fiving each other. A cluster of hot college girls handed out sports drinks to them.

"I thought you quit swimming," Trent said.

Byron shrugged. He hadn't done anything yet except miss some practices. "Let's go talk to them," he said.

Trent sighed and picked up his board. "Fine," he said, as if it were the last thing he wanted to do. He led the way across the grass, straightening his posture as he walked, and threw on his new smirk for good measure. "They do have some fine girlfriends."

They did. The little red-shorts brunette was one of them.

"Ah," she said as she spotted Byron. "You found your date after all."

Byron smiled. It was hard not to like her. "You were a huge help."

She gave him an exaggerated one-shoulder, one-hip shrug, setting her ponytail swaying again. "Sorry. I'm having a crappy day." She held out a bottle of purple Gatorade. "Peace offering?"

Byron took it. "So, how do these guys train? Are they all gymnasts, or martial artists, or what?"

"Little of this, little of that. Mostly they're just fearless and ultra-competitive. Killing themselves to master each move." She rolled her eyes. "In short, typical guys."

A tall, broad, dark-haired guy came over, the biggest guy in the group, all sweaty in his wife-beater tank top and Army fatigue shorts, muscles popping from the workout. "Who's your friend?" he asked the girl. He dusted off his shorts and looked Byron up and down. It wasn't a friendly once-over.

"None of your business," she said. "Where's Stacey?"

Byron sighed. Of course. He'd been sucked in by a pretty girl just to play in some game of hers. He shook his head. "Byron," he said, loud and clear, like he wasn't a high school kid with no business being there. He held out his hand and the guy took his time considering it. "My first time seeing you guys. Your moves are awesome."

The guy shook his hand, still watching the brunette girl. "Dale." He looked over the group, taking them in slow like he owned them or something. "Some of these guys are good. Some need to tighten up. Push harder. Train more in the gym before taking it outside. You into parkour?"

"I'm just learning about it. My friend Betsy, a freshman, she said you guys were the best."

Dale ate it up. He leaned back and shook out his hands, like a swimmer ready for a dive. "Your friend knows what she's talking about."

The brunette rolled her eyes and walked away. "Later, Byron," she said. "Call me." As if he had her number. Or her name. Dale narrowed his beady eyes.

"I just met her two seconds ago," Byron said. "And I don't have her number." He needed to get his loyalties straight.

"Cool," Dale said. Dale watched the red-shorts girl walk away. Byron was pretty sure she knew it, from the way she swung her butt with each step. Clearly her stunt was working beautifully. She dropped onto a stone bench not far away and stretched out with her head back like she was sunbathing. Dale sighed. "So, you want to come practice with us sometime?"

"Seriously?" Byron asked. As soon as he'd said it he wanted to take it back. It sounded childish, like he didn't think he deserved to be here.

"I mean, if you're serious," Dale said. "You know, most guys learn a bunch of tricks off YouTube and come to me thinking they know what they're doing. But they're doing it all wrong. They aren't safe about it. I get them into the gym and have to retrain them and they quit because doing it right is so much harder. You aren't one of those guys, are you?"

"Oh, no way," Byron said. "I'm a perfectionist. No sense doing it wrong." He thought about it after he said it. He figured it was true enough. Running and swimming had come so easy to him that he hadn't really had to try hard to keep up. True, he'd been thinking of quitting because it was getting harder to put in the time. So maybe he was on the verge of becoming a lazy half-assed quitter. But that was before seeing the parkour club. Now he was motivated. "I've been wanting to learn proper technique, I just didn't have a coach."

Dale grinned and relaxed his body. "Well, you came to the right place."

The whole bus ride home, Byron's mind raced about how to get into better shape, and how to get more moves down, the right kind, before the practice session in the gym in four days. He also desperately needed to get his driver's license. And a car.

Byron had his learner's permit, had taken driver's ed and driver's training, but he hadn't practiced enough to take the driver's test on his sixteenth birthday. That had been his original plan. He needed fifty hours, and he only had about twenty, because whenever he drove, his mom practically hyperventilated in the passenger seat, and unlike his friends' parents, his mom refused to exaggerate his practice hours on the form. There was no way he'd rack up thirty more hours in three weeks. Not at his current rate. At least not with his mom. Maybe his dad could help with some, but he was pretty busy and didn't like Byron driving his new car. Uncle Matt could help, though, if he was willing. Byron just needed an adult over twenty-five to sit in the passenger seat and not panic.

He needed to start working on his argument for the car as soon as possible. He could use his parents' separation as leverage. If he had a license and a car, then he could drive himself and Abby back and forth between his mom's and dad's places. So no more awkward parental exchanges. That was the best angle. He could also drive himself and Abby to and from school, so his mom could sleep in on days she didn't have to work. That was a good point, too. And required him to have his own car.

"So, what happened with your big El Camino hunt?" he asked Trent.

"What do you mean? I found the perfect one, of course. Metallic blue. My mom's getting it for me as long as I pull up my grades, which I already did. So I'm just waiting for the report card to prove it."

"No shit?" Byron said. Life was so unfair.

Trent started cackling like a deranged chicken. "You should see your face! Seriously? You bought that?"

Byron shoved Trent into the window. An old lady in front of them turned and gave them the stink-eye.

"How am I going to get to the practices?" Byron asked.

Trent gestured around the smelly bus: it reeked of BO laced with exhaust fumes. "This chariot, of course."

"They can't know I'm only sixteen, though. The school bus pass is a dead giveaway."

"First off, you're fifteen, for three more weeks. Second, why don't you have Betsy drive you?"

"Funny," Byron said.

Trent scratched his chin, faux-thinking. "If I let it slip that there's a little foxy thing after you she might be swayed."

"Are you crazy? Like she'd give two shits."

"You might be surprised," Trent said. "Nothing makes an aloof girl interested like a little competition."

"'Cause you're such an expert on women," Byron said.

"No, but I'm an expert on Betsy, jackwipe."

The old lady spun around and shushed them loudly, finger to her lips and everything. Trent turned and shushed Byron the exact same way. They laughed together the rest of the ride, taking turns shushing each other every time one of them started to speak. Byron did his best to act like he didn't care about what Trent had said, but he couldn't stop thinking about it. Was Trent serious? Was there a chance in hell of making Betsy jealous? It sure seemed to work on Dale.

They got off the bus and Byron turned toward home, in the opposite direction from Trent's house.

"Let me know how it goes with plan Betsy," Byron said over his shoulder.

"Yeah, I'll do my best for you," Trent said. "This should help." He pulled a little scrap of paper out of his pocket and smiled at it.

"What's that?" Byron asked.

"The little fox's number. She slipped it to me while you were panting all over her boyfriend."

"You got her number?" Byron said. He didn't know if he should be more jealous or impressed.

"No, idiot. She gave it to me for you. Try to keep up, will ya?" Trent turned and started walking away, tucking the paper back into his pocket. "The amazing thing is, I don't think she was just faking liking you. I mean, that Neanderthal boyfriend of hers didn't even know she did it, so what was the point?"

Byron chased him down and went for the note, but Trent was a slippery opponent. Byron had to tackle him to get any advantage.

Trent had been a wrestler, so Byron's efforts didn't help much. Every time Byron got Trent pinned to the sidewalk, Trent would use one of his wrestling leg-throwing maneuvers to escape before Byron could get to his pocket. Finally Byron gave up and sat on Trent's chest, pinning Trent's elbows with his knees. Byron was bigger, and that counted for something.

"Quit trying to feel me up. I'll give you the damn number," Trent hollered beneath him. He said it loud enough that Byron knew they must have an audience. Sure enough, Trina and her clique of tramp-in-training girlfriends were coming toward them.

"Well, boys, don't let us interrupt," Trina said. So Byron guessed she was speaking to him again. And her best friend Nicole, the reason she couldn't hook up with Byron, wasn't even in her little clique anymore.

But looking at her now, Byron could barely remember why he'd had such a crush on her. She looked different from last year. Her new makeup, streaked hair, and platform heels took away all the charm she'd once held. Last year she'd been funny, sassy, a little crass, and under all that she'd had a softness about her. Sometimes when Byron looked at her too long she'd blush and look away. The soft underside was gone this year, replaced by this new hardness that Byron didn't get. It was like she was now scared of the real her inside. She was no Betsy, that was for sure. And no foxy red-shorts game-playing college girl, either.

Byron rolled to a sitting position beside Trent and held out his hand. Trent handed him the scrap of paper and Byron opened it to make sure Trent wasn't joking. Sure enough, she'd written down her name and number, and drawn a little heart around the whole thing.

"Chelsea," Byron said, shaking his head. "That's unbelievable."

"Some girl's number?" Trina asked, leaning over Byron's shoulder. "That's what you're fighting about?"

"A college girl," Trent said. "She's after your boy here." Trent never had liked Trina. Byron wasn't sure why. It didn't seem important now.

Byron stood and offered his hand to Trent. He hauled him up

to standing. As they dusted themselves off, Trina and her two look-alike pals tottered off.

"Thanks," Byron said.

Trent shrugged. "If you're cool enough to attract college girls, that makes me cool by association." He adjusted his shirt like it wasn't just a ratty old T-shirt and Byron punched his shoulder.

"I'll put in a good word for you with the college crowd. You know, you still have some good wrestling moves. You'd probably be good at parkour, too."

Trent laughed, getting on his skateboard. "No way. You see how sweaty those guys were afterward? I don't want to work that hard for anything, ever."

13

Lana

It wasn't until Lana had made it to the elementary school teachers' lounge, gathering handouts for the second-grade class she was substituting for, that she realized she'd forgotten to eat breakfast and had left her travel mug of coffee on the kitchen counter. She rummaged through her purse and found a power bar, smashed by the weight of her wallet but still sealed and perfectly edible.

"Breakfast of champions," Mitch's deep, familiar voice said behind her. "Try this instead."

She turned and he held something wrapped in crisp white paper out to her. Mitch was a fifth-grade teacher: handsome, easy to talk to, single, and eleven years younger than Lana. She was too far out of the game to know if his regular attention meant he was interested or just a nice guy.

"I can't take your breakfast," she told him.

"We'll split it." He opened the paper and she saw the bagel was already sliced into two half-moons, slathered in melting cream cheese.

"How do you do it?" she asked, accepting half. It was still warm, comfort in her hands.

"I have a gift." He took a bite and looked over her shoulder at the papers she'd set on the counter. "Mrs. Jennings's class?"

"Yeah."

"Get coffee, too. You'll need it."

The class wasn't as bad as Mitch had made them sound. The kids were in their midweek stupor, sleepy-eyed and slow-moving. The day dragged but was uneventful enough. After school Lana tucked a note into Mrs. Jennings's cubby outlining what they'd covered in her absence. She rubbed her weary eyes and turned to see Mitch smirking in her direction.

"What?" she asked.

"I told you to get coffee."

"There wasn't time. And this coffee's like battery acid."

"You've tasted battery acid?" he asked, smiling, leaning against the counter very close to her.

"No, but I've tasted coffee that my father says tastes like battery acid. And he's an expert on everything, as he'll gladly tell you." She smiled back at him and wondered if they were flirting. It had been way too many years to know for sure.

"We could go grab a decent cup now," Mitch suggested. "Maybe head over to Coffee Cup Café? We can just make it before they close." He checked his watch, nodding, then laid those blue-gray eyes on her. It seemed impossible that Lana could land two coffee dates with two stunning men a mere week apart. She'd been avoiding Nick since the Matt incident. Nick seemed mad at her about the whole thing, but she wasn't sure why. And didn't care to find out. Maybe she'd have better luck with Mitch. She grabbed her coat.

At the café, Lana dove into a mocha Thai: a thick, creamy, warm dessert in a cup, masquerading as coffee. She was going to have to do something about her calorie consumption soon, because even her big jeans weren't big anymore. But not today. Today, like every day since Graham had left, Lana wanted the comfort of food that made her feel loved. Even if it was only self-love. And even if she didn't love herself quite so much when she glimpsed her expanding rear end in the mirror on her way to the shower each morning. Lana's mother had been a lifelong dieter, a calorie counter, and in extreme moments even a binger and purger, and she raised her daughters to follow her example. Which was why neither Lana nor Becca had Gloria's svelte figure. Nothing like being raised by a food tyrant to make you love the illicit pleasure of food.

"Did you know this was my favorite place?" she asked.

"I think maybe you mentioned it once, yeah."

The fact that he knew this about her sent her head spinning. She knew nothing about Mitch beyond his job, beauty, charm, and ability to show up in the teachers' lounge at the exact same moment she did whenever she had a job at Las Juntas Elementary.

"So, are you from San Diego originally?" she asked.

Mitch leaned back and laughed, crossing his arms, which flexed his tan biceps. "Are we doing this now? The getting-to-know-you conversation?"

She tilted her wrist as if to check her nonexistent watch, and nodded. "Yep, it seems about time for it."

He leaned forward, forearms on the wobbly table edge. "Good. And no. Oxnard."

"Ah, close to Santa Barbara?"

"Ish. And you?"

"San Clemente."

"Ah, with the swallows of San Juan Capistrano?"

"Ish."

He smiled at her and she wondered if he had any idea how handsome he was. How easy things would come to him with a face like that: wide slate eyes, prominent cheekbones, a slim jaw, full lips. She had the urge to take a picture of him and send it to Becca, so that she, too, could marvel at the ridiculous beauty of him.

A pierced and tattooed waitress with shoe-black hair streaked with orange leaned over Lana's shoulder to set the check on the table and let them know they were closing.

"No," Mitch pouted. "We were just getting to the good stuff."

The waitress smiled at him and shook her head. "Sorry," she said. "Rain check?"

Mitch turned to Lana, palms up. "She says I get a rain check. That okay with you?"

Lana laughed and nodded. "Sure. To be continued."

"How about over dinner? Maybe Friday?"

Lana wondered how he'd managed to hit the one evening she had free. She briefly wondered if it was fate, then had to laugh at her girlish hope. First Nick, now Mitch. She'd gone from no prospects for eight months to two so quickly that she didn't have time to process whether she was even ready to date again. If either one could even be called a prospect. She reminded herself that one was an ex-boyfriend and the other was a coworker, and that was all. So far. She agreed to dinner.

After coffee they went their separate ways. Lana had kids to pick up from school, homework to supervise, a picky brother to cook for, and Mitch had no such constraints. He was off to meet some friends at the beach, torn between rock climbing and surfing for the rest of his day. As she listened to him rattle off his options she felt silly for entertaining the thought of a romantic connection. Never mind the eleven-year age difference. What did they really have in common?

Friday came quickly. Lana changed her clothes four times in a quest for the elusive perfect outfit. She wasn't sure about the one she'd settled on, but she was out of time to try another. The doorbell rang and Lana checked the peephole to see Graham squinting in the bright glare of the porch light.

"Kids! Your dad's here," she called to them.

She opened the door and Graham smiled. Not a sincere, happy-to-see-her smile, but a resigned one, like he'd been hoping someone else would answer the door.

"They're coming," she said.

Graham reached into his pocket and pulled out a check, folded in half. "Should be enough, for the mortgage, the utilities, et cetera."

"And half the grocery store for Byron?" Lana laughed. It was uncomfortable, receiving a monthly check from her own husband, like amends for leaving her. Severance pay. Becca kept telling her she needed to run the support calculators, make sure she was getting her fair share. But it wasn't Lana's way, demanding money. Lana's way was passive, accepting, adapting without a word to the wants and needs of others for the sake of keeping the peace.

She slid the check into her pocket without looking at it. It seemed rude, checking the amount in front of him. But the truth was it wasn't enough. She knew without looking. It never was. Even with Matt's help on rent she was barely scraping by. At some point she was going to have to resurrect the old money battles with Graham, one of their chief disagreements their whole marriage. But that could come later. Today she had a date with possibility. With someone who saw Lana as more than cook, maid, child care, and underemployed drain on the family bank account.

She stepped aside so that Graham could come in. He remained on the doormat, hands in his pockets, rolling up onto the balls of his feet and back onto his heels. It was something he always did when he was bored or impatient. It had become increasingly annoying to witness the longer they were married. "Come in and sit down like a civilized person," she said. "You drive me crazy with that rocking."

He blanched at the rebuff. This was the new Lana talking. The less decorous version of herself that she'd had to resurrect for dealing with Matt. "It's good for my plantar fasciitis," he reminded her, continuing to do it. "Are you dressed up?"

She was, a little, in soft olive pants and a black blouse with a hint of shine. "Well, I am without kids for the night. I thought maybe I'd try out the bar scene. Hit a rave or two."

"I figured maybe you and Nick Parker . . ." He trailed off and she just smiled, shook her head. The truth would have thrown him for an even bigger loop—first the return of Nick Parker and now another handsome man taking her out to dinner—but she realized that she'd wanted to make Graham jealous only when she had no prospects. Somehow having two men show an interest in her eliminated any need to involve Graham at all. "You look nice," he said.

The compliment confused her. Graham had not been one to dole out flattery freely. So why do it now? Her anger bubbled up. She was tempted to ask: *Why'd you leave me, if I still look good to you?* Good old Graham, who'd kept a running tally of all the ways Lana had disappointed him. Lana, always scrambling to shorten the list, to prove her love. He'd give a weary sigh before launching into a new disappointment. "I need more here, Lana," he'd say, about whatever it was this time: more time alone, more passionate Lana-initiated sex that usually meant a quickie for him and no climax for her, more enthusiastic praise of whatever he was already doling out. When did he scramble to prove his love to her? He didn't. That was expected to be a given. He loved her and she shouldn't doubt it, shouldn't need reassurance, shouldn't need anything he wasn't already willingly giving her.

She pictured the captivating beauty of Mitch to clear her mind, and backed up and turned away. It was easier to talk to Graham when she didn't look at him. "Byron has an essay to write on Japanese internment camps. If he could get the research started with you, that'd help a lot. And maybe you could look over Abby's chemistry labs. And make sure she eats."

"Eats? You think I starve them?" Up on his toes, back on his heels, up on his toes, back on his heels. He was making Lana seasick.

"She seems too distracted to sit down and eat a proper meal these days," Lana said. "She looks thin to me."

Right on cue Abby came trotting down the stairs, light as a butterfly, and into her father's arms.

"She's fine. More grown-up each time I see her," Graham said. Abby smiled, gave Lana a halfhearted wave, and practically skipped toward his car. Byron came tromping toward the door with much more vigor.

"History," Lana reminded him.

"Sucks," he finished.

"Enjoy the rave," Graham said, heading out.

Moments later Mitch's white SUV pulled up, surfboard still strapped to the roof rack. "Are you waiting for me at the door?" Mitch asked, grinning as he stepped out of his car, unfolding his lanky body like a model in a photo shoot.

"Just said goodbye to my kids, off to their dad's house for the night." She stepped aside and Mitch came in, taking a quick glance around the half-empty living room. She needed to rearrange the furniture to cover for the pieces Graham had taken: his recliner, one end table, the coffee table. There was a Graham-void in the room.

"How old are they?" Mitch asked. Lana wasn't sure he knew how much older she was. But he would when he heard she had teenagers.

"Fourteen and fifteen. God help me," she said with a laugh.

Mitch looked her over, dashing as ever in dark jeans and thin blue V-neck sweater, black shoes so shiny Lana wondered if they were new.

"Oh," Mitch said. "So you were a child bride." He shook his head. "No wonder it didn't work out."

Lana laughed and some of her nervous energy dissipated. Matt peeked out at them. Lana introduced Mitch to Matt, and they shared a stilted greeting before Matt retreated. As she climbed into Mitch's SUV, something crunched under her feet. She hoped it was papers and not discarded food. The SUV was pretty messy inside, the backseat full of gear and clothes for Mitch's various hobbies. There was sand everywhere, and the smell of the ocean filled the car. Lana struggled between the desire to clean it up and envy for all the freedom the mess represented.

Mitch's restaurant choice was a noisy, artsy place in the Gaslamp Quarter, brimming with business types and dressed-up twenty-somethings gearing up for a night on the town. Lana wondered if he'd chosen the trendy, upscale place to impress her, but as they made their way to the table, it seemed half the young people at the bar knew Mitch. He briefly greeted them, but didn't introduce Lana.

"Are you a regular?" Lana asked as he pulled out her seat for her, curious to see this little glimpse into Mitch's life outside of school.

"No," Mitch said. "Not really." Lana waited for him to explain. He offered nothing else but his winning smile. They ordered and launched into work talk: school policy changes, the two teachers quitting, test scores, and funding shifts. It felt like any Monday meeting at the school.

"Where did we leave off the other day?" Lana asked, hoping for more meaningful conversation.

"Childhood?" Mitch asked. "Happy or not?"

"Mostly happy. Dad was a lawyer and Mom was head of the PTA. I had three siblings, so it was a lively house. My brother Matt came along and sort of tipped the balance. You know, having a sibling with Asperger's is a unique challenge. And then my brother Stephen was diagnosed with leukemia and everything changed. He went through several rounds of treatment, but it was no use. I was eleven when he died. Stephen was only sixteen. It was like we weren't really a family anymore after that. It became each of us for ourselves." Lana set her wineglass down and picked up her water. She'd overshot her mark on the deep stuff. "Sorry. Two glasses of wine and I lose my filter."

Mitch smiled. "No worries. I'm not much for small talk. Sounds like a lot to handle. Is that when your caretaker streak kicked in?"

"Am I a caretaker?" Lana asked. She wanted to disagree, but he was probably right.

"Two kids and an autistic brother? You have your hands full."

"Full in a good way," she said. "Matt's got his quirks, but he's also brilliant, gentle, funny. It can be hard to get close to someone with Asperger's. We're getting a second chance to bridge that gap."

Mitch smiled, held up his hands. "I like how protective you are of him."

"I've always been protective of him," she said. "Someone had to be. My family was gutted by losing Stephen. Mom went from Mary Poppins to a robot overnight. Dad lost his humor, threw himself into work. My older sister kept busy chasing boys and emulating the popular girls at school. Matt and I were the two left behind. Matt was brilliant, but awkward. He was teased and bullied."

"And who did you become?"

"The good girl. Perfect to a fault. A sealed-up box of tightly contained emotion. Unless someone hurt Matt. Matt had this one tormentor, Tommy. He was big, older. Relentless. I hit him in the face with a metal can of paste and nearly broke his nose. He never teased Matt again."

"I'll be sure not to piss you off," Mitch joked.

"A good plan," Lana said, smiling. What had happened to that fighter in her? Was she gone forever, or just dormant, resting, waiting? "What about your childhood?" she asked.

Mitch took a sip of wine and smiled at her. "Good enough. Loving mother. Nice sister. My parents divorced when I was ten, and I didn't see my father for fifteen years. We're back in touch now, but it's not really a father-son relationship." He shrugged, resumed eating. Lana waited for more, but he seemed to be done sharing. "So are you and your ex on fairly good terms?" Mitch asked.

"We're . . . friendly, but not friends." She wasn't sure if that was true, but it sounded good.

"You think you might get back together?" Mitch asked. Lana was surprised by the directness of the question. It wasn't a typical date question. But maybe it wasn't a date.

"No, I don't think so," she told Mitch.

Mitch was watching her closely. "But you haven't filed for divorce."

"No, we haven't. We hand kids back and forth, he gives me some money every month, but aside from that we hardly even talk anymore. He's dating someone, busy enjoying his new quieter, responsibility-free life, and I'm holding the rest of the family together. I guess we just haven't gotten around to it yet."

"But you think you will? Divorce?"

"Definitely," she said. She switched back to drinking her wine. Mitch ate a few more bites. Lana's plate was empty, though she had no memory of consuming her food.

"What was the biggest issue?" he asked.

She shrugged. "It starts with money battles and next thing you know you're fighting for ground on every front. He's a CPA, so he insisted on being in charge of our finances. I've been self-supporting since I was seventeen and I'm used to living on a tight budget, saving as much as I can for those unexpected bills. Every suggestion I gave on how to cut back expenses was like an insult to him. Every dollar he wasted was like an insult to me. Extrapolate that out to raising kids, home repairs, family vacations, family crises, the finer things he needed as rewards, my fear of being broke, saving for college . . ."

"So he's the controlling type," Mitch said.

It wasn't a word Lana would've used back when they were together, but now that she was the one in control of everything, she realized how rarely she'd been allowed to be the authority on anything. "Maybe," she said. "Maybe we're just both too stubborn. Too much will and too little compromise."

"You're hardly what I'd call stubborn," Mitch said. Lana smiled, not sure if it was a compliment or criticism.

After dinner they strolled around downtown. The dry Santa Ana winds kicked up, gusting dust, debris, and static electricity. The abrasive breeze drove them back indoors. They chose a café where a young couple with long hair, hippie-throwback clothes, and wooden bead jewelry had set up a makeshift stage in the corner. The young man played guitar and the girl played a clawhammer banjo and they sang sweet mountain songs about lost love. The music took Lana back to her childhood, when her southern-born grandfather would play similar music, but one glance and she could see it did nothing for Mitch.

"Not your style of music?" she asked.

He shook his head. "The songs are fine. But there's something about these young wannabe hippies, in their hemp clothing and Birkenstocks, singing sad songs while Mom and Dad pay their way through college. It's like a façade they wear, not who they are. Ask them about politics and they know nothing. Ask what they're doing for the environment and they'll say they recycle. I'd rather they skip the dress-up and find some meaning in their lives."

"Wow," Lana said. "You'd probably think my kids are the most self-centered people on the planet."

Mitch looked up in surprise. "I'm sure your kids are great. How can they not be? They're your kids."

Lana smiled and accepted the compliment, but felt less attracted to him now that she'd seen beneath the cool, gorgeous surface. He wasn't lacking in depth, but maybe in experience. Lofty idealism was great for an early-thirties bachelor, but for a mother in her forties it just seemed like a way of making the world harder to accept than it had to be.

Mitch sipped his loose-leaf tea, set his white porcelain cup down, and sighed. "She also looks a bit"—he held up his index finger and thumb about an inch apart—"like my ex-girlfriend. Maybe that's what I'm annoyed about."

Lana looked over at the girl, lanky and thin with long light hair and dark almond-shaped eyes, her narrow face almost gaunt. She could not have been more opposite from Lana.

"I'll loathe her with you, then," Lana said. She held up her mug, and after a brief moment of narrowing his eyes at the singer, Mitch smiled and clinked his cup to hers. It was the most interesting part of the evening, this glimpse into Mitch's private life, the hint of untidy emotions.

14

Matt

Matt emerged from his room and into the blinding morning light as soon as the garage door's squeaking, grinding, and whole-house vibrating had ceased, signaling the house was now empty. Lana had the loudest garage door he'd ever heard. There must be something loose in it, he decided, because there was no way it was that loud on purpose. After breakfast he'd look it up online, find her garage door opener brand, and figure out how to fix it himself. Matt liked repairing things, especially when taking them apart and putting them back together meant they'd be quieter.

The whole house was quiet, which was exactly what Matt wanted. Except that when he was alone in the house all day, that's when he missed the drinking and the pills most. He needed to keep his mind busy all day and at night to stop thinking about it. He had programming to do for Bill, but he needed more. He needed to think about something even while he was coding. Because Matt's mind was fast-processing. That's what his doctor had told him, and he liked that phrase, because that's exactly how it felt in Matt's mind. Fast. Too fast, sometimes. He needed layers of thoughts to be going at all times. Or one really good topic to focus on, to keep all other thoughts away.

He'd promised both Lana and Nick Parker that he'd never see

Spike again. He wanted to keep that promise, not so much because Nick had been so angry, but because Lana had been so sad. She'd cried when she told him how worried she'd been. He felt her sadness in his chest. It had filled Matt's whole body until he almost cried, too. Matt hated crying. His tears or anyone else's. It was too much for him. It made him want to act out and drive the feeling away with something bigger and more physical. So he needed to never make Lana cry again.

He didn't care so much about how Nick felt. He didn't like to make people angry, but he heard Lana telling Nick to let it go, that it was a family issue and he wasn't family. That made Matt feel better. Lana had sounded mad at Nick as she said it. Matt didn't like to be too close to angry people, because anger got into his chest just like sadness did, but it was easier to drive the anger back out again. The sadness took hold much longer and stronger.

Matt had met Lana's friend Mitch, too. They'd gone out on a date. Mitch hadn't said much to Matt, and Matt liked that about him. He liked Mitch better than Nick, so if Lana was interviewing potential boyfriends, Matt wanted to vote for the nicer one. He told Lana that he liked Mitch better than Nick. He didn't really care about learning to hit a baseball that much. He liked Mitch's quiet over Nick's anger.

Lana had laughed and said, "At this point, I'm not sure what the hell I'm doing. They're both too perfect and too flawed all rolled into one."

Matt had no idea what that meant, but he knew people made contradictory statements on purpose to show when they were conflicted. And he knew how it felt to be conflicted. Matt was conflicted most of the time.

Matt kept his curtains closed and his room dark, but the rest of Lana's house was startlingly sunny. And dusty. It seemed like Lana was cleaning all the time, but mostly it was just messes the kids left everywhere: trails of clothes and papers and packages for things and empty plates and cups. She swept and vacuumed every weekend, but she didn't dust surfaces or scrub hidden corners very often.

Matt kept his room organized, but he wasn't much better about the cleaning. He hadn't dusted or vacuumed in there since moving in, and his dirty clothes and trash kept getting mixed up in piles on the floor and under the bed and desk. But his desk and shelves were neat. Everything on his desk and shelves was there for a reason, and the order mattered. Matt couldn't explain it to anyone else, why the hardback and paperback books had to be on separate shelves, why the hardbacks were sorted by size, from biggest to smallest, while the paperbacks were in alphabetical order by author. Why his journals had to be either blue or green. Why they had to be stacked on the right rear corner of his desk and nowhere else, blue journals on top and green ones on the bottom of the stack. But these organizational details gave Matt a sense of calm that other people's systems just didn't. He was glad that Lana let him set up his room the way he needed, and that she never came in and cleaned it. But he really did need to dust in there at some point. Now that he was out in the sun, he could see how dusty the whole house was. It made his lungs itch just thinking about it. Matt paused to watch a smattering of dust dance through a stream of light. He swept his hand through the beam and watched the dust scatter like silt in a stirred pond.

He hadn't been to his favorite pond in months, not since moving in with Lana. He needed to get back there soon, to little Evan's Pond, to see the families of ducks and clutches of frog eggs that would soon become tadpoles. Tadpoles were one of Matt's favorite things. The tadpoles would be hatching any day, and he liked to see them before they hatched, when they were nothing more than tiny black specks. Looking at those little seedlike flecks, you wouldn't guess how much life was brewing inside, the fascinating creatures that would emerge: capable of growing tails and reabsorbing them, sprouting legs and developing into entirely different beings in such a short amount of time. Matt watched their metamorphosis each year, returning every few days to see their development. He wished he had that ability, to transform himself into another type of creature. Something that functioned better in the world he'd gotten stuck in.

But before he could return to the pond, Matt would need a car. And to have his driver's license reinstated. He was nearly through his four-month suspension from driving under the influence. Then he'd be able to drive again. He didn't have many places to go, but he wanted to have the option. If he didn't get his license and a car soon, the tadpoles might all be gone before he made it back to the pond, their metamorphosis complete. Fully developed frogs didn't hold the same fascination for Matt as tadpoles.

The real trouble for Matt would be deciding which car to get. He needed to research all of his options, check the various safety features, see how well each car held its value. Then he needed to choose the best year, make, model, interior color, exterior color. Matt could hold all of the necessary information at once in his fast-processing brain and parse through it rapidly. But making a final decision, any final choice on anything, usually presented a problem for him. Processing was easy. Decisions were hard.

For food and clothes it was easier when he used a schedule or routine. Chicken every Wednesday. Corn every night. Blue shirts every day but Friday. Levi's every day. He had found a few tricks for getting things done faster. But with a new choice to make, and every car option to consider, the sheer magnitude of deciding could become paralyzing. Matt needed time to weigh the consequences upon consequences of each possibility. That could take months, a year even. The tadpoles would be long gone for sure.

Lana had just left with the kids, off to work and school and the hectic busy days they all complained about but never changed, and left her coffee, again, on the kitchen counter, where Matt stared at it for several minutes. It was in a white plastic travel cup and presented Matt with another case of epic indecision. Knowing what the problem was didn't help him any. It just stressed him out more. He had things to do. He needed breakfast. He had programming work to finish for Bill. But what should he do with the cup of forgotten coffee? Cleaning up was one of his new jobs at the house, but what to do with a travel cup still full of coffee? Empty it and put it in the dishwasher? Lana wanted everything in the dishwasher, she was very specific about that. But she hadn't had the coffee yet, and Lana didn't like to waste food. There was half-and-half in the coffee. Warm dairy products were an ideal environment for growing microorganisms. Lactic acid bacteria. Coliforms. Even *Pseudomonas fluorescens*. Should he put the travel mug in the refrigerator? Maybe it didn't need refrigeration. It was a plastic cup, the kind meant to look like a white paper cup with a bright pink sleeve around it, and not a real, proper thermos. Matt had a good thermos. A metal Nissan one that kept tea hot for hours. Matt touched the sides of the plastic cup and felt the heat within seeping out. That wouldn't do. Not at all. He moved it into the refrigerator.

Matt made his English muffin, spread it with a thick slab of butter, and filled his blue cup with milk. He set up his TV tray by the front window and arranged his food. He settled down and pictured the cup in the refrigerator. It wasn't sealed. Shouldn't dairy products be in a sealed container? He headed back to the kitchen and wrapped the whole thing in plastic wrap, so the drinking and air holes in the lid were covered securely. He put a rubber band around it for safekeeping, then returned it to the refrigerator.

Matt settled by the window again and ate his breakfast. The street in front of the house was busier than usual. Two Toyotas, both white, four Hondas—red, blue, black, and a sporty tricked-out version in saffron-yellow—and a silver Lexus drove by in the first three minutes he sat there. Usually the morning rush was over by now. These cars all seemed to be in a hurry, every one of them exceeding the speed limit. Maybe everyone was running late today. A little red pickup truck went by and it made Matt happy. It reminded him of something from his childhood, but he wasn't sure what. Maybe his grandfather had a truck like that. He'd ask Lana later. He wondered if he should consider a truck instead of a car. He got one of his journals, a blue one, and listed the cars he'd seen in green ink. He put a star next to the red truck. He'd keep track of what he saw and liked, and start narrowing down his options that way. A silver minivan went by. Matt wrote it down and put a big red X next to it. He didn't like minivans.

While he waited for more cars, he noticed there were a lot of dogs out. Matt had never had a dog before, because his brother

Stephen had been allergic to them. Stephen died when Matt was seven, so he didn't remember him that well, except that he was very sick and in and out of the hospital, sick first with leukemia and then sicker with the treatment to kill the leukemia cells. And then Stephen had died, so they could've had a dog then, because no one else was allergic to them, but they never did get a dog.

Matt gave the dogs their own page in his notebook, and wrote a little description of each one in blue ink. The Newfoundland, black and bearlike, was familiar. It passed by every day between eight a.m. and eight-fifteen a.m. But the Great Dane was new. White with black spots. Harlequin. It moved like a smallish horse and his owner ran to keep up with it, but you could see the dog wasn't in any hurry to go anywhere. Then there was a mastiff, beastly and slobbery and taking up more space than any dog reasonably should. The mastiff squatted its huge body down low to the ground and pooped an enormous pile on the lawn of a neighbor. Matt had to look away as the owner used two plastic bags to gather the feces.

Touching feces was something Matt never did. Spike had said that when Matt collected his nail clippings it was the same thing. Human waste, he'd called it. But it wasn't the same. For one thing, nail clippings didn't smell. Matt's especially. He washed his hands thoroughly several times a day, and always cleaned under his nails. Pinworms could lurk there, and all sorts of other nasty bacteria. Matt just thought it was interesting that his body could produce nails endlessly. It was one small way that Matt was like a tadpole. He couldn't grow legs, but he could grow fingernails and toenails. He just kept them to remind him of the tadpoles when there were no tadpoles to see.

Matt looked back out the window just as the mastiff and its trash-bag-toting owner continued on their way. It wasn't just a day for large breeds, but the largest breeds of all. It was like a parade of enormous, exaggerated animals. A Macy's Thanksgiving Day parade, with huge dogs on leashes replacing the big balloon cartoon characters on cables. This thought made Matt smile, but no one was there to see it, his happy smile instead of his stressed or unhappy one. He wrote it down in his notebook, the dogs-as-parade-floats idea. He'd probably never tell anyone about it, because they wouldn't understand, but he wanted to hold on to it, this happy thought to start his morning.

His favorite thing about the big window in Lana's living room was the chance to see so many things without having to interact with them. He found it exhausting, trying to manage the social cues everyone else understood, trying to make eye contact so people knew he was talking to them, remembering not to smile unless he wanted to show he was happy. There were so many rules for interacting with people, and Matt had a hard time remembering them all. Forgetting the rules could make people angry and mean, when Matt never meant any harm to anyone, ever. It was easier just to avoid talking to people unless he had to.

The other nice thing about the big window was that it kept out most of the noises from outside. Matt preferred watching things to hearing them. Noises overwhelmed him a lot faster than visuals did. Unless it was noises he liked, like the bird and traffic noises on the noise machine Lana had given him for sleeping. He could see why all of his rules confused people. He knew he had a lot of rules. He just couldn't understand why everyone else cared so much. He never complained about their rules. Why did they have to judge his?

Matt didn't believe in any gods or afterlife, but he believed there was an order to the universe, even when it felt lopsided. And because of that, he was sure there would be some smaller dogs coming soon to offset all the Macy's parade big ones he'd seen. He waited and waited. His breakfast was gone and he had work to do, not just the programming work for Bill but the noisy garage door opener to disassemble and reassemble. But once he'd had the thought about the smaller dogs coming he was committed to waiting for a smaller dog to pass by. Even a medium-sized dog would do. His leg began to itch, and his lower back started to ache. He became increasingly anxious about the whole thing, the lack of a not-huge dog to set him free from his post. He capped and uncapped his blue pen, over and over, waiting.

Then, finally, a medium-sized, light-stepping, lean red dog passed by, with soft hanging ears and a not-slobbery mouth and a coat so short Matt could see every muscle moving beneath its velvety skin. It was the most beautiful dog he'd ever seen. Matt had to fetch his laptop to look it up. Vizsla, he learned. A Hungarian breed. Because of their color they were easily confused with Rhodesian Ridgebacks, but Vizslas had a rust-colored nose instead of a black one, and obviously no ridge of hair that grew in the opposite direction along their spine. The red dog he'd seen pass by definitely had a reddish brown nose. And no ridge. It had been a Hungarian Vizsla, for sure.

Matt spent the morning learning all there was to know about Vizslas. They were similar in build to the Weimaraner, but smaller in size. And "golden russet," as the American Kennel Club called them, instead of gray. Vizslas were hunting dogs, one of the smallest of the pointer/retriever breeds. Matt wasn't a hunter, but he could see the benefit in having a dog that did both: point out the bird, and bring it back to you after you shot it down. Not that he wanted to shoot birds. Matt loved birds. He loved birds more than dogs. Or had, until he saw that Vizsla loping past. He waited for nearly half an hour for it to pass by again, but the owner must've taken a different route home. He longed for it, that lean, lithe red dog with the springy step and princely air, the long neck and not-too-docked tail, the narrow hips and slender feet. He'd never really wanted a dog before. But now he did. He wanted a Vizsla. He needed one. There was no Stephen with allergies to stop him now.

He gave up waiting for the Vizsla to return and settled at his desk. He had a messy string of code from Bill, an old program that had run fine until the system update broke it. He found several blocks of unnecessary code that needed to be trimmed, but he hadn't found the real problem yet. It was just a matter of time, though. He scanned the code while the dog trotted around in his mind. He was able to work better while thinking about the rust-colored dog of his dreams. Vizsla. He had to look up how to say it. *Veeshla.* That's what it sounded like. It was an affectionate breed. Every website had said so. One even called them Velcro dogs, saying they liked to be in constant contact with their owners. And there was a funny Hungarian phrase that he'd come across: "To own a Vizsla is to have a dog on your head." Matt wasn't affectionate. He didn't like touching. And he never wanted a dog on his head. But the Vizsla might just change all of that. Would touching a dog be like having a person touch you? He didn't like other people's hands on his skin: the germs and the roughness and the sweaty palms or cold fingers. They hurt him, even when they thought they were being gentle. But a Vizsla, with that short soft velvety coat of fur. That might feel nice against Matt's palm. He needed to find out.

Matt printed out two pictures of Vizslas: one poised like a statue as it was judged for a dog show; the other in tall grass, tail extended, nose like an arrow, one paw tucked up to its chest, pointing at a bird you couldn't see in the photo. He hung them on the wall behind his monitor, so he could see both the dog and his work at the same time. Between the Vizsla pictures was a picture of tadpoles, detailing each phase of the metamorphosis.

The coding, Vizsla, and tadpoles, all vying for time in Matt's brain, helped him stop thinking about drinking and Spike's pills for a while. He needed to keep his mind this busy all day every day. He needed to find even more things to write in his notebooks and learn about. Data was the answer. He didn't get outside much to gather new data, but maybe he could find something right in the house to keep track of. Maybe something with the dogs passing by outside or the people who were always inside, to give him something to do with his mind. He liked the idea of using Abby and Byron, of finding something to keep track of when he was around them and trying not to get overwhelmed by their noise.

15

Abby

Abby was so nervous she'd barely slept the night before. Gabe was coming over after school to work on their labs and science fair project together. She'd been so distracted in school that her English teacher had called her a space case and made the whole class laugh. English was an easy class for her, but for some reason she couldn't stay focused on their never-ending discussion of *The Great Gatsby* and what the green light on the end of the dock might represent. To Abby it represented the emerald-green of Gabe's eyes, which she would be seeing in her own house in just a few hours, but that wasn't the sort of thing she could contribute to the class discussion.

Of course, she got to see Gabe in chemistry, or the back of his head a few rows up, but she was never all there in chem anymore. That class had become a nightmare. Having Gabe in chem still made it her favorite class, but Mr. Franks and his watchful eyes, magnified by his glasses, were there, too, which made it Abby's least favorite class. The whole fifty minutes of chemistry was a blur of watching Gabe and being watched by Mr. Franks, feeling anxious and jittery the whole time. How was she supposed to learn anything? Before class Abby waited outside the door to come in just as the bell rang, and she packed up early to rush out as soon as the next bell rang, anything to avoid talking to Mr. Franks. She'd asked Gabe to let Mr. Franks know they were doing the science fair project together, just so she wouldn't have to speak directly to him. But there were still several months of school left, and she knew she couldn't dodge Mr. Franks forever.

She'd also noticed Matt watching her at dinner the night before. Or it seemed like he was watching her. You never really knew what he was up to. She'd pushed her food around like usual, and he stared at the food as it moved around her plate like it was the best TV show he'd ever seen. He had a notebook with him, sitting in his lap under the table, and every once in a while he'd make little notes in it. When Abby gave up playing with her food to go finish her homework, he looked her over in a strange way. Not that Matt ever looked at anyone in a way that wasn't strange. But it was different. Like he was actually seeing her and not just looking in her general direction. Abby wondered what he saw.

Abby had waited while Lana made her a sandwich to take up to her room, a sandwich she wouldn't eat, and wondered if she'd ever find out what was going on in Matt's strange brain and in his little green notebook. It was on her to-do list to find out, but she never would, because Matt never left the house, not since his disappearing act that had been bad enough that Lana had roped in the help of some cop friend Abby had never even heard of before and hadn't seen since. Anyway, with Matt always home, his notebooks would never be left unattended for Abby to spy on their contents. Maybe Abby was becoming paranoid, but there was no harm in that. She needed to stay sharp.

Between Coach Zimmerman, Mr. Franks, Emily's mom, and now Matt, too many people were noticing her lately. Before the separation Lana would've been the first to see it, Abby's distraction and food issues, but not now. Now Lana would only see it if someone told her. Abby thought she had Coach, Mr. Franks, and Em's mom under control. But Matt was a wild card. You never knew what he might say. And he talked more to Lana than anyone else. But how seriously would Lana take Matt? Most of the time when he was talking you had no idea what exactly he was trying to tell you.

On the one hand, it was none of her mom's or anyone else's business how much or how little food Abby put into her mouth. It was her body, after all. But she also had this feeling, buried deep down inside, that it wasn't right that all of these people had started watching her and worrying about her, while Lana didn't even care enough to notice. She pushed the thought from her mind. She didn't have time to worry about it. Gabe was due any minute.

She'd set a notebook, pencils, white poster board, glue, and colored construction paper on the dining room table, and she wondered if she should put some snacks out. Boys ate all the time. At least Byron did. Abby hated food and hated dealing with food. Washing and slicing and peeling and cooking and doing dishes and getting food on her hands. Every step of the process was her least favorite thing to do. Maybe she'd just send Gabe into the kitchen to help himself before they got started.

In the end it didn't matter. Gabe showed up, lavender-smelling and tan and beautiful, holding a Subway bag of sandwiches, two bags of chips, and two huge cups of soda.

"I didn't know what you liked, so I got three different kinds of sandwiches. We can share." He smiled at her and Abby was too dumbfounded to speak. Gabe Connor. Here, in her house. It was as unlikely as having Prince Harry drop by for tea.

Abby loved her house, but she was suddenly embarrassed by it, by the lack of furniture in the front room, just a worn brown couch and Matt's chair by the window. The carpet was shabby and the curtains were old and her cozy home suddenly didn't seem grand enough for the likes of Gabe Connor. He laughed and pointed past Abby and she realized that she was standing in the doorway, blocking his entrance into the house. Perfect. She was already making a fool of herself. She stepped aside and he came in, handed one of the cups of soda to her, and once his hand was free he laid his arm around her shoulders and gave her the brief sugges- tion of a hug. She could smell all of him in that moment: not just the lavender, but his deodorant, shampoo, soap, and a boy smell that was so distinctly Gabe it made her dizzy. He squeezed and released her in all of half a second, but the gesture lasted forever in her mind. By the time she'd processed what had just happened, he was already at the dining room table getting set up.

"So I told Mr. Franks. He said it's good we're doing the project together. He thinks they usually come out better when done in teams."

"Oh. Good," Abby said. She walked over and stood next to him. She wanted him to kiss her so bad that she couldn't stop staring at him. There was no way she could focus on chemistry now. What had she been thinking? Being this close to Gabe, boyfriend to the horrid Caitlin, was going to be an hour of sheer torture. Why would she agree to do this to herself?

Gabe pulled a stack of books and papers from his backpack. "He gave me some books to look over. He marked the projects that were done last year. We'll do better with the judges if we don't repeat something they just saw. Nice of him, huh?"

"Yeah," Abby said. The sunlight coming in the window behind Gabe made him glow. He had a white shirt on that was so bright in the sun Abby had to blink every few seconds to keep her eyes from watering. He looked like a supernatural being. Some kind of spirit brought here to give her whole life meaning.

"Oh, and he wanted me to give this to you. Said it was from something you talked about earlier?" Gabe held out a sealed envelope with Abby's name on it, scrawled in Mr. Franks's notoriously messy handwriting. Gabe looked as curious as Abby. She ripped the envelope open to find a sloppy handwritten note from Mr. Franks:

Abby,

I know you want this to be a closed subject, and I'm trying to respect your need for privacy, but I'm still greatly concerned about your weight and overall health. If you won't discuss the issue with me, your family, or Mrs. Geller, would you please consider contacting my daughter? As I said, she's struggled with anorexia and is doing quite well now. She told me she'd be happy to speak to you. I've told her she might hear from one of my students about an eating disorder, but nothing else. I leave it to you to reach out to her if/when you feel ready. She is an amazing, kind, smart, funny girl, and I think you two would get along well.

Best,
David Franks

He'd put a blue Post-it note on the page with his daughter's information: Celeste Franks, followed by her email address and phone number. Abby's hands turned to ice as she held the note.

"Good news?" Gabe asked. He was flipping through the book from Mr. Franks, but he was watching Abby, too.

"Weird news, but yeah. Good." She forced a smile and put the note back in the envelope, then hid the envelope in her book bag. "I guess my grade's coming up with the extra credit and labs."

"Awesome!" Gabe said, holding up his hand for a high five. It was a ridiculous gesture, so guy-centric and outdated. Abby hadn't high-fived someone since she was about six, but she held up her left hand and let him smack it. They both laughed and sat down.

Abby had just managed to clear her head enough to listen to Gabe's list of project choices when Byron blew in and started crashing around the house like he always did. He poked his head into the dining room, where it was obvious there was serious schoolwork going on, and zeroed in on the one thing Byron cared about.

"Hey, did Mom take you to Subway? Did she get me anything?"

"No and no," Abby said. She flicked her fingers at Byron, shooing him from the room.

"I brought them. There's still one left," Gabe said. "Unless Abby wants it?" He held the sandwich out to Abby, the one she'd already declined twice, and she was tempted to take it just to keep it from going to Byron, but she really didn't want it.

"He can have it," she said. "We're working on our science fair project," she told him. Nothing chased Byron from the room like studying.

"Cool," he said, sitting down. "What are you going to do?" He wasn't talking to Abby. She sighed. Of course. Byron had been trying to ingratiate himself with the popular kids for a solid year. Why wouldn't he fawn all over Gabe?

Abby watched Byron wolf down the sandwich in about three bites, talking around the food like the ill-mannered dork he was, putting on his best cool-guy act to impress Gabe. It was annoying to watch. Pathetic, really. And the smell of the chicken club sandwich was making Abby hungry, which was the last thing she wanted. Her stomach growled and she squeezed her elbows into her gut, worried Gabe would hear. As if he could hear anything over Byron's brown-nosing praise for all things Gabe. She took a sip of the soda Gabe had brought: Sprite, all watery now with melted ice. It tasted like childhood comfort, because that's what Lana had given them when they were recovering from any illness as kids: stomach bug, cold, or flu. Flat Sprite, the wonder cure. But once it slid down her throat, leaving a sugary film on her teeth, it just felt like a thousand calories spreading into her stomach, headed for her thighs. She pushed the soda over to Byron, who blinked at her in surprise at her generosity. Then she ducked into the kitchen for a glass of ice water instead.

Abby had misjudged her food needs. That's why she'd fainted. She could see that now. She had skipped breakfast, and every other meal, that day and the day before and the day before, after promising herself she'd never do that. She knew she needed some food every day. She just got caught up in the challenge of not eating at all. She was only planning to do it for one day, just to see if she could. Then one day turned to three, and down she went, a fainting mess. So, if she was going to keep going with her exercise regimen, she needed a better balance, maybe a few bites of food every few hours no matter what. And always in front of people, so nobody could accuse her of never eating.

She would eat cereal every morning, an apple every day for

lunch, and corn or salad for dinner every night, maybe some baby carrots for snacks in between. She didn't know how many calories that was, but hoped it was low enough to get the stubborn cellulite on her thighs to finally disappear. She threw a bunch of baby carrots into a bowl and headed back to the Byron-loves-Gabe show.

"Yeah, I know what you mean. Gymnasts are serious athletes," Gabe was saying. "They're always these little guys, muscular but lean, no body fat. And crazy strong for their size. Not sure how that'd help you on the track, though."

Byron shrugged. "Yeah, I dunno. Maybe I need to change it up. Lean off track for a bit and try something different. I just want to keep pushing myself, you know?"

"That's a great attitude. Mix it up. Keep challenging yourself. Never slack off."

Byron drank it up. They passed the second bag of chips back and forth, bonding at Abby's expense. They hadn't even noticed she was back in the room. Abby cleared her throat and Byron ignored her, but Gabe got the hint.

"Cool. Well, we really need to get a project outlined for Mr. Franks to sign off on. But we should go running sometime."

Byron beamed like he'd just been asked to the prom by the object of a crush. And in a way he had. Gabe hadn't suggested running with Abby. And hadn't he said she could be an even better runner than Byron? But as Byron left the room, hopping over chairs like a moronic jackrabbit on his way out, Gabe turned and smiled at Abby, and all of her worries disappeared. He was here. That was all that mattered. She held out the bowl of carrots and he took a handful, then patted the chair beside him.

"Time to get down to business," he said. They couldn't decide between two projects: one about mold growth factors using bread and one about fermentation. Abby thought it was funny that Gabe was drawn to the food-related projects. Not her favorite topic, but since both were about rotting food, it was okay. They decided to pitch both to Mr. Franks and let him decide which was better. Then they cranked through their lab reports and in no time Lana came home and Byron took off for Trent's, and then Gabe had to run, because he was going to his father's house for dinner.

"My dad has a new girlfriend," Gabe said, shaking his head. "Tonight I meet her."

"Maybe there's a new watch in it for you," Abby joked. Gabe laughed hard and leaned in for a hug that Abby didn't see coming. Not a one-arm half hug like before, either, but a real, two-arm, body-to-body hug that left her unable to breathe as Gabe picked up his backpack and walked out the front door.

"See you tomorrow!" he called back to her. Abby touched her lips as she watched him go, imagining he'd kissed her good-bye. She adored him so much it hurt.

She turned and there was Matt, in the front window, also watching Gabe go. He settled on a chair with two notebooks. One was the same one from dinner last night.

"Sorry if we were keeping you from your window," Abby said.

"It's not my window," Matt said. He laughed, as if Abby had made a joke, and opened his blue notebook. "Birds," he said, pointing to a blank page.

Abby shook her head. Typical Matt non sequitur.

"So you ate carrots?" Matt asked. "While you were studying?" He pointed at the dining room table, then out the window to the curb Gabe had just pulled away from. "Do you know how many?"

"Were they yours? I thought they were communal carrots."

"Oh, they are." Matt laughed again. "They are communal carrots. I like that. So how many did you eat?"

"No idea," Abby said. "Maybe five?"

"Okay," Matt said. "Five's good. Thank you." He opened the green notebook from the night before and started writing, done with the conversation.

"Sure. Anytime," Abby said, shaking her head. She was living in a crazy house these days. She piled up the project stuff they hadn't even used on the dining room table, and there was Gabe's sweatshirt, hanging over the back of a chair. She held it to her face and it smelled just like him. She carried it upstairs and looked for an appropriate shrinelike location for it, then decided to wear it instead. She pulled it over her head and inhaled. It was like a never-ending Gabe hug.

Lana called her down for dinner, but there was no way Abby could eat.

"Can I eat in my room?" Abby hollered down to her. "I spent all day on the science project and labs. I haven't even touched my regular homework."

"Sure. I'll bring something up to you," Lana called up the stairs.

Lana brought her a grilled cheese sandwich, salad, milk, and cookies.

"Nice sweatshirt," Lana said as she left. "It suits you."

Abby rolled her eyes but couldn't help smiling. It did suit her. It suited her just fine. Abby ate the salad and had a few sips of milk as she did her homework. It only took twenty minutes to do it all. Then she wrote in her journals and did her exercises.

When she put her homework away she found Mr. Franks's note. She read it a few times. She looked Celeste up on Facebook, but her page was secure, so all Abby could see was her profile picture: a smiling girl in a restaurant, a flaming birthday cake before her. She looked normal enough: reddish brown shoulder-length hair, nice complexion, big smile, pretty chandelier earrings catching the glow of the flames. The photo was only of her face, so Abby couldn't see if she was super-skinny or anything. Abby added Celeste's phone number and email address to her phone contacts, just in case, and shredded Mr. Franks's note into a thousand tiny pieces.

16

Byron

Byron needed to figure out how to use the Gabe thing to his advantage. He had no interest in soccer, and no clue why Gabe would be hanging out with Abby, but Gabe was in the most popular group of kids at school. He was one of the lucky ones who fell into it naturally and didn't have to earn his way in. He was so casual about his popularity, like it didn't even matter to him, and that just made him even more popular. He never tried. He just was. Byron needed to be like that.

He'd almost told Gabe about the parkour group, but he didn't want to sound desperate for Gabe's approval. Maybe he could convince Abby to put in a good word for him. Byron drew some of the cooler moves he'd seen at the last practice: thin outlines of guys scaling walls and skimming railings, launching across benches and over tables. Dale was a good coach, despite his bossy nature. Byron was learning a lot about what parkour was and what his own body could do.

Trent was playing a video game that Byron had no interest in, and Betsy was out with a friend, but her laundry was in the middle of Tilly's floor. Byron was dying to ask when she'd be home, but he knew Trent wouldn't like that, just like he wouldn't like that Byron was trying to figure out how to make Gabe his new best friend.

"So are you going to call that Chelsea chick?" Trent asked.

"No way. She's Dale's girl. I'm not getting in the middle of that."

"But she likes you. And weren't you just whining about how no girls like you?"

Byron threw a wad of paper at Trent's head. "I wasn't whining."

Trent eyed the wad of paper like it was giving off a foul stench. "Is that another Betsy drawing?"

Byron unfolded it and showed him that it was a bunch of lame attempts to draw a guy in the various stages of doing a backflip, and Trent shrugged. The Betsy thing was getting to be a sore subject, and it wasn't even a thing. How come life had to be so complicated?

Tilly came home and started cooking dinner, invited Byron to stay as usual, and it wasn't until they were sitting down to eat while Tilly gossiped about the new neighbors with the Mercedes that Betsy came home. She was flushed and giggling, like maybe she'd been running. Or drinking. It was six o'clock on a Wednesday. She patted Byron's head as she walked by him and Byron couldn't miss Trent glaring at him.

After dinner Byron started to help with the dishes, but Tilly wasn't having any of it. She shooed him away and he headed for the living room to find Betsy watching TV and Trent nowhere to be found.

"Phone call," Betsy said, holding her thumb and pinkie up to her ear and mouth to imitate a phone. "Very mysterious. Whispering, and then he ducked into that bathroom. What's he up to?"

"No clue," Byron said. He felt a little miffed that he didn't know. Was Trent keeping secrets from him? They usually didn't hide stuff from each other. But as Byron sat down near Betsy, he realized their friendship was already changing. Parkour, the college crowd, Betsy, Gabe. Byron was leaving Trent behind. And maybe Trent was ditching their friendship, too.

Betsy used her painted toenail, purple this week, to point at Byron's stack of drawings of parkour stunts fanned out on the coffee table.

"You know you're a badass, right?" she said.

Byron smiled at her, not sure if she was teasing or being serious. "Because they're all badasses, like you said, and now I'm one of them?"

"Not the parkour, dummy. The art."

Byron shook his head. "It's nothing. Just a way to kill time."

"You're an idiot if you think parkour and hanging out with my loser brother are more important than this." She leaned forward and picked up the pages. She flipped through them slowly, taking her time to look at each one. "You blow me away," she said. "How is it that you're so insanely talented and you don't even know it?"

Byron didn't know what to say. She was looking at him. Not like she used to: like he was some smelly extension of her brother, some fungus she needed to step around every time she saw him. She was looking at him like she actually saw him, the real him, and liked what she saw.

"Thanks," he said. He wanted to say more, to tell her that Matt had helped him on one of his sketches so he figured he must get his talent from his uncle, because his parents were not artistic in any way. To explain that his dad thought art was a waste of time and that he'd never felt passionate about it until Graham suggested he give it up. But then Trent emerged from the bathroom, still on the phone, and took one look at Betsy and Byron side by side on the couch, Byron's art between them, and headed upstairs without a word. It was a nothing moment but it ruined everything.

"Uh-oh. Is he not speaking to you? Lover's spat?" Betsy asked, and she was back to being the bitchy big sister of his best friend and not the girl of Byron's dreams. He sighed and got up.

"Tell him I had to run and I'll see him tomorrow."

"Tell him yourself," Betsy said. "I'm no messenger."

Byron left it alone, ready to ditch both Trent and Betsy. He thanked Tilly for dinner, turned down her offer to drive him home, and headed out. He was all of two houses down when Betsy caught up to him.

"You forgot your drawings," she said. She was breathless and flushed, like she had been when she first came into the house. She tossed her hair, laughing, as she tried to catch her breath. She was barefoot and beautiful as ever in the fading sun.

"They're nothing. Recycle them," he said.

"They're not nothing," she said, holding them up for him to see, pointing at them emphatically. "Don't ever say that about your art."

"I don't get you," Byron said.

Betsy laughed, shook her head, her dark wavy hair bouncing around her shoulders. "I don't get me, either."

He was torn between the urge to kiss her and the urge to walk away from her and never come back. She was a maddening kind of girl, hot and cold and able to stir something deep in his belly every time she bothered to look at him. She was heartache waiting to happen. He knew it, but he was powerless to do anything about it.

"I have a ton more just like those at home," he said, gesturing to the drawings. "I really don't need them."

"So can I have these?" she asked.

"Sure." He shrugged. He peered at them over her shoulder. He was trying to capture the sense of movement, but the images felt stagnant. He wasn't sure what he was doing wrong. "Only a couple of them even came out close to right."

Betsy swatted him with the stack of pages. "Stop! Stop putting yourself down and acting like this isn't a big deal. I don't have a single skill. Not one. Undeclared freshman college girl. Life of the party by night and utterly forgettable by day. You know how lame that is? You're . . ." She flipped through the papers openmouthed. "Ridiculous."

"Um, thanks?" Byron said. It kind of sounded like a compliment.

"You're welcome." Betsy spun on her heel as if to leave, then turned back to face Byron. She grabbed his upper arm and yanked him down toward her, hard enough that he felt his shoulder pull against the socket. She kissed his cheek, a firm, almost angry kiss, and shoved him away. "Ridiculous," she said. She ran back toward her house, her bare feet slapping on the pavement, his sketches flapping in her hand. Byron couldn't move for a few minutes. He stood there rubbing his shoulder where he could still feel the force of Betsy's pull.

He walked into his house still in a daze. They were just finishing dinner, the smell of roast chicken enough to make Byron hungry all over again. Lana carried plates to the sink while Matt waited patiently for his ice cream. Abby was nowhere to be found.

"I've got the dishes," Byron said, nudging his mom aside. "You can take care of Matt."

Lana stopped rinsing plates and stared at Byron for a minute. Then she leaned over and kissed his cheek, just above where Betsy had. "You're the best son ever," she said. Byron smiled and felt a hint of defiance against his father. Who was Graham to judge him? Graham didn't even know him.

After he finished the dishes Byron hovered outside Matt's door. He'd never really talked to him before, more than necessary. He wasn't sure what he wanted to say to him now. He'd just decided to give up when Matt spoke through the closed door.

"You can open the door," Matt said. "If you need to talk to me. I can hear you out there."

Byron, feeling like an idiot, opened Matt's door. Matt was sitting in front of his computer, entering something from his notebook into a spreadsheet.

"My mom said you like to draw, too. I wondered if I could see your artwork sometime."

"You can see my artwork," Matt said. "You usually use a pen, just a ballpoint. I don't usually use pens. I like drawing with pencils, colored or shades of gray. Some artists like charcoal, but I don't. Too messy. And pastels are so . . ." Matt waggled his wrist, made a motion of smearing something. "I like watercolor. Oil paints when I'm outside. I can't stand the smell indoors. Do you paint?"

"No," Byron said. How could he call himself an artist if he never painted? "Not yet, but I'm interested."

"Interested is good. Interested is how everything starts," Matt said. Byron waited for him to get some of his artwork to show him but Matt didn't move from his data-entry task, so Byron gave up.

He sure was a strange person to deal with. Byron headed up to his room and started gathering his sketches together. They weren't organized at all, just strewn around his room like dirty laundry. He needed someplace to keep them, some way to sort his works in progress into garbage and good stuff.

"A few examples," Matt said from the door, startling Byron. He was holding a nice big blue leather portfolio. That was exactly what Byron needed. "Since you're interested."

Byron reached for the portfolio and Matt withdrew it. He was funny about people touching him, but how else was he supposed to hand people stuff? Matt gestured for Byron to move and he stepped aside. Matt opened the portfolio on Byron's bed and slowly flipped through a series of pictures. There were a lot of tadpole ones. Some of lizards and birds. A series of dog ones. Several landscapes. Some funky shadow people that looked real and dreamlike at the same time. Byron really liked those. There were a few paintings of a person's upper body, the broad chest overflowing with contrasting colors. They were creepy and fascinating, just like art should be. Art was supposed to make you feel something, Byron thought, and those did.

"These chest ones and the shadow people. They're so interesting. I like those the best."

"Oh, the animal ones are my favorite," Matt said. "Those other ones are . . . they're the feelings I get sometimes in my chest. They get too big and then I do stuff I'm not supposed to." He pointed to a painting where red, black, and yellow streaks exploded out of the chest area, turning into shrapnel pieces.

"And the shadow people?" Byron asked.

"That's us," Matt said, as if it made perfect sense. Byron didn't see it, but the simple statement gave him chills. Matt wasn't just a guy who sketched random stuff. He was an artist. And suddenly Byron wanted to be one, too.

"Thanks," Byron said. "For showing me."

Matt snapped the portfolio shut and left without saying anything. Byron shook his head. Had he said something wrong? Matt was just as confusing as Betsy. Byron wished he had a few more predictable people in his life, so he wouldn't always feel so confused. A few minutes later Matt was back, with a black plastic toolbox and a small blank canvas stretched over a wooden frame. He set the toolbox down and opened it up. It was full of paints and brushes.

"You can't have these, but you can use them. The canvas you can have. But you can't paint in here. It's too messy. I mean, your room is messy already, but the paints are messier. Your mom would get mad if you got paint on the carpet. She says I can only paint in the garage. So you should only paint in the garage, too. You can sketch on the canvas in here, but you have to paint in the garage."

"Wow, thanks," Byron said.

"And you need to be able to drive," Matt said. He rubbed his face and looked around the room. "You can take the driving test once you're sixteen. You'll be sixteen in two weeks."

"I don't have enough hours yet," Byron said. "Nobody around here has time to take me out to practice." He sounded like a whiny kid, which he was.

"Okay," Matt said. "I'll get a car. Maybe a red pickup truck. And I'll take you."

"You will?" Byron was confused. How had they gone from art to driving, and why was his uncle suddenly talking to him?

"Yeah. I can't drive. They haven't given my license back. But they will. Soon. And I'll need a car. And you need to drive. So for now you can drive, and I can show you the tadpoles. And then later I can drive."

"Oh. Great," Byron said. He had no idea what tadpoles had to do with any of it, but getting his hours and getting his license sounded good. If he had his license and a truck he could borrow, maybe he could even ask Betsy out on a proper date. If she'd ever agree to that. Maybe he could take her to a park or down to the water to sketch her against a pretty backdrop. She'd probably like that.

Matt left and Byron looked through the toolbox. Matt was right, the oil paint tubes gave off a stinky oily smell. The whole box reeked of it. He checked out the various brush sizes, imagining the fine or broad strokes he could make with each one. He picked up the canvas and felt the smooth texture, the tautness, the promise of something. He drummed his fingers against it and got a nice hollow sound. He got a pencil, took his time sharpening it to a fine point, and started sketching on it.

17

Lana

Lana was out front attempting to trim the hedges with the un-wieldy hedge clippers, missing her unaffordable gardener desper-ately, when a police car pulled up behind her. She knew without looking that it was Nick, and that she looked like a hot mess in her dirt-streaked jeans and the Hawaiian shirt that she'd inherited from Graham years ago.

"I think what you really need there is a machete," he said. "Take out your aggressions and trim the hedges at the same time."

She laughed. What was the point of always wishing she looked better? She'd succumbed to daily vanity rituals to keep Graham's attention, and he'd still left.

"Not a bad idea," she said. She dropped the clippers on the lawn and headed toward the car.

"We still friends?" he asked. He swung the passenger-side door open and Lana took a seat.

"We are," she said. "Old friends." She'd never sat in a police car before. It was terribly busy in there with a radio, a computer, a shotgun, papers, food, water, coffee.

"Welcome to my office," he said. He started to clear some papers from the floorboard to give Lana more legroom, but she waved him off. She wasn't planning to stay long. They sat in silence for a moment before he cleared his throat. "So is Matt okay?"

"He's fine," she said. Matt was sitting in the front window watching them. "I'm sorry I wasn't more grateful for your help that day."

"You're a protective big sister. You always were. It's a good thing. Matt needs that. I get caught up in everything needing to be on the up-and-up. It worked in the Marines. It works on the job. It works against me in personal relationships." His radio bleated something incomprehensible and Nick turned it up to listen, then back down again. "What I'm really saying is, I'm sorry, too. I shouldn't have yelled at him, or you."

"Forgiven," Lana said. She looked him over. He was so handsome, so steadfast, so proper, so contained. But he wasn't the man for her and never had been. When they'd dated, his self-possession made her crave silliness and mess. He still had that effect on her. She thought she wanted a reliable, orderly life. But now she realized that wouldn't be enough. "You remind me of who I used to be," she said.

"I'm sorry, and you're welcome," he said. They both laughed.

Just then Matt banged on the front window, startling them both. Lana was out of the car and headed for him before she had time to think. Matt pointed wildly behind her, shouting something she couldn't make out. It looked like he was saying "dog." She turned to see a petite blond woman running down the street with a reddish dog on a leash. The dog was beautiful: trim and graceful, narrow-waisted and leggy as a dancer. Its color was like polished mahogany. Matt opened the front door and came out on the steps.

"Hungarian Vizsla," Matt said, pointing, nearly dancing with excitement. "Or Magyar yellow dog. They've been around since the 1300s. They were nearly extinct after World War II. There were only about a dozen Vizslas left in Hungary then. They used them to bring the breed back. Vizslas were the hundred and fifteenth breed added to the American Kennel Club."

"It's a beautiful dog," Lana said.

"You scared me there, Matt." Nick laughed. He was out of his car in full-alert mode, arm flexed, hand near his gun. He relaxed his arm and sighed. "So you want a dog?"

"No," Matt said quickly. "Not a dog. A Vizsla, yes, but an ordinary, slobbery, ugly dog, no."

"I see," Lana said, laughing as the tension dissipated.

"You do? You see? Can we get a Vizsla?" His enthusiasm nearly did her in. Matt wasn't good at subtlety, so Lana had to pull out the sledgehammer.

"No, I don't think getting a dog would be a good idea."

"Not a dog," Matt insisted. "A Hungarian Vizsla." He pointed down the street at the place where his dream dog had been.

"Even so, I'm afraid the answer is no. A dog is a lot of responsibility and we're still adjusting to—"

Matt stormed back inside the house, slamming the door behind him, hard enough to rattle the big front window. Lana sighed, turned to Nick, and held up her hands.

"I can't win."

"You care too much," Nick said, climbing back into his car. "And I mean that as a compliment. Don't let this situation with Graham change that. This whole thing is just a process you have to go through right now. It's not who you are."

Lana leaned in the passenger side of the car. "You know you have a knack for showing up just when I need you, and saying precisely what I need to hear?"

He laughed. "That's the exact opposite of what my ex-wife says about me." He smiled and waved and went on his way. Lana headed inside and found the red light on the answering machine blinking. She hit play, hoping for an old friend's voice over that of a telemarketer.

"Hello?" Gloria's voice rang out. "Mattie, pick up the phone, okay? It's Mom. I called your cell but you didn't answer. I'm sure Lana won't mind if you use her phone." There was a beat of silence before Gloria sighed dramatically and hung up. Lana checked on Matt, who was ensconced in his room, sulking.

"Mom called. She'd like to talk to you," Lana said through a crack in the door. Matt was curled into a ball on his bed, facing the wall, his spine a knotted arc of tension.

"I'm too busy," he said. "I need to do this right now."

"Should I tell her you're resting?" Lana said. "That you'll call her back later?" As usual, she felt responsible for the mess around her, for Matt's disappointment, Gloria's need to check in with Matt, and Matt's refusal to cooperate, but she didn't want to be a part of any of it. And none of it really was her fault. But it still fell to her to fix.

"Tell her I don't like talking on the phone," Matt said. Which, of course, Gloria already knew. So then why did Lana always have to remind her?

"I can't make him talk on the phone," Lana said, again, to her fussing mother.

"But I haven't spoken to him in a month. I need to hear his voice, to know he's okay."

It had been three months since Gloria had spoken to Matt, but Lana knew better than to correct her mother. It was just as well, really. Lana didn't want Gloria to find out about the Spike incident. Becca understood what had happened, had commended Lana on how well she'd handled it. Gloria wouldn't be so understanding. Not that she was in any position to judge Lana when it came to caring for Matt.

"He's fine, Mom," Lana said.

"Just because he's fine by your standards doesn't mean he's fine by mine."

Lana paced from the living room to the kitchen and back again. Being on the phone with Gloria always made her restless, like her muscles were surging with leftover teen angst. Gloria was the nervous-energy type, anxious and silence-evading, terminally busy. Lana made herself sit down and relax. She wanted to be nothing like her mother. "He's eating, he's not drinking, he's sleeping better. He's keeping busy with his interests. His newest one is rabies. Did you know marsupials are rabies-resistant?"

"Why in the world is he worried about rabies?"

"He's Matt, you know? He's not worried, he's just interested. And he was talking to Byron about Hemingway and Steinbeck."

"So he's not drinking but he's obsessing about alcoholics and fatal diseases? And you think that means he's fine?"

Lana peeked into Matt's room, through the door still ajar just a crack. He was at his computer, typing away. Happily immersed back into his own little world. It seemed better to leave him there.

"I'll do my best to get him to call you later," Lana said. "Maybe if you could try the video chat again. Then he wouldn't feel like he was talking on the phone."

"I told you it doesn't work from my computer. I don't know why and I don't have time to figure it out. That little camera you sent me is worthless. The directions make no sense. I hope you didn't spend a lot on it. Just have him call me. A mother has a right to talk to her children."

Lana hung up before she lost her composure. Gloria had had Matt's whole childhood to get to know him, but she'd been too busy rushing from one commitment to another to bother. So why cash in on her mother status now? Except to compete with Lana.

To clear her head, Lana headed to Home Depot to see about getting a tool to make hedge-trimming less of a chore. She wondered if they had machetes. She wandered aimlessly, let some burly orange-aproned man talk her into a new pair of shears. She made her way toward the register, and there was Mitch, holding hands with a lean young beauty: long-legged, light-haired, and angular-faced. Lana ducked behind a display of patio furniture to spy unseen. Mitch said something and the girl laughed and tossed her hair in response. Lana wasn't sure, but the girl looked an awful lot like the one from the café, the musician who'd reminded Mitch of his ex. Or possibly it was the ex, and they just looked that much alike: long thin hair, long thin body. So that explained why Lana hadn't heard from him since their dinner together. Just like Graham, he preferred the younger, flirty type. Not that Lana knew if Graham's girlfriend was either younger or flirtier, but Lana had decided that she must be. It made her easier to loathe.

Back home with the shiny new shears, Lana had lost any desire for hedge shaping. She tried again to get Matt to talk to Gloria, with her phone on speaker and her parents on separate handsets in their retirement villa in Florida. He gave a curt hello, then mimed a headache or overstimulation by covering his temples and ears before ducking out of the room. After that her parents took turns lamenting the sad turn of events with Graham, their prized son-in-law and unpaid accountant.

"Is there any hope?" Gloria asked. "Is he really gone?"

"It's not up to me," Lana said. But she really wanted to ask why her mother was still rooting for the type of man who left his family.

"What will we do," Gloria asked, "when tax time rolls around? Do we have to pay him now?"

"It's just tragic, is what it is," Jack chimed in. "You two had such promise. And now . . . I don't even know if he'd finished rebalancing our portfolio."

"I'm very sorry for your loss," Lana snapped. "I guess I should've begged him to stay on your behalf." They sputtered and fussed like cranky toddlers, never once acknowledging that she'd lost a hell of a lot more than they had. She changed the subject back to Matt, instantly regretting it. Her parents had discouraged her from taking him in. Promised her nothing but trouble with him around her kids. It was like they were just waiting to be proven right. Stephen had been the perfect son. Even more idolized after his death. There wasn't room for Matt to move up in the rankings.

"You know Matt will have one of his episodes, and then what'll you do?" Gloria said.

Lana sighed. "Those were brought on by stressful situations that could've been avoided. This is his home. His safe place. If you understood a little more about Asperger's—"

"Don't you start with that again," Gloria said. She never used the term *Asperger's*. Lana wasn't sure if she was in denial or if she thought it was more loving to refuse to label Matt. Her reasons didn't matter. Trying to get them to care about Matt, to love him as unconditionally as they worshiped Stephen, was futile. And as her parents aged they just became more stuck in their ways. Being angry at them wasn't going to change them. But Lana wasn't sure what to do with the anger. She had a lifetime of it stored up.

When Lana had a class to cover at Las Juntas a few days later she ran into Mitch, like clockwork, in the teacher's lounge. She was tempted to ask about the girl, but there was no reason. Mitch owed her nothing. That, and he was offering her a cup of coffee, good stuff, from the café down the street.

"Latte. Better than battery acid," he said.

"Thanks. Did you know I was going to be here?"

"Gerry told me he'd called you to sub for him. Everybody loves Lana." He smiled and nudged her with his elbow. Mitch was the king of mixed signals.

"Everybody but her soon-to-be ex-husband."

"He's an idiot. Don't let him get you down. Get through the divorce and then go celebrate. Head to Cabo for a weekend. Or the entire summer."

"Sounds tempting," she said, but she was thinking: *Spoken like a man with no children to consider*. "I'm running the reading lab again this summer, but before it starts I might take the kids and Matt to Florida to visit my parents. I could sit on the beach there." She hadn't really been considering it, but once she said it aloud, it sounded like a good idea. She could prove Gloria wrong by bringing Matt to her, let her parents see firsthand how well he was adjusting, and show them that Lana wasn't one to give up on her family responsibilities just because life threw her an unfair curveball.

"So what can you do for yourself in the meantime?" Mitch asked. "Something against your caretaker nature. Something just for you."

Lana laughed, not because it was a ridiculous suggestion, but because her mind was blank. What did she ever do just for her? How had she ended up forty-four and single, without one hobby or interest aside from her family? What did women her age do for fun or relaxation anyway? Mitch watched her think it over.

"That bad, huh?" he said, laughing. She shrugged. Nodded. "Okay, what about yoga?" he suggested. "I'm in an awesome class. Very low-key, perfect for a beginner."

Lana wanted to object, but she really couldn't think of a good reason to turn him down, aside from fear of embarrassment. Becca swore by yoga as the best form of stress relief. Lana could use some of that. Plus, she felt she'd made her point to both Gloria and Graham, the anti-snack tyrants in her life, by eating everything she wanted post-separation, and had the extra pounds to prove it. It was time to let those go, before they settled in for good.

"When?"

"Tonight. Class is at seven." Mitch smiled. "Wear something you can move in. I'll pick you up at six-forty."

He arrived right on time, smelling of cologne. Who wore cologne to yoga? Lana started having misgivings about the outfit she'd chosen.

"Do you have a mat?" Mitch asked as he looked her over without a flicker of attraction. Not that she blamed him. She needed to get proper yoga pants instead of wearing her comfy couch sweats.

"No. Should I bring a blanket or a towel?"

"I tossed an extra mat into the car for you, just in case." He flashed a smile, proud of his forward thinking. "Do you have something for your hair?" He made a motion of pulling his short hair back into a ponytail. Lana held up her left wrist to show the hair tie on it, and off they went.

En route Lana made small talk to ease her anxiety. She was not a natural athlete like her kids. She almost never exercised. She liked walking, but that was about it. A lifetime spent watching her mother diet, exercise, and, when all else failed, purge her way to thinness had led Lana to spurn most fitness regimens and avoid scales whenever possible. Gloria's perfectionist streak had affected Lana the same way as Nick's self-control. She had rebelled like some moody teenager. It was time to find a balance.

Lana told Mitch about Matt's Vizsla obsession to pass the time, only to find that Mitch had a good friend with one.

"They're amazing dogs. Smart and eager to learn. We should get them together. See if it'll bring Matt out of his shell," he suggested.

Lana was expecting to head downtown to one of the fancy gyms of glaring lights and pop music, spandex-clad twenty-somethings grinding to iPods before gleaming mirrors. Instead, they turned into the local community center, where low buildings flaked brown paint and eucalyptus leaves blanketed the parking lot so thickly they obliterated the lines between parking spaces. Lana agreed to the Matt and Vizsla introduction without thinking, because her stomach was suddenly a mess. It was like the first day of school all over again, that horrible anxiety of needing acceptance.

The class was in a large empty room with a once-glossy, now-marred hardwood floor. It was made up of a dozen ragtag middle-agers with a handful of hippie-ish youngsters thrown into the mix. Lana felt less anxious at the sight of them. These were her kind of yogis. She rolled out Mitch's purple mat. She wondered if it was his ex-girlfriend's or his current girlfriend's or if he just liked purple.

She put her hair into a ponytail as Mitch made his rounds, apparently buddies with about half the class. The young half of the class. He stretched as he talked to his friends, getting warmed up. One girl seemed particularly interested in Mitch, showing off her sculpted body in a snug camisole and yoga capri pants. She was in the same category as Mitch's preferred type: long hair, narrow face, tall, and thin. Lana suddenly felt self-conscious of her extra twenty pounds of curves. Well, possibly thirty. Abby had moved the scale into the kids' bathroom and Lana had taken it as a sign that she no longer needed to weigh herself.

A handsome, reasonably aged man settled in to Lana's left. He wore gray gym shorts and a blue Cal-Berkeley T-shirt and was so utterly lacking in pretension that his proximity put Lana back at ease.

"First time?" he asked Lana. He had nice broad shoulders, a strong jaw, thick silvering hair, and warm eyes.

"That obvious?" she asked.

"You'll be fine. I'm terribly inflexible, so I'll make you look good."

Lana laughed. She wanted to chat more, but a bearded man took his place at the front of the class and bowed his head with his hands clasped before him. "Namaste," he said. The class echoed him. "Let's begin in mountain pose. Three deep cleansing breaths."

Everyone stood statue-straight on their mat: shoulders back, chins up, arms down at their sides. The handsome man to Lana's left gave her encouraging little smiles as she faked her way through the class.

While many of her classmates looked her age or older, they were all able to bend into positions that Lana couldn't even attempt. Even the handsome man next to her, Mr. Inflexible, could reach his toes while she couldn't. And her balance was crap, too. She nearly fell over several times. Mitch helped her fine-tune her poses a couple of times, but he was such a yoga perfectionist that she felt like she was letting him down with her ineptitude.

Lana preferred to watch the handsome man to her left. He couldn't do every pose perfectly, but he was totally at ease with the constraints of his body. He had a tendency to close his eyes as he held each pose. He seemed off somewhere peaceful and distant, somewhere Lana wanted to go, too. He caught her watching him twice and grinned, guileless and uninhibited. He was the embodiment of what she wanted to be: happy, self-accepting, with nothing to prove.

As the class progressed and Lana's body warmed up, she was able to bend a little bit farther with each pose. By the end of the class she was a limp noodle, her muscles barely attached to her bones. The teacher walked them through a relaxation exercise, breathing and clearing their minds, letting thoughts enter but drift away like clouds in a vast sky. It worked so well that Lana fell asleep. She awoke to the instructor's deep voice seeping into her subconscious, pulling her back to reality.

"Slowly come back into the room," he said. "Rub your hands and feet together. When you are ready, sit up." Lana sat up, spacey and tired, exhausted but invigorated.

"Well?" Mitch asked as he rolled up his mat.

"Amazing," she said, unable to move just yet.

"Told you," he said. A young man walked up and tapped Mitch's shoulder. One of his rock-climbing buddies, judging by their conversation about crash pads and carabiners. Within minutes Mitch was surrounded by the young set, all laughing and telling stories about outdoorsy adventures and drinking binges. The young beauty flirted and flaunted before Mitch, and he gave her the attention she sought. The whole group was so young that their mere existence made Lana feel old and tired. She put on her shoes and socks and smiled at the handsome man beside her.

"Thank you," she said. He was a reminder that beauty came in all ages, shapes, and sizes. He had a good build, a nice face, but, most importantly, a kindness about him, his entire being a peaceful cloud.

"You did great. My first time I couldn't do half of what you can. I'd just had back surgery and I was trying to limber up, only to realize that *limber* isn't a word that will ever be associated with me."

Lana laughed. "I understand completely. But I have no back surgery to blame."

"Oh, I wish I could blame the surgery. I'm just built more for football than yoga. All the more reason to do it." He smiled and held out his hand. "I'm Abbot, by the way."

"Lana."

"Very nice to meet you, Lana. Will I see you again next week?"

"I think I might have to," Lana said. "I feel compelled to master at least one pose." He laughed. "Did you go to Cal?" she asked, pointing at his shirt. He looked to be about Becca's age, in that late-forties to early-fifties range. Becca had gone to UC Berkeley and had been pretty popular there. It was possible they knew each other.

"No, I went to UCLA. My son goes to Cal. A freshman in computer science. I also have a son at Boulder. Business major."

"Wow, college-aged kids. I have high-schoolers. A freshman daughter and a sophomore son. College is coming fast, though. I'm not ready."

He laughed and slid his bare feet into his shoes, dark brown Crocs. Lana liked everything about him but the shoes: the same ones half the kids wore at school. Why would a grown man wear kids' shoes? She glanced at Mitch and he gestured toward the door. The leggy beauty was sauntering off, swinging her narrow hips in her butt-hugging capris for all of the men to appreciate.

Lana and Abbot said goodbye, and as Mitch drove her home she kept thinking about Abbot. A grown man wearing kids' shoes had to be unpretentious. It showed a sense of humor and play. Becca would say he was in touch with his inner child. These were good qualities, Lana decided. The kind she needed more of in her life. Enough with the young, chiseled beauties with their complicated egos and groupies. Enough with the solid gorgeous men with their rigid rules and structures and lack of humor. Lana wanted someone real and deep and self-effacing and utterly approachable. Someone emotionally available. Maybe someone a little more like Abbot.

Mitch looked Lana over. "I think this is the most relaxed I've seen you. Want to get a drink or some tea or something?"

"As nice as that offer sounds," Lana said, "I'd like to head home to make sure my kids and Matt are okay." It was the first time she had left them all alone together.

"Back to caretaker mode," he teased. "At least I got you off-duty for an hour."

"I like taking care of the people I love," Lana told him, fighting her defensive tone. "I'm not interested in changing that. But I think I'll join the yoga class. That gets me a regular hour off, right? Provided my house is still standing."

The house was fine, the kids were fine, and Matt was fine. It looked like Lana would be getting a regular night to herself each week. And a chance to see Abbot again.

18

Matt

The dog, definitely a Vizsla, but the wrong kind of Vizsla, was wiggling like its copper-colored fur was too tight and it needed to escape from it. This dog was nothing like Matt's beautiful running Vizsla. The color and build were right, although this Vizsla was female, therefore slightly smaller in stature, but everything else about it was wrong.

"Why does it move so much?" Matt asked. Lana and Mitch were trying to keep the dog between them, but she was determined to escape, even if it meant leaving her skin behind. They took turns holding her collar while she leapt around like the ground was on fire.

"She's just excited to see you," Mitch said.

Mitch's friend, the dog's owner, had gone inside to answer the phone, and this was when the dog had lost its well-trained composure. She was sitting nicely and being rewarded for it with treats until the phone rang. Then the man went inside the house and the dog turned into this unruly jumpy thing that never had all four feet on the ground at once. She kept trying to leap up to Lana's face, either to lick Lana or break her nose, Matt wasn't sure which.

"Bella!" the owner yelled from the back porch, and the jumping dog immediately sat, but her tail was still alive, wagging wildly against the ground and making a hissing noise as it swept back and forth across the tile. She was a hyperactive rattlesnake in Vizsla skin. Matt looked from the tiled area where they stood to an undeveloped field behind the house, and beyond that to a hill with dried grass, rocks, and rodent holes. It was possible there were rattlesnakes out there. Those shady crevices were perfect for snakes.

Lana and Mitch released Bella's collar and she kept sitting. The man who owned Bella held his hand out flat, palm down, as he walked toward her. When he was right in front of Bella he tipped his fingertips downward in a quick flick. The dog dropped to her belly, sphinxlike. The man tossed her a treat, but it was too far away for her to reach. Bella stayed put. She pricked up her ears and eyebrows, waiting, looking from the man to the treat. "Okay, take it," the man said. Bella lunged for the treat, gobbled it down, and came straight for Matt.

Matt let out a shriek and covered his nose, bracing for the impact. The man yelled, "Sit!" and nothing else happened. When Matt uncovered his face, Bella was sitting in front of him, her entire body rigid with attention, her tail the only thing moving. A rattlesnake poised to strike.

"Wow," Matt said. He couldn't look at the dog. Her amber eyes were fixed on him. She was waiting for something, but he wasn't sure what. She looked desperate for it, though. "Are there rattlesnakes around here?" He pointed toward the hill, turning his body away from the eager dog and her hungry eyes.

"I don't know about here," the man said. "I do hike her in some areas with rattlesnakes. You can do rattlesnake-avoidance training with dogs, but we haven't had any run-ins, so I haven't felt the need."

"What's that?" Lana asked.

The man explained a procedure where the dog is led right up to a rattlesnake safely enclosed in a glass box, and then is shocked with a shock collar. They keep it up until the dog refuses to go near the snake.

"Oh, that sounds cruel," Lana said.

"Better than getting bit by a rattler," the man said. "Like I said, I haven't done it. Vizslas are one of the more responsive breeds. It usually only takes one lesson and they understand."

"Do they ever calm down?" Lana asked, stepping between Matt and the dog. Matt backed up until he was a safe distance from Bella.

"They're a high-energy breed, for sure. But Bella's just a year old. She'll settle down a little as she grows up. I haven't hiked her yet today, so she's all keyed up. After a few miles of hiking, she'll sleep all afternoon."

They left after that. Matt sat in back while Mitch and Lana sat up front. They were in Mitch's 4Runner, which was loud and uncomfortable, but he was the one who had known the way to the man's house, so he drove. Matt hadn't been in many SUVs, though, and it was interesting how different a perspective it gave him, being only a few more inches off the road. Even familiar intersections looked different from up here.

"Glad the kids didn't come," Lana said. "I'd never hear the end of how much they wanted one."

"They're great dogs," Mitch said.

"Way too high-energy for my house," Lana said. Matt knew she meant too high-energy for him, and wondered why she didn't just say so.

"I could have a dog like that, but I'd need that man to control it, too," Matt said. Both Lana and Mitch laughed, but Matt wasn't joking.

When they got back home Matt went straight to his room. He looked at all of the Vizsla pictures on his walls. You couldn't tell from these nice photos of them all poised for show that they were buzzing with uncontainable energy inside. He took some of the Vizsla pictures down. He'd gotten used to the decorated walls, though, and didn't like the empty spaces anymore. He put up some of the rabies-resistant kangaroo pictures that he'd had up before. He sat on the bed to rest. He was exhausted.

When Lana knocked she woke him up.

"Oh, sorry, I didn't know you were napping," she said. She was holding a tray with his lunch on it.

"I didn't know I was napping, either," he said.

Lana smiled and set the tray down. Matt carefully arranged the sandwich plate, the apple, the bowl of pretzel sticks, the blue cup of milk. "Two-percent milk?" he asked.

"Yes," Lana said. "I guess we're not ready for a Vizsla."

"No. I guess not."

"I see you put your kangaroo pictures back up. We could go to the zoo sometime, take a look at some live ones."

Matt took a bite and set down his sandwich. He wiped his mouth with his napkin and nodded. "Good," he said. Lana left him to his lunch.

Before he finished eating there was a lot of noise that could only mean the kids were home from Graham's apartment. His room was close to the kitchen, and he could tell that's where the kids were. Matt's thin bedroom door couldn't keep the noise out. In fact, the noise seemed louder than usual. He realized the sound was growing louder, which meant they were coming for him. He covered his ears, watching the door, but it didn't open. Instead, a thick, creamy sheet of paper slid under the door. The noisy footsteps receded. Matt waited a minute to be sure they were gone before uncovering his ears and picking up the paper. It was a watercolor painting of the same hill and tree that Byron had sketched in his notebook, the one Matt had helped him with, but redone with nice broad strokes and a variety of blended colors. The color was thin, it needed more paint in some areas, but the colors were good, hints of purple in the green grass and a faint orange hue to the blue sky. Matt liked the peaceful feeling of it. He looked at it for a long time. He took down a kangaroo picture and pushed a thumbtack into Byron's painting, hanging it over his computer monitor where he could see it as he worked. Lana noticed it when she came to take the tray away.

"Very nice of him to do that for you. And kind of you to hang it up," she said.

Matt was in the middle of a drawing with colored pencils: a

grassy hill with wind blowing, bending the taller blades down like ripples of velvet, the early spring grass blending from yellow to green.

"It was nice of Byron to do a painting for me," Matt said. "I want to do something nice back. You always try to do something equally nice in return when someone does something nice for you."

"That's exactly how I feel," Lana said. "What were you thinking of doing in return? A picture for him?"

"I can do a picture. He can have this one. But Byron really needs help driving. He needs thirty more hours before he can take the driving test."

"I know. I'm letting him drive us to school every morning. He's getting much better."

Matt did the math and shook his head. "That's a fifteen-minute drive. He needs thirty hours. That'll take a hundred and twenty days. I can help," Matt said. "I get my license back next week." He felt nervous about driving, now that he'd gotten in trouble for breaking the rules. He thought he'd be fine with Byron driving. He'd review every law himself as he taught it to Byron. And he'd have someone to take him to see the tadpoles.

"That's a nice offer," Lana said. She looked down at Matt's drawing, watched him sketch a bird soaring above the tall grass. "But don't you think it'd be stressful for you? It's a pretty out-of-control feeling, riding in the passenger seat while a new driver figures it all out."

"We could start in an empty parking lot somewhere," Matt offered. "I can teach him three-point turns. And parallel parking. And the mechanics of a car. I'll get a car again, now that I have somewhere safe to park it."

Matt wondered if he'd park in the garage, in the space now filled with boxes of stuff and the family bicycles. He could move it all, clear a space, if Lana told him where to put everything. He'd never had a garage before. His car would be protected and safe next to Lana's.

"What happened to your last car?" Lana asked. "You used to have that old Chevy, right?"

Matt had a black car before. It was too hot inside during summer. He'd get a lighter color next time.

"Someone took everything out of it," Matt told her. "The stereo, the floor mats, they broke the glove box so it wouldn't stay closed anymore. They took my rearview mirror. I didn't like it after that. I gave it to Spike. I didn't have my license anymore and he needed a car and I owed him something for the mess. He said there was no way we'd get our security deposit back. Did you ever see the mess?"

"Yes, I saw the mess. Still, you didn't have to give him your car."

"Byron will need help with the written test, too. I can teach him while we practice. I used to know the whole booklet. Every traffic law. But I'll review it. Make sure we both know it all."

"I'm sure you still know it all." Lana laughed. "We can talk about it more later."

She left and Matt returned to sketching his picture. It was time to add the Vizsla. Not the wild Bella jumping out of her skin, and not the poised pictures of Vizslas at dog shows like on his walls, and not even the on-leash trotting one he saw out the window some mornings. He drew a Vizsla racing freely through a grassy field, full sun, shadow beneath the dog, ears flying back, tracking a bird overhead. A happy Vizsla getting all of its energy out so that it would sleep and then maybe Matt could finally get close to it.

When he finished the picture he took it upstairs to give it to Byron. On the way to Byron's room he passed Abby, sitting on her bed, staring at the wall across the room. He paused and peeked inside to look at the wall, too, but he couldn't see anything there. Abby turned and jumped when she saw Matt in her doorway.

"Is there a problem with the wall?" he asked.

Abby laughed but didn't answer him. She sat up and tucked her hair behind her ears and looked at the books and papers on her bed. She had a desk in the corner of her room, but it was covered in jewelry and hair clips and nail polish and fashion magazines. She never used it for its proper purpose.

"You don't like the desk," Matt said, pointing from her pile of schoolbooks on the bed to the cluttered desk.

"I like to spread out," she said.

"You need a bigger desk," Matt observed.

Abby shrugged. "I just like the bed. It's more comfortable. My desk chair's so hard."

"You have very low body fat," Matt said. "From not eating enough and burning too many calories exercising each day. You need to match your caloric intake with the amount of calories you expend each day. You'd be more comfortable in a regular chair if you ate more, or exercised less, gained some weight, had some padding." Matt patted his backside, smiling. "Like me. Not too much, just enough."

Abby laughed. She crossed her arms over her body. She picked up a large book and held it up in front of her like a shield.

"Algebra," Matt observed, pointing toward the book. "That's easy for you. Why aren't you in a more advanced math class?"

"All freshmen have to take algebra. Stupid requirement. But it's AP algebra. Advanced placement."

Matt nodded. He remembered she'd been staring at the wall and checked it again. There was still nothing there. "Why don't you like to eat?" he asked her. She made a little gasping sound but didn't say anything, so he continued. "Cereal for breakfast. An apple for lunch. Salad or carrots for dinner. That's only about three hundred calories a day. You need twelve hundred calories a day at least. You're starving yourself. It's unhealthy. Hard on your heart and other vital organs. It affects your sleep. Your memory. Your moods. Eating is essential for survival. Do you wish you wouldn't survive?" Abby covered her face with her hands and the book fell open on her lap. Matt wasn't sure she understood what he was trying to say—so often people couldn't understand him. "Some food is terrible, but some is quite good. Maybe if you only eat the food you like, prepared the way you like, like I do, it would help."

He rubbed his hand over the wall, feeling the smoothness of the pale lavender paint. He preferred walls with a little texture and flat paint, but Lana's whole house had smooth walls and semigloss paint. When he looked back toward Abby she was staring at him with red eyes. He pointed at them, wondering what was wrong, if maybe she had allergies like his brother Stephen had, back before he died. Stephen had been allergic to all sorts of things: pollen and penicillin and especially animals. They definitely couldn't ever get a dog if Abby was allergic.

"Your eyes are red," Matt said, and Abby rubbed them with the heels of her hands. "Rubbing them makes it worse. If you have debris in there, you could scratch your eye. Is there something in your eye?"

Abby sniffled and shook her head and wiped her nose on her sleeve.

"Oh, no. Are you sick?" Matt asked, backing up a step. He didn't like being around sick people. Abby shook her head and let out a sigh. Some tears spilled out of her eyes and rolled down to her chin. She sniffled into her hands, her elbows resting on the algebra book on her lap. She was crying, which was even worse than her having allergies or being sick, because Matt didn't ever know what to do about crying. Seeing people cry upset him too much, so he turned to leave.

"I don't know," Abby whispered. Matt stopped in the doorway and waited, in case there was more. "I don't know why I don't eat more. I just can't. I know I should but I don't know how to start again. Am I really only eating three hundred calories a day?"

"Yes, most days now. It was more, but now it's only three hundred. That's very low. Way too little for someone your age, your height," Matt said. "I don't really like food, either. I mean, not most food. Or dinner at the table. I like to eat alone. In the quiet. On my tray."

Abby nodded, wiping her tears with the hem of her shirt. "That's good," she said.

"Well, yes. The tray is good. And the window. It's better than the kitchen. The kitchen is noisy and has smells of foods I don't like sometimes. Like brussels sprouts. And salmon."

Abby laughed and kept on crying at the same time. She was

snotty and hiccupping and Matt really wanted her to stop. He went to the bathroom and got the box of tissues and handed her the whole box. She needed it.

"The main problem is you don't eat enough calcium or protein. Your muscles and bones will start to suffer. You're upset, that's why you don't eat. I get upset, too. I used to act out, throw things and break stuff, even stuff that I liked, and sometimes even hurt myself, when it was really bad. I'm on Wellbutrin now and that helps some, but sometimes it's still there. The feeling. It won't go away. Not completely. Not ever." Matt hit himself in the chest, mimicked the sparks and shrapnel flying outward from there, like the painting he'd shown Byron. "You know that feeling? Even if you start eating again, the feelings will still be there. But not eating won't make the feelings go away, either."

Abby coughed and cried some more. "You're right. Not eating doesn't help. Exercising sometimes does."

"Okay. Exercise is good. But you need to balance it. The calories you burn and the calories you eat. I can keep track of it if you can't. I'm very good with numbers. I have spreadsheets all set up."

Abby laughed even though she was still crying. Matt felt better with her laughing. "So, what, you want me to report my eating and exercise to you each day? So you can track it for me? Is that why you asked about the carrots the other day?"

"Communal carrots," Matt said, and they both laughed. "You know, maybe . . . maybe sometimes you could even eat with me," he offered. "If you want. Not on my tray, but maybe on your own. We could put them side by side. In the window. And we could be quiet? And just eat. Not a lot. Just enough."

Abby sniffled and wiped her eyes and didn't say anything else, but after a moment she nodded into her wad of tissues. Matt crossed the hall to Byron's room and slipped his Vizsla sketch under the closed door. He went downstairs and told Lana that he needed a second tray in the living room.

"Oh," Lana said. She was washing dishes and she dried her hands and started digging through the pantry closet. She pulled one out, filthy and unused, and started cleaning it off. It was just like his: the same creaky bronze-colored legs with broken plastic caps at the end and a white-painted surface with a nature scene.

"Good?" she asked as the picture came through the grime.

"Good," Matt said.

19

Abby

Abby sat across from Em in the cafeteria, watching her eat a greasy slice of pizza. It was disgusting, the sauce oozing through the web of separated cheese, the trail of thin brownish oil dripping down Em's fingers. Abby worked on her shiny red apple, taking small bites.

It was still hard, putting food in her mouth and chewing. At some point Abby's jaw got tired and the stuff on her tongue stopped being food. It became something foreign and repulsive, like sawdust or newspaper. It didn't feel like food, and it didn't taste like food. Then came the trouble of swallowing. Sometimes she just couldn't do it, and she'd spit the vile mouthful into her napkin. Not at school, where she usually skipped lunch, but at home with Uncle Matt, where she was trying to eat more.

With all of the things that upset Matt, you'd think he'd be bothered by seeing Abby spit chewed-up food into a napkin, but he just handed her a fresh napkin each time she did it. He never looked at Abby with any judgment. Actually, he never looked at her at all. She never worried how she looked around Matt. And even though he mostly ignored her, she felt less invisible next to him than she did at school. She was surprisingly happy next to someone who never looked at her for more than a second. The kids at school had finally stopped teasing Abby about fainting, so that made school more tolerable. But she was back to being invisible, which wasn't much better.

Gabe was sitting in the back corner of the cafeteria that the popular crowd owned, with Caitlin at his side, stuck to his arm like a barnacle. Or maybe a parasite. Something Gabe might eventually remove. Even through the noisy, packed cafeteria, Caitlin's obnoxious cackle carried across the room and got into Abby's aching head. Usually most kids ate outside in the sun, basking on the lawns in front of the main building. But today the hot and brutal Santa Ana winds were blowing, teasing the girls' hair into a tangled mess, kicking debris through the air and getting it into people's eyes, blowing everyone's stuff away. So they were all crammed into the small cafeteria. The Santa Anas made everyone edgy and restless, and Abby felt exactly like that: static electricity filled her whole body and she couldn't sit still. She swiveled on the bench, turned her back to the Gabe-and-Caitlin show, but she could still picture Caitlin tossing her hair, leaning forward to give Gabe a good view down her shirt, and Gabe smiling and joking with all of his friends, oblivious to Abby's presence across the room.

Abby gave up on the apple, rolled it up in her paper lunch bag, and stowed it in her book bag. She couldn't look at Emily and the greasy pizza, and she couldn't watch Gabe, and she couldn't eat, and she couldn't run. Lunch had become thirty minutes of sheer torture.

"You aren't running today?" Em asked, wiping down her hands with the brown papery napkins that absorbed nothing, just smeared it everywhere. Em had this ability to flip instantaneously from oblivious to mind reader that Abby both loved and hated. Today it was more on the annoying side.

Abby gestured outside. "In these winds? All that crap in the air, getting blown around. I'd have an asthma attack."

"Since when do you have asthma?" Emily asked, abandoning her worthless napkins and pulling a wet wipe from her backpack. Emily was always prepared for every scenario.

"Okay, so an allergy attack, then." Abby didn't have allergies, either, but she wasn't sure Emily knew that.

"If it makes you feel better, he looks kind of annoyed with her right now. He's trying to talk to Mike and Caitlin keeps interrupting. Gabe and Mike are leaning around her trying to see each other without her jumbo-sized airhead in the way."

Abby sighed. She didn't really want a play-by-play on Gabe, but she also didn't want to keep talking about why she couldn't run in this weather when she'd be playing soccer in the same winds in two hours. She nodded. "Thanks."

Byron came over and sat down next to Emily. She blushed so red that Abby was embarrassed for her.

"Can you do me a favor?" he asked Emily.

"Byron, go away," Abby said.

"What?" Em practically whispered.

"Can your mom maybe give Abby a ride to our dad's place after practice today? Just as a backup. I think I have her covered, but in case that doesn't work out?"

"Why?" Abby asked. "Why can't Dad get me?"

"Dad has to work late, and we're supposed to take the bus to his place. But I have plans, and he said as long as I've got you covered that's fine," Byron said, as if sharing this with Abby violated some plan of his.

"And if I call Dad to check on that, he'll confirm?"

"Don't do that," Byron said. "Please." He turned back to Emily. "So?" Emily smiled and nodded at Byron.

"Awesome. You're an angel," Byron said. He patted Em's shoulder as he got up and walked away.

"That was strange," Em said, still blushing.

"Yeah," Abby said. "Wonder what he's up to now." Just as she was formulating a plan, choosing between stalking Byron to find out what he was really up to and turning him in for the sheer satisfaction of doing so, Gabe settled down beside her and her brain froze in the faint cloud of lavender mixed with a boyish smell.

"Hey," Gabe said.

"Hi," Abby said. She did her best not to look at him. Tried not to blush to match Emily. She still had his sweatshirt in her room, folded neatly under her pillow. She needed to give it back.

"Sorry about the science fair project," he said.

They hadn't been chosen as finalists, the ones that got to go on to the district science fair. Abby had been relieved, because Mr. Franks was going to be working with the three students who had been selected. "It's fine," she said. "No big deal."

"Byron said you might need a ride home after practice today?" Gabe said.

"Oh, are you the backup ride?" Em asked. Abby glared at her. "I mean, I think I'm the backup ride, if you can't do it."

Gabe smiled. "I'd be happy to give you a lift." His white teeth gleamed in the dull cafeteria.

Abby, always skeptical, worried about getting her hopes up. "Byron probably didn't mention that I'm going to my dad's tonight."

"He did," Gabe said. "Del Mar. No problem." He stood up, checked his cell phone, and sighed. Abby turned to see Caitlin holding her cell, beaming death rays in their direction. No doubt she'd just texted some command to Gabe.

"Thanks, Gabe," Abby said. "My brother's up to no good, I'm sure. I'd rather stay out of it if I can."

Gabe laughed. "He's definitely got a twinkle in his eye. Maybe we can follow him and find out what he's up to."

At this, Abby couldn't help but smile. "I was actually thinking the same thing."

Gabe smiled at her, so openly that her stomach flipped. Why did he have to keep doing that? "Great minds," he said. "I'll see you at practice. We'll figure out our plan of attack then."

She nodded, unable to speak. He walked away, not back to his friends and the parasite Caitlin, but outside into the gusty winds. Through the glass she watched him make a call. Then her phone rang. Her hands were shaking as she answered it.

"Am I crazy or are things weird with us?" Gabe asked. The wind over the speaker made it hard to hear, but she was sure it was him.

"I hope not," Abby said. "I don't want them to be." Em cocked her head like a dog asking a silent question.

"Me, either," Gabe said. "You're the only drama-free girl I know." Abby's heart skipped at his words.

"Speaking of drama," Abby said, "I'm a little scared of you-know-who. I think she hates me. And the more we talk, the worse it gets." It was easier to say on the phone, when she didn't have to see his face. But she was facing Em and got to see her mouth fall open as she figured out who was calling. Abby turned away so she wouldn't be distracted.

Gabe laughed. "Yeah, she loves her drama. And hates everyone, at least a little. Even me half the time."

"So why are you with her, then?" Abby asked. She was very brave with the wall of the cafeteria between them.

"I'm not. Not really. It's all some big game to her. Half the time I think she likes me and half the time I think she's just using me to make other guys jealous."

"Oh," Abby said. "So why do you let her hang on you so much?" The wind gusted across the line, filling the short distance that separated them.

Gabe laughed. "I guess I'm a little scared of her, too."

The line grew quiet and Abby wondered if they'd been disconnected. Then the wind gusted again. "Look, she'll freak when she sees I'm giving you a ride. And I'm going to have to be either sneaky or an asshole to keep her from getting into my car after practice. You okay with that?"

"I am if you are," Abby said.

He laughed. "All right, then. Our first mission together. I'm looking forward to it."

He hung up and Abby stared at Em.

"What?" Em begged. "You have to tell me everything." Abby shook her head, unable to remember a single word they'd exchanged. Instead she just rested her hand on her racing heart. Em squealed.

Practice was miserable. The hot winds had gotten even worse. Freshly mown grass blew all around them, leaves and twigs kept lodging in Abby's hair, and no matter how many times she smoothed out her ponytail, the Medusa-like wisps just spread bigger. And Gabe was nowhere to be seen.

"Maybe he forgot?" Em asked when she caught Abby checking the sidelines. "You know my mom can still give you a ride."

"Maybe he chickened out," Abby said, trying to sound like she didn't care. She redid her ponytail. She should've worn a braid instead. And a headband.

"Hair spray," Caitlin said over her shoulder as she sauntered by, gyrating her hips like any of the girls around cared about her swinging butt.

"What?" Em asked.

"Your train wreck of a hairstyle," Caitlin said, mimicking a huge afro with her hands. "Spray it down next time, and the wind won't make you look like you just ran into an electric fence."

Caitlin smirked and Abby gave her the same mocking smile back. Caitlin didn't look amused, and Abby felt a little pride in standing up to her, however tiny her rebellion had been.

Practice ended and there was still no sign of Gabe. Abby fetched her things without bothering to change out of her uniform, cramming her disappointment into her duffel bag along with her dirty cleats and shin guards. She followed Em to the parking lot and was about to get into Emily's mom's station wagon when she saw the familiar old blue Honda Civic idling a few cars down. Gabe was in the driver's seat, waving her over like he was the getaway driver and they were in the middle of a criminal act.

"Um, Em," she said, pointing.

"He came!" Emily squealed. "Hurry, before Caitlin sees." Em shoved Abby toward him so abruptly that Abby nearly tripped over the curb. She scurried between the cars and slid into Gabe's passenger seat, forgetting that she looked like a windblown disaster. She waved at Em as they sped past, then caught a glimpse of Caitlin watching Gabe's car gun out of the parking lot. Caitlin was shielding her eyes from the sun with her hand, and her mouth was hanging open.

"Should I duck?" Abby asked.

"Too late, I'm afraid," Gabe said, taking a corner a little too fast. As the tires squealed, Abby worried that if her mother ever found out she let a seventeen-year-old boy drive her home, she'd be in serious trouble. But then she remembered that she wasn't going home, she was going to her dad's apartment, where they lived by a totally different set of rules. It was the first moment she'd ever been happy her parents were separated. "Ready for our adventure?" Gabe asked.

Abby caught a glimpse of her reflection and gasped. She pulled out her ponytail, dug a hairbrush out of her book bag, and got to work on her tangled mess of hair.

"Sorry I look so horrible," she said.

"You look great," Gabe said without looking at her. "You look like an athlete. I hate these girls that laze around the field the whole game and come away looking like they just came out of a salon."

He definitely meant Caitlin with that remark. Abby smiled. "So, my dad's apartment is just off Carmel Valley Road."

"Yeah, I know. But we have a stop to make first. Our mission, remember?"

"Right," Abby said, although she had no idea what he meant. No matter, she was sitting in the front seat of Gabe's car while Caitlin was back on the hot, windy field alone and fuming. Abby felt giddy, almost dizzy. This had been Byron's doing, which was unbelievable. Maybe he wasn't such a lousy brother after all.

"I know where Byron went," Gabe said. "Trent blabbed. Should we check it out?"

"Sure," Abby said. She'd be in huge trouble if her mom found out Gabe had not only driven her at all, but driven her in a detour to track down Byron for no particular reason. But of course the side trip meant extra alone time with Gabe.

"What did Trent say?"

"I said I was giving you a ride to your dad's house, and if he kicked my ass for driving his daughter without permission, I'd need to get ahold of Byron to explain, and he said, 'Well, he'll be at State until five,' followed by a lot of swearing because he wasn't supposed to say anything."

They laughed and Abby was surprised at how easy it was, having a conversation with Gabe. The butterflies in her stomach weren't going quite so crazy anymore. He felt less like some mythical god whose beauty blinded her and more like a boy she knew from school. Maybe even a friend.

"You know, you forgot your sweatshirt at my house," she said. "I keep meaning to bring it back to you, but . . ."

"No worries," Gabe said. "I have, like, twenty of them. One thing about having two homes, you get doubles of everything. Triples sometimes."

"What do you say for twenty?" Abby asked. "Twenty-tuples?"

Gabe smiled at her. "I have twenty-tuples in sweatshirts. Keep it. To remember me by."

Abby's heart jumped. As if there were any chance of her forgetting Gabe, ever.

"I need to change my shirt," she said. Her soccer jersey wasn't muddy, but it was hot, itchy polyester, full of static, and she couldn't stand it for another moment. "I have a tank top on underneath, so don't freak out." Abby pulled the jersey over her head and slipped her T-shirt on. When she looked over, Gabe was staring at the road, but smiling. "What?"

"You," was all he said. And then the butterflies were back. Gabe exited the freeway and headed for campus. "So, Trent mentioned the commons. I think I know where that is."

They took a few wrong turns but soon found the grassy area. And there was Byron, in a crowd of bigger, stronger, older guys, jumping and running and performing the most ridiculous stunts Abby had ever seen. They just parked and watched him for a while, both too captivated to speak.

"I never would've guessed," Gabe said. "I figured it was about a girl." And then a gorgeous girl with a perfect body and tiny dress trotted up to Byron and threw her arms around him. Gabe laughed and playfully smacked Abby's arm. "And I was right!"

The girl seemed more into Byron than he was into her, which made no sense at all. She was gorgeous, and Byron was . . . Byron. Then a bigger, more muscular guy came up to Byron and Byron sort of shook the hot girl off in a hurry. The guy and girl squared off and she walked away.

"Love triangle?" Abby asked.

"Ah, the games women play," Gabe said. Abby hoped he still thought of her as the only drama-free girl he knew. "Well, our mission is accomplished," he said. "What next? Something to eat? I'm starving."

Boys were always starving. And since she'd only had a few bites of apple for lunch, Abby was starving, too. She'd promised to tell Matt exactly what she ate that day, and so far it was nearly nothing. They went to a little sandwich shop on campus and Abby got a salad. She made herself eat about half of it, no dressing. Gabe wolfed down fries and a grilled panini that smelled amazing.

"You should try this," he said, holding the sandwich out to her. She wanted to and didn't want to. Matt would be so excited if she had a bite of real food to report. "One bite," Gabe teased. "Don't be one of those girls that can't eat in front of a guy."

Abby accepted the challenge and took a small bite. The panini was as good as it smelled: salty, buttery, crunchy, cheesy. As she chewed and swallowed she felt conflicted: empowered because she'd done it, eaten food with actual calories, and guilty, like she'd failed herself somehow.

"You need real food after a workout. Not salad," Gabe said. He tore off a chunk of his sandwich for her. She shook her head but he already had her hand in his, was carefully wrapping it around the panini, and the fact that he had ahold of her hand overrode all other senses. She took the sandwich, smiled, and tried to eat it. She took a small bite and chewed and chewed. When he wasn't looking she spit it into her napkin. In the end she had to lie and say she didn't like it. She blamed it on the pesto spread.

They headed back toward her dad's apartment and Abby fought tears the whole way. She wanted to be lighthearted and fun and make witty comments that made Gabe want to see her more, but all she could do was think about that sandwich and how she'd gone so far off track that she couldn't even eat three bites of food. They drove in silence.

"You okay?" Gabe asked when they were almost to Del Mar.

"Yeah. Tired, I guess. But I really appreciate you doing this. Driving me."

"Do you?" he said. He parked outside her dad's apartment and stared out the windshield. A lady was following her toddler down the sidewalk. The kid looked pretty unstable to be out there on the concrete without a helmet or padding, like any minute the cute little stroll was going to end in bloodshed. It was exactly how Abby felt at that moment.

"I do. Especially considering you'll probably catch hell from Caitlin for it."

Gabe shrugged and turned toward her. He was wearing sunglasses and they made it hard to read his expression. "Don't worry about her."

"She's the kind of girl you don't want to make angry," Abby said.

Gabe nodded. "She's called me about six times in the last hour."

Abby shook her head. "Maybe you need to get that whole thing figured out."

"Yeah, I do." Gabe took off his sunglasses. "Sorry to drag you into it."

"Don't be sorry. I'm not. I got a ride home. And now I know Byron's big secret. Two secrets, if you count the girl and the college sport stuff separately. I'm sure I can use that to my advantage somehow. Plus I got to hang out with you."

Gabe smiled at her. "I like hanging out with you," he said. "But you're right. I need to deal with this." He held up his phone and shook his head. "Make that seven calls, nine texts."

Abby sighed. Why did the Caitlins of the world always get the Gabes of the world? It just wasn't fair. "Good luck with that," she said. She started to open the car door, turned back to say goodbye, and found herself wrapped in Gabe's long warm arms, his earthy boy scent and trace of lavender, his shoulder against her cheek and his heartbeat against her chest. She held her breath. It was all she could do not to cry.

"Thanks," he whispered into her hair. "For understanding. I'll call you."

He let her go and she got out of the car and walked toward her dad's place on shaky legs. She looked back when she got to the staircase that led to her dad's upstairs unit, but Gabe was already gone.

She let herself into her dad's apartment, where the stale cooking-oil smell that was always there was the only thing to greet her. She opened the windows to let some fresh air in and sat on the hard couch, just staring at her phone for a while. Then she started typing a message to Mr. Franks's anorexic daughter Celeste.

20

Byron

Byron put Matt's truck in reverse and backed out of the parking space, turning a little too hard and making the power steering squeal.

"Sorry," he said, but Matt seemed unaffected. He was much calmer than Lana with the whole driving thing. He never held on to the dash like he was bracing for a crash, or gripped the handle over his door like he was expecting to be thrown from the car. Byron drove in a large loop around the empty parking lot, picking up speed.

"Slow down before the turns. Accelerate once you're past the midpoint of the curve," Matt said. Matt stared out the window like he was just on a leisurely drive enjoying the scenery and not in the empty, off-season lot of the Del Mar horse-racing track. Byron slowed down for the next curve, then pressed on the gas once he was halfway through the turn, and the truck glided out at a better speed, with less pull.

"Good," Matt said. *Good* was not something Lana or Graham ever said while Byron was driving.

Byron took another lap around the lot. Matt looked up at the ceiling of the truck like he was calculating something. And he probably was. "Parallel parking and three-point turns," Matt said.

He held his index finger in the air, putting some thought on hold. Matt had memorized the whole driver's-test handbook and he was taking Byron through it page by page. "Over there." He pointed at a curb and Byron drove toward it.

They spent the next fifteen minutes suffering through Byron's attempts at parallel parking. Matt got out of the pickup and measured Byron's distance from the curb after each try. Matt didn't seem to care how many times Byron messed up. He wasn't frustrated or impatient. He was just along for the ride, as if there were nowhere he'd rather be than setting up cones for Byron to knock over again and again as he failed to squeeze in between them. Once he finally got it, Matt didn't make him keep trying like Graham always did. Graham wanted three perfect tries before calling it a success. Matt was happy with one.

"Three-point turns," Matt said, sliding back into the passenger seat, the orange cones balanced on his lap. They were cheap plastic cones that Byron and Trent used to set up skateboarding courses, and they were mangled beyond saving now. "When you look back, put your hand on the headrest of my seat. That helps you turn around. Never back up without looking behind you. There could be a dog back there."

Matt used *dog* in the same scenario that Lana always described, except she always said *baby*. Byron had a hard time picturing a world where people let babies crawl across streets left and right, but he definitely could picture a dog darting out without warning.

"I think you might be a better teacher than Mom," Byron said.

"Your mom is a teacher," Matt said. "But she doesn't teach driver's training."

He had a point there. The three-point turn portion of the lesson was a fiasco, because Byron kept turning the wheel the wrong way when going in reverse, making each one into more of a six-point turn. They quit after that. Byron had just over an hour to make it to campus for the parkour club. Matt caught him checking the time on his cell phone.

"It's against the law to text while driving," Matt said.

"I'm not texting. And I won't. I was looking at the time. I need to get going. I have to take the bus all the way downtown. Two buses, actually. So can you drop me off at the bus stop on your way home?"

Byron and Matt switched seats and Matt carefully readjusted the seat and mirrors. Matt had just bought the little red Toyota pickup, but he only seemed to drive it with Byron. It wasn't like Matt had a lot of places to go or people to see. Byron was hoping he'd offer to share the truck with him once he had his license. Maybe Matt would even sell it to him once he realized he didn't actually need a car. Byron could pay him a little each week over the summer. He had a job lined up at a smoothie shop owned by the family of one of his track teammates. It was down near the beach and the perfect place to meet girls. Not that Byron seemed to be having trouble in that department anymore. Now that Chelsea was using him to make Dale jealous, and he was hoping to use Chelsea to make Betsy jealous, and Trina was jealous even though Byron no longer wanted her, he had all the girls he could handle.

"Why don't I drive you there?" Matt said. "Driving is much faster than the bus. We'd have time to get something to eat. There's a restaurant downtown. It has old cars from the fifties inside."

"Corvette Diner," Byron said. "Have you been?"

"No, I don't like to eat in restaurants. There are a lot of germs," Matt said.

"But you want to go? To see it?"

"Could we?" Matt asked.

He was a strange uncle, but he was Byron's only one. Matt finished his preflight check, then drove straight there as if he had the route memorized. And of course he probably did.

Byron got a Rory Burger with peanut butter, extra protein for the workout ahead, and Matt just sat and stared at the decorations in the place. He wouldn't even drink the water they brought him. But he seemed happy just looking around and pointing stuff out. He knew everything about the cars: what year they were, how many had been made, which movie stars had died in one just like it. Afterward he dropped Byron off.

"You can take the bus home?" Matt said.

"Yeah, of course. See you there."

Matt waved and put the truck in reverse. He hadn't even asked why Byron was going to campus. One thing about Matt, you could never call him nosy. Byron was halfway through the workout, breathing hard and regretting the burger and fries, feeling sluggish from the extra weight in his gut instead of energized by the load of calories, when he spotted the rust-colored Toyota pickup still sitting in the lot. Matt had moved the truck from the loading zone over to one of the real parking spaces in the shade, but Byron was sure it was him. Had he forgotten the way home? Was he having one of his episodes? Byron hadn't seen Matt lose it, but his mom had warned him that Matt could freak out without warning. She was worried that it might happen while they were in the car together.

Byron sprinted over to the driver's side of the truck, and Matt looked at him through the closed window.

"Everything okay?" Byron asked. Matt just blinked at him, squinting into the sun. Byron made a motion of rolling down the window and Matt tried, but the truck was off and the power windows refused to budge. Matt looked panicked by this, clicking the button repeatedly to no avail, so Byron opened the door. "Forgot, the windows won't work when the car's off," Byron said. Matt turned the key and rolled down the window, even though it was no longer necessary, what with the door open.

Matt nodded, looking relieved. "Everything's okay," he said.

"I thought you were going to drive home," Byron said.

"I am," Matt said. "What's that you're doing over there?"

"Parkour. Or free running. You keep the body in constant motion. It's great exercise."

"It is. Not a very effective means of travel, though," Matt said.

Byron laughed, but he could see by Matt's face that he wasn't kidding. "No, it's not meant to be. More of a test of your strength, speed, and creativity. Each obstacle is like a puzzle you need to solve, only there's no one right answer. You can go over it, under it, around it, but you have to interact with it in some way, and you can't break stride, and we try not to do what everyone else has done."

"So if I told you that all nine of you went over that railing, next time would you go under it?"

Byron turned to look at the railing beside the steps that they'd been launching across. "Sure," he said, calculating how he'd do it.

"And the picnic table. Most of you slid across the surface. Only the man in the blue shirt jumped from one bench to the other without touching the table at all."

Dale was the one in the blue shirt, Chelsea's ex-boyfriend and the leader of the group, and the one guy Byron both wanted to impress and show up.

"What else?" Byron asked.

"The fountain. The tree at the far end of the grass. The corner of the building there." Matt pointed. "You all did the same thing. Everyone follows the leader. The blue shirt man. The big one. He's the leader?"

Byron shrugged. "Really, there isn't supposed to be a leader. It's an individual sport. Not a competitive one." He was quoting a book he had at home. But he wasn't sure Dale saw it that way. Dale saw it as his world, his sport, his team.

Byron could see Matt calculating, pointing from object to object, designing a new course, moving his lips as he murmured the directions to himself.

"Okay," Matt said. "Can I tell you the answer? Is that against the rules?"

"Nope," Byron said. "Tell me." He leaned against the truck and watched Matt point out a ballsy route he wasn't sure he could pull off. But it was worth a try.

"Do you have your phone?" Byron asked.

Matt held it out to him. "I have two hundred minutes of call time each month. Last month I only used sixteen minutes."

"Does it have video? Can you film me?"

Matt fiddled with the phone and showed Byron that he was ready to shoot a video. Byron bolted from the truck at a dead run, the stairs in his sights. As he launched himself under the railing, barely skimming the concrete beneath, he heard Chelsea let out a cheer. He was up and over the steps in one move, as Matt had suggested, saving his energy for the picnic table. He jumped onto the bench and flipped over the table, landing on the soft grass to one side. He did a forward roll across the bench, his momentum carrying him as he dropped to all fours and gripped the edge of the fountain, kicking his legs over his body. He spun horizontally, ended in a body roll across the grass, popped up just feet from the tree trunk. He launched upward, somehow managed to grasp the lowest branch, and swung himself toward the corner of the library, just at the right height for a wall jump back into the tree, this time grabbing a higher branch and swinging himself back toward the fountain. He landed solid on the concrete, finished a final cat pass across the edge of the fountain, and landed on the grass near the group.

He was winded and dizzy, but proud of his run. He flashed a smile at Matt, a good ending for the video. Then Chelsea took off toward him, cheering in her short blue shorts, for an even better finale. And then he spotted Betsy across the fountain, hands on curvy hips, lips curved into a smile, eyes cutting at Chelsea's approach. Byron didn't waste a second. He jumped up on the edge of the fountain and ran to Betsy, wrapped her in a hug, and, carried away on his high, ducked in for a kiss. She tipped her head back and grabbed his neck and he got lost in the softness of her lips, the whisper of her breath, her minty lip balm. When he pulled back they were both breathless and laughing, the whole crowd of guys was cheering, and Matt was still filming. There are good moments, and then there are perfect ones.

Betsy leaned back to look Byron over, and a wave of doubt washed over him. Then she smiled, shook her head, and punched him in the chest. "You really are a badass," she said. She tipped her head back, grabbed the collar of his shirt, and pulled him in for another kiss.

Byron introduced her to the guys, proud to have a girl there just for him. Chelsea had disappeared, and that was for the best. Introducing them would've been awkward. Dale was ridiculously friendly toward Betsy, which was nice and put Betsy at ease, but Byron knew it was all about Chelsea. It didn't matter, though.

He was one of the guys now, on a college team with a college girl holding his hand. It was his birthday week, and he couldn't think of anything he wanted that he didn't already have in that moment.

Betsy and Byron took their time walking around campus after that. She gave him the full tour, showing him where she usually ate lunch, where her favorite spots were for resting between classes, where the best coffee cart was stationed every morning. Byron had never had coffee before, but he figured he better learn to like it as part of his new life.

Betsy took him to her dorm, an ancient concrete block that needed sprucing up. Her room was a square of four gray walls and thin brown carpet about the size of Byron's room at home, but there were two beds, two dressers, two desks, a microwave, a mini-fridge, and heaps and heaps of crap squeezed into the space. Byron could see why she liked coming home so much.

There was a little girl on one of the beds, with ink-black hair and pale skin, raccoon-eye makeup and tattoos covering both of her arms. She looked up when they came in but said nothing. She had earbuds in and was writing in a journal. She didn't look happy.

"And this is my roommate, Magda. She's a poet." Betsy turned toward Byron and smirked for his benefit.

"Hey," Byron said. Magda peered up at him and pulled out one earbud.

"What?" she said.

"I just said hi. I'm Byron."

"Byron's an artist," Betsy said. Magda's scrunched rodent face relaxed a little.

"What kind of art?"

"Mostly sketches. Some painting."

"I mean what style? Realist? Abstract? Impressionist? Pop?"

Byron started laughing. "I don't know. Landscapes. People."

"Still life? Fruit bowls?" Magda asked. She seemed to be teasing him.

"No fruit bowls. And not still life. I like trying to capture people in motion."

"He's in the parkour club," Betsy said. "So he draws their stunts and stuff."

"Cool," Magda said. "Which classes have you taken so far?"

Byron hesitated, looked at Betsy. She smiled and shook her head.

"He doesn't go here. So I was thinking maybe you could let us into the art building. Show him how awesome it is. Maybe help me convince him to . . . transfer."

Magda looked over her journal, sighed dramatically, and shrugged. "Yeah, sure." She put on some weird rubbery-looking black boots and led the way, ring of keys dangling from her hand.

"Magda works in the printing press side of the art building, but she has access to the whole thing," Betsy said.

"Book art, not printing press," Magda said, laughing. Out in the sun Byron noticed she had a crystal nose piercing, and that under the thick black eye makeup and unflattering hair she was actually kind of pretty.

"She keeps explaining the difference, but I have no idea what she's talking about," Betsy said.

Magda led them into a dark, quiet hallway that echoed their footsteps. The walls were lined with glass cabinets showcasing various art projects: metal sculptures, blown glass, papier-mâché, little figures assembled from toothpicks, bottle caps, and wire, a heap of multicolored cloths that vaguely resembled a human in a fetal position.

"This stuff's crazy," Byron said. Magda shrugged, unimpressed, and waved him on. She led him to a case of small books with natural-fiber covers decorated in pressed flowers, hand-painted and stitch-bound and full of thick pages of calligraphy.

"That one's mine," she said. "Book art. Not printing press." She nudged Betsy and they both giggled. They'd neared the end of the hallway, where the room opened up into a warehouse-sized space of sculptures and paintings: colored plastic pieces hanging from the ceiling like a giant child's mobile, greasy metal car parts in a maze of small shiny mirrors in one corner, an endless spool of unraveled film in another corner, and colorfully decorated pottery lining one wall.

"Holy crap," Byron said. "I had no idea there was this much . . . art in the world."

Both girls nearly dropped to the floor cackling. Byron didn't care. He roamed the art projects, reading the little placards that told about the student, the inspiration, the materials used. He left the giggling girls behind and walked into a room of possibility. There were epic canvases of enormous paint splatters, solid hues with just a hint of another color in the right light, tightly controlled strokes of razor-sharp features that suggested an old man's face, long loose lines of pastels that gave the impression of a woman and child blending into flowers in a breeze, exaggerated cartoonish characters amid stark crooked buildings. Byron was speechless. He didn't know how much time passed, but at some point Betsy appeared beside him. She took his hand.

"Badass enough for you?" she asked. Byron nodded. He wasn't sure what all he was seeing, but he had no doubt this was the world for him.

"Thank you," he said.

Magda left them to it. After a final tour Byron hugged and kissed Betsy outside the art building. He didn't want to leave her or campus or the feeling of students here to party and make friends and fall in love and push themselves and learn about things they never even knew existed. He hated the thought of heading back to his dull old ill-fitting life of high school drama and pointless classes and, worst of all, no Betsy. But she had a class to go to and Byron had Matt, still sitting in the parking lot by the commons, waiting for him. He'd tried to send him home, but Matt had insisted on waiting. He said it was time for Byron to try freeway driving anyway.

"You get it now, right?" she said. "You're an artist. All the rest is part of who you are, but the art, that's the core."

Byron nodded, kissed her again. "I get it," he said. "I never would've known if you hadn't shown me this."

"You would've figured it out, but I'm happy to help."

"I can't believe I get to kiss you now," he said.

Betsy started laughing. "You're adorable," she said. Byron

didn't want to be adorable. But if it meant he got to kiss Betsy some more, then he'd take it.

"When can I see you again?" he asked.

Betsy shrugged, fluffed her hair. She picked up her backpack and smiled at him. "We'll figure something out," she said. Byron wasn't sure if she was being flirty and coy, or blowing him off. He felt a surge of panic, like maybe she was already leaving him behind, ready to move on to some other project more interesting than showing a high school kid what art was.

"Okay," he said, hoping she couldn't see his worries.

She turned like she was ready to go, then looked back at him. "What's the story with that girl? The short shorts."

Byron shook his head. "Chelsea. Dale's girl. She likes to flirt with me to make him jealous, but there's nothing between us. Just a game with him. Hopefully you put it to rest today."

Betsy nodded. She looked very serious. "I'm not interested in being someone's plaything," she said.

"Me, either," he said. "I don't feel like that about you."

"How do you feel about me?" she asked, stepping very close to him.

"Like I kind of love you," he said. She blinked and her mouth fell open. He'd done it. He'd said it. He ducked and kissed her, long and hard, then backed off. "How badass is that?" he asked. He felt giddy, weightless, like he might float right up to the sun. She was blushing, holding her breath. He backed away until he ran into some guys playing hacky sack in his path, then turned and ran, full of fear and power and more exhilarated than he'd ever felt.

When Byron made it back to Matt's truck he was too spacey to drive. Too tired from the Rory Burger and hard workout and too high on loving Betsy and art. Matt just shrugged and agreed to drive. On the drive home, as Byron nursed a sore hamstring, Matt rattled off modifications to the route Byron had tried.

"You're smaller and faster than the other guys, but they're stronger. You can't jump as high as the blue shirt guy, but you can swing your body farther when you use your arms, like in the tree."

"His name's Dale," Byron said. "The blue shirt guy. The leader."

Matt shook his head. "You're the leader now."

"Really, there isn't a leader . . ."

"There's always a leader," Matt said. And of course he was right. Dale had given Byron a hard time about the flip over the picnic table, saying parkour wasn't about showboating, and flips had no place in it. But the other guys thought the flip was awesome. So maybe the other guys weren't following Dale's lead as much as they used to. Byron smiled and stretched his leg, massaging his pulled muscle.

"Okay, enough about parkour. Can we talk more about art?" Byron said.

Matt nodded. "Okay. I like art better. Can I show you the tadpoles?"

Byron laughed. Matt was a nutty conversationalist.

"Yeah. Tadpoles and art. Let's do it."

21

Lana

Between Nick, Mitch, and Abbot, Lana had realized two things about herself. One, that the sleeping romantic in her had been re-awakened. And two, that she wanted to be in better shape for whoever might actually see her naked again someday. She called her friend, neighbor, and former walking pal Camilla and left a desperate message: "I'm getting fat, Camilla. I need your help." Camilla called back laughing, promising to make Lana feel thin by wearing bright purple leggings that showed off her cellulite.

They met at the end of the driveway. Camilla was wearing the purple leggings, but they were under a loose black skirt. When she moved in the light, the lower half of the skirt glittered with sparkles.

"Hey, where's the cellulite?" Lana asked.

"I'm afraid it was too hideous even for you. I don't know what I was thinking. Cute, though, yes?" She twirled, a scattering of sequin flashes. "Why dress my age?"

Lana laughed. Camilla was in her early fifties, but had the heart of a twenty-year-old. "I wish I had half of your energy and spirit."

"And if I had those legs of yours, I'd wear the leggings without the skirt."

Lana laughed. "The legs aren't what they used to be. That's where you come in."

"Well, then, let's get to it," Camilla said. She was an all-business walker, the kind who pumped her arms even on a casual stroll. She'd put on a few pounds herself, but she hadn't lost an ounce of drive. She pushed the two of them hard. The cherry trees were in full blossom, the ground littered in petal confetti, the air pungent with spring.

Lana had left Abby and Matt home alone together, each in their own rooms. Byron was at Trent's. She was surprised to return home to find Matt and Abby seated side by side in the front window, aglow in afternoon sun, eating on matching trays. It was the opening scene from *The Cat in the Hat*, without the rain, and Lana came inside happier than she'd felt in a long time.

"You two are straight from a storybook. I love it," she practically sang.

"Abby's eating with me," Matt said.

Abby took hamster bites from an apple slice. She seemed to be concentrating on gnawing the peel off one millimeter at a time.

"Do you want anything more substantial? A sandwich? I can make it."

"No, thanks," Abby said.

"She's starting with her favorites," Matt said. "She'll eat more if she likes what she's eating."

"Of course," Lana said. She wanted to press Abby to eat something with actual calories, but the memory of her mother's diet-obsessed ways offset the urge. How could she scold a child for eating healthy food when she could still hear the sound of her own mother retching up her binges through the thin veil of memory? Not to mention her own overindulgence of sweets and carbs that she was attempting to exercise away. If Abby wasn't a binger, with or without the purging, maybe she'd dodged the family's unhealthy eating habits and the cycle had finally been broken.

"What else have you two been up to while I was out?"

"We're not talking," Matt explained. "Just eating."

Abby nibbled carefully on a cucumber round, spinning it as she devoured the outermost edge. She looked up at Lana, smiled, then turned to look back out the window.

"Okay," Lana whispered.

In yoga, the instructor told the class to open their chests, inhaling deeply, visualizing their hearts expanding. During class Lana had been too busy concentrating on her posture to feel it, but sitting at the kitchen table, with Matt and Abby bonding in the next room, she felt her heart opening up like the Grinch's on Christmas Day.

Byron came home, sweaty and flushed, crashing through the house with the elegance of a wrecking ball. Abby and Matt had retreated to their separate rooms again. Lana was in the kitchen wiping down spotted counters and a splattered stove. Byron made a double-decker sandwich with three slices of bread and almost an entire container of deli-sliced turkey. He shoved it into his mouth as if it were trying to get away.

"Where have you been?" Lana asked. "You're drenched in sweat."

"Mastering the awesome sport of parkour," Byron said, glowing with happiness. He used his shoulder to wipe a trickle of sweat from his temple.

"What's parkour?" she asked.

"The coolest sport ever," he said. "I kind of need to talk to you about it. I might want to quit swimming." He chewed, swallowed, nearly choking he was eating so fast. "And track. And just do parkour. And maybe tae kwon do again, or gymnastics? I don't know yet. Plus, I need to take some art classes. Actually, lots of art classes."

"Oh," Lana said. Everything he'd listed was out of her price range, but it was the most excited she'd seen Byron about any activity in a long time. "I'd like to know a little more about parkour before we do all that. And these art classes. And we'll have to talk to your dad about the cost."

Byron launched himself up, popping over the back of the chair without touching it, and landed with a grace that was new. He gave Lana a sweaty hug, lifting her off the floor for a moment. "Thanks!" he said. "I'll call Dad right now. Get on the computer and Google parkour. You'll love it. It'll get me into super-good shape."

"I'll do that." Lana held on to his arm. "Just one thing. We were thinking track and swimming might earn you a college scholarship. If you're only doing sports outside of school, does that carry the same weight?"

Byron laughed, shaking Lana by her shoulders. "That's the best part. It's a college team! I'm already in, so I'll be there three times a week. I might need a car to get there and back, once I get my license. I could also get an art scholarship, you know, because I think art is my real calling."

He bounded out the door, enormous puppy feet trailing behind his long, lean body, leaving Lana with her mouth hanging open. Since when did he have a calling?

Lana was in the midst of clicking through a series of YouTube videos of death-defying parkour stunts with Byron watching eagerly over her shoulder, worrying about her child throwing his body off buildings and over walls, when the phone rang.

"Lana Foster? This is Margie, from Dr. Tucker's office? I'm calling because there was an irregularity on your pap smear, so we'd like you to come back in for a follow-up."

"Excuse me?" Lana said, hoping she'd heard wrong. Byron perked up and Lana gave him a lighthearted laugh like it was nothing. But she instinctively headed out of his hearing range.

"You had your annual exam a few weeks ago? It appears there were some irregular cells, so we need to do another test."

"Irregular how? What does that mean?"

"That's what we're trying to find out. When can you come in?"

"Uh, whenever, I guess. I have to drive my kids to and from school, but . . ."

"We have a cancellation for tomorrow at ten," she suggested. Lana agreed and hung up.

To distract herself from the rattling phone call, and not with distressing parkour videos, she asked Byron if she could see some of his art. Aside from his doodles in the margins of pages, she didn't know much about it. He'd never wanted to share it before. He escorted her up to his room and quietly flipped through one amazing sketch after another: sunlit trees, shadowy buildings, athletes midstride, midflip, and midlanding, young girls with down-cast faces framed by flowing hair. He was more talented than she'd realized. A lot more talented.

"I talked to Dad about parkour, and he was fine with it," Byron said. "Not so much on buying a car, though." He stopped at a watercolor of the backyard swing set she was thinking of finally getting rid of. A young Byron sat on the top of the slide, ready.

"Oh, Byron, this is lovely," she said, choking up as she held it. "They all are."

"You think I have talent?" he asked. His voice was as small as the boy in the painting.

"Of course you do. More than talent. A calling. Like you said."

Byron smiled. "I didn't tell Dad about this. He doesn't . . ." Byron shook his head, took the watercolor from Lana's hands, and started piling the pictures together. "He thinks art is a waste of time."

Lana took Byron's hand. "This is not a waste of time," she said in her authoritative teacher voice. "This is a gift. I'm so proud of you, that you can do this. And without training. Just imagine what you could do with some fundamentals under your belt."

Byron smiled, sheepish and unsure. "Thanks. Maybe you can tell Dad."

Damn it, Graham, Lana thought. *What kind of father diminishes his son's passion?* She used her pride in Byron's art and anger at Graham to push aside the scary scenarios that filled her mind all night long. Irregular pap smears weren't uncommon. It had happened to Becca once. They didn't get a clean sample. The second one had turned out fine. Surely Lana's would be the same. But the next morning as she sat in the small, chilly exam room surrounded by fading, curling posters about breast health, pregnancy, and contraception, Lana wasn't so sure.

"How many sexual partners have you had in the past ten years?" Dr. Tucker asked.

"One. My husband," Lana said.

"And as far as you know, you were his only sexual partner?" Prim little Dr. Tucker flipped through Lana's chart and made some notes, as if not the least invested in her reply.

"Um, as far as I know," Lana said, and for the first time it occurred to her that you never really know, do you? An unhappy spouse can be capable of anything. Graham didn't seem the type, but how often did wandering husbands look the part?

Dr. Tucker looked up, her dark eyes magnified by her glasses. "Is it possible you weren't?" She was a lean, compact woman, but Lana felt intimidated by her. Doctors always made Lana nervous. Some inherent fear of being judged.

"I don't know. We separated recently. Well, months ago. I never thought there was anyone else, but do you ever really know for sure?" Lana's voice trembled as she spoke. When would she be able to admit marital failure without feeling wrenched open?

Dr. Tucker remained impassive, but made a note in Lana's chart. "Okay," she said. It took all of Lana's willpower not to lean forward to see what the scribble said. "So, you're aware that HPV causes cervical cancer, and that it's an STD?"

"Yes," Lana whispered. "Is that what I have?" The word *cancer* sent a jolt through Lana's body. Images of Stephen, taken down swiftly from vibrant and strong to pale and weak, feigning a smile and promising to fight as he slid from sick to sicker, a rapid-fire slideshow of Lana's worst fears.

"Oh, let's not get ahead of ourselves." Dr. Tucker laughed, touching Lana's bare knee with her fingers. Her hands were ice-cold, like the room. "But you have tested positive for human papillomavirus, or HPV. It's the most common STD there is, and honestly, almost all women will have it at some point. It doesn't necessarily mean your husband cheated on you and gave it to you. Most women contract it sometime in their twenties. It can lie dormant for years, decades, before manifesting like this. Okay?"

Lana nodded, but her entire body had gone numb. She had an STD? She was in her mid-forties, had been monogamous for two decades. It made no sense.

"Most of the time your body resolves the infection by itself, so we'll test you for it again in about six months, see if it's still coming up positive. Today I want to do a colposcopy to double-check those irregular cells. Once we have the results, we'll go from there. No worries unless we find something to worry about, okay?"

"Yes, okay, fine," Lana said. But of course the avalanche of worries came anyway, buried her alive. "And what if you find something?"

"If we confirm the presence of abnormal cells, we'll talk about the next step. If they're all normal cells, then there is no next step, aside from retesting for HPV."

"Can't you tell me the worst-case scenario now?" Lana asked. "Just so I can . . ."

"Obsess?" Dr. Tucker laughed. She smiled and shook her head like Lana was a charmingly testy child. She patted Lana's shoulder, and the coolness of her small hands chilled Lana through her T-shirt. At Lana's annual exam she'd been completely naked under the faded, worn hospital gown. Today she was pantsless beneath a crisp papery drape across her lap, but fully clothed on top. She was only half undressed yet felt significantly more exposed. Raw. Unspooling. She wished she'd listened to Becca's meditation CD. Maybe brought it with her to tune out the slow-boil panic drumming in her ears.

"This will hurt less if you're relaxed," Dr. Tucker said. "Lean back, no worries, all is fine in the world." She laughed as she tucked a child-sized pillow behind Lana's head.

But how could Lana possibly relax? So every aspect of the simple exam hurt more than usual. Dr. Tucker kept up a steady stream of chatter, asking about Byron and Abby, but even as Lana answered her she was somewhere else, somewhere painful and cold and lacking in oxygen.

By the time Lana got home she was emotionally gutted and cramping. It was just a doctor's visit, just a follow-up for more information. Nothing had changed, really, except for her sense that she had been finally moving into an easier phase. Maybe there was no easier phase. Maybe life would just keep coming at her as ruthlessly as ever.

Lana had a few hours before picking up the kids from school, so she took a couple of ibuprofen and curled up in bed. When she woke it was past lunch and she had a sharp pain in her stomach. She'd forgotten to eat, and to feed Matt. She went downstairs and found him eating at the front window.

"Sorry," she said. "I fell asleep."

"I can make my own food," he said. "I know how. I just like it when you do it."

"I know," Lana said. He hadn't really had that kind of a mom, the kind who doted on him, stocked up on his favorite foods, catered to his dietary whims. "I like to do it."

The truth was, Matt had lost his mother to cancer. Not hers, but Stephen's. From the moment of Stephen's diagnosis, nothing mattered to Gloria but getting Stephen better. Her other three children were forgotten, left to fend for themselves. Lana and Becca survived well enough, but Gloria had no right to desert Matt, a troubled, bullied, misunderstood child who needed extra love and kindness and compassion. Lana vowed not to let her scare get the better of her. Not to let Matt suffer just because a big, frightening thing was challenging her just as they were getting settled into a routine. Matt needed a consistent home environment, and Lana had promised him one.

Lana ate a few bites of yogurt over the kitchen sink to buffer the ibuprofen she envisioned burning a hole in her stomach. She stared out back at the neglected yard. She needed to seed, water, aerate, mow, but these had always been Graham's duties and she wasn't even sure where to begin. She didn't feel like being alone with thoughts of the jobs she'd inherited but didn't know how to do, or with trying not to think about Dr. Tucker's test results, so she tried Abby's trick of pulling up a chair beside Matt in the early afternoon sun of the front window.

"Any Vizsla sightings?" she asked.

"Yes. Two. The same one, twice." Matt polished off his sandwich and wandered off, leaving Lana sitting there alone. Really, she knew better than to think he was the right person for lifting her out of a funk. She was about to call Becca to dump yet another round of fears and complaints on her when Matt returned with two bowls of yogurt-covered pretzels.

"I'd rather not share," he explained. "You were at the doctor's office. There are so many germs there. Most MRSA infections come from hospitals and health care facilities."

"Well, let's hope I don't have that," Lana said, accepting her bowl of pretzels. It was the first time Matt had made a caretaking gesture toward her. It was tiny and enormous at once.

"You're good for us," she told him.

"We're good for each other," he said.

They ate their snacks in silence, and Lana understood why Abby liked the spot. In a world of drama and complications and emotional upheavals, Matt was the one family member impervious to it all. Matt was simply Matt, every day, every hour. Incapable of adapting. Disinterested in change. Free of judgment. Here Lana had thought she'd be the big sister rescuing him, and it was turning out the other way around.

Lana was grateful for her yoga class that night. She definitely had some stress to work out of her system. Mixed-signal Mitch was there, catching up with his young, toned, outdoorsy friends, including the lean, free-spirited young woman. Abbot settled next to her, Crocs and all, and stretched in pike position.

"I can't help thinking of my students every time I see your Crocs," Lana confessed, regretting it the moment she'd said it.

He laughed a hearty cackle. "I have arch issues. I used to wear Birkenstocks, but they started smelling. My niece wears these, and when they get dirty my sister puts them in the dishwasher. Can you believe it? Shoes you can wash. So she got me a pair for my birthday. It's half a joke, but they do have a good foot-bed, and I only wear them here." He pushed the pike deeper, nearly resting his head on his knees. He sat up and smiled, flexing his feet, clicking his rubber shoes together Dorothy-style. "They remind me of my niece. She's nine and brilliant and everything that's good in the world."

"Plantar fasciitis," Lana said, and he nodded.

"Getting old is the pits. Might as well have fun shoes."

In one conversation he'd invoked the most positive words of wisdom from Dr. Tucker, Camilla, and the same type of pure adoration she felt for Matt. There was a cosmic feel of destiny in it.

"Okay, you swayed me," she said. "I embrace the shoes."

"Enough to have coffee sometime?" he asked. "I promise to wear loafers."

They laughed and class began. He stole a glance at her and she nodded, accepting his invitation. It was good to have something to look forward to. With Abbot's help, the week tipped the balance more toward joy and hope than fear and loneliness. So when Dr. Tucker called to follow up on her labs, Lana was fully prepared to get the all-clear.

"Well, I'm afraid we found irregular cells on your biopsy as well," Dr. Tucker said. Her voice was softer than usual. Motherly. Which frightened Lana more than the words themselves.

"Oh," Lana said. *Irregular cells*, while a terrible term, was still milder than its more terrifying counterpart *cancer*, and Lana hoped Dr. Tucker's reluctance to use that word meant it wasn't definite.

"I'm sure you have questions. Would you like to come in, or cover them here on the phone? Is this a good time to talk?"

"Um, now is fine," Lana said. She definitely had questions, tons of them. She just couldn't think of a single one as she sat on her bed and stared at her stunned face in the closet mirror. She'd just stepped out of the shower and was only half dressed. Her hair was wet and it was going to dry flat except for the annoying upward curl at the ends if she didn't attempt to subdue it as it dried, but that no longer mattered, did it?

"Okay," Dr. Tucker said, her business voice back. "I'll just talk and you stop me when you have a question. After the colposcopy, I've determined that you have high-grade squamous intraepithelial lesions, or HSIL cells. With the presence of these cells, I'd advise doing a LEEP procedure." Dr. Tucker paused, and Lana waited, and after a moment of silence permeated by paper-shuffling on the doctor's end, she continued. "What that means is I'll insert a numbing agent into your cervix. Then I use a thin wire loop carrying an electrical current to cut away the abnormal tissue. It shouldn't be painful. The whole thing takes about ten minutes. It has a ninety percent cure rate. Follow so far?"

"Yes," Lana whispered. What about the other ten percent? She pushed the thought from her mind, but it kept bubbling back up.

"You might have some cramping for a day or two afterward. And you should avoid intercourse for three to four weeks after."

"No problem there," Lana said. She was done with men anyway. An STD that led to cancer. If this wasn't the universe telling her to surrender to singlehood, what was it?

"This isn't an ideal scenario, Lana, but it's not the end of the world. Okay? We know what we're dealing with, we have clear steps to take, and a very high success rate. These are all good things."

"Yep," Lana said, mustering both her shaky voice and some false confidence. "I trust you."

"Good," she said. "Let's set up a time."

After they hung up, Lana did a Google search for HPV. As with any medical condition, it was a bad idea. She found tons of articles from respected medical institutions full of terrifying data. Also, very few of them seemed to back up Dr. Tucker's claim that this was likely a decades-old STD she'd picked up pre-Graham. Maybe it was possible, but it was equally possible that it came from him, a gift from some indiscretion of his, and since there was no test for men, she could never know for sure. Not without asking him directly.

She swallowed her fear and finished dressing. Her hair was a disaster and none of her clothes fit right and she was supposed to have coffee with Abbot in two hours. She sent him a text saying she didn't feel well. She sat on the foot of her bed, deep-yoga-breathing, rallying her inner goddess of strength and wisdom. The goddess was busy doing other things, though. Lana gave up searching for inner peace, and wept.

22

Matt

Matt settled by the window. He'd developed a nice daily routine. The routine helped keep his body calm, while the new data kept his fast-processing mind busy. He could go an entire day without missing drinking if he kept busy enough. He flipped the green cover of his steno notebook open, uncapped his favorite green pen, and recorded:

Lunch: baby carrots (3)—7 calories, cucumber slices (2)—2 calories, Triscuits (2)—40 calories, apple (2 slices)—18 calories. Total: 67 calories. 2 grams protein.

He listed these items under the standard header for each day:

Breakfast: Cheerios ½ cup—55 calories, with ¼ cup skim milk—21 calories, 8 oz. skim milk—83 calories. Total: 159 calories. 12 grams protein.

His pages of Abby-data were growing. But she still wasn't eating enough calories each day. And definitely not enough protein. She mostly ate fruits and vegetables, which was good, healthy. But almost everything else was missing. Even good things that went with vegetables, like butter.

Matt had done some research and figured out a healthy, bal-

anced diet based on Abby's age, height, and weight, and the types
of foods he'd seen her eat. When he showed it to her she didn't say
anything, just stared out the window until her dad came to pick
her up for dinner. After she came home from Graham's, though,
Abby told Matt that he could help her eat more of the right things,
but only if he didn't tell anyone about it. Not even her. Matt kept
notes on everything she ate, but he never told her how many calories he wrote down. That was one of the rules. The other rule was
that he could only add one small thing to her diet each day, no
more than a few bites. That was fine. Matt understood not wanting to change too many things at once.

Matt had calculated a steady daily increase in food that would
get Abby up to eight hundred calories each day. It wasn't enough,
but it was a lot more than she was eating now, and when he'd
said she needed to eat at least twelve hundred calories a day she'd
started crying. Eight hundred didn't make her cry.

By adding a few bites each day Matt would eventually get her
up to 250 calories at each meal, plus one 50-calorie snack. Tomorrow she would add half a banana to her breakfast for an additional 50 calories. That would put her at 209 calories instead of
250, which wasn't the exact right number. Eating the whole banana would have been the best idea, but Abby didn't want a whole
banana. Matt tried changing the banana idea for something worth
91 calories instead, but Abby wouldn't let him change his choice
once he'd made it. He was still figuring out the rules. They were
very complicated. But sometimes complex rules were the only ones
that made you feel really safe and in control. Matt understood
that.

Matt was reviewing his notes on Abby's dinners when a police
car pulled up out front. Matt was home alone, and as Nick Parker
got out of the car and adjusted his police officer belt loaded with
police officer gadgets, Matt didn't know what to do. Nick didn't
have a baseball or bat, so he wasn't there to teach Matt to hit a
baseball. He had to be there to see Lana, but she was teaching that
day.

Nick stopped halfway up the front walk and waved at Matt.

Matt sometimes forgot that people could see him in the window. Matt waved back but didn't move. Nick Parker came closer to the window, rested his hands on his hips.

"Can I come in?" he asked. Matt could hear him clearly, so he must've been talking pretty loud. Matt was worried the neighbors would come outside and wonder why a police officer was yelling through his front window, asking to come in. And the only way to stop him was to let him inside. Which Matt didn't want to do. Matt's stomach churned and his ears buzzed and his chest got that funny overfull feeling, but he got up and headed for the front door anyway. Nick wouldn't stay once he knew Lana wasn't home. He opened the door.

"She's teaching. I can't remember where. Not her usual elementary school, but somewhere else," Matt told him.

"Okay," Nick said. He leaned against the wall just outside the door and crossed his arms. He'd asked if he could come in, but now he wasn't coming in. "I actually wanted to see you."

"Oh," Matt said. He wished Lana were home after all. "I haven't been to see Spike. Not once. I promised."

Nick held up his hands and shook his head. "I'm sorry. That's what I came by to say. I'm sorry I got so angry and sorry that I yelled at you. I was upset, worried about you and Lana, but that's no excuse. I was wrong."

Matt nodded and smiled. It was his anxious smile and he hated that he was doing it, but there it was. Nick brought out that smile more than anyone.

"Wait one second," Nick said. "I have something for you." He walked back toward his police car and Matt had a panicky feeling, because there were all kinds of scary terrible things inside a police car and Matt didn't want to see any of them. But then Nick reached into the passenger side and pulled out Matt's favorite cobalt-blue fleece jacket. The only one he'd ever really liked. He came up the walk and Matt went outside even though he had no shoes on, because he was so happy to see his jacket again. "I don't suppose you want to know how I got this back?" Nick asked. Matt shook his head. What did he care how? He had his jacket back and that's all that mattered. It was the perfect color and the perfect softness and his whole day was better now.

"Thank you," Matt said. He hurried back inside with his cheek against the jacket and closed the door. He sat by the window and Nick stared at him from the lawn before waving goodbye and driving off.

When Lana came home Matt showed her the jacket.

"From Nick Parker. I thought I didn't like him because of the anger. I thought I only liked Mitch because he didn't make me talk to him. I wanted to vote for Mitch for your boyfriend, but now maybe Nick is okay, too. You can choose. I don't need a vote."

Lana laughed until she had tears in her eyes and then she didn't look happy anymore.

"Thanks for your approval. But I think maybe I need to be partner-free for a while. Love is too complicated for me."

"Love isn't complicated," Matt said. "If it is, then it isn't love."

Lana stared at him for a long time. Then she smiled. "You just sit there quietly observing and taking notes and we all think you're in your own world. But then you say something like that and I realize you're in our world, and you see it clearer than any of us."

Matt didn't understand what she meant but it didn't matter. He had his jacket back and it was nearly dinnertime, so he was about to get more Abby-data for his notebook. His Abby notes were his favorite part of the day. He put on his fleece jacket even though it was warm enough that he didn't need it, and went to his room to wait for dinner.

For dinner Abby usually ate corn and plain salad for a total of forty-five calories and only one gram of protein. Today Abby had agreed to add one ounce of whatever meat Lana served, which would almost double her calories for the meal. Matt had requested chicken, because it was Wednesday. That would be thirty-three more calories, and would increase Abby's daily protein intake by seven grams, to twenty-one grams total. She was very low on protein for a fourteen-year-old girl. She needed forty-five grams of protein each day, but she didn't like meat or cheese or nuts or anything that had fat in it. She also needed fat in her diet, but like the twelve hundred calories, talking about fat made her cry. So first Matt was focusing on the protein. After the banana day, he was going to suggest that she have milk with dinner for an additional eight grams of protein. Right now Abby only drank ice water.

Matt had made a schedule for the next month, outlining each meal and highlighting the one new thing for her diet each day. It was a nice schedule, written on a thick piece of orange construction paper, with straight freehand lines for the rows and columns and a small picture of each new food in each day's square. He was proud of the chart and wanted to hang it on his wall, but Abby had asked him not to, so he kept it on his desk under one of his kangaroo pictures.

Matt wanted to bring his notebook and green pen to the table, to watch Abby eat and record each bite the moment she swallowed, but Abby didn't like to see the notebook. She also didn't know how to measure an ounce of chicken without a scale, but Matt had an excellent sense of spatial relations and had already figured out what one ounce of chicken looked like when cut up into little Abby-sized bites. Abby was going to cut the meat into small bites and move the pieces toward the corn, one by one, until Matt nodded that she had a one-ounce portion piled there. This all made dinner so interesting that Matt thought that even if Byron was loud he'd stay at the table just to watch Abby's pile of chicken bites form and then disappear. He could do that even with his hands over his ears. So it was just as well that he wouldn't have the notebook there. He couldn't write anything down with his hands over his ears.

When she was not eating, not running, not playing soccer, not staring at the wall, and not doing homework, Abby wrote poetry. Matt had read some of the poems. Abby didn't rhyme or follow any specific meter. Matt preferred meter and rhyme, but they weren't his poems. She mostly wrote about her body. Not her whole body, but parts of her body, as if they weren't even hers. Matt had a couple of the poems tucked into the notebook, behind the daily calorie counts. He pulled one out, written in Abby's purple pen on a lined sheet of school paper with three holes punched in the margin.

Hip bones sculpted into bookends
Beginning and end to the same old story
Legs strong but pockmarked with failure
Dimpled with lard
Juts of collarbone whittled free
Shoulder blades transformed into flightless wings
A hidden fairy emerging from within
Born not from pixie dust but carved from bone
A new sprite carefully shaped yet still unformed
Her magic is invisibility
Her face is angular, striking, but
Still not beautiful enough to be noticed
The scale whispers to her in her sleep, makes promises
To tip the balance of power in her favor
If the fairy achieves weightlessness
Only then will she be able to fly

Matt didn't know much about fairies. He preferred real things to mythical ones. But if Abby liked fairies, that was fine. He didn't understand why she didn't use punctuation, though. As a freshman in high school she should know all of the punctuation rules. He was tempted to add some, to show her how, but it was her poem, so he left it alone. He tucked the poem inside the notebook and left it on his desk, hidden under the photo of the rabies-resistant kangaroo. It was a Tasmanian forester kangaroo, which was endangered.

Matt settled at the dinner table, arranging his plates and bowls as he visualized a one-ounce portion of chicken. He wanted to get it exactly right. Lana set the platters of food on the table and, like always, offered to serve Matt first.

"Abby first," he said. He was bristling with anticipation. "That piece, right there." He pointed at the smallest piece of chicken. Lana slid it onto Abby's plate and Abby smiled, not at Lana or Matt, but at the chicken itself. Then she began slicing it, very slowly, into tiny bites. She made her pile and Matt, watching her closely but distracted by his own heartbeat, nearly missed when the pile was the exact right size. He was supposed to nod subtly toward her when she was done measuring, but instead he smacked the surface of the table with the palm of his hand and made a half-cough, half-bark sound that he'd never heard himself make before. Byron and Lana jumped and looked at him strangely, but Abby understood and just laughed. Matt laughed, too. It was the best dinner he had enjoyed with the whole family in a long time.

Abby ate her chicken very slowly, chewing more times than necessary. Matt watched her throat, waiting for her to swallow. She took so long that he thought she might spit it out. She did that at the window a lot, but he had never seen her do it in front of Lana.

"Water helps wash down the chicken," he told her. She kept chewing, so Matt pointed to her water glass. Twice. Three times.

"Is it too dry?" Lana asked.

Abby shook her head. She took a sip of water, swallowed, and smiled. She didn't usually smile while eating. Matt wanted to write that down in the notebook, too. He waited, too agitated to eat, until her last bite was swallowed, washed down with more water, two full glasses of ice water in all to get the small pile of chicken out of her mouth and down into her stomach. She set the glass down and bit her lip, like she wasn't really happy with what she'd just done, but Matt was happy. He clapped his hands together, smacked the table again, and rushed toward his room, excited to add to his notes. His chair tipped over backward and made a horrible banging sound against the white linoleum as he hurried from the table. He heard Lana say something, but he didn't have time to listen or go back. The notebook was waiting.

A few days later, sitting at the window and looking at the maple tree full of hopeful blossoms and new spring leaves, Abby helped Matt count birds. There were more of them fluttering about the front yard these days, including a couple nesting in the tree. Well, Matt suspected there were more. It seemed like more. It was possible they were just busier, flapping around more than just two months ago. Matt didn't like guessing. He liked data. He wanted to prove that there were more. So now he was counting them all.

He tried to do it every day at exactly eight in the morning and five in the afternoon, when the birds seemed busiest and easiest to count. They were hard to count if they weren't flying around. If he kept counting for a whole year, then he'd know if there were really more in April or if it was just the same birds, happier and busier in spring weather.

Matt and Abby agreed that there were nine different birds right now. Not including the hawk Matt had seen earlier but which wasn't around now. Matt wasn't counting hawks, though. He just wanted to know how many birds were in the tree. Robins, jays, and finches. He wrote down the date and the time and the number nine, and set the notebook down.

"Eggs," Matt said. "Six grams of protein. Seventy calories in the large ones your mom buys. I think there must be more protein in the jumbo ones, but Lana never buys those. Of course, they'd have more calories, too." The birds had made him think of eggs. Another possible protein source for Abby. "Oh, sorry," he said. He wasn't supposed to talk about calories.

"I don't really like eggs," Abby told him. She wrinkled her nose and shook her head. She was eating a Triscuit with a small scoop of peanut butter on it. It was her one change for the day. Matt had suggested three crackers with peanut butter, but Abby was still upset about eating the chicken, so she would only add one cracker today. And it was a very small amount of peanut butter. The whole snack only added three grams of protein. Not nearly enough. Matt had to be careful about the next foods he added. Too much protein, like the chicken, and Abby said it made her stomach hurt. Too little, and he felt anxious that her daily total wasn't increasing fast enough.

"Beans," Matt said. "Black beans, kidney beans, garbanzo beans."

"Beans, beans, the musical fruit?" Abby asked.

Matt shook his head. He didn't understand what music had to do with it. "I like kidney beans. Garbanzo beans make good hummus, but I don't like them by themselves. They have this skin thing on them and they're too dry. Baked beans are good, but sometimes too sweet. Black beans are best. With sour cream. Don't you like beans?"

Abby giggled, leaning to the side and holding her ribs, as if beans were very funny. Matt didn't understand what was so funny about beans.

"Soybeans!" he shouted. Abby jumped and started laughing even harder. Matt nodded, pointing toward the window, down the street, across town, at the little Asian grocery store a mile away. "Yes. Edamame. You like vegetables. It's a vegetable. Surprisingly high in protein for a vegetable, but also low in fat. I know you don't like fat."

"Okay," Abby said, sitting up and sighing, which seemed to stop her laughter. "A vegetable with protein sounds good."

Matt pulled out the notebook and wrote down *edamame*. He used a pencil, just in case they changed their minds. He'd written *banana* in pen and then there was no changing it. But he was so excited that his writing was sloppy. He erased it and nearly tore the page in his haste to revise it. Abby, watching him closely, smiled as he swept the eraser dust away and blew the page clean. Matt wrote *edamame* again, carefully rounding out the letters, giving them a little calligraphy flair for good measure. The second time it came out better. Matt nodded at his work.

"An excellent addition," Matt said. He tipped the notebook toward Abby so she could see his fine writing, but then remembered that she didn't like to see the notebook, so he snapped it shut before she could see it. And then Abby was laughing again. He liked her laughter. It was like a sound a small animal would make. A small happy animal. Almost as happy as the birds outside.

He opened the notebook again, wrote down the date and time, followed by, *Abby laughs. Two times.*

23

Abby

It was every bit as bad as Abby had anticipated, and worse. After seeing Abby and Gabe together, Caitlin went on a full-blown rampage, intent on ruining what little social status Abby had. First came the rumors about her and Carter James, which were ridiculous. Carter was a junior-year jerk: a geek-turned-bully who couldn't seem to carry on a conversation without pissing someone off. He was an obnoxious know-it-all, quick to pick arguments and even more annoying for almost always being right. He made people feel small and stupid as cheap entertainment, and he was toxic to everyone linked to him. The rumor died as quickly as it began, though, because Carter wasn't shy about letting everyone know that he'd never consider dating a freshman, let alone sleeping with one. Which meant, as much as she disliked him, Abby owed him some small debt of gratitude.

The rumor that caught and burned longest was about Mr. Franks. It was a disgusting accusation, low even for Caitlin, but kids love gossip about teachers, and a sordid tale of a chem teacher hooking up with a student in the lab after hours seemed irresistible, and so it just kept going, spreading around the school like a wildfire that died down each night and flared up again each morning. Abby heard snickers in the hall behind her, noticed long looks at soccer practice, felt too many eyes on her in Mr. Franks's class, which did nothing to help her stay clearheaded in chemistry.

She'd also started avoiding Mr. Franks's daughter Celeste. After several text and email exchanges about Celeste's road back to normal eating, chock-full of suggestions for Abby like getting rid of the scale, finding an accountability partner for meeting her calorie-increase goals, cutting back the exercise to only thirty-minute sessions instead of hour-long ones, she felt like she'd betrayed Celeste somehow by getting her innocent father thrown under the bus of high school gossip. Celeste was funny and sympathetic and easy to chat with, but how do you tell a girl there's a rumor going around school that you slept with her father to save your grade? It was better just to lay low, but Abby missed checking in with Celeste each day she added something new to her diet and getting the nicest, most encouraging messages in response.

Gabe sat two rows in front of Abby in chem, and after the third round of giggles rose and fell in class, when Gabe turned to give Abby yet another apologetic smile, Mr. Franks caught it.

"Gabe, Abby, please stay after class," Mr. Franks said. He didn't look at them as he said it, he spoke to the blackboard, where he was listing the elements they needed to study for the next quiz. Which just made it worse. Made it seem like they were all so familiar there was no need for him to look at them. The whole class rippled with murmurs until Mr. Franks turned and glared at them all. Which, again, just made things worse.

"What's going on?" Mr. Franks asked after the class had emptied. He perched on the front corner of his desk like usual, but his arms were crossed tightly and his fists were white balls. Gabe and Abby exchanged glances, but neither said anything. Mr. Franks looked at his watch. "We can sit here for the next hour. I have an open period."

"It's just stupid kid stuff," Gabe said, checking the empty open doorway. Abby realized there must be kids out there eavesdropping, just out of sight, but well within earshot. Mr. Franks crossed the room in his angry stride and closed the door.

"Abby?" he said. She looked at her shoes, the cracked beige

leather of her flats, too worn out to hold on to much longer, too perfectly molded to her feet to ever give up.

"I don't know," she whispered.

"Is someone bothering you?" Mr. Franks asked. "Both of you?" So, he already knew, on some level. Abby supposed you couldn't be a high school teacher for long without learning to decipher all those teenage scoffs and giggles.

Abby was going to cry. The tears stung the backs of her eyelids, threatening to come full force. She had to get out of there. She needed to run, hard and fast, on the track, until there was nothing left of her body but air heaving into her lungs, burning her throat, her mind clear of all other thoughts, even if just for a moment.

All of this over a stupid crush on a boy who would clearly never choose her over bitchy, slutty Caitlin. Abby dug her nails into her palms, then inspected the small half-moon marks she left behind. The tears still loomed, so she did it again, harder. Mr. Franks held his hand out to her, very nearly touching her left wrist.

"Please, stop," he said in such a small, soft voice that her tears came freely. She turned her back to Gabe and Mr. Franks and let her humiliation swallow her whole. As if the rumors weren't bad enough, now everyone in school would be calling her a crybaby. And they'd be right.

"It's my fault," Gabe whispered.

"No, it isn't," Abby sobbed. "It's . . ." But she couldn't say it. She wasn't sure why. There was no need to protect Caitlin. The school had a zero-tolerance policy on bullying. But being a narc was a thousand times worse than being a bully. Social suicide. Abby cried into the crook of her arm like the pathetic loser that she was. She felt a hand on her shoulder and shook it off with a swing of her elbow. She turned to see Gabe reel back, holding his hands up to protect his face. It was all going wrong. She wasn't mad at him. Just hurt and scared and hating everything she felt.

Abby sniffled, wiped her eyes, and took a deep breath. "It's fine," she said. "I'm sorry we were interrupting class. It won't happen again."

Mr. Franks sighed and turned to Gabe with narrowed eyes.

"Gabe, I know whatever this is, you'd like it to stop as much as I would."

Gabe stared at Abby, looking sad and sorry, and it made the tears threaten again. Abby bit the inside of her cheek until she tasted the metallic tang of blood, and that did the trick. She shook her head at Gabe, so slightly that only her dangling earrings swayed. Gabe gave a tiny bob of his head.

"Yeah, we were just . . . goofing around. It won't happen again," he said.

Mr. Franks wasn't buying it, Abby could tell, but what choice did he have? He sighed angrily and pulled out two unevenly cut squares of blue photocopy paper. Hall passes, because now they were both late for their next classes. He signed them and handed them over.

"This isn't over," Mr. Franks said. "If you won't talk to me, talk to someone. Mrs. Geller or Mr. Walsh."

Abby shook her head. The last thing she needed was fake sympathy from a guidance counselor who hadn't been a high school student for fifty years, or a vice principal who thought joining more sports teams was the solution to every conflict.

"I'm fine. We're fine. We don't need to talk about it anymore," she whispered.

She took the hall pass and her book bag and rushed for the door, but Gabe was longer-legged and faster, and he made it to the door with her, opening it for her like a gentleman, which just made it all worse.

"Stop," Abby said, because if she said more she'd risk crying again. Gabe waited for her to pass through, then followed her out. She hurried to get away, to put some distance between them, but he caught up to her easily. He grabbed her upper arm and she yanked it free of his grasp, then blinked up at him in the bright midmorning sun.

"What?" she asked coldly.

"I'm sorry," Gabe said. "I don't know how to fix this." He looked around, as if to make sure it was safe. Luckily, the grounds around Mr. Franks' classroom were a ghost town. Everyone was already in class.

"Clearly we can't be seen together, like, ever. You just go back to doing whatever it is you do with Caitlin, and maybe she'll stop."

"This is low, even for her." Gabe shook his head. "I'm not sure she's capable of it."

Abby turned on him, anger forming a hard, cold place in her belly. "You don't think this is her? Are you crazy? Who else would care?"

Gabe shrugged. "Maybe there's some guy who has a thing for you. We don't know. These things take on a life of their own . . ."

"Nobody else cares about me in this school. Nobody. Caitlin's the only one who would have any reason to . . ." Abby gestured toward Mr. Franks. There were no words to sum up all that Caitlin had done.

"If you're so sure, then I'll . . . I'll talk to her," Gabe offered.

"Please don't. Anything you do for me will just make things worse. We need to steer clear of each other. If you say anything to her, just tell her that I don't mean anything to you and never did."

"But that's not true," Gabe said.

Abby thought of slapping him, the first time she'd ever felt the urge to hit another human being. She decided not to, because she wasn't the violent type. Then she struck him in the center of his chest with both palms before she could stop herself. She snapped her wrists back in the process. She knew it didn't hurt him, but she'd used enough force to knock him back a step. She rubbed her stinging wrists. Of course she was the only one who got hurt.

"Shut up!" she screamed, not caring who heard.

Gabe gave her a wounded look, rubbing his chest. She didn't know what he wanted from her. Or what she wanted from him anymore. She just wanted to disappear, same as always, only even more so now.

"What can I do?" he asked.

"Nothing, apparently," Abby said. "I'm just ruined, that's all. You and Caitlin can live happily ever after and I'll hide in the corners until high school is over. Thanks."

She turned and stalked off, equally disappointed and grateful when Gabe didn't try to follow her. She checked the hall pass. Mr.

Franks had signed his name, but hadn't written in the time he'd dismissed her. Which meant she could put in any time she wanted. She veered left and headed for the track. A twenty-minute run would help. And she'd only be missing algebra, which she could do in her sleep. She settled her book bag into the small of her back, braced it with her arm, and broke into a hard run, her flats slapping the pavement, echoing off the walls of the buildings around her.

The morning was cool, which made running easier. She changed in the bathroom so the gym teachers wouldn't see her. The PE class was playing indoor volleyball, so the track was empty. She ran until she was winded and weightless.

Abby made it through the rest of her day without seeing Gabe or Caitlin by carefully avoiding all of their usual hangouts. She lurked around the field at lunch, where Byron and his smoking buddies gathered. Byron wasn't with them today, which was what she'd hoped for as she crested the hill toward the field. But as she stared at the crowd of hacking, puffing dorks on the other end of the grassy patch, she kind of wished Byron had been there. Just seeing a familiar face in the crowd might have made her feel less anxious and alone. He would've given her plenty of space, but he would've nodded to her to let her know he saw her. To make her feel like she existed.

She texted Em to say she wasn't feeling well and might go lie down in the nurse's office. She didn't want her company. Em wouldn't understand any of this. Nothing like this could ever happen to her.

Abby skipped soccer practice. It was the first time she'd missed one, and she knew she wouldn't get into trouble for it. She needed the workout, but she couldn't bear to see Caitlin, or Em. She hated that skipping it sent a message to Caitlin. A message that she'd won. But she had won, hadn't she?

She called Matt and asked him to pick her up from school. He drove her home in his little red pickup truck in silence. She was glad that he didn't ask any questions. They settled in their seats by the window at home with their usual snacks. When Abby saw his little green notebook tucked under his right thigh, hidden from view out of respect for her, the waiting pen tucked into the metal coil of the notepad's spine, there was nothing she could do to stop the tears from coming again. She couldn't eat today. There was no way. And now she wasn't just letting herself down, she was letting Matt and Celeste down. Matt got up and left her to cry alone. When she was done, empty of tears but with a throbbing headache instead, Matt came back to the window. He set a box of tissues and a bottle of cold water before her, and took his seat beside her again.

"I put the notebook away," he said.

"Thanks," she said. She blew her nose, drank half the bottle in one long pass. "I'm sorry."

"I put it under the kangaroo picture," Matt said. As usual, there was no inflection to his voice, no emotion behind his words. He was as rock-solid as Abby was quicksand. "The birds are even busier today."

"Should we count them?" she asked.

"It's not five o'clock," he said. Matt and his rules. They were annoying and comforting at the same time. Abby nodded, but she counted the birds anyway, silently so Matt wouldn't know. She needed something else to fill her mind.

After counting the birds about ten times, Abby watched the neighbors arrive home from work, fetch their mail, roll beastly plastic trash bins out to the curb. The man across the street was trimming the green hedges that framed his thick lawn, carving the unruly bushes into a perfect right angles. Abby started to feel less alone. Less empty. Maybe, if she could just never go back to school again, if she could just live there in the sun, in the window beside Matt, counting birds and watching people and breathing, she could eat again.

"There!" Matt said, pointing down the street. One of his beloved Vizslas, sleek and elegant, trotted along next to a young woman jogging. "Now it'll be a good day," he said, snapping his fingers. He nodded, bobbing his blond head, looking from Abby's right shoulder to the window. She wanted to feel it, that same simple happiness, but she was a dark hole inside.

"Okay," she said, because he seemed to be waiting for her to say something.

"It's the same thing," he said. "That's you. You're the Vizsla. The Vizsla was the Vizsla, and then I met one and it was too excited and jumpy and it made me feel worse, not better, so then the Vizsla wasn't the Vizsla for me anymore. But then it was you. Sitting here and being calm and not jumping on me. You're the Vizsla."

He was pretty excited, his voice rising in pitch, higher than Abby had heard it before, and she wanted to understand, but he was off in Matt-land, where no one else could see how his random thoughts connected to each other.

"I'm a dog?" she asked.

"That's not a dog. That's a Vizsla. They're not slobbery or ugly and they don't shed thick long hair everywhere and they don't smell. They have too much energy but they're more beautiful than any other dog. The owner runs a different route most of the time, so I don't see him anymore. The Vizsla. Most of the time I don't see him anymore. And I missed him. Even though I don't want one anymore, not a real one, not a rattlesnake-tail jumping-out-of-their-skin one. But then it was okay, because even if I didn't see him anymore, I saw you. You're the Vizsla now."

Matt was pointing excitedly at the window with one finger, and when that didn't seem to be enough, he started gesturing with his whole hand, waving toward the street, smacking the pane of glass with the backs of his long thin fingers. The Vizsla was long gone, but Matt was still signaling wildly toward it.

"I'm the Vizsla?" Abby asked. Something inside her cracked. A tiny speck of light pierced the gloom. She felt like laughing, but Matt seemed so serious, so earnest, so passionate. All of which just made it more ridiculous. He was calling her a dog. And he meant it as a compliment, she was pretty sure.

"Yes," Matt said, leaning back in his seat. His hand was still extended, hovering between them. Without looking at her, he patted her shoulder with it, three quick taps, light as a bird's wing. It was the first time he'd ever touched her. "Yes, I love it, that Vizsla. But I don't need it anymore. You're the Vizsla now. I love you now."

The neighbor finished loading his hedge clippings into the big green trash bin and started sweeping the walkway in front of his house. The mailman came and made his rounds, nodding toward Abby and Matt as he passed. She sometimes forgot that the window worked two ways, and the outside world could see in just as well as she could see out. She raised her hand and waved, and both the mailman and the neighbor waved back.

"Okay," Abby said, smiling for the first time all day. "I'll be the Vizsla now."

24

Byron

One thing about Dale, he knew his way around a computer. It only took him a few minutes to hack into the high school's system. Byron was shocked when Dale said his major was computer science. That had given him the idea.

"So what exactly are we looking for in here?" Dale asked.

Byron shrugged. "Not sure exactly. But I'll know when I see it."

"What do you care about a bunch of high school kids anyway?" Dale asked, typing away, leaning in close to the computer, just like Matt did when he was on a mission. Byron could've asked Matt to do this, and he was sure Matt would've been better at it, faster, but Matt would've known it wasn't right. Dale didn't seem to care.

Byron shrugged. It'd cost him a promise to lay off flirting with Chelsea and admitting that parkour was an art form while free-running was just a sport, to get Dale's help. He wasn't about to add the truth about his age into the mix.

"So this girl in trouble is a friend of yours?" Dale asked, typing away, screens sliding by as he delved deeper and deeper into the system.

"My kid sister," Byron said.

"Oh," Dale said, blockhead bobbing on his thick neck. "Okay, then I get it."

That seemed unlikely, but Byron knew better than to say so. Byron's phone buzzed in his back pocket and he slid it out to see a new message from Betsy.

Hey there :)

She was writing to him regularly now. Byron smiled and tried to think of a clever response, then caught Dale watching him, eyes squinted like he was playing Dirty Harry. Byron tipped his phone so that Dale could see the screen, see that it wasn't Chelsea.

"Your girl?" Dale asked, still squinting at the phone. Maybe he needed glasses.

"Yeah. Her name's Betsy."

"Cool," Dale said, and turned back to the computer. "Just about done here."

Unable to come up with a charming, witty response for Betsy, Byron fell back on the only other thing he had to offer: flattery.

Where are you? Been too long since I've seen your pretty face.

Betsy sent back a photo, poolside, in a swimsuit with a big smile, her cleavage taking up half the picture. Byron was so mesmerized that he missed whatever Dale was saying. She was at home. Byron was spending the night at his dad's. He wondered if he had time to head over to see her first. But then there would be Trent to deal with, too. Byron hadn't counted on how hard it'd be to have a friend and a girlfriend in the same family.

"Dude?" Dale poked Byron in the ribs.

"Yeah?" Byron said.

Dale pointed at the computer screen, his index finger and thumb held trigger-style, and took a shot at the screen, complete with childish gunshot noise. He'd found his way into the student roster, as Byron had requested. Byron held up the note Gabe had given him.

"Scroll down to Edwards. Caitlin Edwards."

It took Byron seconds to find exactly what he needed. He compared Gabe's note to the school's information. The answer was so simple and obvious that he laughed out loud and smacked Dale on the back.

"Awesome. I owe you one."

"Nah, we're cool," Dale said, which meant the parkour brown-nosing and Chelsea promise were enough.

Byron caught the bus home. His driving test was all scheduled, just two weeks away, but he'd come to like the long bus rides. The bus was full of interesting people to sketch, not to mention the landscape that slid by: parklike campus, bustling streets lined with businesses, suburban sprawl. Byron usually passed the time filling the notebook Magda had given him, one of her book art test projects that she hated but Byron loved. He felt so artistic with it tucked under his arm, Magda's thick creamy cover decorated with pine needles and clover.

The bus ride also gave him time to think more about the Caitlin situation, about the fact that some bitch at school had targeted Abby, who had to be the nicest girl there. Byron was sometimes annoyed at how perfect Abby was, but now he felt oddly protective of her, even her prissy side. She shouldn't have to give that up for anyone, especially not a wannabe like Caitlin. Byron had heard the Carter James and Mr. Franks rumors floating around school, and a few lowlifes had even come up to him to ask if they were true. He'd never thrown a punch before, but they had him mad enough to start.

He couldn't figure out how to ask Abby about it, but he started keeping an eye on her at school, giving people the evil eye who dared to look at her funny. Or dared to look at her at all. Parkour had made him stronger, and he wasn't afraid to take people on anymore. Oddly, being willing to throw a punch meant never having to do it. He'd never known that until now. Hallways rippled with chatter when Abby rounded a corner, then fell silent when Byron came around behind her. But it wasn't enough.

Gabe had noticed him shadowing Abby and filled him in, said Caitlin had confessed to starting the rumors, thought the whole thing was funny as hell. Gabe said he was equally guilty of causing trouble for Abby, just by liking her. He'd asked for forgiveness and everything, as if he were to blame for liking the wrong kind of girl before finding the right kind of one. He was a good guy. But that Caitlin. It was totally uncool. More than that. It was bullshit. By the time Byron made it home, he was good and pissed off about the whole thing all over again.

He headed upstairs and there was Abby, just lying on her bed and staring at nothing. She did that more and more lately. When Byron looked at her, he felt fury like he never knew he could feel. Watching her stare into space, so far gone that he didn't know how to bring her back. He crossed the hall into his own room, seething. He wanted to hurt Caitlin for hurting his sister. He wanted her to feel as miserable as Abby did. Worse, even.

He got another text from Betsy:

No comment on the pic?

Damn, in his anger he'd totally forgotten to respond. *Speechless*, he wrote.

And he was. In so many ways. How could his love life finally be taking off, lifting him higher with every text she sent, while his home life was sinking fast? Why couldn't good come with more good?

He headed for Trent's house and found him over a blue mixing bowl, eating a concoction of salsa mixed with guacamole with almost a full bag of Doritos mashed up into it. It was a sorry sight. Not that Byron hadn't done this with him before, but standing there watching him, Byron realized what idiots they looked like. Children. Betsy wasn't in sight, and he didn't want to ask where she was. He sat with Trent and watched him eat.

"Pot roast in the fridge," Trent said around a mouthful. "Pretty good."

Byron helped himself. While he was warming it up he eyed the tower of dirty dishes in the sink. The dishwasher was empty, so he started loading them into it. He'd just shoved a huge piece of pot roast into his mouth, resumed his task of rinsing soiled plates and stacking them neatly on the lower level, the way his mother insisted they do it, when Betsy leaned her hip against the counter on the other side of the dishwasher.

"Look at you go. You're such a stud," she said, laughing.

He smiled and stared at her swimsuit-clad body. Her breasts were a thin, sheer piece of fabric away. Their shape easy to make out. Her nipples little ridges rising in the chilly room. It was unbearable. He picked up speed on the dishes. With his mouth completely stuffed, he couldn't talk. Not that he knew what to say to her.

"You didn't send me a picture back," she said. Trent made a choking sound, first faking it, then maybe the real deal, before slamming his Coke and carrying his bowl of fiesta surprise upstairs. Byron and Betsy watched him go, then turned back to each other.

"Alone at last," Betsy said. She stepped around the open dishwasher and pressed up against Byron, her head back for a kiss. He leaned down and their lips met. He went in for a tender kiss, but Betsy pushed into him forcefully, parting his lips with her tongue. Byron's entire body buzzed with adrenaline and want. Betsy took his hand, still wet from the dishes, and placed it on the fabric covering her breast. Byron's heart raced so fast he wondered if he might be having a heart attack. Had anyone ever died from the excitement of finally getting to touch the girl of his dreams? Betsy leaned into him, the full length of her body against his. He tried to turn sideways, twist away, worried she'd feel his erection against her hip, but she leaned in again, harder, as if that were the whole point. Byron was dizzy, breathless, kissing her and spinning out in space, and he realized his hand was still lying limply on her breast. He wasn't sure what to do with it, so he removed it, regretting it the moment he did.

Then Trent hollered something incoherent downstairs and Byron felt equally annoyed and relieved for the interruption. Betsy pulled away, flushed and quiet. Byron felt like apologizing, but he wasn't sure what for. He felt like he'd done something wrong. Trent came stomping downstairs and got his phone. He stepped just outside the sliding glass door and made a call. Byron wondered who the secret caller was, again.

Betsy sidled up next to Byron and loaded the last of the dishes. She stood close enough for him to feel the heat of her body, but she didn't touch him.

"You're a good guy," she said, drying her hands. She sounded almost sad about it, like it was a bad thing. Byron shrugged, tried to come up with some cool response, but he had nothing.

"I am," he said. Because, while he hadn't been sure before, now with Abby's well-being on his mind full-time, he was pretty sure he was.

"I don't usually attract the nice ones," Betsy said. She looked away, as if embarrassed by her comment. Byron felt a surge of warmth, from his groin to his chest. He loved her so much he couldn't breathe. She was funny and sassy and smart and sexy, but she was also soft and sweet. She was everything he'd ever wanted in a girl.

"Well, this time you did," he said. She turned and smiled at him, a different smile than he'd seen before, not a flirty or brazen one, but a quiet one, a private one, just for him. He kissed her, a slow gentle kiss that built quickly right back to where they'd been before. He was about to try touching her breast again when Trent interrupted. Again.

"I'm coming in for another Coke!" he yelled from the backyard. "Please do not be making out when I do!"

They separated and stared at each other.

"Oh, god," Trent said, coming inside. "That's even worse." He shielded his eyes as he fetched his soda. Halfway out of the room he stopped. "Byron, we're still friends, right?"

"Of course," Byron said.

"So can we actually hang out before you go to your dad's?"

Betsy opened her mouth as if to make a comment, then stopped, smiled at Byron, and shoved him in Trent's general direction. She took off shortly after that, back to campus and Magda and the world Byron envied on so many levels, while Byron watched Trent play video games and stewed in resentment.

He headed home a little later, glad to be out of there. But it didn't get any better when his dad showed up. Graham had been

MIA for weeks, as he always was during tax season, but did he bother to ask them how they'd been doing? He drove and talked nonstop about boring CPA work stuff: tax extensions and how much money he'd saved his clients and how godlike he was to them. Abby was curled into a ball in the backseat, chewing on the sleeve of a sweatshirt that was way too big for her, so Byron had to suffer alone through listening and acting like he cared.

"I was thinking Mexican for dinner," Graham said. He alternated between burgers, Italian, and Mexican for every dinner together. They parked and headed into the restaurant, and Byron knew immediately that something was up. Graham acted strangely self-conscious, touching his hair, tucking in his shirt a little tighter. They headed toward a table for four, where a redheaded woman was already seated. She stood up and smiled at Graham before clumsily hugging him.

"Kids, this is Ivy," Graham said.

Ivy smiled and waved shyly. Byron and Abby looked at each other and said nothing. It was a setup. How ridiculous. They'd hardly seen Graham for the last month and now they had to share their time with him with Ivy.

Abby turned her chair to see the Spanish-channel soccer match on the TV over the bar. She ignored Graham, Ivy, and her plate of food. Byron ate his dinner and Abby's, plus the entire bowl of chips, while Graham and Ivy chatted about work stuff. Ivy clearly wasn't an accountant but she acted fascinated by Graham's tales of superstar tax services.

"Do you want to hear about us at all?" Byron asked when he couldn't take it anymore.

"By all means," Graham said, smiling, but his eyes were tight. He was annoyed at Byron's tone, but hiding it for Ivy's benefit. "I've told Ivy what a star athlete you are."

"I participate in sports, sure, but I'm really an artist," Byron said.

Ivy actually perked up at that. "No kidding? I was a theater major. I used to volunteer for set-design duty every time. I just loved it. Especially the painting."

"Theater major?" Graham said, smiling adoringly at her. "I had no idea. So you were an actress?" He took her hand and Byron hated her for taking his dad's attention.

"Oh, god, no!" She laughed. "I was a playwright."

"Fascinating!" Graham said. "Can I read one sometime?"

"Can we go home?" Byron said. "I don't think Abby's feeling well. Not that you noticed." Abby snapped her head and glared at Byron. "What? You'd rather endure more of this crap, or be back home where you can stare at the walls in peace?"

"Nobody's staring at any walls, or heading home," Graham said. His voice was very soft, the anger nearly hidden beneath it, but Byron could feel it there, and it stirred rage in him. Graham wasn't a father. Just some guy who clocked his time with Byron and Abby like they were a second job. "We're having a nice dinner with my friend Ivy."

"You're having a nice dinner with Ivy. Abby and I are just sitting here," Byron said. "We haven't seen you in weeks. Has it been weeks since Ivy's seen you? Or do you always have time for her?" Byron didn't know why he was making such a big deal out of not seeing his dad more. It wasn't like he even missed him.

"Byron, I'm here now. Let's not make an issue of it, shall we?"

"No," Byron said. "Let's make an issue of it. I want to quit swim team and track and focus on parkour and art. And if you'd seen me more than a half hour at a time in the last month, you'd know that. And if you cared what makes me happy you'd want to see my art. And if you had any sense of talent at all you'd realize I'm good. Better at art than I am at sports." Byron wasn't sure if it was true, but he wanted it to be.

"Don't be ridiculous," Graham said. "You're just testing me, and I get it. Tax season occupies a lot of my time. It's almost over. And I know the separation has been hard on you kids . . ."

"It's not hard on us. We have Mom. We have the best parent. Ivy can have you." Byron got up and walked out, furious to the brink of tears. He sat on the curb out front, breathing hard and wanting to hit something. But there was nothing he could do about any of it. His dad was an ass who no longer wanted the job of being a husband, a father, a decent guy. Byron called Lana and asked her to pick him up. She made it there in record time, stepped out of the car looking panicked. She calmed when she saw Byron, placed her hand on her chest and sighed, then sat next to him.

"Bad?" she asked. Byron nodded. "I'm sorry," she said.

"It's not your fault."

"I know. But I still feel bad. Like maybe if I'd done something different or been better somehow. Maybe my expectations were too high or I was too passive-aggressive . . ."

"You're not the problem," Byron said. "He doesn't even see me, you know? Or Abby. I can't imagine how you put up with him as long as you did."

"Byron, he loves you. In his own way. He really does."

"His way sucks."

Byron felt a presence behind him and braced for another round with Graham, but when he turned around it was Abby standing there. She sat on the curb next to Lana and they just watched traffic for a while. Until the boom of Graham's voice interrupted them.

"Of course," Graham said behind them.

Lana sighed and stood, waved Graham over to the side of the restaurant, as if putting a few feet between them and the kids would keep Abby and Byron from hearing every word.

"Don't," Graham said, and Lana laughed. Not a happy laugh, but a bitter one. "You're the one putting these ideas in his head, right? About the art? Quitting track and swimming? We talked about this. How else can we afford college for him?"

Byron clenched his fists and Abby touched his shoulder. He nodded and relaxed his hands. He was okay. His mom was on his side. Abby was on his side. He had Betsy.

"It wasn't my idea," Lana said. "It's who he is. You need to see him and love him for who he is."

"He's a child," Graham said. "He doesn't know who he is. It's our job to point him in the right direction."

"Because we turned out so goddamn happy? He should follow in our footsteps?"

Ivy stepped out of the restaurant's glass front door, took one look at the action unfolding, and ducked back inside. Abby snorted.

"You always do this, Lana. You can't baby everyone."

"And you can't bully everyone, Graham!" Lana's voice was shrill with emotion. "Stop trying to control everyone. Let go. Focus on yourself more than everything around you. Figure out what makes you happy and leave the rest of us out of it." Byron had never heard her yell at his dad before. Not like this. It made him uncomfortable, but he was also proud of her.

"I left so we wouldn't have to have this fight anymore," Graham said. "You don't need to fix me. I'm fine. I know my responsibilities and I meet them."

"And yet you're still miserable. You stress yourself out and everyone around you suffers for it. I get that you left so you wouldn't have to deal with me anymore, except guess what? We're raising two kids together, so we have to deal with each other. We had this broken dynamic in our marriage, and now that we're separated, we still have that same broken dynamic. Nothing's changed! You still blame me for everything that doesn't go your way. I'm not apologizing to you anymore. I let you be in charge of everything because I loved you and I wanted you to love me. But you still left. I don't need your approval anymore. I don't need you to like me now. I'm taking my children home with me. And if you ever try to break their spirits again, you will never see them again. You don't deserve me. And you don't deserve them."

Abby and Byron followed Lana to her car and Graham stormed back inside the restaurant. Lana started the car but couldn't seem to remember how to drive it. She tried to pull out of the parking spot but the car wouldn't budge because her parking brake was still on. Her hands were shaking.

"Can I drive?" Byron asked.

"Oh, yes, please," Lana said, getting out. While they were switching drivers, Graham and Ivy came out of the restaurant. Ivy and Lana stopped about ten feet apart. They did this old-time Western movie stare-down and Byron waited for the duel to start. Lana just sighed.

"I wish you the best of luck," Lana said to Ivy. "You'll need it."

Byron drove home with Lana and Abby in the backseat, like a

chauffeur. When he looked in the rearview mirror at them, Abby was lying down with her head in Lana's lap and Lana was stroking Abby's hair. It was a tender scene, perfect for a painting. Byron felt the overwhelming urge to capture the moment on canvas as soon as he got home.

25

Lana

Nick was not easily deterred. He either called or stopped by almost every day. Which on the one hand Lana liked. She'd always liked being pursued, wanted. But on the other hand it reminded her of the early days with Graham. Graham had wanted to win her like a prize, cherish her like a valued possession, and had ended up owning her for nearly two decades, holding on to her long after the sense of pride in catching her had worn off. She wanted a different kind of love next time around.

Mitch still brought her breakfast and coffee at school, still asked if she wanted to get a drink after yoga sometimes. And still flirted with every hardbody girl in class. He was a butterfly, flitting from flower to flower. Lana appreciated his attention—warily.

Which left Abbot. Handsome, easygoing Abbot. A man with grown children, though. Free of the daily responsibilities Lana still structured her life around.

She filled Camilla in on their next walk: the Graham fight, the sting of seeing his girlfriend in the flesh, the wonderful confusion of having three new suitors after nearly a year of being single. And then, when she'd run out of means to avoid the biggest issue, she told Camilla about her bad cervical cells and their pending removal.

Camilla broke her relentless stride to give Lana a hard hug, tight enough to squeeze a gust of air from her lungs.

"That's not sympathy, because you're fine," Camilla said, releasing her and continuing walking. "That's sisterly solidarity. I've been there. Terrifying post-mammogram biopsy of suspicious calcifications. It was frightening as hell. But it all turned out fine. And you'll be fine, too. Got it?"

"Got it," Lana said.

She walked hard, feeling the unease slough off as she strode. For most of her life she'd thought being strong meant taking on life's hard issues with somber determination, internalizing fear and stress with a smile on her face. But sharing her anxieties was liberating. She was forty-four years old, and just learning this.

"Thank you for these walks," Lana said.

"Oh, don't go getting all sentimental on me," Camilla said. "So what about this Abbot fellow? Seems to me he's the only one you aren't apprehensive about."

"I don't know. It doesn't seem like I'm in a good place to start something new."

"Funny," Camilla said. "It seems to me that's exactly where you are. Why not throw in some good new stuff to offset all of this not-so-great new stuff?"

Lana chewed on that thought for an hour. Then called Abbot and rescheduled their coffee date. Because of the three men who had recently entered her life, he was the only one who had not once made her doubt herself. And because of this comfort with him, she was only mildly surprised to find herself telling Abbot about her upcoming LEEP procedure over coffee. He had just filled her in on the full scope of his years of back problems, his surgery, his ongoing recovery. She knew he would understand.

"Oh, Lana," Abbot said, coffee cup between his hands. "That's the pits."

"Yes," she said, laughing. "That's exactly what it is."

"Well, as someone recovering from his own health ordeal, I have two words of unsolicited advice," he told her, raising his eyebrows and widening his hazel eyes.

"Bring it on."

"One, stock up on chocolate. That helps everything. Two, let's get out of here. Drive across the border and shop for kitschy nonsense and colorful, scratchy Mexican blankets that we'll never use."

Lana laughed and tried to think of a reason to refuse. She hadn't been called in to work, Emily's mother was picking up Abby after soccer, and Matt was picking up Byron for another driving lesson after school. She had a free day, and an invitation from a kind, handsome man to spend the day enjoying herself.

"I'm in," she said before she could overthink it.

"Great," he said. "Are you wearing good walking shoes?" He leaned around the table to check Lana's feet, and the gesture soothed and warmed her, the simple act of feeling cared for. She held up her tennis-shoed foot and smiled.

Tijuana was a battle against a tide of humanity: vendors, shoppers, college students getting drunk before noon, small kids yanking on her shirt as they waved candy for sale, men in serapes and sombreros calling tourists over for photos with their well-dressed burros. It was brimming with music, food smells, animal scents, exhaust fumes, and every color imaginable embroidered on bags, blankets, dresses, ponchos. Lana and Abbot browsed the open markets, ate small soft tacos, drank Cokes in glass bottles, and laughed in the chaos and sun. Abbot insisted on buying Lana a silver bangle bracelet inlaid with turquoise. It was beautiful, but it seemed too much for a first date.

"I remember the plight of the freshly single parent," he said. "Survival mode, right? Reward yourself, just this once. Please."

Lana nodded and Abbot slid the bracelet onto her arm, then took her hand. They strolled along the street, through the crush of people and noise, but were no longer part of that world. Lana floated in a dream as Abbot's thumb stroked the back of her hand. He bought her a box of Mexican chocolate, fed her a piece, and kissed her cheek. For a couple of hours the assault to every one of Lana's senses left her unable to think about anything other than the here and now. The vibrant colors, the warm day, the taste of cinnamon in the chocolate, and Abbot's warm hand in hers. It was a perfect escape.

Abbot offered to come with her to Dr. Tucker's office for the LEEP procedure. Camilla had planned to join her, but a conflict had come up. Accepting Abbot's offer would alleviate Camilla's guilt at having to cancel. But Abbot was a strange choice for company. A man, for one, joining her for a trip to her gynecologist. A man she only knew from yoga and coffee and one Mexico outing.

Abbot shrugged and said, "Sometimes people just want to feel useful. How can you deny a man that?"

Lana definitely understood that feeling. Finding ways to be useful was her security as well. Lana accepted his offer. She was going to need a distraction in the waiting room.

Abbot was on partial disability, recovering from his back surgery, slowly easing back into a full-time workday. He was anxious to get back to his normal routine, but reluctant to give up his extra hours off.

"Is yoga part of your physical therapy?" Lana asked as they settled into Dr. Tucker's crowded waiting room.

"No, it's my mental therapy. Physical therapy is when sweet little Marianne, who is all of ninety pounds but a lot stronger than she looks, bends me until I'm crying in pain, then tells me how good it is for me."

Abbot was a sales manager for an advertising firm, buying and selling time slots for clients. It was an interesting thought: buying time. Lana tried not to think of her worst-case scenario, and what it would mean: limited time with her children, Matt, herself. Not enough time for more walks with Camilla. Not enough time for Becca's spiritual advice. Not enough time to win her father over again. Not enough time to get to know Abbot.

"I know it's an impossible suggestion, but really, you need to stop worrying so much," Abbot said. Lana laughed. Abbot held his hand out and Lana placed hers into his broad palm. "Because here's the thing. You're going to go in there and have this taken care of. And then life is going to keep right on going. Today. Tomorrow. Weeks. Months. Years. We have time. None of us know how much, but we know we have today. Let's use it wisely. Let's make travel plans and eat good food and walk on the beach and listen to live music and laugh hysterically at absolutely nothing."

He squeezed Lana's hand and she smiled at his gentle eyes. Where had he come from? Abbot had been divorced for four years. His ex-wife was engaged. His children were grown. He was at a point in his life when he could focus primarily on himself. He was learning the truths that Lana had been putting off. But why? She'd figured once her children were grown, once Matt was safe, once everyone else was accounted for, she'd make time for herself. But here was her body sending her a different message, one of urgency, one of warning. Time was limited. The time was now.

"You're a wise man," she said.

"I'm a broken man. I have pins in my back to fix what I ignored for too long, so busy working and managing my stress that I forgot to live. It cost me my marriage and my health. That was my wake-up call. Maybe this is yours."

Lana wasn't a big believer in fate, but having Abbot next to her, holding her hand and telling her exactly what she needed to hear, that felt a lot like destiny.

"I haven't told my kids or my brother about this," she confessed. She felt like a fraud, keeping it from them. But she also felt the need to protect them from this big, scary thing.

"Will you?" he asked. His tone was free of judgment.

"If I have to, yes. But . . ." The tears built, as she knew they would, and she cleared her throat to force them back inside her body. "I had a brother who died of cancer. He was young and strong and smart and beautiful. He got sick and then it was like we all had cancer, as a family. It grew in him and it grew in us, until that's all we were. Just doctor's appointments and worrying about him and trying to stay out of my parents' way, because they only had time and energy for him. Years lost, on hold, waiting and watching Stephen instead of living each day like it mattered, like it was a gift. I missed so much of my childhood because he was sick, and he left us anyway. The hole was even bigger when he died, because he'd become the focus of our whole existence. Without him we had nothing to unite us anymore. My parents never recovered. Matt needed help and they had nothing left for him. I won't do that. I won't let cancer define my kids' childhood the way it consumed mine. I won't let it take what Matt needs from him again."

Abbot stroked her cheek with his knuckle, trailed his fingers down to her chin, turned her face toward him. She worried she'd start crying if she looked at him, so she closed her eyes. She felt his lips on hers. He kissed her very gently, and for that moment Lana forgot every worry she had.

"Lana Foster?" a voice said. Lana startled at the sound of her own name. A purple-smocked nurse, holding a chart against her hip, smiled at her. Lana rose on nervous legs and turned toward Abbot.

He stood and hugged her. "You've got this. You'll be fine," he said.

"You really don't have to wait," she said, trying to sound strong.

"I'm not leaving you," he told her.

The procedure, as Dr. Tucker had promised, wasn't painful, but it was uncomfortable and terrifying in a nonspecific way. It began much like a pap smear, with Lana on her back, feet in stirrups, vulnerable and exposed and desperate for it to be over. After the pinch and burn of the anesthesia, Lana felt a strange flush come over her body. Her breathing picked up. Nothing had even happened yet, but she was on the verge of a panic attack. She didn't want to give in to it, didn't want to admit to Dr. Tucker that she was losing it. Lana focused on her breathing, using the same peaceful visuals they taught in yoga to abate the panicky feeling in her belly, each thought a mere cloud against the backdrop of a perfect blue sky. She exhaled slowly, created a little breeze to blow the clouds away, and it actually helped. After a few minutes Dr. Tucker put away her tools with a definitive cold clang of metal and helped Lana sit up.

"That's it. Great job. We're all done. I want you to take it easy for a few days. I'll call tonight to check on you. Is there someone here with you?"

"Yes," Lana said, and there was such comfort in the simple word, in the fact that she was not alone.

Dr. Tucker hugged her, a brief embrace, more moving for its unexpectedness, and left her to get dressed and wonder, *Now what?*

Lana passed the reception desk and saw Abbot through the glass doors, leaning against the concrete wall just outside, doing something on his phone. Lana got to watch him undetected for a moment. He was a genuine man. That's how she'd describe him. No gimmicks, no posturing, no aggression, nothing to prove. And he liked himself. So different from Graham and his need to shine, from Nick and his need to enforce rules, from Mitch and his mixed signals.

Lana stepped out to meet Abbot, and his face broke into such a broad smile that it gave her butterflies.

"There she is," he said softly. He put his arm around her waist, as if she needed help walking, and although she didn't need any help whatsoever, and doubted it was good for his healing back to walk hip-to-hip with her, she let him take some of the weight off her and guide her toward his car. He helped her inside, and she noticed a bag of groceries in the backseat. He smiled and nodded toward it. "Lunch. If you're up for it. You rest, I'll cook."

Lana was exhausted, but it was mostly emotional fatigue. Resting sounded perfect. Having someone cook for her sounded equally tantalizing. She nodded.

"Your place or mine?" Abbot asked.

Her place had no children until at least four p.m., but it had Matt, bills, reminders of Graham. "Yours," she said. She wanted newness, change, a glimpse into Abbot's life.

His condo was clean and calm: tan carpet, sage walls, a hunter-green couch and upright piano. The furniture was mostly dark wood: earthy, solid, and comforting. He opened his balcony doors to reveal a view of Sycamore Canyon and the mountains of Cuyamaca in the distance. He directed Lana to the couch and carried the bag of groceries into the kitchen. She woke up just as lunch was being served.

"I was trying to be quiet. I didn't want to wake you," he said.

"No, food is good. I was too nervous to eat this morning. And too anxious to sleep last night."

He'd made salmon, brown rice with mushrooms, fruit salad, grilled asparagus. Lana realized how hungry she was the moment she sat down.

"This is wonderful," she said. "I haven't had a man cook for me in . . ." She took a bite, thought it over. "Okay, maybe ever."

Abbot laughed, his hazel eyes twinkling. "Well, get used to it. I made a couple extra salmon fillets, a salad, and got you some French bread. I'm sending it all home with you so you don't have to cook tonight."

"You're too good to me," Lana teased.

"I haven't even started," Abbot said. He leaned forward and whispered, "There may also be fresh-baked cookies."

After lunch he drove her home. They parked in the driveway and kissed in the car like teenagers. Lana was excited, exhausted, cramping, exhilarated. It was overwhelming. But Camilla was right. The best means to combat all of the lousy new stuff in her life was with something absolutely wonderful, something just for her.

After the Graham fight outside the restaurant, she'd been enjoying a newfound solidarity with Byron and Abby. Byron teased her, called her "warrior-mama," pretended to be afraid of making her angry now that he'd seen her confrontational side, but she could see how much he'd needed it, that feeling of her having his back.

Abby was back to eating sandwiches in her room rather than dinner with the family, but she wasn't avoiding Lana during non-meal times. She was like a young child again, sneaking her way onto Lana's lap on a sunny afternoon, cuddling and snoozing against Lana without a word. It was in this position that Lana realized just how skinny Abby had gotten. She was all bones and sharp angles, not a scrap of fat on her. Even her muscles seemed smaller. Lana patted Abby's frail body, felt every surface, searching for flesh, finding almost none.

"Baby?" she asked, barely a whisper. "When did this happen?" She slid her hand down the slope of Abby's arm, felt the knobbiness of her elbow, the lack of meat above or below it. Abby sniffled, then gave in to tears, and Lana held her, and waited.

"I don't know, Mama," Abby whispered. She only called Lana "mama" when she was hurting or scared.

"Oh, my sweet girl," Lana said. "Tell me what to do. How to help." Lana cried with her, silent tears that slid off her chin and onto Abby's flaxen hair. She'd been so wrapped up in cancer fears, struggling to pay bills, fielding interested men, trying to avoid feeling anything toward Graham, that she'd failed at the one job she cherished most. But if she could be Byron's warrior-mama, she could be Abby's, too. She hugged Abby, the notches of Abby's spine carving into Lana's arms like knives. She'd known Abby wasn't eating much. How had she missed just how far it'd gone?

"I don't know," Abby said. "I don't know what happened. How to get back."

"We'll get you some help. We'll do it together, okay?"

"Okay," Abby said. She nuzzled closer. The day outside was warm, the heat pushing itself inside the house. Soon Lana would have to switch the air conditioner back on. But Abby's body was ice-cold.

"I never told you about Grandma Gloria," Lana said. "Maybe I should have. I'd kind of forgotten about it until recently. Or I just didn't want to remember. She was bulimic." Lana let the word settle in between them. "And when she wasn't bingeing she was dieting. Living on these appetite suppressants and practically nothing else. It was like an obsession for her. After Stephen died it was even worse. The more depressed she got, the more control she needed, over something, anything. And that was it. It didn't make her happy, it didn't make her healthy, it just masked the real problem, the sadness she wasn't dealing with."

Abby sniffled and wiped her eyes, nodding.

"I don't know what all is hurting you now, love. But I'm here. If it's me or something I've done, or the separation, or anything. I'm here for you. No matter what. You can trust me."

"I know," Abby whispered. But of course that couldn't be true, or she wouldn't have kept this secret.

"Do you know what you weigh?" Lana asked.

Abby cried and shook her head. "I have a friend. Celeste. She's a recovering . . ." Abby sighed, cleared her throat. "She says it's better not to see what you weigh. You weigh yourself backwards. Have someone else look at the number, but not you. I thought about Matt, but . . . maybe you would be better."

"Okay," Lana said. "We don't have to do it now. When you're ready. And we need to see your doctor. Maybe she can recommend someone to talk to."

"You mean a shrink?"

"I do. It can be a family therapist, and we can all go together. Or you can go alone. Or some combination. Whatever feels most comfortable. But we need to do something. The outside things that have been controlling us, today's the day we stop them. Today we stop being afraid. Start getting ready for all the good to come. Both of us."

"You sound like Aunt Becca," Abby said. Lana laughed. She never thought she wanted to sound like Becca, with her metaphysical spirit-guided proclamations, but maybe Becca was on to something.

"I just had a scare myself," Lana said. She tried to stop herself, because why burden her children with this uncertainty, this threat? But like Camilla and her breast-cancer-scare solidarity, Abby deserved to get something in exchange for her trust. "I had a routine cancer screen, and something abnormal came up." Abby gasped and sat up. She looked at Lana with alarm. Lana cupped her face. "I'm fine. I had a procedure done to cut out all of the bad cells. We'll keep an eye on it to make sure no new ones crop up. But here's my point. It's been a hard year for all of us. We're buried in change, and most of it the kind we'd rather do without. It won't be easy, but I say from today forward, you and I make a pact to help each other focus on the good stuff instead of the bad."

"What if there's no good stuff?" Abby asked.

"Then we make some. We do something we love, every single day. Something just for us. It doesn't have to be big, but it has to bring us joy."

"I think maybe I want to change schools," Abby said.

"Why?" Lana asked.

Abby shook her head. She sighed and tucked her hair behind her ears. "Because I hate my life."

"Being a teenager is hell," Lana said. "I remember it well."

"Is this the part where you tell me it will pass and get better?"

Indeed, Lana had been about to give that very speech. Because it had passed. It had gotten better. She smiled and shook her head. "No. This is when I tell you we're not running. We're fighting. We're kicking this thing's ass. Whatever it is."

"Whoever, you mean," Abby said.

Lana felt the warrior-mama rise to full height within her. "Who's hurting you, baby?" she asked.

"I'm on it," Byron said from the foot of the stairs, startling them both. "She won't hurt you anymore. I promise."

He came to sit beside Lana. Abby wiped her red, tearful eyes, her runny nose, and stared at Byron with a look of quiet awe.

"What does that mean?" Lana asked him. "Should I be worried?"

"No. I won't get into any trouble. I know what I'm doing," Byron said. "So, this cancer thing. You're going to be okay?"

Lana sighed. She'd have to follow up later on the bully situation. She let him change the subject, though. This was just as important. "Yes," she said.

"You don't know that for sure, though. Not really."

"I don't know what happens next. Not really. But I know that whatever it is, I'll be fine. We'll be fine. I'm warrior-mama now, remember? No going back for me."

As she sat, one arm around each of her children, her nearly grown babies who thought they no longer needed her, but clearly still did, she resolved to fight. For them, for herself. To set a better example. They didn't need to see a woman who was taken down by her husband leaving, or one faking that she was fine despite having been left. They needed to see that she'd gotten hurt, knocked down flat, but got up and kept going.

She kissed them both and headed for the phone. First, she made an appointment with Abby's doctor. When they asked what she needed to be seen for, Lana hesitated.

"Anorexia," she said, clearly as she could. It was a frightening word.

She hung up and dialed Graham. He was working, no doubt buried in tax forms, and he sounded impatient as he greeted her.

"I think it's time we filed for divorce," Lana said. "Made it official."

"You sure you're ready for all of that?" Graham asked, as if the act of getting divorced could be more painful than the act of being left.

"I am. Enough of this limbo."

26

Matt

Abby held the notebook before her, balanced in her open hands. They were clean, her hands, but still it made Matt nervous. She carefully turned the pages, reading every word, and Matt tried not to think about the strain on each page, grazing the wire coil as Abby flipped a page up, over, and around the spring-shaped spine of the notebook. They were her pages, after all. Matt repeated this to himself to keep from taking the notebook back. He wanted her to keep reading. The best part was coming, but if even one notch of the spiral-bound page tore, it would ruin the entire notebook.

"Oh," Abby said. She stopped flipping pages and held the notebook closer to her face, and Matt knew she'd seen it. That when she stopped eating and there were no more meals or calories to count, he'd tried counting her smiles, but soon those had stopped, too. So he counted her breaths. It was all she had left to offer him, and Matt needed something for the empty yellow pages yet to be filled. Each page was supposed to cover one day, and the days were marching forward. He couldn't just stop taking notes. He'd already written the date at the top of each page with his heavy black calligraphy pen. The pages needed data.

Abby had taken thirty-seven breaths since she'd begun reading. She took more when she was upset, fewer when she was concentrating. They were slower now, although Matt felt her tense next to him. And then she wasn't breathing at all. Matt wondered what else he would count if she took her breaths away from him, too.

"Thirty-seven," Matt said. "So far. Thirty-seven breaths now." He pointed toward the notebook, toward the waiting page.

At this, Abby let out a long sigh. Thirty-eight. When she looked at him there were tears on her face. She wiped them with the back of her sleeve.

"You don't count tears?" she asked, half laughing while she cried.

"Oh, no," Matt said, shaking his head, turning his body to face the window. He didn't like to watch people cry. "I don't count those."

"Maybe I could . . ." Abby let out another sigh. She was up to forty-two now. "I could eat a slice of apple or two." She held the notebook out to Matt and he took it. He uncapped his green pen and held it up to show he was ready. Abby stood slowly and walked toward the kitchen. Matt recorded the breaths. He wanted to separate the breaths and the food somehow, but he wasn't sure how. They needed to be on the same page. He could include the time for each notation, but he needed more of a division than that. Maybe a second-color pen. He went to his room and got blue and red pens and waited by the window, anticipation mounting, trying to choose a color.

Abby returned with three slices of apple, two carrots, and one Triscuit. They were arrayed nicely on a plate and she tipped it toward Matt to show them to him. He nodded.

"I can't write them down until after you swallow," he explained.

"Of course not," Abby said. "I just . . . which would you eat first?"

"The Triscuit, of course. Brown, orange, white." He pointed from cracker to carrot to apple.

"Is the apple white?" Abby asked, holding up the thin slice to the light. She'd trimmed the peel off, so it was almost white, almost colorless, but for a hint of yellow. It would turn brown soon, from the air, but Matt didn't consider that in his calculations. Only the real, natural color mattered.

"Maybe yellow, but that's still a primary color."

Abby nodded, took a tiny nibble of the cracker. "Primary colors last, I remember now."

Abby was going to see a therapist about her eating. Or not eating. Matt had seen a therapist for a little while after his overdose. A thin man with sleepy eyes who tried to explain what Asperger's syndrome was and how it made Matt different. Matt didn't feel different, though. He felt like himself, every day. The therapist seemed to want to convince Matt that he was abnormal, while everyone else was normal. But Matt wasn't sure. Maybe Matt was the normal one, and everyone else was abnormal. Who was this man to say different? After all, Matt didn't have problems with the people around him. They were the ones having problems with him. Didn't that mean they needed therapy even more than he did, to learn to accept the people and things they couldn't change? He tried to explain his theory to the therapist, who smiled and called Matt high-functioning, fast-processing, and well-adjusted. Then his five free sessions ran out and Matt never saw the therapist again.

Matt didn't know if Abby's therapist was like the calories: something they weren't supposed to talk about. He wondered if the therapist would like to see the notebook. Matt was very proud of it. He wasn't sure he'd trust a stranger with it, but he might be willing to make a copy. He decided to ask later, after Abby had eaten the food. He didn't want to upset Abby and lose the chance to get some new data.

Matt noted the Triscuit, wrote down the time. He didn't put the calories (twenty), because she hadn't finished it yet. She was chewing too long, the way she did before she spit something out, but she didn't have a napkin, and Matt had let his stash of them run out when she'd stopped eating with him.

"Water," Matt said. "You need water. To help you swallow." Abby nodded, but didn't move. Matt knew where the water was, knew which glasses Abby liked to use: the short squat glasses with the heavy base. Highballs. Matt went to the kitchen and got her a glass of water. When he handed it to her she was still chewing, but she was smiling. As soon as the glass had passed from his hand to hers, Matt sat and noted the smile in the notebook. It was a good day for data.

"I like it when you wait on me," Abby said.

"I'm not waiting," Matt said. "I'm taking notes." He showed her the notebook, the page now fuller with its three categories: breaths, food, smiles, in green, red, blue ink. He let her see it because there were no calories on it yet, since she still hadn't swallowed the cracker. As far as he knew it was only the calories Abby never wanted to see.

Abby read the page and laughed, choking a little around her unswallowed cracker, and Matt made a note of the laugh, struggling over which color pen to use before settling on the blue, the same as the smiles. The page was nearly full. The whole day was turning around. By the time he finished making the note, Abby was laughing harder, peering over his shoulder at the notebook on his knee. He hoped she appreciated the nice balance of information filling the page. She swallowed some water, nearly choking on it because she was still giggling. Matt was tempted to record the choking, because there was so much going on and it was all so much more interesting than the breaths, but choking seemed like it was in the same category as tears: better not to remember.

Abby ate the three apple slices and the two tiny carrots, all very slowly, like she might stop at any moment. She had the order wrong, the carrots were supposed to come first, but Matt didn't say anything. He made his calorie notes and counted her breaths and didn't talk. It was like before, and this made him feel calm. He hadn't noticed how much he missed sitting in the window with her until she was back there next to him.

"If your therapist wants to see the notebook, I can show it to her," he offered.

"Thanks. I'll ask. I think it can just be our thing, though. I know you probably don't want anyone else to hold it."

"I didn't mean the actual notebook. I meant a copy. But maybe you won't need the notebook now that you have a therapist,"

Matt said. It hadn't occurred to him until he said it. Maybe Matt wouldn't get to record Abby's breaths and smiles and laughs and calories anymore. Maybe he'd have to find something else to record. He had his license back, and his new red truck. He could go out in the world and find data. But he had grown to prefer his safe, quiet, sunny window. And Abby sitting beside him.

"I don't mind the notebook," she said. She chewed her last carrot and gestured for Matt to record it. He smiled and wrote it down.

Abby drank her water and set the glass on the window ledge, empty except for the last piece of ice, quickly melting within. The sun cut through the glass and cast rainbows all around her. He wished he'd gotten her milk instead of water. Then he'd have more calories and protein to list. But the rainbows were beautiful, and maybe a drained milk glass wouldn't have been clean enough for those.

"You're Rainbow Girl," Matt said. He gestured toward the rainbows on the carpet and Abby's calves, but she didn't look down. She tipped her head back and laughed, her old birdlike giggle, and Matt had to make a note of it, so he didn't have time to explain the prism effect of the glass.

When Lana came in she'd complain about the water glass on the windowsill. It was sweating moisture and would leave a ring on the white paint of the sill. Matt was torn between removing the glass to spare the paint and leaving it there to keep the rainbows. He decided the best thing would be to take a picture to remember the rainbows, then move the glass. He got out his phone and tried to see them through the camera, but it didn't work. The feeling in the narrow box of the photo was all wrong: flat and dark. It felt small in the picture, and much bigger here in the room with Abby. He tried different angles, but none of them worked.

"Let me see," Abby said. She held her hand out for his phone. Matt never gave his phone to anyone else. He saw how Lana let the kids use hers, and they'd already broken one of them: Byron, by dropping it on the concrete front steps. Matt held the phone halfway out to Abby, but he knew he couldn't let it go. He changed his mind, started to pull it back toward himself, and just then Abby leaned toward him, very nearly touching her cheek to his, and grasped the phone, still in his fingers, pressing the camera button. The screen filled with a photo of the two of them. Matt realized they looked alike: same fair skin, same light hair, same narrow jaw, same round eyes.

"Rainbow Girl and Notebook Man," Abby said, smiling. "Send it to me, okay?"

Matt nodded, fumbling with the phone. He wasn't sure how to send a photo. He'd never done it before. His pictures were his. He also needed to record the smiles, two since his last note. He looked from the notebook to the phone to the glass. He still needed to move the glass. And the breaths. He was losing track of the breaths. It was too much to do all at once. The calm feeling was gone and his hands and cheeks were tingling. He couldn't do all of it, which meant he couldn't do any of it. His anxiety was rising, his heartbeat picking up, the rainbows still beckoning to be caught on camera, the notebook waiting for the smiles, the glass sweating on the ledge, the phone heavy in his hand.

"I can do it," Abby said. "Is it okay if I hold your phone?"

"Your mom won't like the glass there. The water. The condensation is getting on the windowsill. But the rainbows . . ." He was having trouble breathing, and Abby's smiles and breaths, he was losing track of them.

Abby jumped up and left the room, left him alone with the rainbows and the notes and the phone still in his hand. She came back with a paper towel, which she folded neatly into a small square and placed beneath the glass. The rainbows disappeared as she lifted the glass, but they returned once she'd set it down.

"Better?" Abby asked.

Matt nodded. "Three," he said. "Three smiles."

"Okay, but I can't write in your book, right?"

Matt nodded. Abby was waiting. He couldn't think clearly. He looked at the three pens in his hand.

"Blue. Blue for smiles," Abby said.

Matt uncapped the blue pen and made the note. He sighed

once that was done. He'd stopped counting her breaths and now he'd never know. "I've lost track of the breaths, though. They're gone forever."

"We don't need the breaths anymore," Abby said. "I'm eating again. Back on your plan. Only foods I like. No spitting it out in napkins. Is that enough data? The smiles and laughs and food and birds?"

Matt nodded, relaxing. It was plenty of data. He could let the breaths go. He'd rather record the calories and smiles. He recapped his blue pen, slid it into the coil of the notebook. All that was left was the photo on the phone.

"Never mind the picture. I'm sorry I touched you. I forgot." Abby leaned back and sighed, folding her hands in her lap.

Matt set the phone down. He still felt overwhelmed. He didn't know what to do.

"I think I'd rather be Rainbow Girl than the Vizsla, if that's okay with you," Abby said.

Matt nodded. He'd forgotten that she was the new Vizsla. He'd lost them both for a little while. The runner must have found a new route. He never saw the Vizsla anymore.

"You can just be Abby," Matt said.

Abby extended her thin, pale arm until one of the rainbows rested in the palm of her hand. Matt picked up the phone, switched it back to camera mode, and captured it. It worked. The darkness was gone. The fairness of Abby's skin and the brilliance of the rainbow brought the calm feeling back. Abby was smiling again.

Matt held the phone out to her. She gently took it, careful not to touch his fingers as she did so. While she dealt with the pictures, he noted the smile in the notebook. It was a very good day for data.

27

Abby

Lana took Abby to her first therapy appointment, but Abby would be going in solo. That's what the therapist, Jennifer Powell, had suggested. Abby wasn't nervous until they sat in the tiny waiting room, just a hallway with a few chairs in a big old converted house. Every step in the dark-paneled house creaked under worn Persian rugs, and the windows were covered in heavy drapes. It was a horror-movie house. A door opened and a young, bubbly, pretty girl, with big green eyes, dark reddish brown hair, and fair skin, appeared. Abby half expected her to have an Irish accent.

"Abby?" she asked. She didn't have a fancy accent. Abby nodded and stood. She was trembling all over. "I'm Jenny," she said, shaking Abby's cold hand. "Come on in and have a seat." Jenny whispered something to Lana as Abby entered the room.

Jenny didn't have one of those long shrink couches for lying on, she just had an ordinary brown IKEA love seat, like the one Abby's dad bought when he moved out. The room smelled faintly of incense, but Abby couldn't find the source. Jenny sat across from Abby and smiled. She was a bit overweight, which seemed strange. Could someone overweight counsel anorexics?

"Would you like to start out with why you're here?" Jenny asked.

Abby shrugged. She wasn't sure what to say. "I don't like to eat," she said lamely. "I mean, I have trouble eating. I guess I have an eating disorder?" She didn't know why she made it a question. She felt like she was being tested, only she'd forgotten to study for the exam. There were blinds in Jenny's office, open to reveal slats of light across the whole room, like jail bars. The room was stuffy and Abby took off her sweater, then felt self-conscious about her body. Lana had made a big deal about Abby's arms, saying there was no meat there at all. Abby thought they were a little bit flabby. She focused on her stomach and legs in her workouts. Not her arms. She put an orange throw pillow in her lap and tucked her arms under it.

"One thing about me," Jenny said. "I've struggled with an eating disorder myself. Obviously not anorexia." Jenny laughed and Abby felt forced to laugh even though it wasn't funny. "It's been a lifelong battle," Jenny went on. "I always wanted to fit some ideal, obtain an unhealthy body type that fashion magazines planted in my head when I was your age. You know the pictures I mean?"

Jenny opened a folder and removed a picture of a supermodel. There was nothing special about it. Jenny watched Abby closely. She pulled out another picture. The same picture, only different. She handed both photos to Abby. In the second one the model wasn't quite so tall, and she had shadows under her eyes and lines around her mouth. She had bigger thighs and meatier upper arms.

"The magic of Photoshop," Jenny said. "You see, that one is the real girl, untouched. This one"—she pointed to the first image—"is what she looked like after they erased every ounce of fat. The ideal that I was chasing? Turns out it didn't even exist."

Abby looked back and forth until she got it, then she looked up at Jenny. Jenny was waiting for her to say something, Abby was pretty sure, but Abby had nothing.

"It makes me mad," Jenny said. "That they set young girls up to hate their bodies to sell some product that nobody needs."

She handed Abby a whole stack of them: before-and-after-being-Photoshopped pictures of models and celebrities. Sure enough, the ones Abby had spread all over her desk in her room, the magazines full of women with flawless skin and perfect bodies, were fake. They'd been stretched like taffy, wrinkles smoothed out, blemishes lightened, thighs and arms carved away until they were nonexistent, breasts enlarged and lifted. The women themselves were erased, leaving some imaginary girl behind. Abby cared and didn't care. She guessed she had fallen for it, just like Jenny. But that wasn't why she didn't eat.

She looked up and nodded. "I'm sure a lot of girls feel like they have to look like this. And that's too bad."

"But not you?" Jenny asked. She had her head tilted to the side like she could see Abby better from an angle.

"I don't know," Abby said. "Sure, I'd like to be perfect. I mean, who wouldn't, right? But the truth is, I just don't like food. I hate certain textures and smells and anything with a lot of grease. I can barely make myself swallow it."

"What is food?" Jenny asked.

Abby laughed, but Jenny looked serious. "It's, um, calories?"

Jenny collected the photos of the fake supermodels. "Anything else?" Abby shrugged. "How about nutrients? How about vitamins, minerals, protein, fiber, the resources we need to have the strongest, healthiest bodies possible?"

Of course Jenny was right. Abby had messed up on her answer. She needed to think before responding. "Yeah, sure. That, too."

"I hear you're quite the athlete," Jenny said. Abby shrugged. It wasn't like she was going to brag. "Why would you rather run during lunch than eat? Why would you work yourself to the point of fainting? Just because you don't like food?"

The only way Jenny could know about the fainting and lunch-skipping running was if Lana knew. Which meant someone had told on Abby. Abby was mortified.

"I just . . . I'm trying to keep in shape."

Jenny gave her a sympathetic smile. "Sometimes, when people have a lot of change going on, hard things, things they can't control, they find other outlets for their fears, their anxieties. Other means of asserting control over their lives. Exercising as much as possible, eating as little as possible, does it make you feel in control?" She did this for a living. She already knew the answer. Abby saw no point in playing dumb.

"It takes discipline."

"And without this discipline, what might happen?"

Suddenly Abby felt angry. She wasn't sure why. "Everything would go to hell." Except everything already had gone to hell, hadn't it?

"And what would that mean? How would it change your life if you ate more, exercised less, gained weight, actually liked food?"

"I'd get fat. I'd be made fun of. I'd be even uglier than I am now. I'd be a failure. I'd be ruined." But of course she was already ruined. Only she didn't want to talk about that. Abby took the pillow by opposite corners and spun it forward and backward.

"Do you think your food aversion might have something to do with the fact that you only see food as calories?"

"I don't know."

"What do you see when you look at your body?"

Abby looked down at her thighs, the fat nobody seemed able to see but her. She shook her head. She was done sharing. She wanted to leave.

"I see nothing," she said. Abby stopped spinning the pillow and set it neatly aside. She felt a swell of anger and she sighed it away, but it didn't quite leave, not all of it.

"It seems to me that you try very hard to be perfect. Perfect student, perfect athlete, perfect daughter. You have very high standards for yourself. Maybe impossible standards."

Abby clenched her teeth. It was all she could do not to start her thigh-clenching exercises right there in front of the eating disorder specialist. She wondered if she could get away with it. A feeling of defiance rose up inside her. She slowly tightened up every muscle in her body, just for the thrill of pulling one over on good old Jenny.

"Perfectionist tendencies frequently accompany anorexia. This belief that achieving perfection will finally bring happiness. That you can't be happy unless you are perfect. Do you ever feel like that?"

Abby relaxed her body, took a breath, tightened it up again.

"Are you happy?" Jenny asked. It was a stupid question. Happy people didn't end up in therapy. Abby snorted. Relaxed her body. Tightened up again. "Right now, exercising in front of me, are you happy?"

Abby felt like she'd been punched in the stomach, and her body went slack in response. "No."

"How do you feel?"

"I feel . . ." Abby felt a swell of tears, laced with rage. She felt humiliated and exposed and like the biggest failure in the world. She looked for one word to sum all of that up, but there wasn't one. "I feel everything. Everything but happy."

"Well, that's a start," Jenny said.

"Of what?" Abby asked.

"A process. Next we let those feelings out. We let go of all of the sadness and shame and self-pity and doubt and rage. Everything that gets in the way of us loving ourselves."

"How?"

"We scream it out, of course." Jenny smiled and Abby smiled back, sure she was joking. Jenny pointed to the pillow at Abby's side. "That'll do. Pretend that pillow is everyone who ever made you doubt yourself. Make a list. Start with the worst person. Who is it?"

"Caitlin," Abby said without thinking.

"Caitlin. And what did Caitlin do to you?"

Tears welled in Abby's eyes and she shook her head to clear them. "She's just your typical popular mean girl. She kind of has it in for me."

"What did she do?" Jenny was nearly whispering, Abby figured to make her feel safe confessing. But there was nothing safe about it. Abby put her sweater back on.

"She started rumors about me. About me and a teacher. They weren't true."

Jenny nodded, her face smooth with sympathy. She pointed to the pillow. "Tell her how much she hurt you. Tell her how furious you are. Tell her you aren't taking it anymore. Yell at her. Scream at her if you can."

Abby laughed, but Jenny was dead serious. Abby couldn't do it. "I'm not really a yeller."

"I'll show you how it's done," Jenny said. She sat facing the pillow, leaned in close with an angry face, her hands on her thighs. "I hate how you made me feel," she hissed. "You called me fat. You made me feel ugly. Worthless. I don't deserve to be treated like that, Mom!"

Abby wasn't sure if Jenny was putting on an act just to set an example, or if her mother had really said those things. Abby wanted to give Jenny a hug. But then it was her turn. Abby stared down the pillow, but her anger was very far away.

"Hit it," Jenny said.

Abby gave the pillow a light-handed smack. It absorbed the blow like Abby was merely air. Invisible. Insignificant. She hit it again, with the side of her fist, hard enough to make a sound, a quiet gust of air leaving the pillow. She tried once more. And again, with both hands. The sound was probably similar to the sound Caitlin would make if Abby hit her in the stomach. Her soft, flabby, stupid, rumor-starting stomach. Abby didn't feel as strong as she used to, physically or emotionally, but she was stronger than this, she was pretty sure. She pulled the pillow closer, raised her fists like a boxer, and let loose a steady stream of punches: left, right, left, right. She was training, just warming up. She thought of Caitlin, chem, the rumors, the years she had left enduring the hell that was high school. And Gabe, whom she still loved even though he was maybe the worst thing that had ever happened to her. She leaned over the pillow, pummeled it with everything she had. Her arms were getting tired but she couldn't stop. She grunted as she punched, found hidden energy reserves in guttural sounds. She was almost out of strength, out of energy, out of will, when she felt a welling inside her, a bottomless anguish for everything that she'd had and lost: happiness, laughter, peace, hope. She hit Caitlin, the rumor-spreading kids, her dad for leaving, her mom for taking so long to notice her again. She even hit herself, for all the ways she'd failed herself. A sob rose to the surface and Abby blocked it with a scream, a primal sound that came from her toes. She stopped hitting the pillow and screamed herself empty at it.

"It's not fair!" she shouted at the pillow, just a stupid orange square that cared nothing for her, just like everyone else in her life. "I always do everything right. I never cause any trouble. I never ask for anything. And for what? None of you care about me! None of you see me! None of you love me! I never hurt anyone! Why do you all want to hurt me? Why can't you just leave me alone? Why can't you just like me? Why don't any of you care how I feel?"

Abby was hoarse and out of breath and a sob came up like vomit, choking her. She cried a hard, airless cry, broken and empty and animalistic, her whole body lurching with the effort. She coughed and choked on her sobs until her breath came back, then buried her face in the pillow and cried it all out. She wept until she had no more tears, just a splitting headache and a runny nose.

She sat up and wiped her eyes on her sweater. Jenny held out a box of tissues and Abby took them. She had the hiccups and her entire body ached. She went through a dozen tissues, blowing until her nose was raw. Jenny waited patiently. Abby glared at Jenny, hating her. Why would she want Abby to feel like this? Jenny had to be the worst therapist ever. This wasn't helping at all.

Abby stood up to leave and swooned. She was too dizzy to take a single step forward. Jenny reached out to catch her. Abby reeled, falling back onto the couch. She threw the box of tissues across the room. They bounced off a wall with barely a sound, leaving a small dent in one corner of the blue box. Abby lurched across the room, using the wall for balance, and stomped on the box, flattened it into a mangled mess. She stormed back to the couch and sat, arms crossed, breathing hard, glaring at Jenny.

Jenny smiled at Abby and clapped her hands in a slow, steady rhythm. "Perfect," she said.

Abby started to laugh, because the whole thing was ridiculous, and her therapist was insane. She'd assaulted a pillow and a box of tissues and she was supposed to be proud of this. But as she laughed, hiccupping and snorting and coughing, she began to feel lighter. She'd dumped her sadness and anger, had made a complete fool out of herself. She was weightless. Drained clean. And she was still here.

"Now what?" Abby asked. She pointed at another box of tissues. Unsmashed. Waiting. And she and Jenny laughed together.

"Now we start the next phase," Jenny said. "We've emptied you of the bad. Now we fill you up with good. List everything you like about yourself."

Abby sighed. "I'm sorry about the Kleenex box," she said.

"It had it coming," Jenny said.

Abby laughed. She wanted to skip this next part, but Jenny was waiting. "I guess I like my soccer skills. I'm pretty good on the track. I like when I get good grades."

Jenny wasn't satisfied. She pursed her lips and narrowed her eyes as she considered something. "Here's an idea. Close your eyes. Picture yourself as a little girl, back when you still had favorite foods, before you noticed fashion photos, before the Caitlins of the world got to you. Now tell that little girl everything you like about her."

Abby closed her eyes and searched her eyelids, lit pink by the sun coming in the window. She remembered a photo of herself from a family camping trip. She was maybe six and shoeless and missing a front tooth and blissfully happy with a s'more in her hand. She imagined kneeling before that girl. "I like your sense of humor," she said. Her voice was small and thin. "I like your silliness. Your animal impressions. Your made-up stories. Your kindness. Your adventurousness. Your tree-climbing skills. Your honesty. Your compassion. Your pretty smile. Your strong body." She opened her eyes and Jenny was smiling.

"Good," Jenny said. "Can we agree that you and little-girl Abby have all of those qualities in common?"

Abby shrugged. She supposed it was true. Some of it was buried, but most of it was still there, inside somewhere. She nodded. Jenny hugged her and the hour was up, just when it was getting good.

Abby was a zombie afterward, completely exhausted. Jenny said a few words to Lana and they left. Abby was quiet the whole ride home, but she could feel her mom trying not to watch her, silently waiting for something. It seemed strange that they had barely even talked about her eating. Or not eating. But in a way that was the best part.

"It was good," she finally said. "I'll go again."

Lana squeezed her hand and held on to it for the rest of the drive. Abby was overcome by sleep before they made it home. She woke up hours later in her bed. She figured her mom must've carried her upstairs like a baby. There was a bouquet of flowers on her nightstand and a card from Lana that read, *I love you and I'm proud of you.*

Matt came by to see if Abby wanted to have dinner with him at the window. She shook her head. "I think I'm too tired."

"The flowers are nice," he said.

"Do you know what kind they are?" Abby asked.

Matt pointed them out one by one. "Mum, daisy, tulip, Stargazer lily, fern, baby's breath. The pollen on these Stargazers will get everywhere. And if it gets on the petals it'll turn them brown. You can cut the stamens here and throw that part away. I can do it if you want."

Abby nodded and watched Matt carefully trim the stamens, cupping his palm beneath them. The pollen dusted him a rusty brown.

"You know everything about everything," she said. "How much do you know about chemistry?"

Matt brushed his hands off over her trash can and shrugged. "I know a lot about chemistry."

"I could probably use a study partner."

Matt smiled. "I'd make an excellent study partner. Can I borrow your book? And look at your class notes? I can make flash cards on the chapters that'll be on your final."

"Perfect," Abby said. She drifted back to sleep, and when she woke up there was a salad, milk, and half a sandwich next to the flowers. And a big stack of homemade flash cards.

The next session with Jenny was easier. Abby was already mad when she got there, about nothing and everything. She'd spent the whole week avoiding Caitlin and Gabe, so nothing had really happened, except that she'd become some kind of mole rat at school, always scurrying into dark corners and hiding places to avoid everyone. It was her best solution and biggest problem, all in one.

Abby yelled at the pillow for ruining her life, for making her hate school, for making her forget everything she once liked about herself. She gave the pillow a few hard punches, dropped it on the floor, and stomped it. She didn't even need to cry out the rest. Her anger and frustration and annoyance at the world poured out of her and into the room. When Abby felt enough emptiness inside her to let in some good, she unearthed her long-forgotten love for little-girl Abby and filled up the space with that. Abby began to feel fiercely protective of that little girl.

"I won't let anyone hurt you," she told her six-year-old self. "Never again. Not even me."

"Good," Jenny said. She pulled out a piece of paper with a chart on it. "Now we need to talk about getting strong again, physically, to better protect that girl."

"By eating," Abby said.

"Are you ready?" Jenny asked.

"I'm ready," Abby told her. She was and she wasn't.

"That's how it is," Celeste Franks told her that night on the phone. "You love it and hate it. Welcome to recovery."

She called Celeste once or twice a week. She understood better than anyone. They laughed at the visual of Abby screaming at the pillows in Jenny's office.

"I wonder what the people in the waiting room think," Abby said.

"They play those white-noise machines so they can't hear you out in the waiting room. I wonder if there's a 'screaming session in progress' setting. Like a tornado."

Abby giggled. "My uncle has one of those. It even has traffic noises."

"Oh, that sounds perfect. Then it'd just be like an ordinary day in New York. Screaming and everything."

Celeste was going to college in Boston and got to go to cool places like New York just for fun. "I wish I had your life," Abby said.

"You don't need my life. You've got a kick-ass life coming. I can't wait to see all of the amazing things you're going to do."

"I'd like to meet you in person sometime," Abby said.

"You will. I'm coming home for the summer. I figured we'd hang out. Won't we? You won't be in my dad's class anymore, so it won't be weird, right?"

"Oh, no, it won't be weird," Abby said, thrilled to hear Celeste wanted to hang out. Maybe it would be weird, but she didn't care. Celeste didn't mind that she was five years older than Abby. She didn't have an attitude about befriending a high school freshman. Or a student of her father's. She was awesome, just like Mr. Franks had said. She was like the big sister Abby had never had.

Abby went to school the next day, relieved to find Caitlin was absent. People were whispering about Caitlin in the hallway. Abby eavesdropped until she had the whole story. Caitlin's parents had bought a new house in Rancho Peñasquitos, and Caitlin didn't want to change schools. So rather than applying for a transfer back into the district and risking getting turned down, they'd lied and used a friend's address. Her parents were just like her, thinking they were better than everyone else, that the rules didn't apply to them. The school board found out about the fake address. It was something they were cracking down on. They made an example of her. And just like that, Caitlin was gone.

The rumors about Abby and Mr. Franks slowed without Caitlin there to keep them going. Plus there was new gossip to distract everyone: Jeff Meeks got busted for smoking pot during lunch, Paulette Rollins was pregnant and keeping the baby, and Sean Billings was sleeping with Milly Mercer while still dating Shelby, his girlfriend of three years.

Abby asked Byron how he'd done it, and he just shrugged and smiled.

"Told you I'd take care of it. I just couldn't let her get the better of you for one more day."

"Thanks," Abby said. She wrapped her arms around him and squeezed hard. He hugged back and nearly crushed her. "Ouch. You're one big muscle now," she said. "What happened?" She playfully poked his shoulder, his bicep, his chest. His whole body felt hard as a rock. "Are you on steroids or something?"

Byron laughed and ducked, grabbing Abby around her hips. In one swift motion he swung her around in a full circle, feet over her head and then back on the ground like a human pinwheel. "And you're the tallest toothpick on the planet."

Abby nodded, her playful mood gone, a sullen one looming. "Yeah. I know."

"Aw, I didn't mean anything by it, Abs," Byron said. He tousled her hair, first gently, then using both hands, until her entire head was a static-ridden rat's nest. "You're awesome. Annoyingly perfect just as you are."

"Whatever," Abby said, shaking her head free. "I'm far from perfect, but thank you."

"Are you kidding? Why do you think an annoying cow like Caitlin is so insanely jealous of you? You're smarter, more athletic, prettier, and you're okay with who you are, so you don't have that desperate need for attention those girls have. I bet it drives her crazy that she can't be more like you."

"Wow. Thanks," Abby said. It was the closest she had felt to him in a long time. Maybe ever.

She was still feeling chummy with him when Graham picked them up for dinner. It was the second time they'd seen him that week for dinner, and they were going to spend the night on Friday. Byron talked about the art classes he wanted to take, and Graham didn't say anything bad about the idea. He didn't say much of anything at all. Graham clenched his jaw and stared into space, so Abby and Byron mostly chatted without him. Graham seemed to be on good behavior after the fight with Lana. Abby and Byron took turns toying with his new silence.

"I think I want to circumnavigate the world in a plane," Byron said.

"Sure, take the easy way," Abby mocked. "Try a sailboat instead. That's a real challenge. Me, I'd like to give the Iditarod a try, after I go backpacking through Europe for a year before college."

Graham flexed his jaws and ground his teeth but said nothing. Testing his resolve got boring fairly quickly, though.

"You know, Dad, you can bring Ivy next time," Abby said.

"Are you sure? I don't want her to take away from my time with you."

"We'd like to get to know her better," Abby said, which was half true. The other half of the truth was that Ivy would be more fun to talk to than Graham. Byron wanted to hear more about her painting. Abby wanted to ask about her writing. Abby was back to writing poetry, at Jenny's suggestion. Her new poems were different. They weren't just about body parts she hated. She wrote about all of the scared girls at school. She could see it clearly, now that she wasn't so focused on Gabe, Caitlin, and food. That same look of bewilderment all around her. She'd thought she was the only lost one, but suddenly she could see that they were all lost, in one way or another.

Abby was eating, three small meals a day and a little snack, as promised to so many people. She had more energy and was sleeping better. But it was still hard. She was gaining weight. She'd hidden the scale and the mirrors so it wouldn't be so obvious, but she could tell that her shirts were more snug around her waist, that her jeans didn't slide below her hips. Sometimes eating made her feel back in control, but sometimes it made her feel out of control. Just like Jenny and Celeste said it would.

Abby thought about what her mom had said about her grandma Gloria's bulimia. They had a family trip planned to Florida to visit her grandparents in a month, and Abby wondered if she could talk to Gloria about it. About how it had felt at the time: like she was in control, or like it was controlling her. And whether she still did it.

Abby dug through her mother's photo albums until she found the picture from the camping trip that she used in her mind in therapy. She put it on her dresser. Every morning Abby stared at the photo for a few minutes, heaping praise on little-girl Abby until her sense of hope felt stronger than her anxiety. Some days the feeling lasted longer than others. She wanted that feeling all the time, but something kept getting in the way.

She asked Gabe to meet her before school, in the upper parking lot where none of his friends would see, and with only enough time for a brief conversation before the bell rang. Short and sweet. She handed him a plastic grocery bag with his sweatshirt inside. She had a whole speech prepared, about letting go of him and Caitlin and everything that had been so hard about her freshman year, so that she could have a worry-free summer, come back stronger than ever her sophomore year. But standing there, inches from Gabe, the most beautiful boy in the world, she couldn't remember a word of it. She figured she'd always be in love with him. Jenny said your first real, hard crush was sometimes like that. Everlasting.

"I wanted you to keep this," Gabe said, peeking into the bag.

"I can't," Abby said. "I mean, I really, really want to. But that's all the more reason why I can't." She cringed, because it was a horribly embarrassing admission, and then she started laughing, because telling the truth did that to her now. Made her feel light and airy and giddy. Free. Gabe watched her giggle with a strange smirk on his face.

The first bell rang, and Abby gestured toward the building, suggesting they head in together. Gabe nodded but didn't move. He sighed and held the bag out to Abby.

"I want you to have it," he said.

"It doesn't fit me."

"I don't want you to forget me."

"How could I forget you?" she asked. Her whole year had revolved around him. They had two minutes to get to class. Abby turned to walk down the slope without him. Gabe, always faster, managed to get in front of her in a flash.

"Please," he said, still holding the bag out to her.

Abby sighed: confused, frustrated, on the verge of being late to English. "Why?"

Gabe leaned in and kissed her. No warning, no warm-up, no chance for her to react at all. He just pressed his lips to hers, briefly, then pulled back and stared at her. Her first kiss. From Gabe, the only boy she'd ever loved. She wasn't sure what to do. She'd written about this moment a hundred times in her journal. But what happened next? She'd never thought that far ahead. She backed up a step.

"Are you still with Caitlin?"

"No," Gabe said. "After what she did to you I'll never speak to her again."

"Aren't you afraid to be seen with me?" she asked.

"Of course not. You're the prettiest, smartest, most athletic, most drama-free girl in the whole school. Maybe the whole world."

He smiled at her, his perfect teeth shining in the morning light, the one crooked tooth that she loved best on full display. He took her hand, wrapped it around the handle of the bag, then held both the bag and her hand as he pulled her down the walkway toward the building. She stopped just outside the doors, switched the bag to her other hand, and took Gabe's hand again. Properly.

As they headed into the building several kids turned and looked at them. The popular boy, the star athlete, Caitlin's toy, holding hands with the fainting girl, the rumor-ruined girl, the anorexic. And the strangest thing happened. Those other kids? They looked right at her. And smiled.

28

Byron

Byron pulled into the DMV lot and parked. He was closer to the car next to him than he meant to be, but it was too late to do anything about it now. He turned off the engine, wiped his sweaty hands on his jeans. The balding DMV test guy with the clipboard made a few marks on his sheet of paper. Then he smiled at Byron.

"Congratulations."

"I passed?" Byron asked. He didn't want to sound surprised, but he was. He'd been so nervous during the test that he'd forgotten everything Matt had taught him, but maybe all of those practice hours actually counted for something. Maybe, even without being able to remember the specifics, his body still knew what to do.

"You sure did," the guy said. Byron followed him inside. They had him pose for his picture and handed him the piece of paper for his temporary license. Just like that. He was a driver.

He went out to lunch with Betsy to celebrate. And he drove, which was a big deal in itself.

"Now I feel like a proper boyfriend," he said. He'd never used the word with her before, just in his head. Once it was out there, floating around Lana's car with them, he wondered if he shouldn't have said it.

Betsy leaned across the center console and kissed him. He turned to kiss her back and she pointed forward. "Eyes on the road, boyfriend!" she said. They laughed all the way to the café. He was having the best day ever.

His mom made cupcakes and let him eat three of them before dinner. It was his dad's night for dinner, anyway. So what did she care if he ruined his appetite?

When Graham picked them up, Ivy was waiting in the car. Lana spotted her as she greeted Graham at the front door. Byron waited for some reaction, but Lana just smiled and gestured to Byron.

"Did you hear? It's official. The powers that be have deemed him roadworthy."

"Terrifying," Graham said.

"Dad," Abby scolded.

"I'm kidding," Graham said. "I'm very proud of you."

"Can I drive to dinner?" Byron asked. Lana and Graham both started laughing, but Byron wasn't kidding. "What? I'm insured."

"Oh, I know," Graham said. "I got the bill. I think buying a second home would be cheaper than having a male teenage driver in the family. Let's just enjoy a nice dinner, shall we?"

Which meant no. Byron figured it was too much to hope for Graham to suddenly become a different kind of guy. He figured asking for a car was totally out of the question.

They let Ivy pick the restaurant, and she chose the little Italian place. Graham did their taxes and always got a break on the bill, which he felt compelled to tell Byron and Abby every single time they went there. After they ordered dinner Graham's phone rang and he ducked out front to talk to whoever it was.

"I'm sorry," Ivy said to Byron and Abby. "About last time. I didn't realize that I was going to be a surprise guest."

Byron shook his head. "Not your fault. That's just how he operates."

They watched Graham through the window, chatting and laughing on the phone. It didn't seem like a business call. What could be that funny about taxes? Ivy had a funny look on her face, sort of scrutinizing with narrow eyes. When she caught Byron looking at her she gave him a big smile like everything was fine.

"So what kind of art do you do?" she asked him.

Byron shook his head. He wasn't sure he wanted to be friends with this woman. It felt like a betrayal of his mom to like her.

"I'm still figuring it out," he said.

"I just love art," Ivy said. "You know the Museum of Art in Balboa Park? Maybe we could all go there. Make a day of it. Pack a picnic. We could educate your dad a bit on art. Maybe help him come around?"

"Why bother?" Byron asked. He was annoyed with his dad, ditching them for a phone call, but the only person there to take it out on was Ivy.

Ivy sighed. "My parents divorced when I was thirteen. My mom married the most boring man alive. Sweet, loved her dearly, but my god, he was dull. My dad couldn't take losing her. It nearly killed him. He was a very emotional person. Too much for her." Byron and Abby exchanged looks as they waited for the moral to the story. "He was an artist. My father. Broke and broken but passionate and so full of . . . everything."

Byron smiled. "That's how art should be."

"Yes," Ivy said. "But CPAs are not naturally wired that way. Maybe I can help bridge the gap."

Dinner came and they all looked at Graham out front, still yakking away. They decided not to wait for him and started eating without him.

"I hope it's okay that I came along tonight," Ivy said.

"Of course," Byron said. "If you weren't here we'd be eating alone." He pointed out the window with his fork and resumed eating. He noticed that Abby was eating, too. Little bites of some veggie pasta thing, mostly just the veggies, but still. He pointed at the pile of pasta she was leaving behind and she scraped about half of it onto his plate.

"I have to eat the rest," she said, in the same tone you'd use to tell someone you needed a flu shot or a cavity filled at the dentist.

"I heard about your . . . struggle," Ivy said to Abby, very softly.

"I just want to say that I'm proud of you." She reached over and touched Abby's hand like she was afraid to say more. Abby looked at her for a while, then started laughing.

"Thanks. I do what I can," Abby said. She speared one of the corkscrew pasta pieces and put it in her mouth, still grinning as she chewed. Abby was so different lately that Byron barely recognized her. Different in a good way.

He patted Abby's head. "Good girl," he said. Which just made her laugh harder.

Pretty soon they were all laughing. At everything. At nothing. Graham finally joined them. He sat down, smiling. "What did I miss?" he asked. "You seem to be getting along swimmingly."

"Abby ate a piece of pasta," Byron said. "It was awesome. She's a master."

They started laughing again. All except Graham, who of course didn't get the joke.

"I'm glad you're eating," he said to Abby, taking the mood from silly to serious just like that. "If you ever want to . . . talk about it, I'm here."

Abby nodded, very serious. Then she speared another coil of pasta and waved the fork around in circles, the way parents make a spoonful of baby food into an airplane to get a fussy kid to eat. She popped the bite into her mouth.

"Woohoo! Another winner!" Byron shouted, and he, Abby, and Ivy erupted into giggles again. Graham smiled, but he looked around the restaurant to see if anyone was annoyed at the noise. Byron could see that he didn't get it. Maybe never would. That being happy and silly and having fun were more important than money. That being responsible didn't have to mean having to be serious all the time.

A text came in and Graham smiled at it before turning his phone over.

"Who is it?" Byron asked, because even though it was rude to be nosy, they were all wondering.

"I'm glad you asked," Graham said. "A friend of mine who used to coach swimming at USD."

"Is that who you were on the phone with? Is he a recruiter or something?" Byron hated when his dad was smug and coy.

"Yes, I was on the phone with her, and no, she isn't a recruiter. But she's well connected there. She said maybe she could get you an in."

Byron looked at Ivy to see if she was bothered that his dad had been on the phone all through dinner with some other woman, but Ivy was unreadable.

"Isn't USD some crazy-expensive private school? Why would I go there?"

"I'm just trying to get some options lined up for you," Graham said.

"Do they have a good art program?" Byron asked.

Graham sighed and started eating. Ivy smiled at Byron. She slid her hand over toward Graham and he put his hand on top of it without saying anything. Byron wondered what Ivy saw in his dad. Did he laugh with her? Or did he just tell her what she could do better all the time? Did she think a good guy would leave his wife after eighteen years and hardly see his kids afterward? Or maybe Ivy had been the reason Graham left.

"So, Ivy, how'd you meet my dad?" he asked. He watched her closely for signs of lying.

Ivy laughed. "It's such a boring story. We were in line together at the DMV. Changing our addresses at the same time." She smiled at Graham and he smiled back.

"We were in line for a good hour, making the best of bureaucratic hell," Graham said. "She was the prettiest girl in there. And smart, and funny, and—"

"And I had snacks and he was hungry."

They laughed together. Graham touched Ivy's hair and she rubbed his back. "Then it took him another month to get around to calling me."

"More like two weeks. I was terribly busy with work. You know it's—"

"Tax season," Abby, Byron, and Ivy said together, all laughing. Graham smiled, but he didn't seem to think it was quite so funny.

So then Ivy hadn't shown up until after his dad had moved out. Byron sighed. Ivy wasn't the enemy. He wasn't sure if that was better or worse.

"Do you still write?" Abby asked.

"Not in a long time. I have to say, hanging out with you kids has me thinking about starting up again. Writing and painting."

"Yeah," Byron said. "How'd you go from being a theater major and artist to dating a CPA and working as a . . . ?"

"Sales rep for a cosmetics company?"

"Whoa," Byron said. She hardly even wore any makeup. He wanted to ask how old she was, but he knew that was rude. She looked younger than Lana.

Ivy shrugged. "Life."

"Well, you should definitely get back to painting," he said. "My uncle is sharing his supplies with me right now. He lives with us. But I need to get some of my own."

He looked at Graham, but his dad was busy eating while checking emails on his phone and not even listening to the conversation.

Ivy smiled, practically brimming with excitement, and playfully smacked Byron's arm. "So, I was at the DMV because I moved, right? Into my father's house. My artist father's house? He's in a home now. But his studio is still there, in a building out back. Just full of endless supplies. Maybe a bit dusty. I keep meaning to go through it all but I have no idea where to begin. I'd love to find a good home for that stuff."

Byron smiled. There was no way he was going to get out of liking her. "Really?"

"Come by and take what you want. Really. It would make my father so happy, to share it with a budding artist."

Graham finally looked up, palmed his phone, turned toward Ivy. He clenched and unclenched his jaw, but didn't say anything. He looked like a cow chewing cud.

"How about now?" Byron said. "Can we go after dinner?"

"A perfect idea!" Ivy said. "Graham, I can show you one of my plays while Byron gathers supplies." She grinned at all of them, but only Abby and Byron grinned back. Graham pursed his lips until they were white. Byron was impressed that he hadn't said anything yet. Graham didn't like it when anyone made a decision for him. He even refused to let waiters suggest their favorite dishes. Byron could already see that Graham's days with Ivy were numbered. He figured he'd better take advantage of her dad's studio while he had the chance.

Ivy wasn't kidding about the art stuff. Byron scored two easels, a stack of prestretched canvases, four huge rolls of canvas, brushes, gouache, wax medium, varnishes, glazes, every kind and color of paint imaginable. Byron didn't even know what half of it was, but he couldn't wait to experiment with it.

The next day Matt helped Byron organize the new art supplies in the garage. They were converting one side of it into an art studio.

"Now you really need to take some art classes," Matt said. "I can pay for them."

"Seriously?" Byron said. He already knew which ones he wanted to take. A whole summer series offered through the Art Academy of San Diego. Lana couldn't afford them, and Graham had shot the idea down. "You'd do that for me?"

"I have money," Matt said. "I would have used it for art supplies. Since you're letting me use these, I can give you the money. Besides, I want you to get better at art."

He made it sound so simple. He was the exact opposite of Graham.

"I can't believe you'd do that. I don't even know how to thank you," Byron said.

Matt started sorting the messy pile of supplies. "You can set up the easels," he said.

Things were looking up for Byron's art career. When he showed Betsy the new studio she said, "Maybe I could model for you. Nude. Except for a necklace. Like in *Titanic*."

Byron wasn't sure if she was kidding or not, but the idea kept him awake at night. She was moving back home at the end of the month. He was looking at a long summer with his hot girlfriend living just a few blocks away. Lazy afternoons lounging around

Tilly's pool, beach days, day trips to the desert, Tijuana, L.A. With his driver's license, they could go anywhere, do anything, finally find some privacy.

She kissed him and he risked touching her breast again. She made a little noise whenever he did it. He was getting to know the terrain of her body. Then they heard someone's footsteps in the house, growing louder, and they stepped apart. Byron thought endlessly about sex. He and Betsy hadn't been alone much yet. Lana or Trent or Magda were always around. But come summer, there would be a lot more chances for alone time. And more chances for sex. The all-the-way kind. Betsy knew he was a virgin, but he kind of wished he hadn't told her.

"You're sure it doesn't bother you?" he said.

"Why would it bother me?" she said. "You know, I might as well be one, too, since I've never had sex while sober. When we do it, it'll be different."

She rested her head on his chest. Byron wanted to know more about that, and he didn't. He didn't like to think of her being with other guys. And he didn't like to think of asshole frat guys taking advantage of a drunk girl at a party. It made him so insanely jealous and protective of Betsy that he didn't know what to do with the feeling. He wrapped his arms around her and held on tight.

"I'll never take advantage of you," he said. "And I'll never hurt you." But all the while his brain was playing slideshow images of taking advantage of her in really fun ways. Ways that she'd enjoy, too.

Gabe and Abby were a cute couple, the hand-holding type. They sat and stared into each other's eyes and giggled and whispered a lot. Byron thought about asking Gabe basic questions about sex, because he was sure Gabe and Caitlin had slept together. But then he realized this was his sister's boyfriend. And that one day they might sleep together. And then he felt suspicious of Gabe. So instead he just told Gabe he better not hurt Abby, or push her into anything. Gabe was quick to reassure him that his intentions were honorable. That was his exact phrase. It was a funny way to say it, but it put Byron at ease.

So then Byron was back to wanting to know more about sex but not knowing who to talk to. It wasn't like he could talk to Trent about his own sister. Talking to Graham wasn't an option. Lana had already given him the sex talk about condoms and not bragging about sleeping with a girl and realizing that once a relationship turned sexual it never went back. All valid stuff, but not the stuff Byron wanted to know.

"You ever had a girlfriend?" he asked Matt as they painted side by side. Matt had taped up a family photo for them to paint. It was of the new family: Lana, Matt, Abby, and Byron. They were both painting an interpretation of it.

"Three," Matt said. "Michelle, Kayla, and Susan." He ticked them off on his fingers.

"What were they like?" Byron asked.

"Michelle had short brown hair and a funny laugh. And she was allergic to peanuts. Just hives, though. She wouldn't die from eating one. Kayla was blond and drank a lot of coffee, which I didn't like, but she used breath mints. Susan had long brown hair. She played the guitar. She had a cat named Murray. He was orange with stripes."

"So, what was it like, being with them?"

Matt painted a little, looking very closely at the canvas. Then he backed up and put the paintbrush down. "Sometimes I don't like when people touch me. That was a problem. Not during sex. I liked the touching then." Matt laughed. "But Kayla always wanted to hold hands. And I can't do that. It's too . . ." He looked at his hands, rubbed them together. "And kissing was good during sex, when I was excited. But other times I didn't like it. There are too many germs in saliva. You have no way of knowing if someone else is getting sick, is already contagious. Michelle was okay with that. Kayla wasn't. Susan didn't seem to care. She never said anything about it."

"What was it like? You know, sex?" Byron asked. He really hoped no one came into the garage during their conversation.

"The first time I was very excited. And it was over very fast." Matt laughed and started mixing some new colors. "And I couldn't wait to do it again. After that I figured some stuff out. How to last longer. You think about other things. Or stop for a minute if you have to. Women don't like it if you rush. And you need to pay a lot more attention to them than they do to you. You need to touch them more."

"You mean foreplay?" Byron asked.

"Yeah. And after. They like to cuddle after. I'm not a fan," Matt said. He picked up his paintbrush, dabbed it in the new color, and got back to work.

Byron sighed, his longing even stronger. He wanted foreplay. He wanted sex. He wanted to cuddle afterward for days.

29

Lana

Lana settled on the crisp paper of the cold exam table for her follow-up exam with Dr. Tucker. She waited all of five minutes, but it felt like hours. Just enough time to run through every worst-case scenario she could think of. Dr. Tucker entered and smiled, her usual polite but aloof self, until she saw how much Lana's hands were shaking.

"Hey, none of that," she said.

"I think I'm a little bit terrified," Lana said, laughing. "I really don't have time to be sick."

"You aren't sick," Dr. Tucker said, settling on a stool before Lana. She performed a quick exam while Lana tried not to panic. "See? Easy." She tossed her gloves in the trash and helped Lana sit up. "You had a procedure and are recovering nicely. The pain is gone. The discharge is normal. In six months we'll do another pap smear. Hope your body has knocked that HPV out of your system and make sure all cells are normal."

"So I just wait on pins and needles for another six months?"

"No, you forget about it completely, go on with your happy life. In six months I'll call you to come in. Don't waste time worrying about it. We found a problem and we dealt with it. You have no reason to worry."

"Right," Lana said.

"I mean it," Dr. Tucker said. She grabbed Lana by the shoulders and looked her squarely in the eye. "I forbid you to put any more energy into this. I'm on it, so you don't have to be. Got it?"

"Got it," Lana said. She was left to dress with her still-shaking hands. She wasn't sure what kind of resolution she'd been looking for, but she hadn't gotten it. It was still a waiting game. Like everything in life.

Lana emerged into the bright sunlight of a cloudless day, almost irritated with the beauty of it, until she saw Abbot leaning casually against her car. He was in a dress shirt and slacks, shirt unbuttoned, chest hair peeking out. He was strikingly handsome all dressed up for work. Lana's agitation was eclipsed by butterflies. For the first time that day she forgot to feel afraid.

"You're here," she said. He'd had his meeting with human resources and his boss about returning to work full-time, had been sorry he couldn't join her for her checkup as a result.

"I am. My meeting finished early. Is it okay that I came?"

She stepped into his arms and inhaled the sweet warmth of him, his broad shoulder a perfect resting place for her cheek, his strong arms the exact comfort she needed at that moment. "It's very much okay." She kissed him, again and again, until the softness of his lips, the mix of their breath, the feel of his arms around her banished everything else from her mind.

"I got the all-clear," she whispered. "For . . . you know."

During Lana's recovery from her LEEP procedure they had been confined to make-out sessions, hand-holding, long hugs. It gave their romance a chaste, puppy love quality. Waiting was the best and worst part. It was exquisite torture. But now she'd had her follow-up exam. She was cleared for intercourse. She kissed Abbot again, deeper.

"So you're saying . . ." He kissed her back, pulled her close.

"I have no kids for a few more hours."

Abbot smiled, kissed her cheeks, forehead, eyelids. His hands wandered down her back, settled just below her waist. He gripped her hips passionately and pulled her against him. "Where should we go?" He peered into the backseat of her car and raised his eyebrows. Lana laughed and shook her head.

"Your place," Lana said. "I'll follow you there."

They met on his doorstep. Lana's body buzzed with anticipation as Abbot unlocked the door. She trailed her fingertips down his spine. He turned and lifted her, carrying her just-married-style across the threshold. He grunted at her weight.

"Abbot, your back," Lana warned.

Abbot laughed. "You're right. You've got me so excited I don't know what the hell I'm doing." He settled her onto the living room floor and kissed her passionately. She rolled him onto his back and sat astride him. She unbuttoned his shirt, ran her hands across the bare width of his shoulders, the naked slope of his chest, the soft down on his belly. Abbot leaned his head back and moaned.

He tugged on the hem of her shirt, and she lifted her arms for him to pull it over her head. He kissed each of her bare shoulders, her collarbone, her breastbone. Lana pushed his shirt off his shoulders, but it was caught on his wrists by the buttons she'd forgotten to undo there. He lifted his shirt-mittened hands to her back and fumbled with her bra clasp, unable to manage it.

"I've got it," she said, laughing.

"I swear I've done this before," Abbot said, laughing and kissing her as he unbuttoned his shirtsleeves. They stood and giggled and kissed and fumbled, bumping their topless bodies together as he led the way to the bedroom. Lana sat on the bed, suddenly self-conscious of her half-naked body. Abbot removed his pants, laid them neatly over a chair, and knelt before her. "You okay?" he asked. She nodded and smiled, not sure if she was or not. "My god, you are beautiful," Abbot said, gazing not at her aging breasts, the little roll around her waist peeking over her pants, but into her eyes with a sincerity that unhinged something inside her. "How did I get so lucky?" He unbuttoned her pants. She stood to remove them. They embraced and kissed, naked except for their underwear, pressing into each other's bodies until it wasn't enough. Abbot slid Lana's panties off and eased her onto the bed. She lay flat, eyes closed, as he kissed every inch of her. Her entire body tingled. When she couldn't take it anymore she pulled him on top of her and kissed him.

"I don't want to hurt you," he said.

"Do you have a condom?" she asked.

Abbot opened several drawers in search of one. There was something comforting in the knowledge that he didn't have one at the ready.

"Please don't let me have to go to the store like this," he said, and Lana laughed as he opened one last drawer. "Jackpot!" He lay beside her, ran his hand over her breasts, her belly, her hips, her thighs. She couldn't catch her breath, from the laughter, the excitement, the smell of Abbot's skin. He slid his hands between her legs and she gasped. He stopped moving his hand and looked at her face.

"Please don't stop," she said, laughing. He kissed her throat, her shoulders, her breasts, her belly.

"How much time do you have?" he asked.

"Plenty," she said. "No rush." But she couldn't wait. She pushed Abbot onto his back, took the condom from him, and ripped the package open. She loved the look of surprise on his face. She was all-powerful, she was beautiful, she was sexy. She attempted to roll the condom on, but found it slick and uncooperative. They both laughed.

"I'm completely charmed that you're inept at this," Abbot said, taking over.

She climbed on top of him and watched him watch her. They kissed and clutched each other and moved together. Abbot kept trying to slow her down and she kept trying to speed him up. He climaxed first, caressed her until she followed suit. She closed her eyes and let the waves of bliss wash over her. She'd needed this, had missed it, more than she'd realized.

"I didn't hurt you?" Abbot asked.

"You did wonderful things to me," Lana said. "Thank you."

Abbot kissed her and held her, traced his fingertips over her shoulder, down her ribs, across the valley of her waist, and over the slope of her hip.

"You are stunning," he said.

"So are you." She touched the tangle of hair on his chest. He was here. He was hers. She was overwhelmed at her bounty. She wanted to celebrate it. "Would you be up for meeting my kids?" she asked. The question had snuck out. It was too soon to ask such a thing. "I mean, I don't want to rush you, or us, I just wondered . . ."

"I'd love to. How's Sunday?"

Lana smiled and cupped his face. She kissed him again and again. How wonderful to be in a man's arms without reservations, to be admired so cleanly without agenda. No power struggles. No strife. Just this perfect moment: the warm breeze fluttering the pale curtains behind her, Abbot's eyes on her body, his hand grazing her thigh. She hadn't been a take-charge lover with Graham. Sex with Graham had been good, satisfying, but like so many things usually more on his terms than hers. Why had she ever agreed to that?

"Do you have another condom?" she asked, sidling up to Abbot.

"Oh, god, yes," he said, tipping his head back as she kissed his throat.

She made it to school just in time to get the kids. She was disheveled, sore, and relaxed. Empty and full at the same time. She was Lana reinvigorated, reinvented.

"Let's go on an adventure," she told them. "Let's have dinner on the beach."

They swung by home for cold cuts, fruit, cookies, and to convince Matt to join them. Lana drove to Del Mar, parked just south of Dog Beach, along two miles of soft sand and lulling waves. They shared the sunset with surfers, paddle-boarders, off-leash dogs romping in the foamy surf just far enough away for Matt to gather dog-related data without any run-ins.

Lana kicked off her shoes and gripped the sand with her toes, the heated surface giving way to cooler grains below. Matt settled in the middle of the woolly maroon and gray blanket she'd bought on her trip to Tijuana with Abbot. The kids headed straight for the water, squinting into the sun and glaring waves. Abby's sundress billowed out behind her, thin as a distant memory. Byron kicked some water at her and she squealed and spun, dancing in the foam. Lana settled beside Matt as he scribbled in his green notebook.

"They grow up so damn fast," she said.

"We did, too," he said. "Remember?"

"No." Lana laughed. "Sometimes I still feel like I'm fourteen and worried about what to wear to impress the cool kids. I wonder who in their right mind thought I was mature enough for this: motherhood, home ownership, a career, adulthood in general. I hope I have them all fooled, that I have any clue at all what I'm doing."

"You do," he said matter-of-factly. He nodded a few times before returning to his notebook.

Lana snorted and it rolled into a giggle. She cherished the touchstone of Matt's frankness. It was such a posturing and gimmicky world. He was the antithesis of that.

"I bought our tickets for Florida," Lana told him. "To visit Mom and Dad."

Matt looked up, squinting at the bright ocean, then toward the dogs running free.

"Do you remember the pond we used to go to?" he asked. "To see tadpoles? And the time we brought a bunch home?"

"Yeah. I haven't thought about that in years. You were only, what, three or four then? How do you remember that?"

"What happened to them, after they turned into frogs?"

"I don't know."

"We put them in that aquarium, and I remember watching them every day, as they grew legs and lost their tails. But what happened to them, once they were frogs? Did we take them back to the pond?"

"You know, I can't remember. But maybe Mom and Dad do?"

Matt nodded and turned back to his notebook. He deftly sketched a series of tadpole pictures, capturing their varying stages of development into frogs. "I think they died," he said. It was a typical Matt-toned comment, void of any emotion.

"Maybe," Lana said. "I don't remember setting them free."

The sinking sun cast the water in blinding, molten gold. Abby and Byron stood in the surf, ten feet apart, not speaking as far as Lana could tell. They were silhouetted in brassy light, the breeze teasing Byron's shaggy hair and snapping the hem of Abby's dress. They were two beautiful tall, lean, strong, loving souls. They were perfect. And they were Lana's legacy. Her good fortune nearly moved her to tears.

"She's eating again," Matt said. "Abby." He pointed toward her with his pen, then carefully turned a few pages of his notebook. He turned the notebook toward Lana, holding it just out of reach. He used his pen to point to a page. Yesterday's date, followed by foods and calorie counts and protein levels. Below that were smiles and laughs carefully annotated.

"You know exactly how much she eats each day?" Lana asked, reaching for the notebook without thinking. Matt quickly withdrew it.

"I'm not sure I was supposed to show you. It's ours. The notebook. I record the data and she . . . well, she eats and smiles and laughs." He laughed, as if it were funny, as if the existence of such a notebook, the necessity of such meticulous recording, didn't break Lana's heart.

"I'm glad she's eating again. It's going to be a hard road, I suppose. But she's strong. And she has us. Hopefully I'm better support for her than Mom was for us," Lana said. "I wish you'd known Mom before Stephen died. Back when she was happy."

Matt closed the notebook, slid the pen into the coiled spine, hid it away in his bag. "Mom was clinically depressed. There's medication that could have helped. Or therapy. But she didn't want help. She didn't want to feel better. She wanted to be sad about Stephen. She felt guilty that she couldn't save him, so she just wanted to be sad. Being sad helped her remember him. Dad was sad, too, but he worked instead. She didn't have anyone to help her. You aren't depressed. And you have help."

The kids started walking north, toward the dogs. They kept the pocket of distance between them, but moved as one entity. Lana knew if anything happened to one of them she'd be just as gutted as her mother had been. Of course she'd been depressed. She had lost a child. How does anyone ever recover from that?

"I meant me." Matt laughed, his one-huff, almost cough of a laugh. "I meant that I help. I don't actually help. I just watch. But Byron can drive now and Abby eats for the notebook and his art's getting better and he's the parkour leader and her poetry is about her and not just her body parts now and I don't see the Vizsla anymore but there are rainbows some days and I know how to send a picture from my phone now and it helps. I help them and they help me."

"We're helping each other, I guess," Lana said. She had no idea what Matt was talking about, but the details were less important than the love behind them. "We're a good family. We look out for each other."

"I stopped drinking, because you said so," Matt said. "And no more pills."

"Good," Lana told him. "It was making you sick. Hurting your liver. And now it can heal."

"Yes," he said, nodding. "I didn't understand. Why healing mattered. I mean, more than drinking. Everything hurts something else. No matter what. But this is better." He gestured toward Lana, the waves, the kids, with three quick flicks of his wrist. "The dogs are better here, too. They prefer the water. They stay over there."

Lana smiled at him. "I was thinking of having a family barbecue this weekend. I'd like to introduce you all to my friend Abbot. Is there anyone you'd like to invite?"

Matt sifted handfuls of sand through his fingers. "I'd like a girlfriend again. I thought after Susan that I just wanted to be alone. Because of the touching and kissing. But Abby has Gabe and Byron has Betsy and now you have Abbot? So maybe it's okay. The touching. Not always but sometimes. Maybe I could try again. Can I invite Susan?"

"I think that's a wonderful idea."

Tilly, Betsy, Trent, Camilla, her husband Carl, Abbot, and Emily crowded into the small backyard on Sunday, but Susan was a no-show. Matt chose to hide out inside, away from the crowd. Lana made a plate of food and brought it to Matt's room.

"So Susan couldn't make it?"

"She didn't want to meet the whole family yet. She just wants to talk on the phone with me for now. She's happy I'm not drinking anymore. Her cat Murray died. She's thinking of getting a kitten."

"I'm sorry it didn't work out. But anytime you want to have her over, you go ahead and invite her. If you need me and the kids to disappear, we will."

Matt smiled. "You can't really disappear," he said. "You mean leave the house. So we can have sex."

Lana laughed and Matt laughed with her. It was getting easier, talking with him and understanding how his mind worked. It reminded her of dealing with Byron and Abby when they were little. Nuance had been wasted on them. Everything was taken literally. Each word mattered. As it should.

Abby ate grilled mushrooms, bell peppers, and grape tomatoes, juices dripping down her hand as she slid them off the brochette and into her mouth one by one, laughing with Emily. She was a wisp-thin fairy, twirling in a skirt that revealed reedy legs. But she was eating. She'd decided to become a vegetarian, and Lana was hoping that she'd get enough calories and protein that way.

Abbot brought Lana a plate of her favorite foods: Tilly's potato salad, Camilla's coleslaw, fruit salad, two brownies. He had a knack for noticing what she liked and remembering for next time. And he never begrudged her sweets.

Lana speared a piece of watermelon and smiled. "You're going to make me fat, indulging my sweet tooth the way you do."

Abbot carefully looked Lana up and down and shook his head. "Lana, you have the body of a bombshell. You put pinup girls to shame. You're every man's fantasy. Enjoy the brownie."

She took a risk and kissed him, right there in front of everyone, and nothing terrible happened. Maybe she could be a mom, sister, daughter, professional, and a desirable woman, all at once. Maybe this new version of Lana could have it all in a way the previous one never quite had.

The back gate opened and Gabe stepped in. Always well mannered, he strode up to Lana and thanked her for the invite. He was perfectly charming. He wandered over to Abby, both of them seeming shy for a moment. He took her hand and they looked into each other's eyes without saying a word. Lana loved seeing Abby strong, loving, and loved. She was both back to her old self and transformed into an entirely new girl, all at once. Lana hoped that meant the worst was over.

Abbot eased the empty plate from Lana's hands. "She's fine," he said. Lana laughed. It was nice to have him around. So unobtrusive that sometimes she forgot he was there, yet he was always tuned in to her, always seemed to know which direction her thoughts had wandered, how to bring her quietly back from the brink of unhappiness.

"I should've invited you to Florida with us," Lana said.

Abbot slid his arm around Lana's waist, kissed her temple. "Couldn't have gotten the time off, I'm afraid. But I appreciate you saying that."

Abbot stuck around after the guests left. He packed up leftovers, did dishes, wiped down tables. When Matt emerged for his nightly ice cream, Abbot whisked a bowl of ice cream out of the freezer, already carefully scooped into three round snowballs and drizzled with chocolate sauce, and handed it over. Matt accepted it without comment. Lana turned to Abbot in surprise, and he shrugged as if it were no big deal. And really, it wasn't. It wasn't like Lana hadn't told him that around eight p.m. Matt came in for a bowl of vanilla ice cream with chocolate sauce every single night. But, still, it was impressive.

"You're amazing," she told him. "You manage things like . . ."

"A dad? A polite guest? A good partner?" he finished for her.

"Like me."

Abbot laughed. "The best compliment I've had in a long time."

"Is this how you were with your ex?" Lana asked. "Cook? Dishwasher?" There was nothing sexier than a man pitching in around the kitchen.

Abbot shook his head. "I was expected to help out, but when

I did I was frequently scolded for doing it wrong. And then when I resisted getting set up for failure, I was branded as lazy. Some relationships you just can't win, you know?"

Lana nodded. "I know the feeling. So many marriages end up being power struggles, don't they? Each partner just vying for ultimate control."

Lana set the plates in the cupboard. Although the kitchen had been her domain, the entire room was arranged around Graham's preferences. His favorite plates were down lowest, the ones she liked up on the higher shelf. The glasses he liked were in front, the ones she used stored in the back. It had been her doing as much as Graham's. She emptied the cupboard, stacking its contents on the counter. It was time to rearrange.

"So how do we not do that to each other?" Abbot asked. He'd finished the dishes and was leaning against the counter drying his hands, watching her work. It was the first time they'd mentioned a future beyond their next date.

"I think we've both learned a lot in our travels. Hopefully we can be together without trying to change one another."

"Sounds simple enough," he said. He figured out Lana's new order for the cupboards and joined her, putting the dishes back in the new arrangement.

"What's the main thing you've learned in your travels?" he asked.

Lana thought it over. The dull ache of losing Graham. The cold business of separating finances and possessions. The ongoing fear of dangerous cells taking up residence in her body, and that awful, fear-inspiring word: *cancer*. Her mother's vocal dissatisfaction. Her father's constant distractions. The ebb and flow of her children's joy and pain and strength and confusion. Matt moving in. Rekindling her friendship with Camilla. Becca's meditation CDs. Abbot and his soft voice and broad shoulders and brown Crocs and the way he smelled like home.

"I think the main thing I've learned is that no matter what the problem is, the answer is love. It isn't about control or success or doing the most, having the most, or knowing the most. Love my kids fiercely, protect them with all that I have, and be the kind of parent that I wish I'd had. And forgive myself when I falter. Keep my heart open. Trust my judgment. Accept others. Love myself. That's what I've learned."

Abbot reached up to stop her hand in the steady motion of lifting mugs from the counter to the shelf one by one. He turned her toward him and placed her palm on his chest over his steadily thumping heart.

"You're right," he said. "And that's exactly why I love you."

30

Matt

The phone calls weren't working. The problem was that Matt hated talking on the phone. It seemed like it should be easier, because there was no eye contact and the caller couldn't see whether Matt was anxious-smiling or not. But after the third phone call with Susan, where she did most of the talking and Matt did most of the pacing around his room trying to figure out what to say, she said they'd be better off meeting in person.

Matt drove his red truck to the café Susan had selected. He brought himself a thermos of tea from home, because he couldn't eat or drink at the café. He didn't like restaurants or restaurant germs. As soon as he walked in and saw Susan he realized how much he missed her. She had the same brown hair, hanging straight just below her shoulders, and her brown eyes were just as he remembered them, but she looked different around the mouth.

"You're wearing pink lipstick," Matt said. "I've never seen you in pink lipstick before."

Susan laughed. "Hi, Matt. It's nice to see you. Can I hug you?"

Matt set his tea down so he wouldn't spill it or burn her and opened his arms. He turned his head to the side so she'd know not to kiss him. Susan didn't move.

"Tell you what. We don't have to hug," she said. "I'll be right over here if you feel the urge, but I don't need to touch you if you aren't up for it."

Matt liked Susan a lot. She was funny and nice and smart. And she smelled good. Like some sort of flower and spice. He stepped forward and gave her a quick hug, smelling her hair as he did. It smelled like cherry blossoms. She raised her arms to make space for him, but she didn't put her hands on him. She had always been like that: fine with whatever he wanted as far as the touching went. Which made him want to touch her more. He even wanted to kiss her. Not her pink lipstick, though. The lipstick made him think of the lip balm he'd bought for Florida. Mint, with sunscreen in it.

"I'm going to Florida," Matt said. He was already better in person. He hadn't even thought of telling her about the trip over the phone.

"Really?" Susan smiled and sat at a table for two. "When?"

"Tomorrow. For seven days. To visit my parents."

"Oh, Matt, that's wonderful," Susan said. "How long since you've seen them?"

"Two years and seven months," Matt said. He knew that was too long to go without seeing your parents, because Lana had told him so. "They don't travel much. And I don't travel much. And we live two thousand four hundred fifty-six miles apart, according to Google Maps. If I drove. On the ten. Which I won't. I'm flying. I don't know if I like planes very much. So many people and so many germs and not enough space, but my doctor gave me a pill that's supposed to help keep me calm on the plane."

"Do you have an iPod? If you listen to music on the plane it'll keep you busy, distracted from all those people."

Matt hadn't even thought of that. It was an excellent idea. He pulled out his notebook and wrote it down. "Good," he said. "What else would help?"

Susan pointed at the notebook. "That. Write down everything interesting you see. Then when we talk on the phone you can read it to me." The sun coming in the window lit up Susan's face in the nicest way.

"My parents live close to Cape Canaveral," Matt said. "Maybe

I could go to the Kennedy Space Center. Then I could tell you about it." He made a note about that in his notebook. Looking at his notebook reminded him of all the other things he had to tell Susan about. The waitress brought Susan her coffee and scone. Matt made a point of smiling at the waitress when she looked at him. "I stopped drinking. And taking the pills that were bad. I don't live with Spike anymore. I live with Lana now. And I'm painting again. Oh, and I'm on Wellbutrin now." The waitress turned and looked at Matt, so he smiled at her again. "It helps me with my impulse control. I haven't acted out in a while. And I can stop the thoughts before they come out. Sometimes. Usually. You're very pretty. Especially in this light. I wish I could do a painting of you just like this."

Susan laughed and was even prettier when she did. The waitress laughed, too, as she walked away. Matt could feel the happiness all around him. It got into his chest in a good way, pushing aside all of the anxious feelings until all he felt was good.

"Do you have a boyfriend?" Matt asked Susan.

"I told you I'm single," Susan said.

"That was three days ago," Matt said. "I want to know if you still are. You had a boyfriend after me, right? You could be back with him."

"I'm not back with him. He's too . . ." Susan sighed, looked out the window, squinted in the sun. "Moody. Dark. Unhappy. Unpredictable. It was exhausting." Susan turned back to Matt and smiled at him. "You look really good, Matt. I can see how much calmer and clearer you are now. Living with Lana must be good for you. Having someone to look after you a bit, help you out."

"We help each other out," Matt said. "I'm not unpredictable. Ever. Do you think you could be my girlfriend again?"

Susan blushed and laughed. "I like the thought of being friends again, for now. We'll see about the rest, okay?"

"*We'll see* usually means no," Matt said.

Susan tipped her head and studied him. "I don't mean no," she said.

"So you still like me?" Matt asked. He made it sound like a joke, but he wasn't joking.

"Of course I still like you," Susan said. "How could anyone not like you?"

And she meant it. When they said good-bye she kissed Matt. Most of her pink lipstick had come off on the coffee cup and she'd wiped the rest off with a napkin. Her lips were soft and even though she tasted like coffee Matt didn't want the kiss to end.

Matt was so happy after meeting with Susan that he stopped feeling nervous about flying. The kids were excited and Lana was anxious, but Matt took his pill and listened to his music and wrote in his notebook until he fell asleep. When he woke up the plane was already descending. He'd filled his notebook with so many thoughts and he couldn't wait to share them with Susan.

Matt's parents met them at the baggage claim.

"Oh, how lovely you all look," Gloria said. "You kids are nearly grown." She hugged all of them, even Matt, but she did the arm hug without hands, like Susan. So she remembered. Gloria looked older. And shorter. She was skinnier around the shoulders but she had a new roll of padding around her middle. Matt's dad, Jack, was fatter, in his face as well as his body. His head and neck had merged into one solid thing. Both of them had thinner, whiter hair and more wrinkles.

"Do you use sunscreen?" Matt asked. Florida was very sunny, and that was bad for wrinkles. They laughed and everyone started talking at once. Matt turned to watch for the luggage. He liked watching each suitcase slide down the ramp onto the carousel, guessing which way it would fall, which person each item belonged to.

They took two cars back home and Matt was in his dad's car, which was the slow one. Jack was too busy talking to pay much attention to driving. He stayed in the slow lane and talked to Byron in the rearview mirror the whole drive. When they made it to the house, Gloria, Lana, and Abby were already in the kitchen making food.

"I didn't know what everyone would want, so I just got a little of everything and figured we could make our own sandwiches," Gloria said. Byron made two huge sandwiches. Abby used the fix-ings to make a salad. Jack stood there commenting on everyone's food choices. Matt got the English muffins out of his suitcase and made one for himself. He could feel Gloria watching him while she talked to Lana about the flight, the week's plans, the weather. "He's so different," she said.

"I told you," Lana said. "Amazing what a stable environment, clean living, and meds will do."

"Yes, but where's his sparkle?" Gloria asked. "He's lost it."

"Oh, Mom," Lana said. "Really?"

Gloria helped Matt set up his bed in the guest room. He was going to sleep in the bed and Byron was going to sleep on the floor on an air bed. Matt didn't like sharing a room but there wasn't a choice. At least he wasn't in the living room like Abby and Lana.

"It's very crowded in here," Matt said. "Six people and only two bedrooms."

"At least there's two bathrooms," Gloria said. "Are you sure you're okay here? It's a big change, and I know change can be hard for you."

"I've had a lot of changes lately," Matt said. "I had my first hospital stay. I didn't like it. And I moved in with Lana. That's a good change. And no more Spike or drinking or pills. And I got to know Abby and Byron. I lost my driver's license and got it back. I'm painting again. I know what parkour is. And Vizslas. And I have so much data in my notebooks that I had to get a whole pack of them. Lana got them from Costco. I have twenty blank notebooks now. All blue and green covers, with yellow lined paper. I can't wait to fill them up."

Gloria was sitting on the bed staring at Matt. She patted the bed next to her and he sat down near her.

"I'm sorry it's been so long since I've seen you," she said.

"I know you don't like to travel. I don't, either. We live so far apart."

"You seem very calm. So different from before. Do you like it? The way the medication slows you down?"

"I have a fast-processing brain," Matt told her. "Even on the Wellbutrin. I can still think about several things at once. I mean, I can't not think about several things at once. I like that I don't feel that feeling anymore." He rubbed his chest, mimicked an explosion coming from within it.

Gloria nodded. She was the one who'd called it *that feeling*. When he was a kid she'd see him starting to squirm and she'd say, "Matt, are you having that feeling again?" And if he was, she'd clear the room of other people and start moving fragile objects away from him. A few times he'd hurt her. Hit her with fists or heavy objects, drove her from the room because he didn't know what to do with the feeling.

"I'm sorry that I hurt you. When I was having my episodes. I didn't mean to."

"Oh, I know that," she said. She smiled at him and held her hand out. Matt took his time. He touched each one of her fingertips. They were dry and cool to the touch. He pinched each nail until the skin beneath it blanched white, then watched the pink return. He touched the back of her hand, traced a thick blue vein from her middle finger to the back of her wrist. He turned her hand over and traced the lines on her palm. He'd spent hours doing it when he was a kid. He didn't like to be held or hugged. But he could do this. When he was touching her it didn't hurt him. He finished tracing every interesting line on her hand and when he looked up she was smiling with tears in her eyes.

"I missed you, my baby boy," she said.

"There are a lot more lines now," he said, pointing to her hand.

Gloria laughed. "Don't I know it."

They were all tired from their trip and went to bed on Florida time even though technically their bodies were still on California time. When Matt woke up he heard a new female voice coming from the kitchen. Not Abby. Not Lana. Not Gloria. He didn't want more company. There were too many bodies already crammed into Jack and Gloria's two-bedroom condo. But when Matt looked in the kitchen, it was his sister Becca sitting there drinking coffee.

"Morning, baby brother," she said, smiling. "Surprise!"

It was a good surprise. Becca was wearing a long flowered sundress and lots of sparkly crystal jewelry. She had no shoes on and when she stood she only came up to Matt's chest.

"You're so short," he said. "I forgot how short you are."

"Petite," Becca said. "And don't forget that if it weren't for us short folk you and Lana wouldn't be tall, you'd just be average."

It was what Becca had always said, and it made Matt laugh. "Mom is getting shorter. Soon you'll be the same size," Matt said.

"Hey," Gloria said. "No fair picking on the little people. Can I make your English muffin?"

Matt nodded and sat next to Becca. She looked at him for a while and smiled. "You look so good, Mattie." She had tears in her eyes when she said it.

"Clean living," Matt said, quoting Lana. Becca laughed hard. She wiped her eyes and leaned over until her temple was resting very lightly on Matt's shoulder. He put his arm around her and let it rest there. A flash went off, startling Matt.

"Gotcha!" Jack said from the doorway. He was holding his camera.

"Who let him have that thing?" Becca said. "He can't be trusted with it."

"I have all of my kids and grandkids together. I want to record it for posterity."

"You mean blackmail," Becca said. Jack laughed and came over to show the pictures he'd taken of Abby and Byron sleeping, of Lana on the phone out back, of Becca coming through the front door, mouth open, saying something. "Delete," she said.

Matt ate his English muffin while everyone around him talked. He didn't want to leave the sunny room full of his family, even when the noise got too much. He got his iPod, put on some Hawaiian slack-key guitar music that Susan had given him, and sat back down. The music was very soothing. Matt had never been to Hawaii. When he looked up everyone was smiling and looking at him. He took one of his earbuds out.

"You're still here," Lana said.

"I'm still here," Matt said. "Can we go to the Kennedy Space Center? I want to tell Susan about it."

"Who's Susan?" Jack asked.

"My friend. My ex-girlfriend. Hopefully my girlfriend again. I kissed her two days ago, so maybe she's my girlfriend again. I should ask. When I call her about the Kennedy Space Center I'll ask."

"Well, I'll be," Jack said. "Of course we can go. And then you call Susan and get to the bottom of this dating thing. I'm on pins and needles here."

"Oh, Jack, leave him alone," Gloria said. Then she just stood and stared at Matt for a while.

They spent several hours at the space center. Matt read every plaque and took notes for Susan. Byron and Abby took turns posing for pictures in front of the various displays. Gloria and Jack got tired fast and spent most of the day sitting on a bench. Lana and Becca talked and giggled the whole time. It was a good day.

As soon as they got home, Matt called Susan. He read her his whole list of interesting facts about the space program, but he forgot to ask her about being his girlfriend. He'd forgotten to write it in the notebook.

Becca gave Matt one of her meditation CDs to listen to at night, and at first it felt strange: having another person's voice in his head while he tried to sleep. The woman talked in a soft voice, with soothing music playing in the background. But as she talked about relaxing waves of light washing over Matt's body, starting with his feet and moving slowly up his body, relaxing every cell in his toes, arches, heels, ankles, calves, he must have drifted off. The waves of light never made it above his chest. He woke up with his iPod earbuds all tangled around him, but he had slept better than he had in a long time. He headed for the kitchen to tell Becca, but stopped before he made it to her. Something was different. He could feel it in the empty kitchen. Tension, coming in from the patio. He ate his English muffin at the kitchen table while Lana, Becca, and Gloria had coffee on the patio and talked. But they weren't just talking. They were too loud for that. Matt could hear them right through the glass.

"He's doing so well," Lana said. "We all are."

"He's a robot," Gloria said. "My vibrant, spirited boy is gone."

"Mom," Becca said. "He is loved and healthy: alcohol- and drug-free for the first time in decades. He's bonding with Abby and Byron. He's making huge strides."

"It hasn't been decades. He was drug-free when he was still living with me," Gloria said. "He didn't need medication. I managed him myself."

"He was self-medicating: drinking and smoking pot as early as high school," Lana said. "Maybe even before that. It started in his teens."

"Don't you go blaming me for his drinking," Gloria said.

"Nobody's blaming anyone," Becca said. "Let's focus on the positive. On how well he's doing."

"He's so different. Like a different person," Gloria said.

"He is different," Lana said. "He's a grown man, earning his own living, caring for himself. He's sober."

"He's all wrong," Gloria said.

"You're all wrong," Lana said. Becca tried to stop her but she kept going. "You have no idea what he needs. What makes him feel safe and happy. How Asperger's even works. You just dumped him in one school after another and left him to fend for himself. Left all of us to fend for ourselves. You didn't manage him. You ignored him."

"I loved and cared for all of my children. All four of them. I still do."

"Of course you do, Mom," Becca said.

"Just none quite as much as Stephen," Lana said.

They were quiet after that. Abby came in and looked from Matt to the three women on the patio through the closed sliding glass door.

"They're arguing about me," Matt said. "Lana thinks I'm better and Mom thinks I'm worse."

"What do you think?" Abby asked. She got a mango and sliced it into long thin pieces and ate them one by one.

"I think I like my new life," Matt said.

"I do, too," Abby said.

Matt opened the sliding glass door and looked at his mom and sisters. "I'm happy, Mom," he said. "You don't need to worry about me. It started when I was thirteen. The drinking and pot. And then I didn't know how to be without it. But now I do."

Gloria looked at him and didn't say anything. Jack came along with his coffee and nudged past Matt.

"Got room for an old fart out here?" Jack asked. He sat down and put his hand on Gloria's shoulder. She turned away. Matt didn't like the feeling. He wanted there to be something else, anything else, going on.

"What happened to those tadpoles?" he asked his parents. "The ones we caught and kept in the aquarium."

"Tadpoles?" Jack asked. "We're talking tadpoles now? What tadpoles?"

"They turned into frogs. I remember watching their legs grow. I was three or four. We caught them at the park, in the pond. Did we set them free? Did they die?"

Gloria and Jack looked at each other.

"Tell him," Lana said. "If you remember. He can take it."

Jack sighed and rubbed his big face. "One died, I'm afraid. I didn't want you to see it. Get upset. I set the rest free without you. I'm sorry about that."

Matt nodded. He felt better knowing. "I thought maybe they all died. So only one did? And the rest were okay?"

Jack nodded. "I saw them swim off myself."

"I bet the one that died was sick or something. I bet it would've died even in the wild. They might've all died in the wild. Of course, either way they're all dead now."

"See?" Lana said, smiling.

Gloria clucked her tongue and Jack burst out laughing. It was so loud Matt backed up, just inside the open sliding glass door.

"Are you okay, Mattie?" Gloria asked him. "Are you upset?"

"He's fine, Mom," Lana said. "That's what I'm telling you. No acting out. No episodes."

"I'm not upset. But I'm still hungry," Matt said. "I think I want another English muffin. And I want to go to Lake Jesup. They have hawks, eagles, ospreys, egrets, ibis, great blue herons, even alligators. I really want to see an alligator."

"Me, too," Abby said behind Matt.

"Abby wants to see an alligator," Matt said.

"Well, hot damn, let's go see an alligator, then," Jack said. He clapped his hands together and rubbed them, then rested a hand on Gloria's shoulder. She shook her head. Gloria stayed home when they went to Lake Jesup. And they did see alligators. Yellow-green reptile eyes peeking up out of the swampy water, and the ridges of their bumpy backs and long tails. They were just as fascinating as tadpoles. Matt couldn't wait to tell Susan about it.

31

Abby

Abby was all ready to head to the pool, but first she fetched the bag with Gabe's blue shirt inside. She opened it just enough to bury her face in it for a good long sniff.

"Do I want to know?" Byron asked behind her. He was wearing his swim trunks and had his goggles dangling from his hand.

"Nope," Abby said, laughing. She resealed the bag, fetched the oversized sun hat her grandma Gloria had loaned her, and followed Byron out.

She talked to Gabe every day, and they texted, sent pictures to each other, and emailed, but it still wasn't enough. She wanted to feel his warmth next to her. They were just getting started before having to spend a whole week apart. Who knew what could happen in a week? What if he forgot about her?

They'd exchanged shirts, straight off their bodies. Put on clean ones and stowed the worn ones in sealed freezer bags. Gabe's shirt smelled of lavender and his boyish scent. Abby had no idea what hers smelled like. She couldn't smell it, but Gabe said he could. He said she smelled like summer breezes and grassy fields.

"Maybe if you sleep in my shirt it'll make you dream of me," he said.

"I always dream of you," she told him. Sometimes they were

anxious dreams, where she couldn't find him in a crowd, or spotted him through a window kissing Caitlin, but she also had lots of good dreams, about snuggling up to him, his warm tan arms wrapped around her, his breath on her hair.

Abby didn't sleep in Gabe's shirt, because then it would smell like her instead of him. She just kept it in the bag and sniffed it a hundred times a day.

Abby settled on the deck chair with her book while Byron swam laps. The pool in her grandparents' retirement villa was nice, a great big oval with a rock waterfall on one end, and it was empty most of the time. Probably because the air was a thousand degrees in the middle of the day. Abby had borrowed her grandma's mister to take the edge off the heat. As it coated her in a fine, cooling spray, she filled out a postcard for Gabe. She sent him one every day. This one had a picture of the space shuttle. The whole family had gone to the Kennedy Space Center, because that's what Matt wanted to do. He was cool like that. He wanted to do fun stuff and not just sit around talking all day like Gloria or watching TV like Jack. They'd also gone to Lake Jesup and spotted some real live wild alligators. She had a postcard from there to send tomorrow.

Abby finished the postcard, gave up on the romance novel, and leaned back and closed her eyes. It was ridiculously hot, but at least out here it was peaceful. The condo was air-conditioned, but the air in there was tense. There was something going on between her mom and grandma, and Abby didn't want to be a part of it. For some reason Gloria was mad about Matt, that he was calm and happy and not all freaked out about things like the dead tadpole.

That night, on the phone with Jenny for their weekly appointment, shut into the guest room for the only privacy in the entire condo, Abby talked about it.

"And how are you dealing with the stressful environment?" Jenny asked.

"I'm getting nice and tan," Abby said.

"So you don't need to scream it out?"

Abby laughed and Jenny laughed with her. Was it strange to miss your therapist as much as your boyfriend?

"Are you running?"

"Nope," Abby said. "Too hot. I'm being a lazy beach bum. Pool bum. I read, lounge in the sun, I write in my journal, then I cool off by floating in the pool. I don't even swim laps. I'm a manatee."

"Why would you say manatee?" Jenny asked.

"Oh," Abby said. "That wasn't a fat comment. I just meant . . . they're peaceful and happy just being in the water, you know? At least they look happy in the pictures."

"So you're happy?"

"Yeah, mostly. It's different here. And I miss everyone back home. But it's just one week, right?"

It was nice to talk to Jenny, to keep their regular appointment, but doing it on the phone wasn't the same as sitting in Jenny's office. Abby missed the orange pillow that had been the object of her anger those first few sessions. Just sitting on Jenny's love seat every week reminded Abby of how far she'd come, how strong she really was. Abby worried that being thousands of miles away might undo some of the work she'd done on herself. She worried that just being around her bulimic grandmother might make it all come back.

"I don't think she's doing it anymore. My grandma. Throwing up."

"You've been watching her?"

"It's a small place. We're all on top of each other. She doesn't eat a whole lot, but she never disappears into the bathroom after meals. And it never smells like throw-up in there."

"You were thinking you might want to talk to her about her eating disorder. Do you think you still will?"

"I don't know. She talks all the time, but she doesn't seem that easy to talk to, you know?"

"Sometimes people need help opening up. Maybe you need to make the first move. But only if you feel it might help. If it's better not to think about it, then don't think about it."

As if Abby were able to turn off her thoughts about food. She thought about it all the time: how often she ate, how much she ate, how much she hated food in general. She wished there were a pill she could take that would give her the exact vitamins and protein she needed each day, so she'd never have to eat again, but she didn't want to tell Jenny that. Sometimes she still had trouble swallowing the food in her mouth, all chewed up and disgusting, like it was someone else's chewed food that Abby was expected to choke down. She still thought of food more as calories than nutrients. But she was doing her best.

The next day Abby ended up alone in the kitchen with Gloria. Abby had just come in from the pool and was drinking ice water to cool off. Gloria was drinking hot coffee, which seemed bizarre on such a horribly hot and humid afternoon. Abby thought about bringing up the family tradition of eating disorders, but didn't know how. Then Gloria kind of did it for her.

"Are you supposed to be eating?" Gloria asked her. "I can't keep up with all of the rules for each of you."

Abby laughed but Gloria didn't seem to be kidding. "Yeah, I guess I should have some lunch. Do we still have mango and strawberries?"

"I'm pretty sure your mother wouldn't consider fruit lunch," Gloria said.

Abby wondered why Gloria blamed Lana for everything, but it wasn't the sort of question she could ask. "Is there cottage cheese? I could put fruit on that," Abby said.

"Oh, that sounds good," Gloria said. "I'll join you."

They sliced fruit side by side, and sat down across from each other.

"So you know about my eating issues?" Abby asked.

"Your mom mentioned you were getting help. I guess that's what everyone does these days. It was different in my time. We toughed things out on our own. None of that paying people to listen to you whine."

It seemed hopeless, but Abby didn't want to give up on her grandma. "I don't whine to my therapist," Abby said. "But the first few sessions she had me scream out all of my feelings at a pillow." Abby laughed, speared a strawberry. It was delicious. The cottage cheese she had to will herself to eat, but the fruit went down without much effort. "Maybe that's more your kind of therapy?"

Gloria smiled. "Is that some new-age therapy technique?" she asked. "Screaming?"

Abby shrugged. "It helped. I think when we carry everything around inside, not just our own stuff but everyone else's, it gets too heavy, you know? It was a way of dumping all of that. She says we let go of the negative stuff and then fill the empty space inside ourselves up with positive things."

Gloria sipped her coffee. She hadn't touched her food. "Sounds like something Becca would say."

"Are you not hungry?" Abby asked.

"I'm never hungry. It's like my taste buds don't work right anymore. Nothing tastes good."

"I know the feeling."

Gloria took a bite of food, studying Abby's face. "Don't let them make you feel like there's something wrong with you," she said. "You're a beautiful, strong girl. Don't let anyone take that from you."

Abby smiled. She opened up her locket and showed it to Gloria, the teenage pictures of both of them, side by side. "Mom says I look just like you at the same age."

Gloria leaned forward and touched the necklace. Her hands were cold against Abby's skin. "There's definitely a resemblance." She shook her head. "But I was a timid thing at your age. There were so many boundaries for girls then. You have no such limitations. You can do anything."

Abby liked the sound of that. She wondered if that had something to do with Gloria's bulimia. That feeling of being trapped.

"So when exactly did your eating issues start?" Abby asked. "My age?"

"What eating issues?" Gloria asked.

"Oh. Um. I . . ." Abby had stepped in it now. She wasn't sure how to back out of it. But Jenny had told her she might have to make the first move. "Your bulimia."

Gloria flinched like she'd been slapped. "My what? Whatever made you think that I have an eating disorder?"

"Oh. I don't. Not now. I mean, I haven't seen anything. It's just that my mom mentioned that when she was a kid you—"

Gloria clucked and shook her head in disgust. "Your mom meddles too much in things that don't concern her," Gloria said. She rose from the table and put her bowl of food in the fridge. "I'm going to go lie down."

Abby had trouble finishing her own lunch after that. She ate the fruit, but that was the best she could do. She couldn't touch the cottage cheese. She set the bowl in the fridge next to Gloria's.

Abby ducked into the bathroom to change out of her swimsuit. She tried not to look at the mirror. She knew better. She just wanted to see her tan lines. The mirror was above the sink and Abby could only see her upper body in it. Unless she stood on the ledge of the tub. And that was her mistake. She not only saw her tan lines, she saw the fullness of her butt, the doughy spread of her thighs. The cellulite. It was back. She squeezed her flesh here and there, saw the dimples emerge, puckering her skin.

Abby eyed the toilet. It was a nasty thought. She hated throwing up. She'd had the stomach flu before, and there was nothing worse. Why would someone want to feel that terrible? She opened the toilet lid and leaned over. Toilets were just as disgusting as throwing up was, although Gloria had done a nice job cleaning hers. Abby stared into the bowl, the clear water, the possibility. She put her finger in her mouth, poked here and there, but nothing happened. She repositioned herself over the toilet, tried two fingers, reached farther back, jabbed until she gagged. Her whole body heaved upward, but no food came up, just the burn of bile in her lower esophagus. The dry heave hit like a punch to her gut. What the hell was she doing? This wasn't her. Abby emerged from the bathroom sweating, shaking. She felt dizzy and weak, like she needed to lie down, except she couldn't sit still. She called Jenny, got her voice mail.

"Help," she said. "I don't know how to do this." Abby hung up and waited. She paced the small living room, sat, resumed her old habit of flexing her abs, glutes, thighs, over and over. Byron was at the pool. Lana and Becca were out shopping. Gloria was napping. Matt was holed up in the guest room. Jack was wandering the condo grounds, visiting with various friends, a daily ritual for him.

Abby knew she shouldn't be alone, but who should she call? Her mom? What would that do? She'd probably just blame Gloria, and they were already fighting.

Abby called Celeste from the patio, paced in the stifling wet heat as she listened to the phone ring.

"Hey, Abs," Celeste said, light as a breeze. "How's manatee-land?"

Abby sobbed with relief. She wasn't alone. She wasn't totally lost.

"Oh, crap," Celeste said. "Hang on." She heard the rustling of fabric, muffled voices, the click of a door being shut. "Food, Gabe, or family?"

"Food," Abby hiccupped. "I don't know what happened. I was fine. And then . . ." Abby was crying too hard to finish.

"Yeah, okay," Celeste said. "Those setbacks are no joke. But here's the thing. You're stronger than this thing. You have no idea how strong you are. But I do. Okay? We'll get you back on track. What happened? Step by step."

"I went to the pool. I had lunch. I tried talking to my grandma. It was fine until I mentioned my mom. Then she just shut down."

"Some people don't want help," Celeste said. "Be glad you're in therapy, or that'd be you in sixty years."

Abby laughed. Celeste always knew what to say.

"And then I went to change in the bathroom. And the mirror was right there. So I got curious. You know, about how tan I'm getting."

"Uh-oh," Celeste said. "Is there a scale in that bathroom?"

"No. No scale. Just this little mirror that I can hardly see myself in. But I got up on the tub to see my back, and then I saw my thighs . . ." Abby started crying again.

"Yeah. I've been there. What you saw? That's the hardest part. That reprogramming. You and I have this skewed idea about what our own body looks like. We see other bodies and they look normal enough: skin covering muscles and bones. And we envy them, like they have something we don't. We see our own flesh and it's like a container of Crisco. But it's all wrong. We're looking in a funhouse mirror at ourselves. Seeing stuff that isn't even there."

"I tried making myself throw up," Abby said. "But I couldn't do it."

"Oh, Abby," Celeste said, with such kindness that Abby started sobbing again. She was crying so hard that she didn't hear Matt open the sliding glass door. She didn't know he was there until the box of Kleenex and glass of ice water appeared on the table before her. Matt sat with his sketch pad on his knee and worked on drawing alligator tails while Celeste finished her pep talk.

"You are strong. Beautiful. Brilliant. You are amazing. Nothing can stop you. Not even this. Setbacks will happen. But you keep fighting. And I'm right here with you."

"Okay. Thanks."

There was a stirring of voices around Celeste. Some group gathering in her midst. Abby said she was better, that Matt was with her, promised to check in later, and hung up. She blew her nose and drank the water.

"You tried throwing up?" Matt asked. So he'd heard the whole conversation. "Like my mom?"

"You know she did that?"

"Bulimia," Matt said. "Very unhealthy. The stomach acid erodes the enamel on your teeth." He pointed at his smile and Abby shuddered. "It's also very wasteful. Of the food."

Abby laughed and nodded. "All good reasons not to start," she said.

"I agree," Matt said. He returned to his notebook.

Abby sat with him, drinking the cold water to survive the heat, watching him sketch away, until she no longer felt so panicky. She closed her eyes and pictured little-girl Abby. She knelt before her, looked her squarely in the eye. *You are strong. You are beautiful. You are brilliant. You are amazing. Nothing can stop you. You are safe. I will protect you.*

She went inside and removed her necklace. She didn't want Gloria's face touching her body. It was like it was contagious. Or maybe just genetic. She got her lunch out of the fridge and sat down with it.

"You can do this," she said, scooping up a tiny bit of cottage cheese. She was staring her spoon down, still trying to get it to her mouth, when Gloria came into the kitchen for yet another cup of coffee. Gloria opened a drawer for a spoon, mixed creamer into her coffee. She pulled a tiny silver spoon out of the drawer, too. She held it out to Abby.

"This was your mother's. When she was a baby."

Abby took the spoon and stared at her reflection. She was upside down in the bowl of the spoon, right side up on the back of the spoon. Inside a funhouse mirror either way.

"It started with the baby weight," Gloria said. She sipped her coffee, added more creamer, stirred it again. "I was thin my whole life. Never had to think about it. Until I had Stephen. And then the others. Four babies so close together. I think my body just couldn't go back. I played tennis. I swam. I took Jazzercise. I dieted."

Gloria sat across from Abby. She held her cup in midair and stared off into space.

"When you hear your whole life how beautiful you are on the outside, I think it's hard to trust you're still beautiful on the inside, once the body changes."

"Do you still do it?" Abby asked.

Gloria rolled her eyes and gestured at her own body. "Clearly not."

"But you're beautiful, Grandma. Without it."

Gloria's eyes shone with tears and she dabbed them with a napkin. "And so are you. Inside and out. So smart. Such a good heart. This stuff is . . ." She gestured toward Abby's bowl. "Neither the problem nor the solution."

"The problem is that we don't love ourselves as we are. One solution is listing all of the things you love about yourself, every single day."

"Your therapist's idea?" Gloria asked. Abby nodded.

"I like my teeth," Abby said. "They are straight and white."

Gloria laughed and picked up the baby spoon, looking at her reflection in it. "I like my eye color. Blue-gray."

Abby took a bite of cottage cheese. "I like my hands. The long fingers."

Gloria got her bowl from the fridge and took a bite of her food with the baby spoon. "I like my toes. I've always had good toes." She kicked off her shoe and waggled her bare foot at Abby.

"I like my speed and strength on the field."

"I like my grace on the dance floor."

Matt came in with a newspaper tucked under his arm and rifled through drawers until he found tape, then left the room. Abby raised her eyebrows at Gloria and they laughed together.

"I like my wacky family," Abby said.

"I adore my granddaughter," Gloria said. She picked up Abby's necklace from the table, pooled the chain into the palm of her hand, and looked at the photos in the locket. "We could be twins."

"Can you help me put it back on?" Abby asked. She lifted her hair as Gloria laid the necklace around her throat and gently did the clasp.

When Abby went to the bathroom later she found the mirror covered with newspaper, taped down with enough tape to withstand a hurricane. Matt was in his room, drawing in his journal.

"Thank you. For the mirror," she told him.

"We're all on vacation," he said. "We shouldn't care what we look like anyway."

32

Byron

Two things sucked about Florida: the hot sticky weather, and there was no Betsy. Aside from that the trip was fine. Byron's grandpa Jack liked to call him "son," and used words like "strapping" to describe him. It was hilarious. Jack was funny, loud, and not the least bit concerned with whether or not anyone was actually listening when he talked. He had a comment on everything. If a breeze blew outside, it'd take him three seconds to say: "See those palm trees swaying? Wind's picking up. Those fronds make a ruckus when they fall. Not to mention a huge mess."

No one could outtalk Jack. Jack read all of the mail out loud, even junk mail.

"Anyone need an oil change? Only fifteen dollars with this here coupon! Hell of a deal!"

Byron spent the first day setting up the webcam for his grandparents. His grandma Gloria said it was broken or something. It looked like they'd never even taken it out of the box. Byron got it working on the first try. That way they could use it to video-chat with Matt later, and Byron could use it to chat with Betsy during his week in Florida. Except the only computer Betsy had access to with a camera was Tilly's laptop, so every time Byron tried calling, he just ended up trapped in a video chat with Tilly about neighborhood gossip.

Becca also showed up for a surprise visit, which made the whole week better. She was artsy and laid-back and talked about things like manifesting abundance and spirit guides and drove Jack and Gloria crazy with it. And Becca always brought gifts for everyone. Byron got a set of pencils, a sketch pad, and a bunch of T-shirts. The clothes were all super-cool: retro styles, faded colors, old logos.

"Are those used clothes?" Gloria asked, horrified.

"They are. Preworn to soft perfection," Becca said. "Recycle and reuse, Mom."

Gloria left the room shaking her head and Becca laughed. She was so sure of herself. Byron guessed with a cold mom like Gloria and a bizarre brother like Matt, Becca had just given up trying to be anyone other than who she was. Byron drew her a sketch of a seated Buddha with flowers all around and a huge pointed crystal in one hand. Becca hugged him and swayed like there was music going, which there wasn't.

"I hope you recognize your gift, Byron. Don't let anyone diminish it. Not by shaming you or commercializing you. You're going to do great things. Ask the universe for truth to come through your art. You'll be unstoppable."

Unstoppable wasn't a word anyone had ever used to describe Byron before. His aunt Becca was nutty, but she was so encouraging it was impossible not to like her.

"You think so?" Byron asked. He liked the sound of doing great things. Maybe he'd even be famous someday. He pictured himself up on a stage accepting a prize. Did they give out prizes for artists? Big ones, like Oscars? He sure hoped so.

"You're channeling your higher self through your art. It's all there." She pointed from Byron's heart to his head, to a space above his head. "You've got so much work to do. So much to teach us. You better rest up." She smiled and hugged Byron again. She left him with a funny feeling of possibility. Of hunger. Of impatience to find out what would come next. He spent the rest of the day sketching, waiting to see what messages the universe had for him. Apparently they were about lush green landscapes, space shuttles, alligators, and Betsy. Byron reviewed his entire sketchbook with a more critical eye and wasn't satisfied with much in there. It wasn't world-changing, that was for sure.

Then he watched Matt sketch a whole series of alligator tails. Matt worked on every ridge, every shadow, every ripple in the water until he liked what he'd drawn. And then Byron felt better. Surely he needed to get his skills up before the universe started beaming wisdom down to him. He had his art classes coming up the week after they got home. That was a start.

Byron tried to balance his days between art and keeping up his parkour skills. The retirement villa grounds had thick spongy lawns for soft landings, low-hanging branches, and plenty of stone benches for trying new moves. The rest of the day he spent sketching, swimming, watching TV with his grandpa, and texting Betsy.

Every time Byron's phone dinged for a new text, Jack would yell, "Heart line! Another message from the girlfriend! Man, she's a loquacious one, isn't she?"

Jack was a lawyer and liked big words. He also did the *New York Times* crossword puzzle every day, in pen. He was retired, but he was still a lawyer, always wanting to argue about something or prove some point even when the people around him already agreed with him.

"You see, the thing is that nobody in Washington wants to live under the same laws they pass for the rest of us! Governed by the people, my ass. That's the elite in charge there. Put them all on Medicare, Social Security, and those systems would be fixed in six weeks."

"I know, Dad," Lana would say. But Jack would just keep spouting his theories anyway, like she'd just disagreed with him.

One day, out of sheer boredom, Byron made the mistake of doing parkour in the full sun of the afternoon, when the air was so swampy it was like breathing steam. He came in red-faced and hyperventilating, dripping sweat all over his grandma's nice white carpet, and headed straight for the kitchen. He mopped up his face with a wad of paper towels and guzzled a bottle of water. Jack came into the kitchen, looked Byron over, and shook his head. He got two beer bottles from the fridge, opened them both, and set one on the counter next to Byron.

"Man's work deserves a man's drink," Jack said. Byron knew his mom would kill him if he drank it, but hadn't she always taught him to politely accept whatever a host offered him? She said even if you don't like what they make for dinner, you have to eat it anyway. Was this any different? Byron checked the doorway before taking a quick swig of the beer. Jack laughed and grabbed his belly like Santa, then gave Byron a hard smack on the back that almost made Byron drop the beer.

"I'll be the lookout!" Jack said. He scampered to the dining room, where he hunched over, hands on his knees, looking in every direction. He really hammed it up, like he did everything. "All clear!" he said, looking around with his hand shading his eyes like some soldier on patrol. "Drink fast!" Byron was laughing so hard he could barely drink. He couldn't wait to tell Betsy about it. He didn't remember his grandpa very well from their last visit, but he definitely wasn't cool and funny before. Maybe that was a retirement thing. Or an old age one.

Matt came in and sort of eyed the beer. Byron hoped he wouldn't tell on him. Then Byron remembered that Matt had had a drinking problem, and figured drinking in front of him was a bad idea.

"Grandpa gave it to me. I just—"

"No apologies there, son!" Jack said. "Matt, you want a beer?"

"No, I'm not allowed. It's bad for my liver. And it can cause seizures if I drink while on my medication."

"Yeah, okay, got it. Here, have a Coke, then. You like these, right?" Jack pulled a can of Coke from the fridge and handed it to Matt.

Matt took the Coke and looked at it like he'd never actually touched one before. "Mom never let me have Coke. She said it made me too hyper."

Jack nodded, leaned in close to Matt. "It'll be our secret," Jack said. They watched as Matt opened the can, flinched from the hiss and snap of the metal popping free, sniffed the carbonated syrup, and laughed. It was like watching an alien creature discovering something earthly for the first time. Byron was laughing before Matt even took a sip. Matt took a swig, made a face, but then he smiled.

"Good stuff, right?" Jack asked.

"Good stuff," Matt said. "Did you know the carbonic acid in Coke can take rust off chrome?"

"I know it goes perfectly with Jack Daniel's," Jack said, laughing. "So you like living with your sister Lana there in San Diego?" Jack slowed down every syllable in *Diego* as he said it: *dee aye go*, like it was three words and not one.

"I have a nice room. And a weighted blanket. Blue. And blackout curtains. They're red, not blue, but they help keep the sun out. I'd rather have blue."

"Blue-out curtains," Jack said. He and Matt laughed together. They looked a bit alike when they laughed: they had the same way of squinting their eyes and showing all of their teeth. A little airplane engine whined overhead and Jack looked up toward the ceiling. "Cessna?"

Matt stopped sipping his Coke to listen. He nodded. He gave a brief lesson on the various Cessna models. He preferred the small, sleek, carbon-fiber composite Corvalis model. Jack asked a stream of questions about engine types and body shapes and lift and drag and Byron was so bored he didn't listen to the answers, but he liked watching Matt and Jack interact. He could see how much Jack liked Matt's brain: the fact-memorizing part. They were a bit alike like that. But total opposites in the talking part. When Matt was done with the airplane lesson it was silent for a whole second, and Jack never let it get quiet.

"So, what was the Susan verdict?" Jack asked. "Do we have a girlfriend or don't we?"

Matt got up and left the room, leaving his soda on the table.

"Something I said?" Jack asked, and he and Byron laughed together. Jack was like a stand-up comedian. And the beer probably helped. Byron put his beer next to the Coke, so that if someone came in, they'd think the Coke was his. "Just don't ever drink and drive," Jack said, pointing at the beer. "No joking. I've seen some cases . . . people's entire lives ruined. Careers, marriages, dreams ended on a single night from one bad choice. Got it? We're not just talking sky-high insurance rates. We're talking jail time."

"Got it," Byron said. The stand-up comedian was gone and Jack was back to being a lawyer. Then Matt returned and Jack perked back up.

"Susan says yes," Matt said. "She'll be my girlfriend again, if we take it slow." He sat down and took a long swallow of Coke. "I think that means no sex yet."

Byron choked on his beer and Jack howled with laughter.

"Oh, I know that drill," Jack said. "Good ones play hard to get a bit. She wants to see your heart before she sees your . . ." Jack pointed at his lap and laughed as Byron sputtered again. Matt smiled and drank his Coke. "Son, am I making you uncomfortable?" Jack asked Byron. "If so, you're too damn sheltered."

"No, sir," Byron said. "I'm fine with it. I like it."

"Good, good. But I'm no sir. I work for a living. Or did, from fifteen years old until those bastards forced me to retire last year. That's sixty-one years working nonstop. Now I'm just Grandpa Jack. Got it?"

Byron did the math. "Wait, that means you're seventy-seven? How's that possible?"

Jack laughed good and hard. "I know, right? I don't look a day over seventy-six!"

The next morning Matt came out with Byron early for his parkour session, to videotape it and give him suggestions. Byron did some of his best stunts, finally acclimated to the Florida weather. The heat wasn't so unbearable first thing in the morning, and the freshly watered grass was refreshing to land on, if a little slippery.

After that Byron jumped into the pool to cool off. The house was air-conditioned, but it felt stuffy in there, too many bodies for too little space, and the tension between Lana and Gloria sucked up what little air there was.

Byron swam a few laps, long slow strokes pulling him along in the muted underwater world. He was thinking about heading home, looking forward to seeing Betsy, of course, but also to hanging out with Gabe more. Gabe was a senior now, and not a bad guy to be in with when school started back up.

After Byron got out of the pool he sent one of his best parkour videos to Gabe. Then he remembered how Trent accused him of dumping him, first for Dale, then for Betsy, and then for Gabe. He'd already sent the video to both Dale and Betsy. So he sent the video to Trent, too. He could see how being popular was a lot more work than being nobody. He showed the video to Jack, too, who was every bit as impressed as Byron had hoped.

"Did you see this, Glo?" Jack shouted toward their bedroom, where Gloria was lying down for her daily rest. "Our grandson here is gravity-defying!"

Jack offered Byron another beer, and he took it, because Lana and Becca were out shopping. Abby caught him drinking and rolled her eyes, but Byron knew she wouldn't say anything. They were friends now. And at least he'd finally quit smoking for real. Smoking was worse, right? Byron took a picture of himself with the beer and sent it to Betsy. She always looked so sexy and sure of herself in the photos she sent him, and Byron wanted to look cool enough to have a girlfriend like that. In most of his pictures he looked like a loser sixteen-year-old with a huge acne blotch on his forehead and a lame look on his face.

Behave yourself, Betsy wrote back. Then Byron remembered the frat parties where everyone was wasted and she'd slept with guys she was too drunk to remember the names of. Guys who were too drunk to care how they treated a girl. He went to the kitchen and poured out the rest of the beer. He was drinking a Coke when Lana and Becca came back, giggling and carrying shopping bags.

"We were wondering if we should brave Disney World before we head home," Lana said.

Byron shrugged. He was too old for Disney World, but what else was there to do?

Gloria came in from her nap for a cup of coffee. She drank hot coffee all day long. She and Lana kind of squared off, so Byron tried to break up the tension.

"Grandma, we were talking about going to Disney World. You in?"

"Matt can't handle Disney World. I'll stay here with him," Gloria said.

"Oh, stop it, Mom," Lana said. "It's a little late to play the protective parent."

"Both of you stop, okay?" Becca said. She stood between them, which was useless, because she was so short they could still glare at each other right over her head.

"She woke him up at six this morning," Lana said. "We've been working for months to regulate his sleep cycle, and she decides to get him up a couple of hours early for no reason. First denies him the sleep he needs, then tells him to stop taking his melatonin."

Becca turned and looked at Gloria. Gloria just sipped her coffee, staring right at them both. It was like a fuse had been lit. And in a few seconds the bomb was going to go off.

Byron grabbed his phone and Coke and left the room. He didn't need to be a part of whatever was unfolding in there. He needed to call Betsy. To tell her he wasn't a drinker, never would be. She answered on the first ring.

"Hey, babe," she said.

"I poured the beer out," he said.

"Why?"

"Because I love you. I'm not going to drink around you."

"But you aren't around me," she said, laughing, but he could hear the relief in her voice. "And I love you, too."

33

Lana

"I'm just a chicken," Lana said to Becca. "I keep telling Abby how brave and strong she is. I praise Byron for coming into his own. Turns out I'm the scaredy-cat."

They were back at the mall, their favorite retreat. It was teeming with scantily clad teenage girls and aloof boys in low-slung jeans, but it was air-conditioned, there was food, and they could spend hours window-shopping to avoid their parents' condo.

"You're just a normal human being," Becca said. "Recently heartbroken and afraid of getting hurt again."

"But I don't feel afraid of Abbot. At all."

Lana had been avoiding Abbot ever since he told her he loved her. It was a childish response and made no sense. Hadn't she wanted love in her life again? Lana wasn't sure how to remedy the problem, because she wasn't sure what the problem was.

"You're not afraid of Abbot," Becca said. "You're afraid of opening your heart up and getting hurt again."

"Oh, here's the solution right here." Lana paused by the cookie counter, inhaled the fresh-baked chocolate chip aroma deeply. Becca laughed and nudged her along.

"We better get back for lunch," Becca said. Lana sighed. She wanted to check on her kids and Matt, but she felt no desire to see her parents. Which made her feel just as guilty as leaving Abbot's proclamation of love hanging in the air, just a blue trail of fear streaking across the country from San Diego to Sanford in response.

Being in such close quarters with her parents, now visibly slower and more frail, made Lana edgy. Gloria's memory of the distant past seemed to be slipping. She went through old photo albums by the armload, asking Lana and Becca to fill in the gaps.

"Remember the time we went to Yosemite, and it snowed, and we couldn't leave?" Gloria asked. "When was that? Easter?"

"Christmas break. But it wasn't Yosemite," Lana said. "It was Tahoe."

"Yeah," Becca said. "North shore, right? At that cabin we borrowed from Dad's friends. That woodsy place with the rats in the attic."

"The Stillmans," Jack said. "Nice people. You know their son is gay? You remember the crush you had on him, Becca? Turns out you never stood a chance."

Becca, Lana, and Jack laughed, but Gloria was displeased, a wrinkle of unhappiness forming between her eyes.

"I'm sure it was Yosemite," she said, returning to the photo album. Gloria, always proper and polite to a fault, had recently become impossibly stubborn.

Lana mentioned it to her dad and he just shrugged. "She's had her share of hardships. Some recent health challenges. She's got a little fight left in her, and I think that's a good thing."

Jack, on the other hand, was having trouble retaining the present. He was starting to repeat himself. He'd always had a flare for the dramatic, a lawyer's courtroom air about him, posturing and pontificating with the best of them. But he asked three times what Lana's plans were for summer, and three times she explained that she was running the summer school's reading lab. Each time he regarded it like new information. Lana wondered how much he was retaining.

"You'll keep an eye on them, right?" she said to Becca. "Seems fair. I have Matt."

"Nothing fair about that deal in the least," Becca said. "But yes, I'll look after them."

Lana handed Matt his Wellbutrin pill at breakfast the next morning. He studied it in his palm before swallowing it with milk.

"I feel slower now," Matt said. "On the meds. I thought that was a good thing. I have a fast-processing brain, you know. Maybe too fast. But maybe it's too slow now."

"Where's this coming from?" Lana asked. "Did you want to try a different medication? Are you having side effects?" There were a ton of frightening possible side effects for every medication they'd considered for Matt. Lana had just hoped he'd have a high tolerance after his long history of self-medication.

"Mom said I might be better off without it."

Lana braced for battle. She found Gloria in her bathroom, freshly showered, wearing a pink terry-cloth robe, holding the hair dryer aloft in her left hand and a brush in her right hand. Gloria deftly lifted her thin hair up and away from her scalp in practiced strokes as if she were blow-drying it, but the hair dryer wasn't on. Lana's anger subsided in a wave of confusion. What was Gloria doing, pointing a sleeping hair dryer at her head?

"Mom," Lana said. "Is everything okay?"

Gloria lowered her spiky round brush and looked at Lana in the mirror. "Are you and Becca going to the store? We need paper towels. And creamer."

Lana nodded and waited, watching. Gloria set down the hair dryer, touched her hair, and seemed perplexed to find it still wet. She started the process again, this time with the hair dryer blasting appropriately.

Lana didn't mention the scene to Becca. There was something intimate about it, too personal to share. And something alarming that Lana wasn't ready to face. She also swallowed the anger about Matt. They were leaving in three days. He'd be out of Gloria's grasp soon enough. How much damage could she do in three days?

But the whole scenario made her miss easygoing and doting

Abbot. She wanted to call him to complain, to get advice, to hear the way he said, "Lana, dear, that's the pits." But first she needed to get past the hurdle of words, or to be able to explain to him why it was a hurdle for her at all.

Lana sat with Matt as he ate breakfast and wrote in his journal. She drank her coffee and tried to figure out what was wrong with her. Why life had to be so complicated. How she could be forty-four years old and still not have a clue what she was doing. For all the times people had thought Matt had insurmountable issues, maybe he actually had a better grasp on happiness than the rest of them: eat only foods that you love and in reasonable portions, worship and record beauty whenever you see it, spend all day learning new things, work hard when you work, stay organized, and never get pulled into other people's drama.

Lana gave in and called Abbot. "It's time to discuss the elephant," she said.

"Scared the hell out of you, didn't I?" he said. "Not my intention." Lana laughed and felt the bubbles of anxiety dissipate. Really, there were so many things to fear in the world. Love shouldn't be one of them.

"Yes and no. It was exactly what I wanted to hear, the same thing I'd been thinking myself, and yet it just . . ."

"Scared the hell out of you." He chuckled.

"I guess so. Sorry."

"No worries. I get it, trust me. I've been single a lot longer than you. I'm a little more ready for this than you are."

"I want to be ready," Lana told him.

"I'll wait until you are," he said. "Don't rush on my account."

The visit was winding down, the kids bonding nicely with their grandparents, which Lana had wanted. She had to remind herself of this fact as she watched Jack dote on Byron, heard him call Byron "son" repeatedly, while barely acknowledging his actual son, sitting right in the same room sketching his alligators and tadpoles.

Lana handed Matt his melatonin before bed that night, and

Gloria put her hand out to stop Matt from taking it. It was the third time she'd interfered with Matt's medication.

"Enough," Lana said. She pushed Gloria's hand aside and handed the pill to Matt. "He needs this to sleep."

"He needs to live and laugh and be happy and silly," Gloria said. "You're muting the best parts of him with these drugs. You remember how happy he used to be?" Gloria looked from Matt to Jack. "With those dances? You remember how he would make up tap dances with Kleenex boxes on his feet?"

"Mom," Lana said, shaking her head. "That was Stephen. Mocking Becca's tap class. Matt was only a baby then, not even walking yet. You're thinking of Stephen."

"I was here with him all day, every day. I know my own child!" Gloria shouted.

"No, you weren't," Lana said. "You were home with Stephen. But you weren't home with Matt. The Masons watched him for you. Then that church day care. Then the Montessori preschool. Then the YMCA. Then the Eastman Academy. You stuck him in one place after another, anything to avoid caring for him yourself."

"Okay, Lana," Jack said, stepping between them. "It was a hard time for all of us."

But Lana was all warmed up and couldn't back down. "I get it, that you lost a child. I know how hard that must've been. But you had three more kids. And you just quit on us. Both of you. Dad, you worked twelve-hour days, and Mom, you just . . . disappeared. Volunteering and exercising and puking your guts out four times a day to fool the world into thinking you were fine. But you weren't fine. None of us were."

"You think you're any better?" Gloria asked. "You drug your brother, your daughter's starving herself, your son is already drinking, and you think you're better than me?"

"What?" Lana snapped, turning to face Byron. Byron held up his hands, shook his head.

"Now, now," Jack said. "This is getting out of hand. Gloria, you should go get some rest. Hell, we all should. It's just about bedtime, and if we all get a good night's sleep—"

"Start packing," Lana said to Byron. "We're leaving."

"Of course you're going to blame me," Gloria said. "You always do."

"Stop it!" Abby yelled. "You're upsetting Matt."

Lana turned, and there was Matt, leaning back against the wall, holding his ears, rocking, coping the only way he knew how. He struck his ears with his fists once, twice. Swung his arms wide to do it again and Byron lunged for him, planted his palms on the wall over Matt's head, his elbows beside Matt's ears, so that Matt's blows landed on Byron's biceps. Matt pummeled harder, fighting to get to his skull through Byron's protective bubble.

"Hey, man," Byron said, gritting his teeth to fend Matt off. "It's okay. Let's get out of here. We can sketch in the bedroom. We can go outside and see some of those monster bugs."

Matt swung harder, wilder, struck Byron's shoulders, rib cage, flailing. Byron stood strong, refusing to let a single punch land on Matt's body. Lana tried to step in.

"I got it," Byron said. "He'll tire out."

"He's hurting you," Lana said. "It should be me."

Matt landed a punch hard near Byron's kidneys and Byron flinched, lost his footing. As he fell, Lana stepped forward, but Abby beat her to the spot. Abby got her arms around Matt, her hands in fists behind his shoulders. Matt's entire body shook, and Abby shook with him, but she didn't let go. She flopped around like a rag doll.

"What about calling Susan?" Abby asked. "Have you told her about the Vizsla? The Rainbow Girl? The picture we took together?"

Matt was tiring out, trying to shake Abby off, but unable to do so. He made a bleating noise as he pivoted his body repeatedly. He tried to face the wall, but Abby's body got in the way. He tried again and again, slamming Abby into the wall.

Lana wedged herself between Abby and Matt, eased Abby's arms from around his neck. Once free, Matt turned and struck his forehead on the wall. He planted his hands on the wall and drummed his head against it, like he had when he was four. A steady, even rhythm, knocking his brain about in his skull.

"It's okay, Matt. It's over," Lana said. Matt kept bumping the wall with his head. She put her mouth next to his ear, tried whispering a soothing "Shhhh," like she had to her kids when they were toddlers winding down from a tantrum. Matt started humming. Lana felt him coming back. "We still need to get you your ice cream. You didn't have it yet, right?"

Matt stopped hitting his head. He still had his forehead against the wall, but he twisted to look at Lana, peering at her sideways. He nodded slowly. "Yes," he said. "I still need my ice cream. Vanilla. With chocolate sauce."

"I'll get it," Becca said.

"No," Lana said. "I'd like to do it."

Lana glared at Gloria as she escorted Matt to the kitchen. He so rarely had episodes like this anymore, and this one was small compared to the ones he used to have. Surely she could see the meds were helping to curtail them? Gloria just shook her head at Lana, stubborn to the end.

Matt sat down at the kitchen table and continued rocking, ever so slightly, and humming a tune Lana couldn't place. He had a hard red lump forming on his forehead. She served him and then got herself a heaping bowl as well. To hell with the calories. She sat across from Matt and watched him eat. Each bite seemed to soothe him a little more, until he wasn't rocking at all, just eating steady, perfectly measured bites.

"Their freezer is set too cold," he said. "The ice cream gets too hard." He held up the chunk of ice cream on his spoon to show her.

"Maybe they just have too much stuff crammed into the freezer. It doesn't run right when it's too full."

"I like your ice cream better," Matt said.

Lana smiled. "Me, too."

A few minutes later Byron came in, then Abby, then Becca. They all huddled around the too-small table and ate dessert in silence. Abby had fresh fruit with whipped cream on top. She took one bite, smiled at Lana, and nearly brought Lana to tears.

"I love you," Lana said to her. "My fierce little girl." Abby smiled and opened her mouth, baby-bird-style, to show Lana the pulverized food in there. It was something Abby had done as a child: disgusting and adorable at once. Lana covered Abby's mouth, but couldn't help smiling.

Byron was sweaty and disheveled, eating the remainder of the ice cream straight from the container. His muscles were still flexed, the tendons in his neck straining against his skin. Lana rubbed his shoulder. "We'll talk about the drinking later."

"I don't drink. She misunderstood," he said to his ice cream. "I swear."

"Okay. Good. Hey." Lana shook his tense shoulder until he looked at her. "I love you. And I'm crazy proud of you. The way you jumped in there to protect him." Byron lowered his shoulders, shoveled a heaping scoop of ice cream into his mouth, opened his mouth Abby-style to show Lana the melting ice cream in there.

"Disgusting," Lana said, smiling. Byron laughed so hard the ice cream rolled off his tongue and back into the container. He shrugged and scooped it back into his mouth. Everyone at the table groaned.

Lana locked eyes with Becca, who gave her a nod of approval. "You love me best, right?" Becca asked.

Lana snorted. "Despite the fact that your positivity is a royal pain in my ass, I mostly love you, yes," Lana told her.

Becca laughed. "I do what I can."

Lana turned to Matt. "I'm sorry I lost my temper, Matt. And—"

"I love you," Matt said quickly. He looked up and smiled, playful and happy, bright eyes flashing, the episode long gone. "I said it first."

"You did," Lana said. It was the first time she'd heard him say those words. She wondered what they meant to him. If he had any idea how much they meant to her.

Jack came in and took in the scene. "Your mother went to bed. She isn't feeling well," he said.

"Is she okay?" Lana asked. "For real?"

Jack came up behind Lana and stroked her hair. "We all do the best we can with what we've got." He kissed her head, bade them all good night, and went off to bed.

One by one the rest followed suit until only Lana and Becca were left, loading the ice-cream dishes into the dishwasher.

"I know it's hard, but you have to forgive them," Becca said.

"The hell I do. That'd be basically telling them it was okay to forget about us."

Becca leaned against the counter, blocking the dishwasher until Lana met her eyes. "No, it isn't. In my first session, my Reiki healer told me: forgiveness isn't forgetting, it's just saying, *Here, this is yours, and I will no longer carry it.* Think about that."

Lana sighed and settled at the table. She rested her cheek in her palm, her elbow on the sticky surface. "It is too much to carry."

"So let it go. Drop the burden of other people's shortcomings. Stop trying to fix them. That's their job. Yours is to take care of you and those kids and be happy."

Lana rolled her eyes. She loved Becca and her metaphysical spin on everything. And deep down she knew Becca was right. But anger had been Lana's only comfort for all those lonely years in her childhood. In her marriage. "Next you'll be telling me to forgive Graham." Becca shrugged and Lana shook her head. "Why should I?"

"Ironic that you're so pissed at Dad for working twelve-hour days, putting his job ahead of family, but you married a man who is the exact same way. Until you forgive Mom and Dad, you'll just keep creating the same scenario. I'm having to learn this, too."

Lana buried her face in her hands. "Why does healing have to be so damn hard? I'm not sure I have it in me."

"He is able who thinks he is able," Becca said.

"Is that your Reiki lady, too?"

"Close. Buddha."

The next morning Lana rose early. She and Becca did yoga out on the mossy lawn, deep-breathing themselves back to center. When they came in Gloria was up, drinking her coffee. Becca headed for a shower, giving them a moment alone.

"Okay," Lana said, sitting next to her mother. "I'll mention your concerns to Matt's doctor and see what he has to say. There may be milder meds to consider."

Gloria took a slow sip of coffee. "No. You're right. He's better on the medication. Those episodes . . . nobody should have to feel that much. If it helps him, even a little, to not go to that scary place anymore . . ."

"Okay. Thank you," Lana said. "I do talk to his doctor, though. And Matt. We are monitoring the side effects. If the bad ever outweighs the good, we'll take him off the meds in a heartbeat. Nobody's saying they're forever. We're transitioning him from self-medicating with drugs and alcohol to being happy and in control sober. The meds seem to be helping for now. But they're only part of the solution. We're finding ways to help him sleep better, eat healthier, keep his mind busy. He's not all wired and amped up anymore, if you want to call that his 'sparkle,' but he is happy. It's working."

Gloria nodded, stirred her coffee, her thoughts clearly elsewhere. "It should've been me," Gloria said. "To get him sober. To start him on medication. To stop the episodes. What kind of mother can't even keep her own child calm? Make him happy?"

Lana shook her head. "There's a learning curve with Asperger's. You were flying blind. We know so much more about it now than we did when Matt was a kid. You did the best you could with what you had."

Gloria studied her spoon and shook her head. "You don't really think so. You think I failed him."

Lana took a deep breath, released it with a sigh, visualized a lifetime's worth of emotions pouring out of her body and draining down through the floor, back into the swampy earth below the condo. "I don't. I'm just pissed. I have decades of pent-up emotions I never expressed and they're all coming out now. I blame Graham."

"Not me?" Gloria said, batting her eyes playfully. "I thought it was always me."

"Not always." Lana smiled. "Look. About Stephen. I'm sorry. I know it was hard for you, but it was also terrifying for me. I was eleven. I was alone. I was sad, scared. Nothing felt safe anymore, like anything could be taken from me without warning. I lost my big brother. My idol. Then I felt like I lost my parents, too. I needed you guys to reassure me that it would all be okay, and . . ." Lana let a few tears fall. She hated crying. Especially in front of her stoic mother. She'd always felt weaker than Gloria: too emotional, too insecure. "But I forgive you. It's time. That child inside me is still hurting, still misses her big brother, still misses the house full of laughter that died along with him. But as a mother, I cannot imagine your pain." She touched Gloria's hand, surprised at the chill of it on such a warm day, the frailty of her mother's bony fingers, the dryness of her wrinkled skin. "I honestly don't know how you survived it. Losing a child."

"I didn't," Gloria said, staring at the table but gripping Lana's hand with surprising strength. "That was the problem. I think maybe after losing Stephen it seemed easier . . . not to get so attached." A single tear slid down Gloria's cheek. She was not one to cry, and it touched Lana to see her vulnerable. Gloria sighed. "You're a good mom. You have good kids. You're better at this than I was. Even with Matt." She shook her head. "Especially with Matt."

Lana put her arm around her mother's shoulders. "Thank you for saying that. Of course you're a hell of a lot better at marriage than I am, so you've got that going for you."

Gloria smiled. "Oh, don't beat yourself up about Graham. Never trust a man who spends that much time looking at himself in a mirror."

They laughed together. "He really does spend a lot of time primping."

"He doesn't know who he is," Gloria said.

"Do any of us?"

"Don't you?" Gloria asked. "I always thought you were the only one who did. College, marriage, kids, career. You're the only one of my children who managed to have it all."

"Too bad it didn't last," Lana said.

"You'll find love again. I have no doubt."

Lana squeezed her mother's shoulder, which was so much thinner than she remembered. Jack came in and found them sitting in silence, holding hands.

"Well, look at this," Jack said. "We should finally get a break from all this heat, because hell must surely be freezing over right now."

"Oh, Dad," Lana said. "You should know as well as anyone that this ridiculous heat is never letting up. You two should come out to San Diego to visit. It's seventy degrees year-round. Can't beat that."

"What do you think, Glo?" Jack asked. "Brave the perils of cross-country travel for this troublemaker of ours?"

Gloria tucked Lana's hair back behind her ears. She nodded. "I'd like to see all these paintings Byron and Matt keep talking about. And meet this boy who's stolen little Abby's heart."

"Don't forget that garrulous girlfriend of Byron's," Jack said. "My kinda girl."

Matt came into the kitchen, sleepy and quiet.

Gloria rose. "Take my seat here. I'll get your milk and English muffin. You take your medication with breakfast, right?"

"I do," Matt said. "I thought you didn't want me to take my pills anymore."

"I think maybe they are good for you after all," Gloria said. "I really just want what's best for you."

"Oh," Matt said. "Then can you put extra butter on the English muffin? I like lots of butter."

"Of course you do," Jack said. "What's the point of a smidge of butter? So if we come to California, will we get to meet this Susan of yours?"

Matt started on his generously buttered English muffin. He looked at the ceiling. "I think we should have another barbecue. Like when we all met Abbot. This time Susan will come. She said so."

"Wait a minute," Jack said. "Who exactly is Abbot?"

"My boyfriend," Lana said. The word sounded lumpy and ill-fitting. A teenage label for an adult relationship. But it made her smile like a schoolgirl, so maybe it wasn't far off.

"Well, I'll be damned," Jack said. "Look at you. Love lost. Love found. He's not another accountant, is he?"

Lana laughed. "No. He's in sales."

"Oh, lord," Jack said. "Gloria, talk to her, will you?"

Gloria put her hand on Lana's shoulder, kissed the top of her head. "She's just fine, Jack. You leave her be."

34

Matt

The barbecue was on a warm, sunny Sunday afternoon. Susan came just like she said she would. She wore a pale blue sundress and no lipstick.

"That's my favorite color," Matt said, pointing to the dress.

"I know." Susan laughed. "You like it?"

"I like the dress, and I like you," Matt said. Susan laughed and twirled for him. The happy feeling was so big in his chest that he felt dizzy. He had to sit down on the back steps. There were a lot of other people at the barbecue: Abbot, Gabe, Betsy, and some neighbors, but Matt and Susan were having their own private party in the side yard, away from the crowd.

"I want to paint a picture of you," Matt said.

"I'd like that," Susan said.

Matt took her into the garage to see his and Byron's art studio. She admired their supplies, which Matt had organized nicely on shelves. She took her time looking at the row of canvases already painted, propped up against every wall to dry. Matt liked how her dress swayed as she moved. It gave him an idea for the painting.

"Those paintings over there are Byron's. These here are all mine," he said.

Susan turned back toward Matt's paintings. She pointed to the green hill, the bird in flight, the long spring grass bowing in the breeze, the dog-shaped shadow beneath the bounding red dog, its ears flopped back and tail high.

"Your beloved Vizsla?" she asked.

"Of course," he said.

"Beautiful," Susan said. "You're so talented."

Matt put a blank canvas on the easel, looked around the garage for a good spot for Susan to stand, but the light and setting were all wrong. Too dark, too many shadows, too many tools and bikes and Graham's bins of clothes. None of it would make a nice enough backdrop. He handed the canvas to Susan and lifted the easel. "Follow me," he said. He walked out to the side yard and spun in a slow circle, looking for the best background.

"You mean you want to paint me now?" Susan said.

"Are you busy?" Matt asked.

Susan laughed. "Actually, no."

Matt decided to have her stand near the fence, with the grass under her bare feet and the ivy behind her. He set up the easel and went back into the garage for the paints. He had an image of her in his mind and he wanted the real her to match the image.

"The sun needs to be on your face more. Turn to the left a little. Put your chin up. And your hair, I need more of it forward, over your shoulder." He tried telling her how to pose without touching her, but it wasn't working.

"I'm a statue," Susan said. "You can adjust me however you want."

She held very still while Matt tilted her head, moved her arm, rearranged her hair.

"You smell very good," he said. He just about had her posed right, but then he had the overwhelming urge to kiss her. So he did, which messed up the pose. Susan kissed him back without moving her body any closer to his. He liked it when she played statue. He could get as close as he wanted without being distracted by her touching him. He stopped kissing her and stroked her hair. It was soft, silky, the perfect feeling against his fingers. She closed her eyes while he touched her, and smiled.

"You're always so gentle," she said.

"Yes," Matt said, because he knew how it felt to be touched in a less-than-gentle way, knew more about it than anyone else, felt the pain of hasty, rough contact through every nerve ending, all the way down to his bones. "You know someone is happy with you when they are gentle," he said.

Susan opened her brown eyes and smiled at him. "I'm happy with you," she said.

He put half of her hair down her back and half over one shoulder, and the sunlight shone off her hair just right, bringing out copper highlights in her brown hair. He couldn't wait to paint that color, the same color as the Vizsla's coat. So maybe he didn't only like blues now. Maybe Lana's love of the color red wasn't so strange, since he liked some reds now, too. Maybe he even liked his maroon blackout curtains, so close in color to Susan's highlights, to the darkest tones of Vizsla fur. He posed Susan's arms and head. He stepped behind the easel and sketched her outline on the canvas.

"I like having you as my girlfriend again," he said.

"What does that mean to you?" she asked. She hardly moved her mouth as she talked. She was a very good statue. "How is a girlfriend different than a friend to you?"

"I don't kiss friends," Matt said. "And I never have sex with friends."

Susan laughed. "Is that the only difference?"

Matt thought about how Gabe and Abby sat together, not even talking, sometimes for a half hour, just being together. "A friend is someone you do stuff with. Like Lana walks with her friend Camille. And Byron does parkour with his friends. But a girlfriend is someone you want to be with all the time, even when you don't do stuff together. You just want to be with them. Even doing nothing is fun with a girlfriend."

Susan laughed. "Matt, even when you're doing nothing you aren't doing nothing. You have the busiest brain I've ever seen."

Matt had her face, hair, shoulders sketched right, and he liked the flow of the dress, the way he could just draw loose lines that weren't exactly like the dress right at that moment but were the right idea of the dress. That was the fun of art. He could paint exactly what he saw, or he could improve it, just a little, making a tiny adjustment to the hem of a dress, create an imaginary breeze to change the whole feel of the image.

"There's a breeze blowing in the painting. But not in real life," he said.

Susan laughed. "If I have to stand here in the sun for hours we'll need a breeze in real life."

"This won't take hours," he said. "Only minutes. I'm very fast."

Matt wasn't as fast as he wanted to be, not with the drawing. He had to erase the outline of Susan's legs and start over, the curve of her calf down into her ankle was giving him trouble. He took a deep breath and it helped him not get frustrated. He listened to Becca's meditation CD most nights now, whenever the melatonin wore off and the weighted blanket and noise machine weren't enough. He liked the lady's soft voice talking about the ripples of light warming and cleansing every cell in his body, one by one, from his toes to his head. He pictured it during the day whenever he started to feel anxious, and it helped sometimes. It slowed his brain down, focusing on the waves of light passing through him.

The lady's voice and the light waves of cell-cleansing calmness were like sitting in the window with Abby. And painting with Byron. And writing down data about everything interesting that happened in the house. And the tadpoles. And the way Lana prepared his ice cream every night without him even having to ask.

He remembered the darkness and the mildewy smell of Spike's apartment, and Spike's anger and yelling, and the pills he needed to stay calm there. He looked up at the sun, heard the rise and fall of the other party guests laughing and talking just far enough away not to overwhelm him, but close enough to remind him that he was safe and not alone. His whole family of people who cared about him and never yelled at him and wanted his liver to get better so he could be with them for a long time. Everything seemed better now. He talked to his mom on video and she held up her hand for him to trace on the monitor, and he didn't even have to talk sometimes.

Susan sneezed and laughed. "Sorry," she said. She returned to being a statue, but it wasn't the exact same pose. Her head was a little different, angled down more than it had been before she sneezed, but he already had her head sketched, so it didn't matter. He only had her legs left to do and after a few more strokes he got the legs right. He nodded, pointing from her to the canvas, before he remembered that she couldn't see herself.

Focusing on Susan gave Matt that same warm calm feeling. She was soft and smelled good and let him be the way he was and never gave him that anxious feeling.

"You're right. I'm never doing nothing," he agreed. "I have a very fast-processing brain. I tend to think about several things at once. But when I'm with you all I think about is you. That's what a girlfriend's like." Matt smiled, not an anxious smile or a confusing one, but the real kind, the kind that showed the happy feeling coming from his body, but bigger than his body, so it poured out of his chest and into the air around him and onto the canvas that she couldn't see yet. Matt was surrounded by the good feeling.

35

Abby

Abby was meeting Emily at the movies. She took a long look up and down the street, searching for those long legs of Em's, and that's when she saw her. Caitlin. Fluffy, sprayed, bleach-blond hair. Shoulders back to emphasize her busty figure, hips swinging with every step. She was alone and headed right for Abby. Abby backed up, tried to blend into the crowd waiting for tickets, but Caitlin stepped into line right behind her.

"Abby?"

Abby turned and faced Caitlin. Her heart was racing. Did Caitlin know about Abby and Gabe? What would her punishment be for that? "Hey, Caitlin," she said lamely. She didn't know what else to do. There was a good crowd around. Hopefully Caitlin wouldn't make a scene in front of all of those people.

"How's your summer going?" Caitlin asked, like they were just any two kids from school. She seemed so normal. It just stressed Abby out more. Where was Emily?

"Um, fine. We just got back from Florida."

"Cool. Family trip?"

"Yeah, my grandparents live there." There was an awkward pause. The line inched forward. Every muscle in Abby's body was tense. "How's yours?"

"Oh, you know. Great to be done with school. Sucks to be home with the parents all the time. You can't win. My mom's a total busybody. She's all over me. You know how that is." Abby shrugged, because she didn't. Lana watched her from a distance, never pestered her with questions, gave her plenty of space, maybe too much. Although lately it had been better. Sometimes they snuggled together on the couch like when Abby was little. Lana smelled the same as she always had, like safety and comfort, and Abby loved those moments. Close, without having to talk. Abby appreciated the space even as she wondered why they needed it. Why she didn't want her mom close to her all the time, why she didn't want to share everything with her the way she had when she was little. Caitlin sighed and stomped one foot, startling Abby. "Okay," Caitlin said. "So I guess I kind of need to say sorry. You know. Things got out of hand, and . . . well. I didn't mean anything by it. Boys are stupid anyway, you know?"

"Right," Abby said. Her heart was hammering. She figured Caitlin was setting her up for something, a rude remark or a cheap shot, but she was trapped. What else could she do but play it out? "So, I heard you changed schools?"

"Yeah." Caitlin smiled, as if thrilled about it. "I guess now the soccer team will be a million times better, without me on it."

"You weren't bad," Abby lied.

"Please. I hate soccer. My mom just told me I needed a sport because I was getting fat. The best part about switching to Madison, aside from the fact that the kids there are awesome, is that I missed team tryouts. Win-win. I'd much rather be in drama club anyway."

"Oh," Abby said. She was so confused. Who was this girl, and what had happened to the old Caitlin? "You'd be great up onstage."

"I know, right? Totally where I belong." Caitlin flipped her hair and giggled.

They both bought two tickets and stood near each other, fidgeting while they waited for their guests. Emily finally showed up and took her ticket from Abby with her mouth hanging open as she stared at Caitlin.

"Hey, Emily!" Caitlin said, like they were friends or something. Em looked at Abby and Abby shrugged. They were seated inside the theater when Caitlin came in, hand in hand with a handsome guy they'd never seen before.

"I guess that explains that," Emily said.

"There's no explanation for that," Abby said. The guy was carrying Caitlin's drink, food, even her purse. "But whatever."

"Not your problem anymore," Emily said, which was true. Abby smiled and nodded.

"She kind of apologized," Abby whispered as the lights dimmed.

"Really? Did you say you forgave her?"

Abby replayed the conversation in her mind. She shook her head. "Nope."

"Good for you," Emily said. Being unforgiving was totally out of character for Em. Abby laughed and hugged her.

The next day she went over to Mr. Franks's house, to meet Celeste in person for the very first time. Abby was nervous, standing on the doormat, Byron idling at the curb to make sure she made it safely inside before taking off.

Mr. Franks opened the door. He was wearing shorts and a faded T-shirt with a surf company logo on it. Out of his teaching clothes he seemed less intimidating.

"Hi, Abby," he said, smiling. "She'll be right down. Come on in."

He waved at Byron, who would be in his class next year, and Abby took a deep breath and stepped in.

"Can I get you something to drink?" he asked. She followed him through the living room, where the coffee table was hidden under stacks of papers and magazines, into the kitchen, where there were dirty breakfast dishes still sitting in the sink. It was all so normal. She wasn't sure what she'd expected, being in a teacher's house, but she hadn't expected it to feel like any old home. "Lemonade?" he asked. "Homemade."

"Sure," Abby said. He poured half a glass of lemonade, filled it the rest of the way with sparkling water, slid it across the counter toward her. "Thanks, Mr. Franks."

He cringed like a cartoon character, overdramatically. "Oh, no," he said. "In my house please call me David. I'm on vacation. You call me Mr. Franks and I feel an instant compulsion to take roll."

Abby laughed and noticed his wife was out back, kneeling in a vegetable bed, picking ripe red tomatoes and placing them into a basket. There was a girl with her, sitting on a chair and talking to her, but not helping.

"That's Marie, Celeste's older sister. It's so nice to have them both home."

They were such a normal family. Abby had to reconcile it with her image of him as her teacher. Except that he was more than just her teacher. He was the first person who'd really seen her. She sipped the sparkling lemonade, perfectly tart and sweet and bubbly and refreshing.

"Thank you," she said. "For, um, talking to me. I guess Celeste told you that I'm getting help."

He smiled at her and nodded. "You look happy. Healthy."

Abby heard a clatter of footsteps down the stairs and coming up behind her. She turned just in time to see Celeste running toward her, arms open. "Abby!" Celeste nearly toppled her off the barstool with the force of her hug.

They pulled back and looked each other over. Mr. Franks was right, they had very similar body shapes. Celeste was lanky and lean, but strong, and developed. They laughed and hugged again. They spent the afternoon on an old tire swing out back, sitting knee to knee and catching up.

"So, I need to hear more about this boyfriend," Celeste said. Abby gushed about Gabe until she was sure Celeste was sick of it, then asked about boys in college.

"Oh, they're still high school boys, in a lot of ways. Immature. But taller, filled out. And better-looking." They laughed and ate off the platter of fruits and vegetables that Mrs. Franks served them, freshly picked, sweet, ripe, and juicy. They spun in circles on the tire swing until they were dizzy.

"College is exhausting," Celeste said. "Classes, studying, epic finals. Plus staying up all night with the cool people you meet. I just want to lay low this summer. Recharge my batteries. Lounge around the beach with you and see tons of movies. That sound good?"

Abby was thrilled to hear that Celeste wanted to spend more time together. Abby adored her. She was everything Abby wanted to be. "That sounds perfect."

"But I won't cut into boyfriend time. New love keeps you very busy. I have old high school friends I need to catch up with, too. Don't you worry about me."

"No, I want to see you. A whole summer of you and Gabe and the beach. I have a best friend, too. Emily. She doesn't get all of this, really. But she's trying."

"I'll share you with her, too. Maybe we can all see sappy girlie movies together. The ones boyfriends can't stand." They giggled and ate tiny red strawberries, freshly picked by Celeste's mother and still warm from the sun.

Abby and Gabe saw each other every day, except when they were with their dads. She missed him terribly on those days.

Gabe came over after a whole day apart, and Abby was so happy to see him that she jumped into his arms. He laughed and swung her around in a circle. Once he settled her down on the ground again, she held up the bag holding his shirt. She'd brought it to her dad's the previous night, slept with it on her pillow next to her.

"I need to exchange this shirt," she told him. "The smell of you is fading."

Gabe laughed and pulled his shirt off, right there in the living room. He handed it to her, took the one out of the bag, and put that one on instead.

"Done," he said. It was the first time she'd seen him without his shirt on. He was even more beautiful than she'd imagined: tan and lean around his ribs and waist, with defined muscles across his chest. She blushed and looked away even though he was already dressed again.

"I need a new one, too," he said. "Before I go."

"How long can you stay for?" she asked.

"How long do you want me to stay for?"

"Forever?"

"Forever, then." He smiled and put his arm around her. Abby led him to the couch. He sat and she sidled up to him, resting her back against his chest. Gabe wrapped his arms around her and held on tight.

"You said you were going to explain it today," he said.

"Or we could just cuddle and not talk at all," she suggested.

He kissed the side of her head. She turned to face him and he rubbed noses with her, then kissed her. "Nope. Talk."

Abby sighed. She'd told him about finally meeting Celeste Franks, how awesome she was and how excited Abby was to spend time with her. Then of course Gabe asked how she ended up getting to know Mr. Franks's daughter in the first place. An innocent question, but it had freaked Abby out. Gabe didn't know the truth about Abby, and she liked it that way. But he could tell there was something there, the way she'd shut down suddenly. He wouldn't let it go. She'd promised to tell him today. She turned away from Gabe, rested the back of her head against his shoulder.

"Celeste is like me, that's all. We both have issues with food. Somehow Mr. Franks knew. He gave me her number." She snuggled deeper into his arms.

"Okay. So what are the issues?" he asked.

Abby tensed. She wanted to be the drama-free girl of his dreams. She didn't want him to know this about her.

"I don't really like to eat," she said.

Gabe laughed, the rumble of his chest passing through Abby's back. "What does that mean?"

Abby chewed her lip and laced her fingers through his. She shook her head. Jenny had told her she needed to do this, draw Gabe into her support circle. But it was too hard.

"Hey," he said. "I'm sorry I laughed. I just don't know what you mean." She nodded but couldn't respond. Her insides were doing battle against themselves. "You know you can tell me anything," he said.

"What if it's a bad thing? What if you don't like me anymore after you hear it?"

"Seriously?" he said. "Abby, I'm crazy about you. Nothing you say right now will change that. I promise." She turned and looked into his deep green eyes, got lost in there, and had to look away. "Trust me. Please?"

Abby took a deep breath, closed her eyes so she couldn't see his reaction. "I'm anorexic," she whispered. "That time I fainted at school? It was because I hadn't eaten in three days. Celeste is, too." Abby ducked her head, eyes still shut tight, withdrawing. "I have a therapist I see every week about it. I'm getting better, but it's still there."

Gabe hugged her, kissed her temple. They sat like that for a while, just quiet and thinking and feeling. His arms were still around her, but Abby was sure she felt him slipping away.

"It's okay if you don't like me anymore," she said.

Gabe turned her to face him. "Of course I still like you," he said. "How could I not like you?"

"You want a no-drama girl."

"You are a no-drama girl. Look at you. Even now. Steady as a rock."

Abby smiled and he smiled back, and she suddenly felt exactly as steady as a rock, like maybe she could do this after all. With Gabe and Celeste and Jenny and Matt and the window, with her and Lana having their close moments again, with Gloria on her side, and even Byron looking out for her. Fight this fight against food and have the perfect boyfriend and best family and good friends and be happy and whole and not scared anymore.

Gabe touched her hair, traced the line of her cheek, rested his thumb on her chin. "You know how I keep saying you're the prettiest girl I know?"

"Yeah." Abby held her breath.

"Well, I don't mean anything to do with being thin. I mean the whole package. Your eyes and smile and hair and speed and strength. Your brain. Your humor. Your heart. The way you light up when you look at me. But here's the thing. You're an amazing athlete. And athletes are eaters, you know? I mean, it can be smart eating, just healthy stuff, but every calorie translates into energy, speed, stamina. Food isn't your enemy. It has no power over you. It's just fuel. I'm sure you already know all of this, from your therapist, and I'm not doing anything to help right now."

Abby let her breath go, and a landslide of worries went with it. He didn't really understand the food thing, not completely. But how could he? He was a teenage boy, an eating machine. But she liked his analogy, of food as fuel and nothing more. And she really liked that he admired all of those things about her. She was going to write it all down in her journal later, the list of good Abby qualities, as seen by the perfect and beautiful and amazing Gabe Connor.

"You are helping. Really. Just by listening and not judging. By reminding me of the other things you like about me."

"Love about you," he said.

"There's a lot that I love about you, too," Abby said.

"Well, then, I'm glad that's settled."

He grinned, big enough to show his one crooked tooth on the bottom, her absolute favorite. He kissed her and held her and she let go, fell safely back into his arms, into the moment, her head resting on his chest, his heartbeat soothing and strong against her cheek. She nuzzled into Gabe's arms and closed her eyes, drifted away on a sea of lavender and Gabe-smell.

She pictured little-girl Abby, and felt exactly as safe and loved and happy and capable as that little girl. They held hands and skipped off together, Abby and six-year-old Abby. They were fearless together.

36

Byron

All of those secret phone calls Trent was making? Turned out they were to that girl, Fiona, the one he'd hooked up with last summer. She was coming back to town, to spend her summer break with her divorced dad again. They were making plans to see each other as much as possible. When Trent finally came clean, Byron was so relieved. He felt less weird about Betsy if Trent had a girlfriend, too.

"I guess it's different this time, you know? Not just a hookup thing. But, like, I like her. And I guess she likes me, too."

"Wow. Good for you," Byron said.

Trent looked him over. "This doesn't mean it isn't weird that you're with my sister, you know. It just means that I've got my own girl."

"Sure," Byron said. "Hey, maybe we could even double date sometime."

"That's disgusting," Trent said.

Byron shook his head. "Whatever, jackass. At least you're no longer obsessed with my mom."

"Nah," Trent said, leaning back on the couch with his hands behind his head. "Lana and I, we had our chance, but that's over now. I'll try to let her down gently."

Byron launched into a handstand on the arm of the couch, right over Trent's head. "Take it back or I drop right on you."

"Don't get all aggro," Trent said. "Just a damn joke. Betsy's got you so hard up you lost your sense of humor?" Then he jumped off the couch just as Byron dropped down, aiming to squash him. Byron was even more annoyed because Trent was right. He and Betsy had fooled around a bit, lots of kissing and pressing their bodies together with their clothes still on, but they still hadn't gone all the way. Byron thought he was going to explode sometimes. But other times he wanted to take it slow, to show Betsy he was nothing like those college jerks. He was in it for the long haul.

"Don't you talk trash about my girlfriend, asswipe." Byron jumped off the couch into some mock-karate position he'd seen in a movie.

"Don't you tell me how to treat my sister, jerkwad." Trent picked up a ruler from the coffee table and held it, swordlike, out to defend himself.

"Are you two morons kidding me?" Betsy said from the bottom of the stairs. She sashayed in between them, hands on hips, and gave them both a stern look. "Grow the hell up." She tapped her foot in irritation. Byron looked down to see she was wearing pink fuzzy slippers with bunny ears that flopped whenever she tapped. The three of them broke up laughing and fell onto the couch. Byron took Betsy's hand and she squeezed it. Maybe they weren't sleeping together yet, but Betsy was a lot more fun these days. She rolled her head in Byron's direction and puckered up, blew him an air-kiss. He caught it in his stomach, like a sucker punch of love, and grinned back like an idiot. She still had that effect on him. He was hopelessly gone on her. She used her pink-painted nail to trace a heart on the inside of his wrist and it tingled all over his body.

It was almost time for him to head to campus for the parkour meeting. Sometimes Betsy came along, but today she had a dentist appointment. It was always hard for Byron to leave her, but he couldn't see skipping parkour to sit in a dentist's waiting room with bad music, terrible magazines, and that horrible drill sound in the background. There weren't as many of the guys getting together for parkour now that it was summer and half the group had headed home to Mom and Dad until fall rolled back around, but Byron still went twice a week. Graham was giving him a ride. He'd come a few times to watch. He sat on the grass with the hot coeds and cheered Byron on, which was equally embarrassing and cool.

After finishing his run, Byron sat next to Graham and guzzled the water and ate the sandwich Graham had brought.

"You're crazy, doing those stunts," Graham said. "I don't know how you haven't broken something."

"We're more careful than we look," Byron said. "We practice a bunch in the gym before we take it out here."

"You're a smart kid," Graham said. Byron thought it might be the first time Graham had called him smart instead of athletic. Abby was the smart one, everyone knew that. He shrugged and smiled. Graham was better these days. Calmer. Tax season was long over and he wasn't such a stress case. He worked reasonable hours and sometimes even blew off work early to take Byron to parkour. Sometimes they grabbed dinner together after. A couple of times Graham even invited Betsy to join them. He was becoming a normal dad, a real one, not a cardboard cutout, and not a disappearing-act one like Trent and Betsy's.

Graham and Ivy had broken up, as Byron had predicted. Graham was tight-lipped about the details. All he said was, "A realist and an idealist. Not the best match." Graham had more free time now that he was single again, and Byron was happy to be getting a fair chunk of it. He hoped it would last and wasn't just a phase.

"I have a little something for you." Graham pulled a white envelope out of his pocket and held it out it to Byron.

"What's this?" Byron asked.

"Tuition for that art class you want to take."

"Seriously? You'll pay for it?" Matt had already paid for the first session. This would cover the second session, giving Byron a full summer of art training. His summer just kept getting better.

"On one condition," Graham said, picking up Byron's empty sandwich wrapper and rolling it into a ball. "Don't quit swimming. Or track. Do it all. Just because you can."

Byron tapped his lip, faux-thinking. "I'll be pretty busy, trying to keep up with all of that. I might need some transportation."

"Enough about the damn car, Byron. I got my first car when I was nineteen. I worked for three years and saved every penny to buy it myself. You buy your first car yourself, you take pride in it. You get it as a gift, and it means nothing to you."

"Okay, okay, I get it," Byron said. "No car." He smiled at Graham, still so easy to rile up over money. And yet. Byron balanced the envelope on his palm. Seemingly weightless, but in fact the most substantial thing his father had given him in a long time. "So what changed your mind?"

Graham looked around the campus, which was summer-quiet and drenched in shade, June gloom in full effect. The temperature was perfect, but San Diego had mostly overcast skies in June, the whole city holding its breath until July came and full summer perfection broke through.

"You shouldn't quit something you're good at," Graham said. "I mean really good at. Once you stop, it's hard to go back. You're not at the same level as everyone else anymore. You get left behind."

Byron wondered what Graham meant, wondered when he had been left behind. But it wasn't hard to agree to the terms. Swimming in Florida already had Byron doubting his decision to quit swim team. He just loved the feel of the pool, the smell of the chlorine, the pull of the water too much. And he and Gabe had just started running together some mornings. They were planning to be on the cross-country team together. Byron didn't want to give that up, either.

"Deal," Byron said. "Swimming, track, parkour, and art."

"A quadruple threat," Graham said, smiling.

"I seriously didn't see this coming. Thanks."

Graham brushed the palm of his hand along the tips of the blades of grass. "It's not that I don't believe in you, Byron. In your art as much as the sports. I didn't have the opportunities you have. Or the skill. I don't want to see you walk away from something you have natural talent for." Graham tugged a fistful of grass free, tossed it aside. "I envy you: out on the track, in the pool. You make it look so easy. And out here with these guys, doing these stunts." Graham smiled at Byron, tossed a handful of grass his way. "You're a sight to see."

Byron couldn't help smiling. "Wait'll you see my painting skills. After these classes." He waved the envelope. "I'll be a sight to see in the art studio, too. Aunt Becca says I'll be unstoppable. That the universe is speaking truth through my art."

"Aunt Becca . . ." Graham began, then he stopped himself, just shook his head, smiling. "I have no doubt you'll be unstoppable."

A few guys were practicing moves still, grunting and whooping as they launched halfway up the exterior wall of the library to a window ledge, gripped it, and hoisted their legs. They were trying to do a backflip midair. Byron narrowed his eyes, watching, calculating how he'd do it. When he looked back at Graham he was watching him, smiling. "Can you do that?"

"I think so," Byron said. "They need to be turning faster. Get their head and shoulders back before their knees even hit their chests."

Graham laughed. "You're all crazy. You know, I've never been much of an athlete, but I always wanted to be. It was always the athletes who got the cool girls."

"You got Mom, though."

"I did. Took her from one of those athletic types." Graham pointed at the guys practicing jumps and rolls off the picnic table, the buff guys of the group. "Stole her right from under his nose." Graham stared into space, drifting away, thinking about something that made him look sad, then he came back, looked Byron over, and grinned at him. "Of course, I also have no artistic skill. I'm just a numbers guy. That's it. Nothing cool about it."

Byron shrugged, slapped the envelope against his palm a few times.

"It's kinda cool. I mean, Abby's a math whiz like you, right? And she's pretty damn cool."

Graham smiled and nodded. "She is. Both of you are."

37

Lana

Matt was spending more time away from home, out with Susan. Sometimes Abby sat at his window by herself, eating and watching the world go by. Lana made herself a sandwich and settled into Matt's chair beside her.

"Don't tell him I sat here," Lana joked.

"He'll know." Abby smiled. "He's got psychic powers or super-sonic smell or something."

Lana held up half of her sandwich and Abby considered it, then lifted the top layer of bread, spotted the mayo there, and shook her head. "No sale."

Lana took a big bite and made a rapturous sound. "Mmm, mayo." Abby giggled and the sound filled Lana up. "That's my favorite sound in the world," Lana said. "You laughing."

Abby gave Lana a hearty fake belly laugh, Santa-style, that set her chuckling for real. In no time she was snorting and doubled over with giggles. Abby still had her distant moments, her occa-sional sullen moods, but for the most part Lana had her back, her cherished child. She wasn't going to let her go again.

"It's like a dance," Lana said. "The tenuous relationship be-tween teen girls and their mothers. The pull of independence. The changing roles. The fact that you can always love your mother even though you don't always like her."

Abby looked Lana over, serious again, and pursed her lips. "I'm sorry if I make you feel like I don't like you. That's not true. I actually always wanted to be more like you. You're so nice to everyone. And you're the prettiest of all the moms. Everyone says so."

"Do they?" Lana laughed. "Is there a mom beauty competition I never knew I was in?"

"Of course there's a competition," Abby said, rolling her eyes. "We're teenagers. Everything's a competition."

It was news to Lana. "Funny. I wish I was more like you. Your athleticism, your intelligence, your fair hair, delicate skin, and those beautiful eyes, like peridot gems."

Abby made a face and they both laughed. "I guess people always want what they don't have. Take for granted whatever comes easy to them."

"See?" Lana said. "If I'd known that at your age, my whole life would've been different. You're the wisest kid I've ever met."

"How do you wish your life had been different?" Abby asked. She was eating stalks of celery cradling peanut butter, taking small bites, washing each one down with little sips of milk.

Lana looked out the window at the sunny summer sky and thought about how much had happened in the past year, how hard it had been, losing Graham and finding the cancer cells and fighting for Byron's art and getting Abby help. She smiled at Abby, her beautiful girl, and remembered the unflinching, fearless child she'd been.

"Not a thing. Because then I wouldn't be right here, right now, with you."

"Aw," Abby said, patting Lana's head. "My sappy mom."

Lana laughed. "You know, when you were little, you hated it when guests left. You'd run out that door after them, clinging to their hands, trying to get their keys from them. Eventually I'd have to pull you off of them, and we'd stand on the grass watching them go. You'd wait until they were backing out of the driveway and you'd scream, 'Goodbye! I love you!' with such force that half the time they'd get right out of their cars and come back to you. Because we all need more of that. That depth of love."

"I'm sorry I don't do that anymore," Abby said. "I do love you."

"Oh, I know it, sweetie. Remember, I was once a teenage girl myself. I waged major battle with Grandma Gloria over everything under the sun. It's the plight of teen girls. We need to knock our mothers off their pedestals so that we can figure out who we are through our own eyes, not theirs. You go ahead and do that, okay? I'm strong enough to take it."

"You're the best kind of mother," Abby said. "Not the overbearing type, not the kind that noses into my business."

"I don't want to hover. To make you feel like I don't trust you," Lana said. "But I'm not sure that was the right approach. I should've interfered more, sooner. Maybe then . . ."

"I'm fine, Mom," Abby said. "Just like you, I'm right where I'm supposed to be."

Lana patted Abby's shoulder. "Just promise me that while you try to find your way, you'll call me in when you need help, or push me away when you're ready to be independent. And that you'll forgive me when I misjudge your mood and get too close when you need space or too far away when you need me beside you. This whole motherhood act is one big guessing game. I really have no idea what I'm doing most of the time."

"I promise," Abby said. She got up off her chair and settled on Lana's lap. She wrapped Lana's arms around her, a seat belt of affection. "But I think you're pretty good at this motherhood gig."

"Gabe seems like a very nice young man," Lana said. Abby nodded, the sun flashing off her blond hair. "But know that if he breaks your heart I'll hurt him. Bad."

Abby laughed, turned, and kissed Lana's forehead. "I'll warn him. Nobody wants to make warrior-mama mad."

Summer was unfolding before them: quiet and kind. Lana's mornings were spent in the reading lab, her afternoons free for walks with Camille, her evenings for her kids, Matt, her weekly yoga class, and precious dates with Abbot. She was building a new life, moment by moment, on her own terms. But she still had the divorce to deal with.

Lana realized at the first mediation appointment that she'd been suffering a week of anxiety about it for nothing. The mediator, Allen Greer, was a soft-spoken man in his late fifties, portly and calm and all business. He went over his rates, the basic structure of future appointments, explained the various ways to determine temporary spousal and child support during the divorce.

"Talk it over, decide if you want to hire me, and get back to me," he said as he shook their hands. "If it's a go, simply pay the retainer and I'll get you the paperwork to start filling out."

Graham and Lana stood on the sidewalk out in front of his office smiling uncomfortably at each other. They'd been seated elbow to elbow in Allen Greer's conference room for only twenty minutes, but it was the most time they'd spent together since Graham had left.

"Here we go," Graham said.

"He seems nice enough. Competent."

"Sure, he's fine. I guess I'll head in and give him the retainer fee now. Sound good?"

"Sounds good."

Lana headed for her car as Graham headed back into the law office. She had lunch plans with Abbot at a nice restaurant in La Jolla overlooking the cove, his idea, to have something nice to look forward to afterward. She was nearly an hour early, since the mediation appointment had been so brief. She had time to wander along the cove, watch kids frolicking in the baby waves at the tiny inlet beach, spot a seal's glossy black head gazing shoreward about a hundred yards out to sea.

She was staring at the ocean, endless and peaceful and full of possibility yet ultimately unchanging, feeling lost in its vastness, when she heard a familiar trill.

"Lana, dear!"

She turned, already smiling, and spotted her old neighbors Dixie and John, walking arm in arm down the paved path. They took turns hugging and remarking on the beautiful day.

"You look wonderful," Dixie said. "I haven't seen you since that time in the drugstore."

"Valentine's Day," Lana said.

"You must've taken my advice and given Janelle a call." Dixie touched her hair and laughed.

"Dixie told me about you and Graham," John said. "I sure am sorry to hear it."

"Thanks," Lana said. "We actually just started the divorce process today. It's time." She shrugged, smiled, felt nothing but resolution at the words. Bad news about her marriage had lost its power over her.

"Well, we must have you over for dinner," Dixie said. "You and the kids. I haven't seen them in so long."

"Actually, we're having a party at the beach for the Fourth of July, if you'd like to join us," Lana said.

Dixie and John exchanged smiles, such a long-running couple that they no longer existed as separate individuals, and agreed.

Lana headed into the restaurant and found Abbot waiting for her.

"There she is," he said. "You look happy."

"I am." She smiled. "Ridiculously so."

She was even happier when Allen Greer got back to her with the support amounts. She looked over the numbers and felt a wave of relief wash over her. She'd be able to live on it. Not extravagantly, but between the support and her income and Matt's help, she could keep the house and the lights on within it, and they would all have clothes and food and a little left over for some fun.

Graham was back to seeing the kids more often. Lana hoped it wasn't just because his support amount was based on how much time he spent with them. She figured whatever the incentive, the kids deserved more time with their father, and it was good they were getting it. But she also took to writing down every minute they spent with him, in case he tried to artificially inflate his percentage of time with the kids to reduce the support amount. She was learning to look out for herself and her children, unapologetically.

But she was also learning to love again.

On the Fourth of July they headed to the beach early to stake out a prime spot, a grassy picnic area just steps from the sand. Abbot and John took turns manning the grill while Lana and Camille caught Dixie up on the neighborhood gossip. Lana had brought sparklers for the kids, who were probably too old for them, but some traditions were worth keeping no matter how much time marched forward.

Abbot's two sons were visiting him, on summer break from college and fresh from their mother's wedding in Colorado. They were handsome, broad-shouldered boys like their father, gentle and genuine and easy to get along with. One of them played guitar and sang old Bob Dylan tunes while Abby and Gabe snuggled nearby. Byron was teaching some parkour moves to Abbot's younger son while Betsy videotaped it and cheered them on.

Matt and Susan walked down the beach, shoes in hand, talking. Lana could see Matt gesturing out to sea as he spoke, waving his hands emphatically toward the setting sun, and Susan laughing and shaking her hair in the breeze as she listened.

They had all come so far, but still, thankfully, had so much further to go, so much more to do, and more time to do it. Lana inhaled the briny tang of the ocean, took in the endless swath of blue, the world laid out before them.

Abbot appeared at Lana's elbow, holding a brownie, waggling his eyebrows.

"Bad influence," Lana said, holding his hand still to take a bite.

"Good influence," Abbot said, wrapping his arm around her waist.

"I love you," Lana said.

"That must be one damn good brownie," Abbot said. Lana laughed and leaned against him. Abbot kissed her temple, held her a little tighter. "And I love you."

The kids lit the sparklers, took off down the beach with them, streaks of light carving a path in the darkness.

Acknowledgments

I had many supporters as I worked on this novel, and I sincerely appreciate every one of them. I am particularly grateful to the following people:

Harvey Klinger, agent extraordinaire, mentor, and motivator, for bringing out the best in me as a writer.

Everyone at Touchstone Books and Simon & Schuster who gave their time and energy to this project, especially Miya Kumangai.

Stacy Creamer, for turning a dream into reality.

My beta readers: Jessica Harris and Dav-Yell Grant Bruce for their feedback and support.

My dedicated Sunday babysitters: Bob Dunn and Kathie Dunn, for watching my girls while I write, and for being such terrific parents and grandparents.

Carol Dunn, proud mom and spoiling grandma, and Tracy Dunn Arrowsmith, best sister ever and fun auntie, who have watched me grow from a quiet little dreamer girl into whatever I am now and loved me fiercely the whole time.

Heather Swift and Holly Coleman, for their guidance and insight.

Meg Waite Clayton, Ellen Sussman, and Michelle Richmond, for their encouragement and advice.

Jeanene Nehira, Liz Radding, Rhea Karahalios, and Tracy Voeller, for always listening. And Sue Devries, Dana Dee Little, and Janie Ellison, my back-up mothers, for always knowing just what to say.

Jeffrey Harris, for giving me my best motivation ever: the two little girls that I love with all my heart.

My sweet Vizsla Toby, my favorite hiking buddy, for keeping me company while I write.

My vast network of family and adopted family: the Dunn, Jaeger, Branstetter, Harris, Whitfield, Bass, Kempster, and Boice clans, for being there, believing in me, and reminding me often.

My bright, talented, funny, athletic, artistic, beautiful daughters, Zoe and Maia, who turn even my hardest days into the best days I could possibly imagine. This novel is my proof to you that no dream is too big. Dream your own huge, ridiculously impossible dreams and go for it. I've got your back.

And most sincere love and gratitude to my uncle, Michael Dunn, for all he taught me about love, brilliance, quirkiness, kindness, self-acceptance, and the challenges and rewards of living with Asperger's. I love you and miss you.

The Art of Adapting

Cassandra Dunn

Adapting to change is never easy—especially when that change involves your husband moving out and your brother with Asperger's moving into the home you share with your two teenaged children. This is what Lana has been dealing with for the past few months, and not all that gracefully. She's been finding comfort in calories instead of trying to move on with her life, and she's not the only one having trouble adjusting. Her brother, Matt, is settling into a new home with new rules and all the unfamiliar sights and sounds of two noisy teenagers. Byron is a fifteen-year-old boy busy trying to fit in and find himself all at once, while his younger sister, Abby, is eating less and less, though nobody seems to notice. As they each face their own challenges and begin trying to pull themselves up, they realize that having each other to lean on may be the key to getting back on solid ground. *The Art of Adapting* is a moving debut about self-acceptance and love, and what it takes to grow and adjust—both individually and as a family.

For Discussion

1. *The Art of Adapting* rotates between four different perspectives: Lana, Matt, Byron and Abby. Whose story were you most interested in? How do you think their stories would have been affected by the use of an omniscient third-person narrator instead? Is there anyone else's perspective you would've been interested in reading?

2. When Lana thinks about all the clothes Graham left behind, never to retrieve, she wonders, "How did people do that? Simply let loved ones go and carry on like they never mattered in the first place? Lana had the opposite problem. She kept everyone" (p. 36). Can you let people go like they never mattered? Does Lana manage to let go of Graham or anyone else by the end of the book?

3. How did reading Matt's story affect your understanding of Asperger's? Did it change any notions you had or illuminate anything about the disorder for you? Do you know anyone with Asperger's? If so, how did Matt's struggles compare to those of the person you know?

4. Compare Lana's relationship with her mother, Gloria, to her relationship with Abby. How does Lana differ as a mother and a daughter? Does one role affect the other?

5. Many of the characters have a very particular way they relate to food, though clearly it is the biggest issue for Abby and Gloria. Discuss the important role that food plays in the story and how the act of eating was interpreted by different characters.

6. With his dad in his ear about sports all the time, it takes Byron a while to realize art is his calling. What do you think of Gra-

ham's parenting throughout the book? Did you ever feel pressured to follow someone else's passion instead of your own?

7. When Susan asks Matt what a girlfriend means to him as opposed to a friend, he says, "A friend is someone you do stuff with. . . . But a girlfriend is someone you want to be with all the time, even when you don't do stuff together. You just want to be with them. Even doing nothing is fun with a girlfriend" (p. 328). What do you think of his response? How would you define the difference between a friend and a significant other?

8. Lana regrets that it took her so long to realize the severity of Abby's eating disorder and get her the help she really needed. Why do you think she didn't see the problem sooner, when it was already obvious to both Mr. Franks and Matt? Who do you think played the biggest role in getting Abby back on the right track?

9. Do you agree with Lana's decision to tell her kids about her cancer scare? Should she have told them earlier? Not at all? How do you think parents should decide what to share with their kids and what to protect them from?

10. Lana and Abbott are going to try to learn from their past relationships in order to not make the same mistakes with each other. Abbott asks her, "What's the main thing you've learned in your travels?" Reread her response and share your thoughts on the idea that "[N]o matter what . . . the answer is love" (p. 282). What would you say is the main thing you've learned from your personal experiences so far?

11. By the end of the book, there are wonderful new romances in bloom for each of the main characters. Discuss each of these relationships: How did they play a role in each person's growth and adaptation? Were they cause or effect? Do you think they are built to last? Is there one relationship in particular that you're rooting for?

12. Discuss the title *The Art of Adapting*. Everyone is at once adapting to the major changes involved with Graham moving out and Matt moving in, but in their own different ways. How do each of the characters adapt throughout the novel? Who do you think has come the farthest?

Enhance Your Book Club

1. Want to see what kinds of gravity-defying moves Byron was practicing with the parkour club? Visit www.parkour.com to learn more about this unique sport and watch videos of live performances.

2. As Abby's therapist recommends, it's important to fill ourselves up with the positive. Make a list of things you like about yourself and have everyone pick one thing to share with the group during discussion.

3. Paint Nite is taking the country by storm. Take a cue from Byron and Matt and embrace your inner artist for a night of good friends and fun drinks at a guided painting class! Visit www.paintnite.com to find a location near you, or host your own version at your next book club meeting.

4. To learn more about Asperger's and autism, get further reading recommendations, and find out what you can do to help, visit http://www.autismspeaks.org/what-autism/asperger-syndrome.